THE MISSION

Faintly, in the darkness, she could see the figure of a woman, a large statue. It was twice man-high, garbed in a white gown with a golden girdle tied around the waist. Then the head of the statue appeared to turn, looking down at Eleanor.

"Why are you afraid, daughter?" It was a wonderful voice, like honey and sunlight and music all at once.

"I...don't know."

"There is nothing to fear, daughter."

"Yes...Mother."

"I know that you are tired and that your mind is weary. But there is little time. You are here for a purpose—my purpose. You must bring Albion, my Albion, back to the Light. You must drive the Shadow back into the Void and you must restore the rightful king to his throne."

Other Avon Books by
Adrienne Martine-Barnes

NEVER SPEAK OF LOVE

THE

FIRE SWORD

ADRIENNE MARTINE-BARNES

AVON
PUBLISHERS OF BARD, CAMELOT, DISCUS AND FLARE BOOKS

THE FIRE SWORD is an original publication of Avon Books. This work has never before appeared in book form. This work is a novel. Any similarity to actual persons or events is purely coincidental.

SCI FIC

AVON BOOKS
A division of
The Hearst Corporation
1790 Broadway
New York, New York 10019

Copyright © 1984 by Adrienne Martine-Barnes
Published by arrangement with the author
Library of Congress Catalog Card Number: 84-90971
ISBN: 0-380-87718-X

First Avon Printing, November, 1984

AVON TRADEMARK REG. U. S. PAT. OFF. AND IN OTHER COUNTRIES, MARCA REGISTRADA, HECHO EN U. S. A.

Printed in the U. S. A.

WFH 10 9 8 7 6 5 4 3 2 1

In Memoriam

Vernon R. Forgue

THE FIRE SWORD

PART I

Candlemas

I

The silence woke her. Eleanor sat up in bed and looked into the darkness, listening for something that was not there. The small alarm clock beside her bed, with its friendly glowing face, was simply gone. She reached out for the lamp, and her hand met empty air. A frown, a flicker of panic, and a shiver. The shiver grew, and she knew the room was actually cold.

It was so quiet that she could hear the thump of her heart, the soft hiss of her own breathing. There were no street noises at all. Only silence. Since this was more puzzling than frightening, she stuck her feet out of bed, groping for slippers that were not there. Cold, bare floorboards met her toes, and she drew back for a moment, then, thrusting the covers aside in a firm gesture, she went to the window.

The window, all the little diamond panes that were such a bother to clean, and which her house-proud Yorkshire mother insisted be washed once a month, was right there in the wall where it belonged. Eleanor reached out and touched the glass, icy under her fingertips, to assure herself of its reality, then opened the catch and pushed with both hands. The funny wooden hinges gave a creak, and one side stuck a little, warped from centuries of weather.

Eleanor looked out onto a broad expanse of snow. The houses across the mews, all solid brick, the mews itself, all gone. For a second she just gaped, not feeling the cold air rushing into her face, craning her neck around for a glimpse of some familiar structure. Her hands gripped the windowsill.

Panic swept over her. She tried to scream and found her throat so tight, she made only a little squeak, like a rabbit being strangled. She balled up her hands and banged them down on the sill. The cold and the pain pushed the panic back a little.

"This isn't a dream," she whispered. "I'll just shut the window and go back to bed." But she didn't move. The white landscape seemed to mesmerize her. The moon was just rising, a sickly sliver of silver. A fox raced across the snow, leaving deep holes in the virgin whiteness. It vanished into a small grove of trees, the only object in view.

Eleanor stared until the cold began to pierce her bones, and she was sure that there was nothing more to see. She drew the windows in and fumbled the catch closed, her hands stiff and clumsy. She rubbed them together and blew on her fingertips, then caught a glimpse of her tiny face reflected in the many panes. She peered at her face almost anxiously.

It was her own, the straight black hair framing the narrow, pale face. Her generous mouth and wide, green eyes were distorted in the glass a little, so she looked to herself like some bizarre clown. She realized that she had almost been afraid that there would be no features there, that her face would have vanished like the buildings. She turned back toward the bed.

It was less reassuring than she had expected. When she crawled back under them, the sheets felt harsh under her hand, and the coverlet was unfamiliar. Instead of the rather worn quilt made by Gramma Leighton, there was a rough blanket of wool. She rubbed the material between her fingers and looked around the room.

The walls were bare wood instead of the cheerful, flowered paper she had chosen herself when they bought the house. There was no furniture beyond the bed and a large trunk. Like the lamp, clock, and nightstand, her desk, chair, and bureau had vanished. Ellie gulped convulsively and clutched the blankets. She looked at the bare plank floor and grieved for the fluffy carpet.

"I must be losing my mind," she said. "Or else this is all some elaborate hoax. Someone moved me in my sleep. Don't be paranoid. Why would anyone do that? *They* even stole my robe."

The absence of that garment seemed to her to be the

last straw, and she wept a little. She brushed the tears away on her sleeve and sniffed loudly.

"Damn. Not even a Kleenex." This made the tears stop, and she almost laughed at herself. Eleanor shook herself all over and got out of bed.

She opened the trunk and peered at the contents in the pale light. There were garments folded up, and she pulled one out. It was a thick wool robe, a simple tunic-like garment, and she pulled it on over her head. It fell to the floor in deep folds. She fingered it suspiciously, as if it might vanish on her body, then hugged its warmth to her. She saw a long, narrow piece of patterned stuff and she tied it around her waist. The ends dangled onto the floor, so she untied it and crossed it back and forth before retying it.

"Swell. Basic early Norman," she said, looking at the belt. "Just what I always didn't want. No bathrooms, no aspirin, and no Kleenex. I have to stop talking to myself, or I will be crazy."

What do I do now? I would give anything for a marching band playing John Philip Sousa under the window. My feet are freezing. Socks. Find some socks. Keep it simple. Concentrate on real things. What is real? I am, and the clothes are, and the fox and the snow. Somehow that isn't comforting.

Ellie knelt down in front of the trunk and removed the various garments. She finally found a pair of woolen hose and wriggled into them, tying the drawstring around her waist. "No elastic," she muttered.

There were boots in the bottom of the trunk, beautiful leather things with thick soles. She sat on the floor and struggled into them, hampered by the wide sleeves of the tunic. Much to her surprise, they fit. She sat there wiggling her toes.

"Nothing like shoes and socks to make you feel right with the world. I wish there was a light. Damn. Talking to myself again. Candle? I couldn't light it anyhow. No matches. How did they manage?" She sorted through the garments on the floor, folding them after she examined them, one pile on the floor, the other in the trunk. She lingered a moment over a soft, velvety dress, the neck and sleeve edges worked in embroidery, and put it back.

The pile on the floor consisted of a couple of shifts of very fine linen, two heavy skirts with drawstring waists, another robe, and a cloak. There was also a second pair of hose, a second belt, and a leather pouch. Eleanor sat on the cold floor and looked at the stuff for a long time.

"Now what? Explore the house and see if I'm really alone. Oh, Lord. Mother." The thought of her parent both comforted and distressed her. If there was anything Elizabeth Hope hated, it was a lack of amenities. She had spent a lifetime gathering the stories of people who did very nicely without bathtubs or penicillin, but she secretly disapproved of them, and Eleanor knew it.

Eleanor got up and opened the door of her room cautiously. There was only a wide field of snow beyond the door. She stepped out onto it and walked a few steps, then looked back. There was nothing but a small wooden building, her "room." The house itself was as gone as the street and the row houses. She fled back inside and slammed the door behind her, leaning against it and panting.

Her head buzzed, a slight nauseating feeling, as if she had a glass of champagne somehow sloshing just above her brows, within the high bones of her skull. It was a feeling she associated with kneeling and the smell of incense, the chill, drafty feeling of old Irish churches on Sunday mornings, ignoring the giddiness of no breakfast, the drone of the priest's voice leading her mind into a dizzy trance. She had never cared much for those occasions, not that there were many. Her parents had been fairly casual in their religious duties. There had always just been something slippery about Mass—especially in Ireland—as if she might slide out of her young body into some foreign time and place.

As she had clutched the pew back as a child, palms sweating and knuckles whitened, she now scrabbled at the rough wood of the door, pressing a moist cheek and a damp forehead against the panels. The smell of old wood filled her nostrils as she made herself breathe deeply and slowly. Eleanor kept her eyes closed as the buzzing in her skull subsided.

Be logical, she told herself sternly. Don't panic. This is quite impossible. That's not logical. Now, the room is bare wood, but the window is modern; well, modern for England. When were paned windows invented? I don't know. It doesn't matter. My room is part of the original house, but that was Elizabethan. No, wait. Why didn't I pay more attention to Mrs. Bixby when she was talking about the house?

Eleanor pressed her forehead against the wood of the door and thought. Let's see. Our house was built about 1875 after fire destroyed the Tudor house. There was another fire, earlier, I think, and that's when the Duncannons built the Tudor place. Philip Duncannon did something nice for Henry VIII, and he got the place. Why would anyone be nice to a nasty poop like Henry Tudor? Before Duncannon, the land belonged to a Randolph Gretry. That bit of open land is still called Gretry's Meadow. Not to mention the trench called Dolph's Ditch. Gretry is a French name, so it's probably an Anglo-Norman family.

There was a lot more forest then, I think, so a wooden house is right. Castles were for knights, but a wooden room nine hundred years old is a little hard to believe. Worms and rot should have done it in long ago.

Except, here I am, in clothes that are new but old, in a room with a glass window but older, with no food and no fire and no map. I don't even speak the language. Modern French is different. Latin? I couldn't even manage Chaucer, but Latin I can do. Except it's modern, too. I'll probably get burned as a witch the first time I open my mouth—if I ever find anyone to talk to.

A witch! Didn't Mrs. Bixby say the Gretrys had a reputation as magicians? Swell. That's what I need right now, to start worrying about whether magic is real. I can't see any buildings around. What was around that's vaguely contemporaneous with these clothes? That priory. St. Bridget's. I walked over to the ruins once. It's about two miles, I hope.

What should I do? Sit here and starve to death. Or freeze. No. First I dress as warmly as possible, and then I walk to St. Bridget's. Or somewhere.

Relieved to have come to some decision, Eleanor removed her belt and took off the robe. She put one of the shifts over her nightgown, then the two skirts. She put the tunic back on and redid the belt. The rest of the clothes she made into a bundle with the blanket on the bed. Then she drew the cloak over her shoulders.

After taking several deep breaths, she picked up the bundle and slung it over one shoulder and opened the door. She stepped out resolutely, the snow crunching softly under her boots. She took a moment to orient herself and then began to walk in the direction in which she thought the priory lay.

Eleanor began to count her steps, ignoring the cold and the darkness. The moon provided a sickly light, just enough to help her avoid larger obstacles, such as stones and logs, but not enough to let her see depressions in the earth. Several times she stepped into holes, her foot sinking into the snow to her boot tops and even over. Icy trickles ran down her calves into her boots.

When she had counted twenty-five hundred steps, a generous half-mile by her reckoning, she paused. There was a dark line of trees before her. The moonlight did not penetrate below the twisted branches. She tried to remember what wild animals might inhabit the woods. Bears, she decided, should be hibernating. Wolves, on the other hand, would be awake and hungry. She almost turned back, but that felt *wrong*.

Her father had teased her often about her "second sight," and her mother had regarded those occasional irrational reactions to places or situations with well-bred silence. Eleanor suspected that her very reserved mother was subject to similar sensations. She had asked Elizabeth about it once. "Your grandmother used to do that" was the only answer she had received.

Eleanor squared her chin and walked into the woods. She began counting her steps again, moving cautiously to avoid tripping over any logs lurking under the snow. The slender trunks of birches gleamed in the pale moonlight, and she followed what seemed to be a trail. Then the birches gave way to oaks, dark and majestic, and the trail vanished. She moved more slowly between the oaks and lost count of her footsteps.

She felt the panic return in the darkness under the trees and forced herself to continue walking. The cold seeped into her feet and crawled up her legs. A faint breeze rattled the branches and drove bits of moisture into her face.

I should have waited for morning. But I couldn't. Maybe it's the Twilight of the Gods, and there is no morning. Maybe that fox is the only other thing alive in the world. Stop scaring yourself, you damn fool! There's nothing but trees and snow and moonlight. Nothing to fear. If only it weren't so quiet.

The trees seemed to thin a little. Eleanor put down her bundle and flexed her hands. They ached with cold and strain. She rubbed her shoulders and twisted her neck from side to side. She was just about to pick the bundle up again when a faint sound made her stop. She looked up at the slender moon, glad of its light.

A large animal trotted toward her through the trees. Eleanor froze in mid-movement. A wolf loped up to her, its tongue lolling between shining teeth. It stopped a few feet away from her and sat down in the snow.

They looked at each other for what seemed an eternity. The wolf made no move to come closer but remained grinning at her in canine fashion. Perhaps she was mistaken and it was only a very large dog.

"I'm not good to eat," she said in a shaking voice. "I'm all full of preservatives and chemicals that would probably give you a terrible stomachache. Besides, I am not going to grandma's house. There must a nice rabbit around for your dinner. Much tastier than tough old me."

The animal whined and brushed its tail back and forth on the snow. Eleanor looked at it very carefully, sure it wasn't a dog, and confused by its behavior. She began to back away slowly and the wolf growled.

She stopped moving. The wolf appeared to run out of patience and got up. It bounded toward her, whining and wagging. A warm, wet tongue touched her hand. Puzzled, she reached out to pat its head tentatively. The wolf gave a sharp yelp and butted its head against her leg. It was clearly a greeting.

Eleanor felt sweat dripping down her body despite the cold. The animal tore around her in a circle, sending snow flying, barking sharply, then tore back through the woods in the direction it had come from. It ran a short distance, then stopped and looked back at her hopefully and trotted back up to her. When it had repeated this several times, she shrugged, picked up her bundle, and walked after it. Obviously the wolf had decided they were going the same way. How could she argue?

"I hope you're not taking me home for dinner," she said. "You ought to at least call your wife and tell her you're bringing a guest."

The wolf responded with a sharp bark and trotted on. Eleanor kept up as best she could until she was nearly breathless. The woods thinned slowly until they came out onto a broad expanse of snow.

Out from under the trees, the wolf appeared even larger than before. He was as big as any mastiff Eleanor had ever seen, though not as massive. His coat was black with a silvery ruff, and there seemed to be a sort of nimbus of light around him, as if the moon shone more brightly off his black body. She slowed her pace, wiping her face with the sleeve of her robe.

"Hey, wolf! I only have two legs. Slow down. What am I saying? Wolves don't speak English. But, then, wolves don't fawn on people, either."

The animal looked at her and appeared to understand. Instead of leading her, it dropped back and paced slowly beside her. Eleanor found this both reassuring and disturbing, but somehow the wolf felt *right*.

She remembered her father shaking his head over some old Irish romance. "We Celts are all fatalists. We rush toward our fatal destinies like drunken lovers, cheerful as the waters close over our heads." He said the same thing many times, but this was the first occasion on which Eleanor felt she understood it.

Finally, a small building was silhouetted against the darker sky on a small rise. Eleanor could just make out the gleam of a modest cross above the roof. As they crossed the field, she tried to remember everything she could about the early Church. The difference between a monastery, a priory, and an abbey eluded her, but she did remember that one of the first things William the Conqueror had done was to put Norman bishops all over the landscapes. She was thinking so hard, she almost forgot that her companion was a wolf.

They climbed the rise, Eleanor moving more and more slowly. The building looked dark and uninhabited, and she was almost afraid of what might be inside. Her parents subscribed to a vague Catholicism and went to church on Easter and Christmas, and her knowledge of the Church was mainly from her wide, if somewhat undisciplined, reading of history. She knew that monks stayed up all night praying and wondered if priors did as well. And, unless there was a war, which seemed unlikely in the winter, the chapel should be unlocked. She decided she would just creep in and sleep on a pew until morning.

"I'll just be very quiet and I won't disturb anyone. I don't think God will mind if I sleep in His house, do you?" The wolf made no answer.

But when they came to the large wooden door, she hesitated. She was tired and cold, and her legs and back ached. Her stomach growled, and her dinner of steak-and-kidney pie seemed very long ago. She just stared at the door.

The animal watched her for a moment, then took matters into its own paws. Standing on his hind legs, the wolf reached up and took a piece of rope by the door in his great jaws. He yanked, and Eleanor heard a bell ring somewhere inside.

All her fears rushed back. She stood trembling as the slap of sandals echoed on the other side of the door. She was too tired to run. The wolf leaned against her body again. She felt the warmth of his breath on her hand. The door swung open.

II

"Lady Alianora! You have returned. Praise the Lord!" The man who opened the door said these words, then raised his hand to his eyes as if to shade them from a bright light. He frowned. "Where have you been? Were you ensorceled?"

Eleanor was too busy being relieved that the man spoke words she understood to pay attention for a moment. She studied him, a thin brown man in a blue wool habit. It did not look like the simple garments she mentally expected, for the sleeves were deep with embroidery. He looked about forty. Then she focused on his last question and felt herself stiffen.

"Good evening, Father. You appear to know me, but...I don't know you." Her father always said to tell the truth whenever possible.

"Are you bewitched?" He asked the question frankly and without emotion, as if it were a commonplace.

"I don't know. I am cold and tired and hungry. I don't *feel* bewitched, just confused. And, if I am, then you can fix it, can't you, Father?"

"Come in, child. My, what a start you gave me. What a wonder. A daughter of the Darkness would hardly seek sanctuary here. Still, it is very odd. I am Brother Ambrosius. Do you not recall? I mended the cups you broke in happier days."

"I have never seen you before in my life."

"Oh, I see. No, I do not see at all. Here. Let me take that. Who *are* you?" He took her bundle and led her inside. The wolf followed her and flopped down on the stone floor beside the door. The priest closed the door behind them and barred it with a long piece of wood.

Eleanor thought furiously. What possible answer could she offer that would not sound mad or worse?

12

Saying she was Eleanor Melissa Hope of 23 the Dells, Lorinton, Wiltshire, simply would not do.

"I...I am myself. I woke up some hours ago in a small room. I dressed and walked across the snow. In the woods, I met *him*, and he brought me here. That is all I know." It was part evasion, almost a lie, and she hated it, but she felt trapped.

"Come along. We have soup in the refectory." They went down a long hall together. It was dark, and yet she could see. Like the wolf, Brother Ambrosius had a glow about him, but there was no moonlight here. Still, she got the impression of dust along the edges of the corridor and a slightly musty smell, like in an empty house.

They came to a long room with a huge fireplace on one wall and a bare wooden table before it. Eleanor looked around at the smoke-darkened beams and the smooth stone floor. The room smelled of ashes and burning logs with a faint tang of onions. Some herbs hung in bundles from the rafters. The brother seated her on a bench beside the table, and she stretched her legs toward the fire, watching the flames leap on the big logs. He bustled away and returned with a steaming bowl and a large chunk of bread.

"Thank you." She swung her body around to face the table and dipped the spoon into the soup, then stopped. He was looking at her very closely. "Thank you, Lord, for the food on this board," she muttered, crossing herself. He relaxed visibly, and she began to eat.

The soup was thin and greasy, but Eleanor thought it was the best stuff she had ever eaten. The bread was coarse and dry, so she dunked it in the soup and munched on it quite contentedly.

"Would you like more?"

"No, thank you." Some instinct told her that the poor quality of the food was due to neither religious scruples nor inhospitality but simply to poverty. Eleanor could easily have eaten another bowl with a small horse on the side, but the man across from her looked so thin, she was afraid she was taking food from his mouth. "Now, would you please tell me who I am—or who you think I am?"

"Why, you are the Damoiselle Alianora Gretry, or

her twin. On this night, twenty-one years ago, you vanished from your bed. You were as you are now. I was a young man then, and you caused me some trouble with my newly taken vows. My confessor, rest his soul, no doubt found me as tiresome as I now find my brothers. But you would kilt your skirts up in your girdle and run across the fields with that wolf of yours." He spoke simply and without embarrassment.

"Forgive me, Brother Ambrosius." Eleanor had never been aware of stirring even the mildest interest in a member of the opposite sex, and yet she felt guilty. She was vaguely aware of her own body drives, more now since her father's death, but they were private demons not to be used to make others unhappy or uncomfortable. Her father's occasional flings with his graduate students had hurt and infuriated her and how they had injured her mother she did not care to remember.

"No, no. You were the very soul of innocence, a boy-girl yet unawakened. You are. Besides, God made pretty girls to test one's faith. And, in any case, you were promised to your cousin Randolph, your father having no other children. Your wedding was to be tomorrow, February the third. They searched everywhere for you, but you were gone. It was the talk of the shire until the Darkness came. Your father died fighting it, and your cousin—"

"What?"

"He went over to the Darkness. Randolph laid waste the fields, and the minions of the Dead marched back and forth over a track until it was a dark slot in the earth where nothing grows. The hall, Gretry Hall, was burnt one May Night, all but your chamber." He shook his head. "Every year more folk come under his aegis. If it were not for the Marshall, the Darkness would have long since covered the land. And now you have returned, not one day older than when I saw you last."

Eleanor looked at him in the flickering firelight. "Who is this Marshall?"

"Guillaume the Strong? Why, he is the Savior of Albion."

The words *Marshall* and *William* niggled her memory, for one man in English history bore that name, a real man who was almost a legend in his own time. She had waded through parts of his own telling of his life, partly for her father and partly in her amazement that he was lettered. The Plantagenets had had many liege men but none so loyal or good as William Marshall. "Is there a king?"

Brother Ambrosius snorted and rubbed his hands. "There is a whelp of Darkness who sits on his father's high seat and worships death, yes. Some say he usurped the throne by killing his cousin, the rightful heir, and some say the boy lives yet."

"What is the year?"

"The year of our Lord, twelve and twenty, milady."

Eleanor blushed at the title and then frowned. She knew her history of that period moderately well, though her study had been more of troubadours and gleemen than of kings and wars, but it must be different here. The person she knew as William Marshall died in 1219, but he seemed to be alive here. Or else word of his death had not yet reached Ambrosius.

"This king..." Henry? "How long?"

"Twenty-two years in May."

"John?" Her John had died in 1215, but in this here-and-now, who knew?

"Yes. Then you *do* remember."

"Brother Ambrosius, I feel I must try to tell you my tale. It will sound quite mad, so be patient with me. To the best of my knowledge, I am not your Alianora, though I am twenty-one. I...come from a time in the far future, and I come from an island called England, which is also your Albion." She was not about to try to explain Brown University and the United States to him. "But in my world, King John was dead in 1215 or 1216. His son Henry was king under the regency of William Marshall, but William died in the year 1219. I know nothing of the Darkness of which you speak, but there is a trench in my world called Dolph's Ditch. I was born and reared in a land over the sea and only settled in England a few months ago. The house we bought seems to— No, I can't explain that."

"Try."

"As you will. My mother and I live in a house made of bricks, one of a number of such structures, all in a row. The house was built on the site of an older house that burned down, a timber-and-plaster house. The older house was also built on the site of a still older house, which belonged to a Randolph Gretry. My room— Well, I thought it was part of the Tudor...uh, the timber-and-plaster...house. Is any of this making sense?"

"You seem to find the idea of parallel times difficult to discuss."

"Yes."

"But the Darkness is from another Earth. At least, the Pope says it is. The concept of the multiworlds has been accepted as part of the teachings of the Church. Adrian IV first declared it in 1179. His successors uphold it. The Darkness is not unique to Albion. The first occurrence was in Iberia, in 1169."

Eleanor strained to understand. "You mean the Moors?"

"Who?"

"The Moslems, the followers of Mohammed. They overran Spain in about 900 and stayed until...1490 or so."

"This I do not know of."

"The Crusades?"

"Crusades?"

"To free Jerusalem from the infidel?"

He shook his head. "No. The city of Jerusalem belongs to the Jews. They charge pilgrims a stiff tariff to visit the holy places, for they ever worship money, but it is open to all the faithful. Who is this Mohammed?"

"It doesn't matter. He obviously missed the boat in your history. You missed a lot of wars." She thought of the Children's Crusade and shuddered. "Tell me, in this world, did four knights of Henry the Second murder Thomas à Becket, who was Archbishop of Canterbury, and did Henry lock his wife Eleanor up for years and years?"

"Hardly. What a violent world you have traveled from. Thomas refused the see and kept the purse strings instead. He died of old age and rich food. As for good Queen Eleanor, she spent her declining years dashing about the kingdom meddling in the lives of her children and grandchildren."

"Grandchildren." She wrinkled her brow. "Arthur and Eleanor of Brittany...were there others?"

"I see your world is very different. The young king, Henry, the first son of Eleanor and Henry, wed Alais of France. Their son—if he is—now sits on the throne. The second son, Richard, was king for a time because his nephew was not only very young, but also because his legitimacy is very much in question. He was born ten months after his father's death. Richard willed the throne to his nephew Arthur, the son of his younger brother Geoffrey, who was already dead, because Richard never married, despite his mother's meddling. John removed his cousin and claimed the throne, there being no other claimants strong enough to nay-say him."

"Did not Henry and Eleanor have a son called John?"

"Yes, but he died very young. Why?"

"Curiosity. In my world, that John lived and was such a bad king that no other ever used the name. And the oldest son, Henry, never sat at the throne. He got killed fighting his father, which is why Eleanor, in my world, was locked up. She sided with her son."

"Oh. Here, the old king lost and died, and the young Henry took the throne, reigned for ten years, fathering a girl, then died. To you, this is history. To me, it happened in my lifetime, or my father's. I met Queen Eleanor when I was a boy. A splendid woman."

"I have always thought so. I am glad Matthew Paris had no opportunity to blacken her name."

"Matthew de Paree? He was an early convert to the Darkness. They tore him to pieces in Oxenford before I took my final vows."

"Oh, my. And I thought it was just small differences. This Guillaume the Strong, is he the same man who was the teacher of your ... no, of my Richard the Lion-Hearted? He must be old."

"No, he is the son of the old marshall."

"Really? As I remember, in my world, none of his sons outlived him, and his daughter's descendants became hereditary Earls Marshall. My, I am tired. I am not used to long walks in the snow. I was beginning to think that the wolf and I were the only things alive in the world. Are there other brothers here?" There were too many ideas and too much information for her to sort out. The food and the warmth of the fire made her eyes heavy.

"There are four, and a novice. The rest have died or gone over."

"I'm sorry about that. Is there somewhere I can sleep? Otherwise I'll curl up in front of the fire."

"Yes. We lack the facilities of a great abbey, but we do have travelers' rooms. It has been so long since it was used, I fear you will find it a bit dusty. We five cannot do the work of twenty, certainly not when we can barely keep our stomachs full. Come along."

They went back the way they had come. The wolf stood up and wagged its tail. Eleanor patted its head, reassured by its presence, no longer afraid, and feeling the animal a true friend in a strange world. Then she paused. A wolf, perhaps this wolf, had been companion to Lady Alianora. But that had been years before. How long did wolves live? There were so many things she did not know.

Eleanor followed Ambrosius through a door off the hall, the wolf behind her, its toenails clicking on the floor. Ambrosius carried the bundle but no light. The strange nimbus glowed around him and the wolf, and she was puzzled. She suddenly remembered that there had been no candles in the hall or the refectory.

Then the lingering smell of incense told her they were in the chapel. Beyond the circle of Ambrosius's radiance were soft shadows, but Eleanor could not distinguish anything.

"Would you like to speak to the Lady before you sleep?" He did not whisper but spoke in a normal, quiet voice, which reverberated off the stones of the chamber.

Eleanor stopped behind him and looked where his hand pointed. Faintly, in the darkness, she could see the figure of a woman, a large statue. She moved closer to it, and it appeared to emanate its own light.

It was twice man-high, garbed in a white gown with a golden girdle tied around the waist. An enormous blue cloak billowed out behind the figure, with stars painted on the blue in glittery silver, so they almost appeared to twinkle like real stars. In one hand the statue carried an enormous sword, edged with flames and painted red and gold.

Eleanor took all this in at a glance, for her eyes were drawn to the face. It was a stern face with wide blue eyes and golden red hair unbound except by a silver circlet above the noble brow. There was a crescent moon in the center of the circlet, which seemed to shine more brightly than the moon outside had done. The lips of the woman were full and generous but unsmiling.

She walked closer. Eleanor did not need to be told that this was Bridget, for whom the priory was named. The face bore a striking resemblance to the Botticelli painting of Aphrodite, and Eleanor could not help wondering who had been the model. The beautiful Simonetta Vespucci was not due to be born for a couple of hundred years yet.

Then the head of the statue appeared to turn, looking down at Eleanor. The mouth appeared to soften into a grave smile. Eleanor stopped in her steps. A faint hint of laughter seemed to echo in the shadows.

"Why are you afraid, daughter?" It was a wonderful voice, like honey and sunlight and music all at once.

"I...don't know."

"Come closer."

Eleanor, numb with awe, did as she was told, her feet dragging across the stones. She brushed her skirts under her knees and knelt because it felt correct.

"There is nothing to fear, daughter."

"Yes...Mother."

"I know that you are tired and that your mind is weary. But there is little time. You are here for a purpose, my purpose. You must bring Albion, my Albion, back to the Light."

"Me?" squeaked Eleanor.

"Not alone, of course. You will meet helpers along the way. But you must drive the Shadow back into the Void, and you must restore the rightful king to his throne."

Eleanor barely suppressed a sarcastic reply. Tired as she was, she could not break a lifetime habit of courtesy and respect to persons of authority. Part of her rebelled at the orders, and another dwelt on being the good little girl and satisfactory daughter whom her parents had often boasted never gave them any trouble. Her Celtic fatalism told her it was all preordained, and the hardheaded Yorkshire shrewdness she had gotten from her mother railed that nothing was that deterministic.

She reflected for a moment on her walk across the snow, her meeting with the wolf, her memory of the ruined priory. Eleanor was not so exhausted that she could convince herself that she had been dragged from her comfortable bed in the twentieth century to this strange place for no good reason. Everything had a reason—she felt that in her bones—but one could not always know what the reason was. She had tried, during the last months of her father's terrible, agonizing death, to find some reason, but she never had. Still, her mother had brought her up to undertake any task gladly, and after a second, she decided that her choice was doing what she was told or asking for a ticket home. Somehow, looking at Bridget's stern face, she didn't have the courage.

"How will I know the helpers?"

"By the moon."

The ambiguity of this response frustrated her, but she repressed the feeling. "I don't know what to do, Mother." She had a sudden, sharp sympathy for all the heroes in stories who, when consulting goddesses and sybils, had failed to ask the correct questions. She found she couldn't do any better than they had.

"First you must find the sheath of the Sword of Fire. Also, you must sheath the sword in yourself. Then you must free the sacred well from Darkness. These tasks must be accomplished by Midsummer's Eve. Then you will journey to the North Wind and recover the Harp, the Pipes, and the Heir. When this has been done, I will come to you again. My cloak shall cover you and my light will always shine for you, however dark it may be. You may call me by my ten thousand names and I will be with you."

"Yes, Mother." She wanted to protest or ask the hundred questions whirling in her mind, but her throat closed up and she could not. The statue seemed to shiver. The cloak fell to the floor, and the sword slipped from the carven hand and lay at Eleanor's feet. The face resumed its grave expression, and the chapel was silent except for the breathing of the priest and the wolf.

Eleanor folded the cloak over her arm and took the

grip of the sword in her hand, noting that it had shrunk to human size. Her knees and hands shook slightly as she gripped the thing awkwardly. She felt a surge of something go from the grip to her hand, up her arm, and into her skull. It was like a blinding white light. It dimmed a little, and she looked up at the statue. Then the world began to swirl and darken before her eyes, and she felt a pair of strong arms catch her before she knew nothing.

III

Eleanor snuggled into the pillow, fighting off wakefulness. But the rough texture under her cheek disturbed her. She yawned and stretched, then finally opened one eye and sat up. She took one look at the bare stone walls surrounding her and lay down again quickly, pulling the blanket over her head.

She peeked out again after a minute and sighed. The events of the previous night came back as she stared up at the ceiling. Her back, arms, and legs ached, evidence of the reality of what might have been a very real dream. She sat up again and forced herself to touch her toes several times to move her rebelling muscles.

The wolf was curled up beside the narrow bed, taking up most of the floor in the small cell. He lifted his head at her movement and hung his tongue out in a canine smile.

"Good morning, old fellow." The wolf moved its tail slightly. "You seem to be very attached to me. Do you have a name? Ambrosius might know. I'll just call you Wrolf, which is unimaginative. And redundant. I must warn you, I am not at my best before my second cup of coffee. Oh, my, no coffee. Maybe not ever again." Somehow this was worse than the strangeness of the situation or being sent off to slay dragons with magic swords. Eleanor almost wept for the rich, dark smell of fresh coffee and its splendid bitterness. Instead, she took a deep breath and looked about the room carefully.

It was very narrow, and the cot filled half of one long wall. Next to the bed was a chair. The bundle she had brought from Gretry Hall and her cloak were on it. She still wore the clothing she had come in, except the boots, which stood next to the door. At the foot of the bed lay the blue cloak studded with stars, surrounding a long, hard object which was clearly the sword.

She looked at her right hand, expecting to see a burn where she had touched the sword, but the palm was bare of any mark except a slight chafing where she had carried the bundle. Eleanor hugged her knees to her chest and found that her hose were still damp. Obviously Ambrosius's modesty or his vows had prevented him from removing them, and Eleanor hoped she wouldn't get a cold. She giggled a little at that, a heroine with the sniffles. She wondered how the brother had managed her, for though she was no more than five foot seven, he was a bit shorter.

Then she wriggled out of the offending garments, the hose and the petticoats, also a bit moist around the hems, and folded her legs under her tailor-fashion to keep her toes warm, pushing the lumpy pillow into the small of her back and drawing the shabby blanket over her. The chill of the room seemed to bite into her, so she drew the blanket up around her shoulders.

"What I would like, Wrolf, besides some coffee, is a long, hot bath, a cigarette, and a rum toddy. Well, 'if wishes were horses,' and all that."

There was the chiming of a distant bell somewhere, and the sound of feet passed the door. She tried to remember the order of the monastic day, but all she could think of was vespers, which she knew was in the evening. She gave up after a moment and concentrated on the one thing she did not want to think about, her eerie experience in the chapel. The blue cloak at her feet reminded her of it, and she could not look away.

St. Bridget, she knew, was an Irish character, sometimes called the Mary of the Gaels. Eleanor knew she was a pagan goddess who had been christianized. She had listened to her father on the subject of myth, folklore, and religion often enough. She wasn't going to mention this to Brother Ambrosius or anyone else, since she had no idea how the Church stood here on the subject of earlier religions. Just because some pope had decided there were many earths was no reason to assume they had other liberal attitudes. Bridget's feast was in February, an occasion of candles and lights and, recalling Ambrosius's words, Eleanor knew that she had come to the priory on that feast day.

"Wrolf, who spoke to me, the saint or the goddess? There are so many things I don't know. Like, which sacred well? England is covered with holy wells. That's one, Holywell. Then there's Bridewell, which is sacred to St. Bridget, I think. And Glastonbury, of course. What a riddle! What a muddle. No, first I have to find a sheath for the sword. And I have to be a sheath for it, too. Does that mean I have to fall on it? It is a little long to swallow, isn't it? And I am going to find helpers—by moonlight. I hope all of them are as nice as you, Wrolf. Do you think I am your Alianora? I wonder what happened to her."

There was a light tap on the door. Eleanor sat up a little straighter and said, "Come in."

It was Ambrosius, carrying a steaming earthenware jug, a large basin, and a rough towel. "Good morning, milady. Here is hot water." He set the stuff down on the floor at the foot of the bed.

"Bless you. And good morning, if it is morning. It's very dark still, even for February."

"It is always dark in Albion now. We eat in a quarter-hour. You will hear a bell. Come to the refectory then." He seemed a little distant this morning.

"Thank you."

He left, and Eleanor threw back the covers. She poured water into the bowl and removed her remaining clothing, shivering in the cold. She splashed water on her face and body, then rubbed herself vigorously with the towel. She opened the bundle and pulled on the remaining clean shift and then the other tunic. Then she sat on the edge of the bed and pulled her skirts up and put her feet into the basin. The water had cooled down to tepid, but it still felt good. She rubbed them hard with her hands, then dried them carefully. Then she donned the second pair of hose, wriggling her toes at the warmth.

She piled the clothes on the bed and moved the bowl onto the chair. Adding the last of the warm water, she washed the filthy hose she had worn and wrung out as much water as possible. She draped them over the back of the chair to dry and glared at the dirty water. Finally, she spread her smelly shift out on the bed to air with the two petticoats.

Wrolf had retreated to the corner near the door while she dressed. He watched her belt her robe about her. She reached down and picked up the little pouch she had brought with her, and it made a faint jingling noise.

Eleanor opened it. Inside there was a small knife, about seven inches long, with a plain wooden handle, and a curious ring. She turned the ring over in her hand. The band was chased with a complex interlace that met in the center in the shape of some grotesque beast. It slipped itself onto her left forefinger almost without her volition. She stared at it, curious about both its shape and the finger upon which she placed it. Then she heard the bell ring again.

She dragged on her boots, still damp, and undid the belt to slip the pouch onto it. Then she left the cell and looked up and down the hall. Where was the refectory?

Wrolf whined and bumped her with his head. Eleanor shrugged and followed the animal, wondering how he knew his way around. Maybe he had been a brother in a previous incarnation.

The refectory was much as it had been the night before, except there was a little more light coming in the single, long window. There were several men at the table, Ambrosius and three others. Another man stood at a lectern, opening a volume. Ambrosius motioned her toward the table. He handed her a bowl of thin porridge. She stood while he said a blessing. Then they all sat and began to eat while the brother at the lectern read aloud.

Eleanor found that the only thing to recommend the porridge was its warmth, but she ate it gladly. She took several glances at her companions and found they were all thin, solemn men, except the reader. The meal was over very quickly, but the brothers continued to sit and listen to the reader. She gave him very little attention, the text being on spiritual cleanliness. Only after he closed the book did Ambrosius say another prayer and the brothers leave the table.

Wrolf lounged in front of the fire, apparently undisturbed by the lack of wolfly victuals. The reader served himself a bowl of porridge from a pot over the fire and sat down. Eleanor waited, unsure of the correct behavior.

"Did you rest well, milady?" Ambrosius asked.

"Yes, thank you." She studied the brother who was still eating. He seemed rather fatter than the others, and that bothered her. There was also something else about him she could not put a name to, a whiff of something wild, as her mother would have said. Realizing the danger of staring, she looked around the room again, noting the absence of candles or light other than the grayish sunlight and the fire.

That puzzled her, for candlelight was inextricably bound up with her idea of the Middle Ages. Then she remembered that Ambrosius had told her that Randolph Gretry had burned the fields year after year. Candles were made of tallow, the fat of sheep. If there were no crops, or few, then there might not be many sheep and therefore no candles. Beeswax? The same thing applied.

The plump brother finished his cereal and gathered up the bowls from the table. Eleanor watched him shuffle away. Ambrosius sat across from her and fingered the cross around his neck. It was wood and very simple in shape, but carved on the face was an interlace, like the bands on the sleeves of his habit. The silence was broken only by the popping of the wood on the fire and the sound of Wrolf worrying something out of his paw pads.

"Tell me, Brother, what is the history of the figure of St. Bridget in the chapel?" she asked finally.

He gave her a thin smile. "You call it a figure, not a statue. It is our local miracle. The tale goes that seven monks of St. Benedict all received a vision of the Virgin, which instructed them to come to this place. After many hardships, they arrived and set about building a small church. Each morning they awoke to find the stones they had set up thrown down again. Finally, one had a dream telling him to face the door of the church west instead of east. They did this, and the next morning the chapel was complete with the figure of the saint already in place. They did not know who the saint *was*, but since this all happened at St. Bridget's Day, they assumed it was she.

"The figure is of wood, three ells high. There is not a mark upon it made by any chisel, nor are the colors on it any we can create. The colors have not faded in two hundred years and more. The Pope has sent investigators, but they know no more than I have told you. Were you lettered, I would show you our own history, which records many cures and—"

"But, I am. Or I was when...I was before." Eleanor had no idea whether she could actually read the language of this time and place. She still didn't have any idea how she could speak and understand Brother Ambrosius, for she knew she wasn't speaking the English of her own time.

"Oh. It did not occur to me that you could read." He seemed slightly bemused. "Why do they waste learning on women?"

"In my time, most people can read."

"You mean...farmers and butchers and...?"

"Everyone." She didn't think getting into a discussion of universal literacy was a good idea. "What is the significance of the sword? I cannot remember ever seeing anything like it. Female saints are usually praying. That flaming sword seems more appropriate to Michael the Archangel."

"Very true. It is. And, as far as I know, nothing like it exists anywhere in the world. One of the Vatican investigators went so far as to hint that it might not be a saint at all. It is truly unfeminine and more like those ancient queens of Albion, Morgiane and Gunnifer, who led men into battle."

Eleanor felt the war in her breast. Part of her wanted to know the local folktales of these women, especially Gunnifer, and the rest of her knew she ought to be on her way as soon as possible. "Tell me about St. Bridget, then. All I know about her is that she is from Ireland."

"She is a patron of trees and fields, and wells in particular. She blesses animal and plant alike and has a special joy in the young of any kind and a delight in bees and honey. Before the Darkness, the priory was famous for its honey and its mead. Now we are lucky if our hives yield a pot each of honey. As for mead, it is a fast fading memory."

"You all look...very thin, except the reader."

"Brother Jerome? I . . . did not introduce you, did I? I am afraid my thoughts are in great disorder after . . ."

At least now she had an idea what was bothering him, for he was very distant compared to the previous night. "Did you hear what she said, Brother?"

"I did. And it frightened the wits out of me. Twenty-two years I have been praying in front of her and I have never heard a word. Oh, yes, milady, it all happened. She smiled and shed her light on you and gave you the sword and the cloak, though the statue looked just as before this morning. I said nothing to the others. You must not think I am envious, for I would not have the tasks she set you for all the world."

Eleanor spent a moment wondering why she was not scared witless, herself. She felt very sorry for the man; he had seen a miracle, and he hadn't cared for it much. "I was thinking about it when you brought my water. First a sheath for the sword and then the sacred well. The Harp, the Pipes, and the Heir. Do you know what any of that means?"

"I sat up the rest of the night thinking on it when I properly should have been praying and reading in such books as we have here. The scabbard is mentioned in our chronicles as follows: 'St. Bridget left Hibernia in such haste that she did not sheath her terrible, swift sword.' One assumes, then, that the thing is still there."

Eleanor did not allow her face to show the dismay that these words brought to her heart. "Splendid. I only wish I had the ability to fly across the sea."

"I am sure you will find a way. Now, I have given much thought to the well. I feel it must be the well at Glass Castle, for the Darkness came there very early."

Eleanor made a silent thanksgiving to her father and mother's profession as folklorists. She had grown up with discussions of Arthur and Merlin, Finn and Cuchulain as dinner-table conversation, and she knew most of the variants of names and stories. "Glaston-bury?"

"I do not know a place by that name."

"Uh, there is a white hawthorn that flowers there at Christmas, brought over miraculously by Joseph of Arimathea. At least, that is the tradition I know."

"'Twas brought in seven days and seven nights from

Jerusalem by the great St. James, who left Joseph behind to spread the word of the Lord. So, I suppose it is the same. Do you know, when the Pope divined the multiverse, it seemed all neat and simple. But I find that actually confronting it is not."

"I am sorry. All right. First I go across the Irish Sea in midwinter and find this sheath. Then I come back and expel the Darkness at Caer Wydor. Then I travel the length of Albion to the North Wind Country, and find the Harp and the Pipe and the Heir. All in four and a half months. I know. I sound cross. I am. It seems like a great deal to do in such a short time. I do wish I knew what I was doing and why I was picked. You will never see a more reluctant heroine, Brother Ambrosius." She gave him a nervous grin before she continued.

"Where I come from, food is gotten in large stores, and one travels in self-propelling vehicles. A horse is not a common animal and is only used for pleasure. I don't even have a horse. Which means I should begin walking. Tell me, out of curiosity, what was the day of your Alianora's birth?"

"Let me think. Why, 'twas the last day of the year, as I recall."

Eleanor did not answer. That was her own birthday, New Year's Eve. "You ... and the wolf, you seem to glow in the dark. How is that?"

"Why, it is part of the teachings. 'And let your light so shine before men.' Have you never heard it?"

"Yes, in the litany, but I never thought to take it literally."

"Literally? But words have precise meanings."

"'A word means what I say it means, no more and no less.' I can see I have a lot to learn. If I survive this, I would like to come back and talk to you. But now ... can you spare me some bread? And what is the closest town? Bath?"

He didn't look too thrilled at the prospect of her return, though Eleanor did not believe he wished her any ill. She had gone from a curiosity to a troublesome guest, and he would be glad to see the back of her. "Bread and cheese, though not much of either. Avoid Bath. There is much Darkness there. Let your wolf lead you. He will keep you safe from harm."

"Brother, what is the Darkness?"

"It is a great evil which hates all living things."

"You said my...cousin had gone over. Is he still alive?"

"His body lives, but it is empty of spirit. That is what happens to *them*." His eyes were a little wide with nerves, like a shying horse.

"Zombies," she said, without thinking.

"What?"

"Oh, just a word for the living dead. Can the bodies be...disanimated?" She had a scholar's objective curiosity on the one hand, and a great need for information on the other.

"Yes, by light, by hope, and by faith."

"No more tangible means."

"Milady, the light you cast is almost blinding. I do not think you need more than that. But, if you see a thick black smoke with no flames under it, run. The Shadow Fire is very terrible. I shall pack you a bag while you gather your things."

IV

Eleanor walked to the door of the priory with Ambrosius. She had rolled Bridget's sword into the blue cloak, then tied her blanket around it. Then she had used the wide girdle to secure the ends and had slung it across her shoulders, bow-wise, the hilt above one shoulder, the flat of the blade resting across the opposite hip. The extra garments, including the still damp hose, she had made into another bundle, which she tucked under her arm. With the cloak on, she made a very lumpy sight.

Ambrosius handed her a heavy leather bag, and she slung it over her left shoulder. The length of the sword was already beginning to chafe her left hip, and she knew she would be heartily sick of the burden by evening.

"Richard the Third was right," she said aloud.

Ambrosius jumped. "What?"

"It is a play—or rather a line from a play that never may be written in Albion. It is about the last descendant of Henry and Eleanor. Betrayed on the field of battle, and on foot, he says, 'A horse, a horse, my kingdom for a horse.' Except, I don't have a kingdom. And if there was a horse, Wrolf would probably want it for dinner." Eleanor was worried about many things, not the least of which was her companion's appetite. At the sound of his name, the wolf looked back and barked.

Ambrosius decided, after some thought, that she was being funny and laughed slightly as he opened the door. No new snow had fallen, and the whiteness was still marked with the footprints of the night before. "Go down the hill that way. When you reach a high oak, turn right. Go west then. The sun will be some help but little I fear."

Indeed, the landscape was so shadowed it might have

been dusk—not almost ten by her internal clock—on a winter's morning. Eleanor looked up and saw that the sky was not clouded as she mentally expected but was clear and gray. The midmorning sun made an amber blot in the dingy sky.

"Thank you for all your help. I hope I come back someday to return St. Bridget's sword and cloak. I don't feel worthy to bear them. I mean, I *know* God moves in mysterious ways, but this is—"

"Was Christopher worthy?"

"I have no idea."

"Go then, and be not afraid. Bless you, Alianora. Godspeed and farewell." Ambrosius vanished inside and shut the door. She listened to the bar being slid into place and felt very small and helpless. Clearly the sooner she left the neighborhood of the priory, the happier Ambrosius was going to be. Eleanor shrugged her burdens into less uncomfortable positions and trudged down the hill. Wrolf, at least, was uncomplicated.

Hours later, the sun was a dirty orb sinking slowly down the horizon before her. She had gone back to silently counting her steps to measure the miles, knowing that her stride was probably more than a foot, and counting five thousand to the mile. By her reckoning she had walked sixteen miles but only twelve of them in a western direction, for there were hills, and twice Wrolf had led her aside, to circle some unknown danger.

Eleanor had met no one and passed no habitations except a long burned-out cottage, its stone blackened and its roof fallen in. There was little sound; a few birds but nothing else. Wrolf padded beside her, ears alert and nose sniffing. The trees she passed were bare, except where the birches put out a few hopeful buds. In all, it was a desolate and depressing landscape, and were it not for Wrolf's air of cheerful unconcern, Eleanor knew she would have fallen into one of her black moods.

She came upon the circle of standing stones quite unexpectedly. Eleanor stopped in her tracks and looked around, because the stones looked both right and wrong. The solid mass of a hill dimly visible to her left, and south, reassured her. This was Avebury Circle, which she had visited the previous October. The hill was Silbury, a man-made earthwork about which there was much speculation and little certain data. It, too, looked different to her, but she supposed it was the lack of centuries of weathering.

Eleanor looked back to the stones. They resembled the decaying teeth sticking out of the white gums of some old woman. Then she remembered that some stones had been hauled down by Cromwell's Roundheads, but here they were all standing. The previous autumn, she had gone across stiles and pushed her way past sheep and cows to get to the stones. Now there were neither fences nor animals.

The stones seemed to cast a pale light of their own. She moved forward slowly, stepping between two huge stones and entering the first circle. She knew she must have crossed the surrounding ditch at some point, but the snow seemed to have filled it.

A faint sound broke the utter stillness. Eleanor stopped moving immediately. The sound continued, a faint throbbing, not steady but changing, and after a few seconds she decided it was some kind of music, though what kind she would not have cared to say. It was something between singing and harping but neither. After hours of silence, she found it a glad sound. As if in response to her pleasure, the music swelled and the stones began to gleam with pale fire. There was a melody of sorts, but it was like the tunes the winds play in the branches of trees, a sighing, rushing refrain that is always different and yet the same.

For the first time since she had awakened the night before, Eleanor felt safe, despite cold feet and aching back. The priory, she realized, had made her slightly uneasy, the bare lands between, acutely uncomfortable. But this spot felt like home, though there was neither bed nor shelter. She wondered if this was what people meant when they said home was where the heart was, though she could hardly have thought of a less likely place for her cardiac organ than a megalithic monument.

"Wrolf, can you hear the music? Isn't it lovely?" He whined in response. "I'll camp here tonight. Why don't you see if you can find yourself a nice fat bunny or a squirrel? You must be ravenous. Or are you an ethical vegetarian?" Wrolf lolled his tongue out at her and loped away.

Eleanor walked along the circle of stones slowly, moving from east to north, studying each one carefully. She noticed that each one had a voice and a color, quite as distinct from one another as people.

When she had gotten about a quarter of the way around the circle, she came to a stone with no snow about it. Puzzled, she bent and touched the earth. It felt slightly warm. Was there a hot spring under there?

"Hello, stone. Do you mind if I camp by you tonight?" There was a low throbbing vibration she took for a yes. "Thank you very much. I appreciate the hospitality." She almost laughed at herself, being polite to a rock. Her father had chided her once that if she were being cooked for lunch by cannibals, she would probably teach them grace.

Eleanor unslung her burdens, remembering her father, who was often rude, and how she had developed the habit of being extra polite to compensate. She unwrapped the blanket from the cloak and sword, folded it in quarters, and sat down on it with a deep sigh. She wriggled her aching toes inside the boots. For a long time, Eleanor just sat and listened to the music, feeling herself filled with the strange beauty of the stones' song.

Finally, she pulled the leather bag open and poured the contents into her lap. There was a small loaf of coarse bread, a slab of hard cheese, and an earthenware jar. She opened the jar, and the smell of honey rose to her nose. Mead, from the priory's small hoard, she decided. That extra kindness touched her. Eleanor closed it up carefully and put it back into the bag. There was another bottle, very small and made of glass, a wide-toothed wooden comb, and a cloth-wrapped object. She ran the comb through her long, black hair, hitting tangles and muttering for a brush for several minutes before she opened and unwrapped the last item in Ambrosius's bag. It was a small book.

She looked at it in amazement, for she knew that books were uncommon and precious. This one did not appear to be a missal or Bible, but was a slender volume, too small to be either. She opened it.

The first page read "The True Chronicle of St. Briget

of Hibernia," in a clear, clerical hand. Below that, in a different and less elegant hand, it read, "Milady Alianora. This is an incomplete copy of this history, penned by Brother Guillaume before he died. I hope it will be of service to you. God be with you, always. Bro. Ambrosius."

Eleanor broke off a small piece of bread and munched on it as she hunched over the book in the fading light. In a few minutes she was lost in an adventure of epic proportions, full of evil wizards (some of whom she recognized as thinly disguised Irish gods) and great monsters. She read until she found her nose almost pressed to the page. She closed the book and rubbed her neck to ease the crick she had given herself. She sighed because, even with the light from the stones, it was too dark to read further.

"'A book of verse, a jug of mead, and thou, Beside me in the Wilderness, Ah, the Wilderness is paradise, enow,'" she said to the air. "I apologize to Omar Khayyám, but I am not sure he has been born yet. And if there is no Mohammed, if he ever will be. Which will make Mr. Fitzgerald very cross," she said, thinking of the Victorian translator whose entire reputation depended on the *Rubáiyát*. She cut off a small piece of cheese with the knife from her belt pouch and put everything carefully back into the bag except the little glass vial. This she opened and sniffed. There was no odor, confirming her suspicion that it probably held holy water. She tucked it into the pouch with her knife, then spent a few minutes braiding her hair. "Why didn't I think of this before it turned into a mare's nest?"

Eleanor got up and unfolded the blanket, propping the still bound sword at one end and the lumpy bag of food at the other. She unfolded the extra clothes and spread the robe and shift out on the blanket, shaking the still damp hose out vigorously, then spreading them on the warm ground nearby. Then she wrapped herself in her cloak, glad for its rough warmth, and lay down on her back, looking at the sky but seeing no stars.

She felt the earth beneath her, through the layers of cloth, complaining and groaning. Eleanor heard a faraway noise, like someone dragging a chain across a piece of metal and knew she really did not hear it. There was the sound of waters as well, as voiced and colored as the stones around her, green and golden, and one dark river that was as cold as sin. She moved her hand and felt the stiffness of Bridget's sword under it. She sat up abruptly, realizing that resting her head on the cloak and sword was causing her strange auditory hallucinations.

Wrolf came bounding up the curve of the circle, his tongue hanging out and his muzzle matted with blood. He barked sharply, then flung himself down beside her, wagging furiously and panting. She looked at his black fur in the silver glow that surrounded him.

"Hello, handsome. Did anyone ever tell you you're a messy eater?" He responded to her question by licking his chops and then his paw pads. "No matter, unless you killed some farmer's sheep. And if you did, and you didn't bring me any, I would be very annoyed. You are the best friend a girl ever had. I'm still a girl, you know. Twenty-one and never been kissed. What will Mother think when she finds my bed empty? You're a lucky wolf. I'll bet you're a bachelor with no responsibilities."

Then she turned her head, as did the wolf, his ears pricking at some noise yet beyond her hearing. Eleanor listened, noting the sighing of the stones and the faint murmur of the earth beneath her, until a sound, a regular crunching noise of footfalls, made her tense her shoulders. Wrolf looked into the darkness but did not move.

A figure, glowing faintly, emerged from the gloom. It was a girl, perhaps sixteen, with pale hair and a dark cloak around her body. She paused beside the pulsing stone and lifted her hand as if to shade her eyes.

"Hail to thee, bright lady," the girl said. She bowed deeply.

Eleanor said nothing for a moment. Then, responding to a feeling of sureness she did not trust, she said, "Greetings, Rowena."

The girl's eyes widened. "Thou art truly She. My father begs you will come to our house. We would be honored."

Eleanor hugged her cloak about her. She had named the girl from some inner voice, and the knowledge that she had gotten it right bothered her a little. "And why did he not come himself?"

"He was afraid to approach you, milady."

"And thy mother?"

"My...mother sent no message."

Wrolf gave a low growl. Eleanor smiled and said, "Come closer, child. I won't bite. Give me your hand." She found an icy hand thrust into her left one.

Leaning on the cloak and sword with her right hand, she "saw" the house to which she had been invited, a tumbledown hovel squeaking with rats. The father had empty eyes, and she knew him for a creature of the Darkness. The mother was a poor miserable soul, frightened into speechlessness. Eleanor looked into Rowena's eyes and found a kind of gentle madness there.

A fire filled Eleanor. It seemed to race along her right hand, into her veins, up her throat, then into her brow. She was afraid and yet steady. The stones hummed around her, and she knew that Rowena's father was some kind of trap. A kind of light seemed to suffuse her whole body, extending upward like a pillar of fire.

"No, thank you, Rowena. I prefer to sleep under the stars."

"What stars?"

"Look!"

They both raised their heads, and the gray blanket of shadow parted a little. A tiny diadem of lights twinkled overhead.

"Oh! How glorious! I have never seen stars, only the moon, a little."

"You will see them again, whenever you wish. Let me kiss you." Eleanor placed a kiss in the center of the girl's forehead. "Now go home. When you get there, kiss your mother as I have kissed you, and tell your father ...nothing."

"Yes, lady." Rowena stumbled to her feet like one dazed or drugged. She trudged off across the snow and finally vanished from sight.

Eleanor felt herself begin to shake all over, not from cold but from sheer terror at her presumption. She knew she had believed in the goddess from the first time her father had told her of Eiru and Badh, ancient deities of Ireland. But this was the first proof she had ever had of her own ability to embody the attributes of that entity. It was not a pleasant feeling.

Finally, she relaxed a little, telling herself she had done no harm. She stretched out, pillowing her head on the sword again, for the folds of Bridget's cloak cushioned it nicely, tucked her own cloak around her as closely as possible, and sighed. "Thank you, Bridget. I think. I never realized that hiding your light under a bushel basket could be so hard." Then she slept.

Eleanor found she slept very lightly. Wrolf lay beside her, his back pressed against her side, and drowsed with an alertness common to the canine, ears erect and nose twitching at the slightest sound. After a couple of hours, as near as she could estimate, Eleanor woke fully. Her body was still tired, but her mind seemed fully aroused. She sighed and grumbled a little under her breath, but weary as she was, sleep would not return. She knew herself well enough to know that this was a signal that she was supposed to do some hard thinking. She indulged in some crabby thoughts about bossy subconsciouses as she stared at the dull sky above. The slender moon was rising again.

She reached a hand out from under her coverings to touch Wrolf's rough coat. The harsh feel of the hairs was reassuring, though she had never touched anything like it, except possibly a German shepherd in his winter coat. Then she listened to the quiet harmonies of the stones around her.

Let me see, she thought. I am at Avebury Circle, about twelve miles from the priory. This is the early part of the thirteenth century, but history is different enough that I shouldn't make any assumptions. The Catholic Church seems pretty mellow compared to the one in my world, but I guess not putting all that energy into fighting Islam might make them less hidebound. On the other hand, didn't the Crusades help wake Europe up from the Dark Ages? Maybe this culture is stagnant, or would be without the Darkness. If a pope had declared the theory of multiple earths in my world, he probably would have found himself drinking hemlock. I wonder how St. Francis does here? Has he founded the Franciscans yet? I can't remember. No, wait, he was contemporary of St. Bernard, the poop who preached the Second Crusade, the one that Richard went on. I think. I never did really pay attention to dates unless they interested me. Anyhow, maybe there are Franciscans. And Benedictines, because the priory was founded by them. But, blue habits? Blackfriars is Dominicans, white is St. Bernard's Cistercians, brown or gray is the Franciscans. I guess it doesn't matter, but I wish I had asked about the embroidery. Those interlaces must have some significance.

Stop getting sidetracked. Think! Magic seems to be sort of accepted here. At least, miracles. I feel different. Brother Ambrosius asked me if I was bewitched, but it didn't seem to bother him much, as if people popped in and out of elfmounds all the time. Lord, if I had come to the door of a monastery with a wolf in my world, they would have locked the door against me. Or burned me on the spot. Hmm. I wonder if Joan of Arc gets to escape martyrdom. That's going to play hell with future playwrights. I wish I had enough magic to conjure up my single-volume world history. Or, better yet, this world's equivalent.

No, wait. That's the whole point. If the Darkness isn't driven away, there may not be any history. And why did I get picked as a prime mover? I can't believe I was picked at random.

What special qualities do I have that St. Bridget should entrust me with her sword and her cloak? I am not brave. I'm fairly smart, but I'm not sure intelligence is a good quality in a hero. It's too easy to start wondering about the meaning of life when the bad guys are shooting at you. Maybe it's because of Daddy.

Eleanor remembered her big, laughing, black Irish father, not as he had been at the end, wasted with disease, but as he had been in front of a classroom, roaring out the story of Cuchulain or Oisin or Grace O'Malley of the Clares. The university would never have put up with his unorthodox teaching of Irish literature, except that Daniel Sean Hope had the panache of success upon him. Every two years he produced another book of folktales, mythology, or criticism that was either an academic triumph or an immodest money-maker. He took dry scholarship and gave it artificial respiration. Until Eleanor was ten, she was certain that Queen

Maeve still lived and that leprechauns were real. Her father had breathed so much life into ancient traditions and stories that his collapse from lung cancer had been more than a shock; it had been an affront.

She had loved him as only a single and somewhat spoiled child can. Eleanor had memorized virtually every word he had ever written, whether it was about O'Casey and Yeats or Finian and Conlabar. Every summer in Ireland, she had struggled with Gaelic until she could speak it fluently. Her mother, true to her cool Yorkshire upbringing, had stood outside the cheery circle of the father and the daughter.

Elizabeth Leighton Hope was a woman of great strength and reserve. She stood up against her husband's all-consuming ambition to pursue her own quiet academic career. She had been overshadowed by Daniel's success in many ways, though her work in Scottish and Yorkshire folklore was highly respected in the small world where the names Briggs, Thompson, and Coffin were bywords.

At heart, Daniel had been a pagan and Elizabeth a dour Calvinist, in spite of which they got Eleanor as far as her first communion. Somehow, she had never been confirmed. Elizabeth had borne the disappointment of eleven miscarriages and one small, rather sickly daughter, and then kept to herself. Daniel had lavished his love and energy on his daughter and his work, and Eleanor had chosen the laughter instead of the silence.

Lying there, searching the gray vault of sky above her, Eleanor realized for the first time what an essentially selfish man her father had been. Whatever personal desires and ambitions she might have formed had been swept away or submerged in the full-time job of being Daniel's daughter. Unlike girls her own age, she had not dreamed of career or marriage. She had entered college halfheartedly, studying folklore as if it were the only discipline in the world when she already knew as much as most of her father's graduate students. She had stopped that almost gratefully when he had gotten sick. Folklore was not her greatest love, but she had never told Daniel that.

What would I have wished to do with my life if I had had a free choice? she asked herself. Write, paint, dance, philosophize? I can't remember ever wanting to be a nurse or a ballerina. The only thing I've ever cared about is horses. I'm too big to be a jockey, and I would hate being a vet. God, what a useless soul I am. And a barbarian. My mother can carry on an intelligent conversation with anyone, a physicist or a theologian. She really knows about music and history and art. Oh, Mother. I never appreciated you, and now you are too far away. No wonder you were almost relieved when he died. He didn't leave you any room for yourself. Well, I hope you can be happy now. You're well shut of both of us.

If I ever get back, I'll try to love you, Mother. I hope you're not worried about me. I hope that whatever brought me here made things tidy. Maybe you got the real Alianora. I wonder what happened to her?

Enough maundering. Back to business. This Albion. Where magic is rather commonplace, I think. The book Ambrosius sent might have been cribbed from any number of old tales. Briget of Hibernia is no more a saint than I am. She's a goddess, pure and simple.

What does that make me, a student heroine? I don't even know why I was picked, except that I was pretty useless where I was. I do like the out-of-doors. Even the snow. I respect nature, I suppose, and I think I still believe in dryads and fairies. Maybe I've always been a little pagan.

Now I'm about twenty miles from Bath, which I should avoid. In order to get to Ireland, I have to get to the sea. So I'll go west another day, then swing a little south and head for where Bristol will be someday. A boat? I know from nothing about sailing, and besides, the craft of this time are pretty primitive. I can just see me persuading some sailors to cross the Irish Channel in midwinter. But, at least I know Ireland. That's a comfort. I wonder if they have tried to conquer it this time?

She drifted into a light sleep. Sometime later, she heard Wrolf give a low growl. Eleanor sat up instantly and looked around.

There was something outside the circle of stones that was blacker than night. It was a heavy, oppressive presence, like a thundercloud on the ground. She peered at it and saw little specks of red, like eyes.

A sound reached her ears over the singing of the stones. It was a low moaning, like something in pain. There was also a deep rumbling, almost like an animal breathing, and a dragging, shuffling noise. The blackness crept closer to the circle.

With icy fingers, Eleanor undid the blue cloak from around the sword. She put her hand on the grip a little tentatively, remembering her experience the night before, and felt the shock race up her arm again. But it was less violent this time, and she found she could hold it. She stood up, drawing the sword from the folds of the cloak, shaking and wondering what she was doing. Again, she felt a sense of correctness, shrugged, and waited.

Pale fire coursed along the blade. She held it awkwardly and thought, Let there be light. The stones around her swelled their glow until each was a great beacon.

The blackness beyond the circle took on a shape. It seemed to be a great snake with many eyes on stalks. There were legs of a sort, large misshapen limbs. The breath of the thing was dark, and she could feel a cold from that breath that was like death itself.

Wrolf stood beside her, bristling and growling. Eleanor put her left hand on his thick mane and saw him become a beast of flame, with great gouts of fire dripping from his jaws. She had a sense of déjà vu, then realized Wrolf looked like a poster for the *The Hound of the Baskervilles*. She turned her attention back to the thing.

"Begone, thou worm of death," she shouted at the blackness. Her words sounded small and pitiful in the night.

It made no reply but shuffled onward. One of its large legs seemed to snake out and come to rest a few feet in front of her. The nearby stone made a screaming cry.

Eleanor released her hold on Wrolf and stepped forward. She took the sword in both hands and brought it down on the leg with all her strength. She felt the sword cut into the noisome flesh. The beast gave a terrible shriek and yanked back at the leg. She hacked again, and a foot fell off at her feet. A spurt of some liquid gushed out of the severed limb, and then the foot burst into white fire.

Making a horrible, gurgling scream, the animal thrust its head into the circle. The glowing light cast by the stones revealed something like a crocodile with many eyes. Eleanor stepped away from the long jaw and terrible breath while Wrolf circled and snapped at the eyestalks. The thing moved with painful slowness, but its dark breath almost froze Eleanor where she stood.

She moved to one side of the giant head and hacked at the eyes. The beast began to turn its head back toward her, and a horrid foreleg groped at her. Eleanor chopped at the leg until it retreated, then brought the sword down between two prominent bones behind the head. The sword flamed brighter and brighter until she was almost blinded by the light it gave. She hacked at the vertebrae until her arms were numb, the beast screaming and trying to reach her. Its long tail lashed the ground beside her and finally swept her aside.

Eleanor lay breathless on the cold ground for a second, the skirts of her garments pressing wetly against her hose-shod feet. The half-severed head began to inch toward her. She gulped a deep breath and dragged herself to her feet. She staggered around the head, giving the beast's breath a wide berth, as fast as her legs would move.

Wrolf leaped over the huge beast in a glow of light. He closed his jaw on the tip of the lashing tail. Fire dripped from his mouth, and the tail seemed to flame up. Eleanor waded in and went back to work on the thing's neck. After a time, she lost all consciousness of anything but bringing the sword up and down, up and down. Twice she was knocked aside by tail or leg, and twice she struggled up and returned to her grim decapitation. Wrolf's light was here and there, and the terrible keening of the beast mingled with the howls of the wolf in a dreadful cacophony.

Finally, the beast stopped screaming, and a moment later, head and body parted company in a sickening gush of dark fluids. Eleanor stepped back, almost tripping over her skirts in her eagerness to avoid contact with whatever the beast had pumped through its veins.

Then flames raced along the body in both directions, going from red to white, and Eleanor had to turn her head away to shield it from the actinic light.

She sat down on the bare ground with a thump, her legs quivering and her hands shaking. She noticed in a dispassionate way that her bootless feet hurt and that her hose were torn, her feet cut and bruised by small stones. The sword lay across her lap, flickering faintly. Wrolf sat nearby, licking his paws, once again a large black wolf. If it had not been for the burning body of the beast, she might have thought the whole thing a very nasty dream.

As she sat, Eleanor heard the odd moaning continue, and realized it came from the ground under her. She patted the earth affectionately and watched the white fire continue to consume the beast, the leathery skin melting away, then the muscles beneath it, and finally the huge skeleton. The cold crept into her bones, and she got up and went over to her tumbled pallet. She slumped in the middle of her bed, dazed and exhausted, until a slight lightening in the grayness to the east told her that dawn, such as it was, was rising.

Eleanor looked down at the sword beside her. There were dark smears on it, and she dragged it down to the snow and scrubbed the blade until her hands were aching with cold. When it was clean, she rose with soaking knees and carried it back. She dried it carefully with her blanket and wrapped it up again.

She rubbed her hands together vigorously, then shuddering a little, she stripped off her robe and shift, casting them a distance away onto a small patch of snow, then pulled on her other clothes. She slipped out of the ruined hose and put on the first set she had worn, still a little damp from their washing the previous day but clean. She struggled into the boots, bruised feet protesting, then huddled in her cloak and damp blanket against the warmish ground beside the stone.

Eleanor opened the leather bag and took out the bread and cheese. She ate without tasting and would cheerfully have killed for a good cup of hot coffee. Her thoughts were aimless and pointless, and she only stopped eating when she realized she had consumed half the remaining food. She sighed and tucked the rest away. Then she opened the bottle of mead and took a swallow. The smell of honey seemed to linger after she had capped the jar, and she realized that she could still smell the beast.

The offending hose lay nearby. She picked them up and carried them a distance away. She picked up the smeared robe and shift and looked at them. The shift was beyond recall, but the tunic was mainly dirty along the hem. After a moment, she took out the little knife and hacked the bottom off the garment. She shook it out vigorously and took it back to her little pile of stuff. She put on one petticoat, which, in her haste to dress, she had not donned, and packed the other into the leather bag with the food and the book.

She looked at her meager possessions gravely. "Wrolf, you don't happen to know a nice horse with an urge for travel, do you? I'd settle for a donkey. I wish I didn't have such modern notions about cleanliness, or that I could go to Bath and use the hot springs. I also wish I had a needle and thread. Skirts are pure hell to fight in, not that I want to do any more fighting, you understand, but I have to expect it. I just hope I don't meet anyone who knows how to use a sword. I sure don't. I hate to ask, but why me?"

The stones hummed their endless tune as Eleanor began to gather her belongings and arrange them about her person. Her back protested as she slung the sword into position, and she could feel that she was chafed across the shoulder blade from the day before. She slipped the bag over her shoulder, clasped the cape around her throat, and started to leave.

Wrolf whined and danced around her, blocking her movement each time she started to leave the stone under which she had slept.

"What is it?"

He barked and bounced over to a dark patch where the beast's blood had touched the earth. Wrolf scrabbled frantically at the patch, sending bits of dirt flying into the air. Then he charged back to her.

"What? I didn't have time to file an environmental impact report. I should clean up the mess, right? Yes, I can hear the earth moaning, too. How in the name of...?"

Eleanor removed her cloak and slipped the bag off her shoulder. She took out the bottle of holy water from the pouch and stared at it. Wrolf gave a tiny growl. She put it back and took the mead from the bag at her feet. She stood thinking for several minutes.

She could see her father, bristling with vitality, speaking on ritual, magic, and religion. "All ritual was spontaneous once," he had roared. "It was a matter of necessity. A shaman did something, said some words, and if they worked, they got codified and repeated. So, when you study a ritual, remember it is a mire of traditions, but it began life as pure, dumb luck." Her father had never been very romantic about his work.

"Oh, Mother Earth," she began slowly. "I sorrow for this desecration of your holy body. I hear the pain you suffer. I do not know how to heal the hurt, but perhaps if together we remember sunlight and flowers and honey-laden breezes, the pain will diminish." Eleanor walked over to the largest patch and poured a splash of mead on it. "Dear Gea, take this in token of happier times and be renewed." She repeated her prayer at each place where the beast's blood had fallen and gave each a drop of mead.

The music of the stones changed subtly. Its tempo quickened slightly. When Eleanor turned back to get her cloak and bag, the first patch she had treated was rich with grass. It seemed to flow out like an unrolling carpet of merry green. A few brave crocuses pushed their heads out of the ground and waved their gold and purple banners. Eleanor stood and stared at the ground around the stone.

"My mother always said crocuses were a small miracle," she told Wrolf as she picked up her things, "but I never thought to see anything like this. No wonder Ambrosius was eager to get rid of me." Then she shouldered her burdens and cut across the circle to the south.

V

As Eleanor came to the two smaller circles of stones that stood in the middle of Avebury, she paused. In her time, the tiny village of Avebury stood right in the middle of the circle, its church, museum, and houses all crowded together in the midst of the remaining stones. There was no village here, but only a kind of blinding whiteness in the air, like a shimmering snow cloud.

The two center rings made a different music than the sarsen stones of the outer circle. It was a higher, sweeter song, and she thought she could almost make out the words, though they seemed to be in no language that she knew. She could see nothing beyond the brightness. Even the solid blue of Silbury Hill was invisible.

After a moment, she swung to the right, planning to go around the western ring. She stumbled forward a few steps and ran smack into the face of a stone.

"Huh! Pardon me," she said reflexively. "Wrolf, where are you?" She groped out, blinded. A cold nose touched her hand. "Can you see?" There was a bark she could not interpret. "I do wish they had offered Wolf and Stone in the language department," she grumbled, moving cautiously, and banging into another stone. After she had repeated this experience twice more, Eleanor was convinced that the stones were moving. She was beginning to sweat despite the chill of the day.

"Okay, fellows, enough is enough. I see you have a good sense of humor, but I don't want to play Blind Man's Bluff. I sure don't want to be It." The music sounded like laughter or a stream bubbling over rocks. "What do you want from me?" she screamed in frustration.

A voice inside her said, "Why, to dance, of course,"

as clearly as if it were written. The whiteness blinding
her faded, and she could see the stones vibrating in
their places. Eleanor could hear the joyous laughter in
the music as she stepped inside the circle and bowed to
the first stone. "Waltz or minuet?" she asked.

Eleanor was not much interested in folk dancing and
had regarded square dancing as some form of major
penance. In addition, she was clumsy in skirts touching
the ground. But she decided that she was going to do
it wholeheartedly. So she bowed, skipped, lifting her
skirts awkwardly, and do-si-doed around each stone in
the circle until she was breathless and warm. She flopped
down against the nearest stone, wiped a slight film of
sweat off her face, and grinned. She had to admit she
felt better. She glanced around and found Wrolf loung-
ing in the middle of the circle, observing her antics with
an air of lupine superiority.

A great feeling of warmth and happiness filled her.
"Thank you for the dance, folks," she said, patting the
stone beside her in a friendly way. "We must do it again
sometime." Only the laughter answered her.

Eleanor wiped her face again and moved out of the
ring toward the south edge of the outer circle. The snow
seemed less thick under her boots and the air was positively warm, but she attributed this to her recent exercise. She found herself humming "Skip to My Lou"
under her breath and chuckled.

At the southwest edge of the circle was a long, double
row of stones called the Kennet Avenue by the archae-
ologists of her time. Eleanor remembered this from her
visit the previous fall. It began with an enormous single
stone called the Devil's Chair. When she reached this,
she was surprised to find a building, or rather the remains of one, pressed against the side of the stone. The
building had been constructed of stones cut into oblongs
and mortared together. The floor had been flat stones,
but it had the appearance of something exploding from
beneath it. The walls and floor were flung outward.

She stepped closer to the destruction. There was a
dark pit in the middle of the mess. A stench, sickening
and familiar, rose to her nostrils. It was the beast's lair.
Eleanor gagged and stepped back.

Something rustled under her foot and she jumped.

It was a page from a book. She picked it up gingerly and tried to make out the words. It looked to be from a Bible or missal. She sat down on a fallen stone and smoothed the page across her lap. The hand that had copied the words was terribly ornate, so that each word was almost a picture. After a while she gave up trying to read it.

She got up and picked up a few more pages scattered in the litter of blown leaves and broken branches. Books were her great love, from her shabby use-worn *Oz* books to the signed copies of her parents' works, and she felt she could not bear to just ignore these rumpled remnants of what had probably been the only volume in the village.

One of the pages was a calendar of some kind, pillars dividing the sheet into four parts with the name of the month at the top of each pillar. Eleanor suddenly realized that she had to keep track of time, which, without writing implements, defeated her for a while. The page in her hand was for June to September, the days marked off by saints' feasts.

Overturned amongst the debris was a large stone bowl with carvings on it. She squatted down and looked at it. There were stylized cups on stems, which might be flowers, and an interlace of arches, like rainbows, leading from one cup to another, two away. These were almost undamaged. There was the figure of a man on one side, standing on his head from her point of view, holding a long thing in one hand, which might have been a spear or a sword. Where the long thing rested near the man's foot, it crushed the neck of a serpentine figure Eleanor had no trouble identifying. The man had been hacked at with something, and his figure was a broken mess.

"This was some kind of church, Wrolf—St. George's, maybe—and the beast was trapped underneath once, but it got out. I don't think I can make this right. But a little mead couldn't hurt. Ugh! The smell." She took a deep breath, pinched her nose, and went over to the pit. She poured a generous dollop into the earth, praying silently, then backed away.

Something screamed. It was a terrible sound, and it

lingered and finally faded. Eleanor looked around, but she could not find the source. She shivered all over.

"Come on, Wrolf. Let's go. I'll never get there if I stop to play amateur archaeologist. I just hope that thing didn't have any little brothers."

She picked up the pages where she had set them down to get out the mead and put them into the bag on her shoulder. They walked down the Kennet Avenue, a slightly winding trail set with stones on either side. The shape of the stones alternated, a straight-sided one next to a vaguely diamond-shaped one, and Eleanor marveled at the work it had taken to shape them. All the stones were taller than she was, and she knew they weighed tons and tons.

The avenue dipped down to a warm, marshy dale with a small stream gurgling through the thin snow, then rose again to a small hill. There was a modest ring on this hill, and Eleanor stopped and looked back the way she had come. In the dusky grayness of the day, Avebury seemed pale green between the stones.

The small rise gave her a chance to orient herself. Silbury was now almost west of her, and she realized that unlike most of the rest of the landscape, it was not covered with snow. She walked around part of the hill-top and then began to pick her way down the west face of it, slipping and sliding while Wrolf sort of tobogganed on his rump. He shook himself all over, spattering her with snow.

At the bottom of the hill was a stand of trees. In the trees there was a huddle of huts. A stream of smoke came from one. Eleanor stood and looked at the hovels for a moment. She found her need for companionship was less than her desire to avoid any people of the Darkness.

A man came out of one hut, shouldering an ax and whistling merrily. He came toward her and stopped.

They eyed each other carefully while Wrolf wagged his tail.

"Good day to thee," he said. He regarded her with outright suspicion and moved no closer.

"Good day, sir. I was just passing and saw your smoke."

"Where have you traveled from?"

"Why, St. Bridget's Priory." She waved vaguely east.

"St. Bridget's, eh? Are you a pilgrim, then?"

"Yes, you could say that."

He still watched her closely, searching his mind. "I was to St. Bridget's once. Master Overton sent me to take his sheep to the fair, and I stopped there. Did you see the Lady?"

"Yes."

"A marvel, is she not, in her black cloak all set with suns upon it?"

"Yes," she said, laughing a little at his clumsy trap, "but the cloak is blue and covered with stars. She wears a white gown and carries a flaming sword. The moon crowns her brow and her feet are unshod."

He gave her a slow grin and doffed his cap. "These are hard times, lady, and I am a right cautious man. You look cold. Come in and warm your legs by our fire awhile. There is only me and my good wife and our baby. If you have seen the Lady, you are untouched by...'tis best not to speak of it."

"Thank you. I would be glad of a fire."

They went to the hut, Wrolf loping behind. The man gave the wolf a curious look or two but apparently decided not to ask questions.

It was dark inside, lit only by a fire in the dirt floor, warm and smelly. But Eleanor identified the smells as wood and sweat and baby, plus the good, rich smell of something cooking on the fire. A woman bent over a pot suspended over the flames, stirring, and balancing a fat toddler on one hip.

"Sarah, we have a guest."

The woman stood up and peered at them. Her eyes widened at the sight of Wrolf's large shaggy head. "Oh! Sam! What's this?" She clutched the child.

Sam scratched his head. "Don't be a fool. This here lady is a pilgrim from St. Bridget's."

"But...that animal." She pointed a shaking finger at the wolf. Wrolf whined and lolled his tongue out. But his "smile" only seemed to panic the woman further.

After two days in the company of the wolf, Eleanor had forgotten how frightened she had been in the forest. He had become her trusted companion, and while she would not have beat him with a stick to measure her dominion over him, neither did she fear his fangs any longer.

"Wrolf! Sit outside the door!" He gave a great sigh and a look of rebuke and settled down in the doorway, his paws and head inside, the rest out. "You see, he is quite tame," Eleanor said calmly.

"Yes, my lady, if you say so." The woman shuffled the baby higher on her hip and dipped a stiff curtsey. "It just startled me, is all. Will you sit?" She gestured toward a rough bench on one wall. "Wipe your feet, Sam."

"Thank you," said Eleanor. She ignored the bench and sat on the ground next to the fire, extending her hands toward the flames. The silence was broken only by the hissing of the fire and the child's cooing. Finally she said, "I am Eleanor Hope, and I am happy for a chance to warm my hands and feet. That is a very good baby."

Sarah relaxed a little at these amenities, especially the mention of her child. "He hardly cries at all. It is so terrible. We cannot even get him baptized, since the Black Beast destroyed the church. I keep tellin' Sam we oughta move, but he says it is not better anywhere. We just call him Baby, but when we get a priest, we'll call him Christian, for he was born on Christmas, and it was my father's name besides."

"He's a big boy then, if he's only two months old." Eleanor was glad of the woman's need to chatter. She found the sound of a human voice comforting.

Sarah giggled at her ignorance. "Nay, 'twas the Christmas before. But he's big enough to be a mischief. And eat! Don't just stand there like a lump, Sam. I never saw a man so hard to stir! But he caught a hare yesterday, so there's stew. Would you care for a bit? Can't you see she's dizzy with hunger? Get a bowl."

Sam seemed quite unmoved by his wife's sharp tongue. He chuckled and chose a bowl from a pile of stuff on one wall. "Now, Saree..."

"Don't you 'now Saree' me," she said, snatching the bowl from his hand and setting the baby down at her feet. Then she spooned some stuff from the pot and handed it to Eleanor. "Get a spoon. Do you expect her to eat with her fingers?" He picked up a spoon, and

Sarah grabbed it from him to rub it on an apron not much cleaner than the floor. "Here you are, my lady. You'll haf to pardon him. He was raised in a cow byre."

"A right good cow byre it were, too," Sam answered with no ill humor as Eleanor began to eat. "Saree never lets me forget her ol' gaffer wus bailiff to Master Overton. But he came to a bad end for all that." He gave a deep chuckle.

The baby crawled around the fire into Eleanor's lap. He looked hopefully at the bowl in her hand, so she gave him a spoonful, though she was almost too hungry to pause. The stew consisted of stringy lumps of meat and a great many onions. Some salt and pepper would have improved it greatly, but Eleanor was content with the flavor of such herbs as Sarah had put into it.

The child finally decided that no more food was forthcoming, so it crawled out of Eleanor's lap, got to its feet, and headed for the door on unsteady feet. Wrolf, meanwhile, had inched his way forward until only his tail was outside the door. Sarah gave a shriek and stood transfixed as the toddler stumbled into Wrolf. Wrolf gave the child's face a slurpy licking, and the little boy sat down between the great paws with a merry gurgle. Wrolf showed all his teeth and looked so smug that all three adults laughed, Sarah a little hysterically.

"He will not bite, will he?" the mother asked.

"No," Eleanor answered, her mouth full of meat. The bowl was nearly empty now. She opened her leather bag and took out the bread, broke off a piece, and mopped out the last of the juices. It wasn't elegant or even good manners, and she didn't care. Eleanor was warm for the first time in what seemed like days, warm inside. "That is truly the best thing I have ever eaten, Sarah. Thank you very much."

Sarah rubbed her work-worn hands together and smiled shyly. "I wus a good cook once. But there's little to cook now, since—"

"Yes, it must be very hard for you. I see you have a spindle there. Do you have sheep?" Even on the contentment of a full stomach, she didn't want to speak of the Darkness.

"A few what Sam found two year ago. A ram so old he can hardly stand, a young ewe an' an old one, and three lambs now. If this snow keeps on, starve they will. We put by as much fodder as we could, but it's most gone. Still, we are better off than many. If the grass comes, we'll slaughter the old ram, for one of the lambs is a ram. My mouth fair waters when I think o' mutton. I dream sometimes I'm back at Overton before the troubles. There's a great table with cheese and bread and wine and meat and fruits. There wus big barrels of flour in the kitchen, for the lord was very fond of bread and cakes. It don't bear talking about." She ended with a forlorn expression on her face.

"What do you do with the wool after you spin it?" Eleanor asked.

"Nothin'. Sam's going to make me a loom someday. I just spin to keep my hands busy."

"Don't you knit?"

Sarah looked at her curiously. "How do you mean?"

Eleanor hesitated to try to explain the intricacies of knitting without tools. "It's two pointed sticks and you...loop the yarn back and forth and make cloth." Rarely without a piece of knitting or crocheting near her, Eleanor was surprised that Sarah didn't know what she considered a primitive form of textile making. Still, the state of their clothing was terrible, yet they had wool to use, so why not repay their hospitality with a little time and instruction. "I'll show you, if Sam will whittle some sticks for me."

But Sam was already rummaging in a stack of smoothed wood in the corner. After a time he chose one straight rod, smaller than his finger, but long and polished. "I made this for the loom, but it is too short." He pulled out his knife and cut the rod into four pieces about a foot long. In a few minutes, he had whittled points onto each.

Sarah produced a ball of thick, greasy wool and gave it to her. Eleanor, who had been knitting since she was seven, had to think to try to remember the basics that had long since become entirely automatic. She demonstrated casting on and found that Sarah was quick. In an hour she had communicated the basics, including increasing and decreasing and how to make an opening in the middle of the piece. The result was an odd-looking sampler indeed, a serpentine thing with holes in it.

Sarah obviously saw the possibilities, and Eleanor had little doubt that she would invent most of the well-known stitch variations in short order.

While Sarah bent over her work, muttering, Eleanor told Sam that carving knobs on the ends of the knitting pins would keep the work from slipping off. Wrolf and the baby were asleep together, the child's head pillowed on the animal's side, and Sarah's fears forgotten. The scene was so safe and so domestic, Eleanor longed to stay.

She guessed it was sometime after noon, and her inner sense told her to get moving. She thought she had about five hours of decent light, if the constant twilight could be termed decent. Eleanor was certain she would be offered a place to sleep if she wanted one, but she knew she must go on.

Sam rubbed the points of a set of needles with some abrasive stone and smoothed them. He inquired in his slow way about sizes, and Eleanor tried to explain the relationship of thread thickness and needle size.

Finally, she said, "I must leave now. I have a long way to go."

"It will be dark in a few hours," Sam said. "We'd be pleased if you'd stay the night."

"Thank you, but I...feel I have to go on farther today."

"As you wish. Saree, stop yattering. The lady has to go."

"Oh, must you? Just to hear a new voice is a blessing, and this knitting! Do you know, now I see it, I think I seen it before. Mistress Overton had some hosen of fine linen. I washed them once and they looked like this, but so soft and fine I wus sure fairies had made them. I was a silly girl then."

"An' yur a silly woman now. Fairies, indeed!" Sam snorted good-naturedly.

"Yes, you can make stockings, but it's a different method. It takes four needles, very thin, with points at both ends, three in a triangle and one to knit with. Cast on the same number of stitches on each needle, then point the first to meet the last. If you do it right, you'll get a tube." Eleanor tried to explain circular knitting simply.

"We don't need stockings as Sam's got leather leggin's, but I think I follow the notion. Where did you say you learnt this?"

"My mother taught me, and she learned from hers. Now I must go." She reached for her cloak. "Sam, can I have a short stick to take with me?" She had suddenly remembered her need for a calendar and had thought of a way to keep one.

"A moment, milady." Sam got up and went into the shadowed corner where he kept his wood and tools. He brought back a staff, over five feet long, straight and carved with the four phases of the moon on its head, and a piece of dowel about eight inches long.

He lifted the staff. "I took this from the wreck of Aveburn Hall last summer when I wus grazin' my sheep. The best grazin' is in these stone circles, for they seem to be proof against...it. I'd build our house atop this hill, but Saree won't have none of it. Still, *it* don't bother much with the likes of us.

"The Hall went...under a year since. You must have passed it, if you came from St. Bridget's. No matter. Oh, the old lord is still there, an' his woman an' his girl—not his wife, mind. He's never wed, but fathered bastards on half the countryside. But he's mad an' his light is gone. The ol' woman, she says naught, an' the girl is wild but clean. Her name is Rowena, an' a good name, too.

"I think this staff was made for her, for it is quickbeam wood, which no evil can touch. I asked her if it was hers, but she jus' ran away. But I think it would be good for you to take on your journey. An' here's that bit you asked for." He held both out to her.

Eleanor reached out and took the staff slowly. A rosy glow ran up its length, and the moon figures seemed to pulse with silvery light. "Thank you, Samuel. I have no doubt it will be a good companion. Thank you both for everything. And, if I ever pass this way again, I'll come and knit and tell you of my adventures."

Sarah set aside her work and rose and kissed her warmly. Then she pressed a set of knitting pins and a lumpy ball of yarn into Eleanor's hands. Eleanor thanked them again, feeling they had given her more than she had returned, and said more farewells.

She put her cloak around her after stuffing the wool and the pins and dowel in the leather bag, and went and picked up the sleeping child. She kissed his forehead and whispered a blessing under her breath.

Then Eleanor and Wrolf walked out into the clearing. The complaints of sheep were audible from one of the huts. She turned west through the trees, carrying the staff in her right hand. Eleanor turned back and looked at the huts. Sam and Sarah were standing in the doorway, the child still asleep in Sam's arms, and she waved to them. They waved back. She trudged on, feeling both strengthened and depressed.

VI

When she came out of the woods, the dark mound of Silbury Hill was directly before her but some distance away. There was a kind of mist rising around the hill, so she could not judge how far away it was.

Eleanor decided to swing around the hill to the south, subject to Wrolf's approval, and stepped forward with renewed energy. The snow was very thin here, and the ground was muddy. She walked along, keeping the hill to her right. She was surprised then when she came out of a small thicket of trees and found it before her and much closer. She turned south again and found herself walking along a sort of ditch.

"You ever read Tolkien, Wrolf? No, of course not. Now, if you were a Narnian animal, you could talk. Poor Daddy. How he hated Lewis and Tolkien and Paxson and Duane. Not to mention Lloyd Alexander, who mainly wasn't mentioned. Daddy despised anyone who made new stories out of what he thought of as his own private preserve of myth and folklore.

"I'll bet you don't even know the legend of Silbury Hill. I have to admit I paid more attention to the folklore than I did to archaeology or geography last fall. You probably don't realize that a lot of very educated people have spent a great deal of time trying to figure out *why* a very small population spent their time dragging stones all over Britain, and other places, setting up circles. There's a big one south of us called Stonehenge, which was for observing the sun and the moon. But they have terrible disputes about stone circles, with snotty academics snidely suggesting nasty habits and frog ancestry for anyone holding a different theory than they do. If you are outside watching, I guess it's funny. I was a little too close.

"Now, Silbury is another matter. It's an earthwork, the biggest one in Europe. And the legend is that it is the burial place of one King Sil and a golden horse. You may well ask why I was muttering about Tolkien. Well, he wrote about some barrow mounds, which is another kind of earthwork, which had some really nasty inhabitants. You sure are a good listener. Yes, it's still in front of us, just like those barrows. Do you know, my mind doesn't like this at all, but my stomach says forge ahead. Tom Bombadil, where are you now when I need you?"

A few minutes later, she said, "No, we seem to keep hitting the hill, no matter where we turn. I should have stayed with Sam and Sarah. The idea of camping on Silbury, or under it, makes me very nervous, and the notion of crossing it at night appeals to me even less. It's big, but it's not that big, and we should have come around it now. Either it's moving or all roads lead to Rome." She knew she was talking to steady her nerves, that inner sense of right and wrong that had guided her so far. Right now it was humming inside her, a wasp's nest of anticipation, hinting not of danger, but of something simultaneously pleasant and unpleasant.

They crossed a marshy meadow and came to a stand of willow trees, bare of leaf but graceful in their nudity. Eleanor paused and looked at them, but they were only trees. She hoped. She cursed her imagination, her excellent memory, and a certain respected Oxford don, and entered the trees.

"Well, *Salix babilonica* is only inimical to Jews," she told the wolf with forced gaiety, "which is one thing I'm not. But I do wish Mother had bought a house in Yorkshire. Or Africa. Or Mars! To continue my lecture, there is some academic speculation that King Sil is a corruption of 'sal' or willow. Various people have dug holes in the mound and found nothing. I should be so lucky. I hate to tell you this, Wrolf, but I am not a very brave person. Yes, I slew the Black Beast, but that was Her, not me. Well, here we are at the base. Left, right, or over?"

It was warm at the bottom of the hill. Eleanor could see that the meager light was fading fast and that she had a choice of camping in the willows or using the last light to try to circle the mound. She knew its base was only a few acres, but standing under the bulk of it, it loomed like Everest. The path to the left looked clearer, but she was now suspicious of ease, so she walked north, to the right, and Wrolf trotted along beside her. She counted her steps and pushed aside low-growing bushes.

Quite suddenly, an opening yawned in the face of the mound. She stopped and stared at it. Wrolf sniffed and wagged his tail. Then he bounded into the tunnel a few feet and barked at her.

She paused, staring into the darkness at the faintly silvered form of the wolf. He was her guide, and she trusted his instincts and his choices. But she hesitated a long moment. Trust or not, she had no desire to go traipsing into the bowels of any ancient mounds.

Finally, Eleanor took a deep breath. "You know best, old fellow." Then she followed him.

The tunnel bore straight into the mound for a short distance, then branched off. The floor beneath her boots was smooth, as were the walls around her. Eleanor found the regularity of the walls uncomfortable. She wondered what could have made the tunnel and found images of great, blind worms boring into the earth floating in her mind. She banished them as firmly as she could and followed the wolf.

A soft, rumbling noise made her pause. She looked over her shoulder and saw the entrance vanish behind her. It was not, she found, entirely unexpected, but she didn't like it much. "Why didn't I stay with Sam and Sarah?" she whispered as she went after Wrolf. The passage branched, turning right into the center of the mound. The feeling of tons of earth around her was oppressive, and she moved on slowly. The rowan stave seemed brighter in her hand.

The tunnel changed color subtly, the walls beginning to give off a golden glow, making Wrolf a silver-and-black shadow. Ahead, Eleanor could see a larger golden area and eventually they came to a chamber. It was circular, perhaps forty feet around, with a smooth floor. In the middle of the room, there was a pool of water, a spring, and beside it stood a silvery willow tree, the long branches trailing into the bubbling water.

Eleanor stopped at the entrance to the chamber. She

felt a great reluctance to enter—not a fear but a sense
of intrusion. She studied the room. On one side of the
fountaining spring was a great chair, carved with moons
and blossoms. On the other was a short bench. The
water played up into the branches and she heard a faint
sound, like someone being tickled.

"May I enter, oh, well and willow tree?"

There was a sound of vast laughter. "Your welcome
should be obvious, child," said a female voice, which
came from the walls or the air.

"Thank you, whoever you are." Eleanor stepped into
the room timidly. Wrolf walked in with his lord-of-the-
manor air and flopped down beside the pool. Eleanor,
more cautious, dropped a curtsy in the direction of the
spring and another toward the chair.

"You are very polite, aren't you?"

"I try to be."

A woman stepped from behind the chair. She was
very beautiful to look upon, yet terrible, too. Her skin
was so white, the sun had never touched it, her lips a
deep red, and her hair as black as Eleanor's. But her
eyes were all white, and they seemed to speak of dreadful suffering. Eleanor bowed her head to release herself
from that chilling gaze and curtsied again, feeling the
point of the sword bang her leg.

Laughter. "Don't be frightened, girl. I won't harm
you. I've had enough trouble getting you here. You are
a very tough nut to crack, you know. Now sit, and we
will talk. You can call me . . . Sally."

The snort of laughter this name produced escaped
before Eleanor could suppress it. She clapped a hand
over her mouth, then said, "I beg your pardon."

"You haven't forgotten how to laugh. That is good.
And why not Sally? It's a good enough name for a simple
country goddess."

Eleanor found the courage to lift her head and look
at the woman. In the black hair and pale skin, she
caught a glimpse of her own features. The half-mad girl
Rowena had mistaken her for this woman, and Eleanor
wondered if she would be chastised for impersonating
a goddess. All she said was, "If you are a simple country
goddess, then I am Maria of Rumania."

"That fellow Graves has a great deal to answer for.

I think he positively enjoyed frightening people. I am not nearly as bad as he painted me. Sit down, there's a good girl. You have a great many silly notions in that pretty noodle of yours."

"Yes, ma'am."

"I know all your mind, your history, everything. No, you haven't nipped back to your century and your world; yes, I could speak directly to your mind, but I have a great fondness for the human voice. It is such a wonderful instrument when it is used well. Besides, the whole purpose was the entertainment. It's all meaningless without that."

"Entertainment?"

"I see that surprised you." The woman climbed into the great chair and leaned back. "I myself do not know if in the beginning there was but one of us or if we were many to start with. We are many now. Once, I think, we were much as you are, as the race of man. There is such a great deal I have forgotten.

"But we changed. Time ceased for us. Time is the measure of all things, but we did not create it, though some of our company have presumed to pretend to have made it or ruled it. Saturn!" Sally made a derisive, snorting noise through her nose. "And some of your people have given the dominion of time to us. But, time *is*. I have no doubt it existed before any creatures came to measure it.

"Time is more than a way to count the passing moments. It is a measure of change, of growth. And when it stops for any organism, there is no change. No change begets boredom. So, for millenia we have watched you with your brief lives and great violences. But you change. Thus, you are our entertainment. It is rare we even need to put our fingers in the pot to keep it interesting."

"Excuse me, but was I dragged back to thirteenth-century Albion for amusement?" Eleanor lost her awe of the goddess before her in a very human rush of rage.

The woman sat forward in the chair and opened her eyes, which had remained closed while she mused about the old gods. The blank orbs stared at Eleanor. "Oh, no, my dear, no." Sally shuddered. "Do you know what you did at the circle last night?"

"I killed a mucking, great, ugly snake."

"It wasn't really a snake, but you did destroy it. Now, why didn't you just run away? It was slow. Why did you stand and fight?"

Eleanor had no ready answer, so she considered for a while before she spoke. "I . . . was offended by it. When I set aside the assumption that Bridget meant me to kill the beast, which isn't clear, because I'm not sure I was ever *meant* to wield that sword, and ignore the underlying premise that the beast was evil and therefore killing it was the right thing to do, I think I have to say it was an aesthetic decision." Despite the complexity of her sentence, Eleanor felt very clear in her mind. "Evil seems to be a matter of viewpoint, at least it does a lot of the time. On another level, I killed it because the circle had offered me shelter and hospitality, and it was going to be violated. I did it for a lot of reasons."

"An aesthetic decision! Can you regard life as art, then?"

"Yes and no. I'm not Japanese. It has to do with value, which is so subjective that you can't even talk about it without getting confused. Uh, take this tree and the spring. It's a very beautiful tree, but in and of itself it has no great value to me. However, as a symbol of all willow trees, and by extension, all living things, I would regard it as valuable. The well, on the other hand, is water. Water has an immediate value to me, and I don't need to get symbolic about it. I can value it as good, clear water. People will often fight to defend a symbol of something they value as hard as they will defend the thing itself. And everything is both, I guess."

"Do you really believe that evil is all simple and relative?"

Eleanor thought again. "No. I believe true evil exists, just as true good does. But most of us never have to deal with the final absolute of either. Instead, we cope with small . . . shadows of a reality too big to encompass. But, I believe in life, probably because my mother struggled so hard to bring me forth. Now it's almost like she invested me with all the life she had in her. I don't like to think of her suffering my loss, because I know she would miss me. Am I dead, back there in my world?"

"Would it be cruel if you were?"

"Cruel? No, but very hard. I suppose I am feeling guilty because I've never valued my mother as much as she deserved. I shut her out, and now I want to say I'm sorry. I'm very good at being selfish, almost as good as my father." Eleanor, embarrassed at these revelations, yet unable to dodge or hedge under the blind stare, gave a crooked grin. "When does the bench turn into a couch, Dr. Freud?"

The goddess laughed. "My sister Bride has always had a talent for people. But she seems to have none for direction. Or perhaps she is more fortunate in her confidence. Laughter is easier than tears for her, and I am the other way around. I am something of a bitter pill to take."

"It must be all the salicylic acid," Eleanor answered without thinking. Then she reminded herself that she was talking to a powerful and capricious deity, not a nice old lady.

"Do you think so? Is the symbol different than the object? Or is it the same? If I changed the nature of the willow tree, would I alter in turn? No, I don't believe I want to do any tinkering. You have a good share of bravery, child. No one has made fun of me to my face in eons. It's quite refreshing. You can't imagine how tedious it gets to have no one pay attention to you at all."

"What do you mean?"

"You call me 'goddess' and offer me reverence. I am, indeed, what you call me. But I am also a reflection within you. We, my brothers and sisters and I, have speculated endlessly as to whether we created you, as we claim, or you created us, or something outside made both of us. If the last is true, then, for what purpose?

"Long ago," Sally continued, "I withdrew much from the company of my family and so have had a great deal of time for thought. I was always a bit solitary in my nature, but as my relations became more meddling and what you would call decadent, I became more reclusive. All that clamor they made. Perhaps that, too, comes from the willow and the water. I am not haughty as much as austere; I am not cruel as much as stern. I see in your mind the joylessness you perceive. Laughing willows are only in tales for babes.

"But I saw my kind demand more and more adulation from your people, until they were like fiends. There was no giving, and this troubled me. And then we stopped changing and growing. After a time, the worshipers grew disenchanted, and we began to fade. So, I think we are two voices intended to sing in harmony. I believe our disharmony has brought the Darkness."

"Will you tell me about that?" Eleanor had decided she was never going to get her question answered, but the more information she had, the better. Besides, did it really matter why she was chosen to be a heroine?

"Yes. As much as I know. First, there are many worlds of Earth. They exist only a breath away from each other. Do you remember that day in Ireland, you and your father lunching in a circle, and he began to recite an old tale? You fainted and were unconscious for some hours."

"I remember, yes." She did but very vaguely.

"You nearly slipped into the world where that story happened. Only your deep attachment to your father prevented it. I do not think any agency could have dragged you away while he lived."

"All right." A question rose in her mind that she did not like at all. Had "they" killed her father just to get her? Eleanor tried to dismiss it as paranoia or vanity, but the nagging worry persisted.

A deep resentment arose in her again, for being pushed about and ordered around, for getting cryptic answers or none at all to questions, when she could frame the queries at all. She had an impulse to just say "Go jump in the lake" to the powers that were using her. The words gathered in her throat and died there.

Something else stirred inside her, beyond the resentment and the anger. It was a feeling she did not have a name for, though it was rather a pleasant sense. She looked inwardly at it, and finally Eleanor could recognize what it was. She was being treated as if she were an able person. Haven't I always been? she wondered. And then she knew that she had always been used, fettered by her father into a fleshy extension of himself, excluded by her mother into an anxious, spiky child. She felt, in that moment, no anger at them, just a kind of vague disappointment that neither of them had been big enough to leave her some room for herself.

But, now, here, she had a sense of space and freedom. Bridget and Sally were no less demanding in their needs, but she felt as if she had a choice. No, not really, she reflected. I took the sword. Why did I do that? Of all the dumb moves, that's got to be some prize. I've always wanted to do *something*. What? Special. Important. I think my brains are made of noodles.

Sally began to speak again, and Eleanor was aware that she had been observed and monitored in her thoughts, and that she had passed some undefined test. "Each of those worlds is a little different, but if you laid them all in a line, the two ends would be very contrasting. Some of the worlds are already utterly dark, some gray, and silver, and some white.

"The Darkness is a force. It seems to be greater than life or death. Its origin is not known, but what it does is. It stops growth. Nothing dies and nothing is born. It is like a moment of the most intense agony, prolonged forever. And it creeps from world to world."

"Swell," said Eleanor. "It makes Mordor sound like a picnic. I'm supposed to stop that, here, in Albion? I am almost afraid to ask, but why me? Why not...my father? He was big and strong and very brave."

"Because he did not *believe*. His work was intellectual. It never touched his being. In order to invest a human with some of the powers we possess, the person must be able to give us...reality, first. And, too, a female is a better vessel."

"I still don't understand."

"Did you say to yourself, 'I am having a hallucination,' when my sister spoke to you?"

"Well, no."

"You just accepted it, didn't you?"

"Yes."

"You *know* us, in your bones."

"Oh. But, why don't you goddesses chase the Darkness away?"

"By ourselves, we are not strong enough. It must be two voices singing in harmony."

"I guess it's too late to say I wish someone had asked

me first. Great flaming owl turds! They say no man can escape his destiny. Which leaves free will out in the cold. But, dammit, I never wanted to be Wonder Woman."

"You don't *have* to do it."

"Don't I? What, go back and give Bridget her sword and cloak and spend the rest of my life feeling like a rat? I can't. My mother always said I was as stubborn as a pig, and she was right. I'm damned mad about being dragged into an adventure with too much knowledge on the one hand and not enough on the other. I wouldn't have come if I had been asked. You know how Daddy taught me to swim."

The chamber rang with Sally's deep laughter. "I do," she said finally. "But you lost your fear of water in that rough baptism, didn't you?"

"Maybe. I *hate* it when people do things for my own good."

"You are tired and hungry and dirty. It is hard to be hopeful in such a state. I think you will find the well a good temperature for bathing. Then you will eat and rest."

"Me? Wash in a sacred well?"

"Now, you told me a bit ago it was only water. Do you see how much you believe and why you were chosen?"

Eleanor gave no answer. Instead, she stood up and began removing her cloak. Sacred well or not, she was not about to pass up a bath.

She soaked luxuriantly in the steaming water. It was hot enough to satisfy a Japanese bather. Eleanor let her mind go blank. The aches and tensions of her body faded slowly, and she could feel herself turning into a giant prune. The tips of her fingers were already wrinkled, but she felt no inclination to end her bliss.

Eleanor saw the dead-white hand out of the corner of her eye a second before it shoved her head ruthlessly into the water, just enough time to take a sharp breath and hold it. The water, where it touched her face, was cold. She counted seconds in her mind and used swimmers' tricks for breath control, swallowing and expelling small amounts of air every twenty seconds or so, until her lungs were empty. She could vaguely feel Sally's hand twist into her long black hair, but she was powerless to get away from the iron grip.

She knew that in a few seconds, her inhale reflex would draw water into her lungs, but it didn't seem to matter. Eleanor wasn't even frightened, just a little sad at her betrayal. She liked Sally, and could not think of any offense she had given to the goddess. But after all, what did it matter? Death by water or death by fire, what possible difference could it make? She couldn't even conjure up the energy to be angry with the lady of willows for leading her down the garden path.

The now icy water filled her mouth and nose. It flowed down into her chest and abdomen, and the sense of great cold seemed to reach her fingers and toes, so warm a moment before. She hung frozen in the water for what might have been an instant or an eternity, void of any thought or emotion, until a pair of strong hands hauled her gasping to the edge of the well.

She clung to the slippery stones, feeling their hardness under her hands and against her chest. Eleanor gulped air and felt the ringing in her ears subside. Then Sally caught her under the arms and dragged her up out of the pool, cradling her body and crooning softly. Eleanor pillowed her head against Sally's breast and shoulder and gave a little mewling sob.

"There, there, dear child," Sally murmured as she stroked Eleanor's wet hair, "it's over now. Yes, I played a nasty trick on you, but you hadn't gotten over your fear of water, not really. Shh. Don't try to talk. Just be still and rest against me. It's been a long time since I held anyone in my arms. I had forgotten what a pleasant feeling it is. It almost tempts me to take a lover again, but they always seem to get possessive. Neither man nor god had dominion over me. Poor baby. Soon you will meet my sister, the sea, and you must not be afraid of her, for she's capricious enough to kill you."

Eleanor could feel the beat of a heart under her head. It was a steady, comforting rhythm. She found, as she lay there, that she could trace the flow of blood up and down Sally's body and even feel the net of nerves. She followed the nerves over the body until she touched upon the sexual center. The sensation of exploring this private sphere, even with her mind, was frightening and exciting.

She started to draw away in mind but found that the healthy animal part of her, dormant during her father's illness and annoyingly persistent since, was too strongly awakened. Eleanor wrestled with needs in herself that had been denied, the desire for love expressed as lust, the desire for any love at all in an environment where it was a rarity, and finally the need to offer love completely. She suppressed her body's desires sternly and found that there remained a vast reservoir of unexpressed affection.

Trembling slightly, she raised her head off Sally's breast and lifted herself a little. Then she clasped her arms around the goddess's neck and placed a fervent kiss upon the smooth cheek. Sal smiled slightly, then bent her head and returned the gesture.

The sensations Eleanor felt under the kiss were totally conflicting, simultaneously wild and calm. Her body experienced a prolonged climax that made her cry out sharply, but her mind seemed filled with cool green light that pulsed to gold as the kiss continued. She found her lips pressed against the goddess's, shutting off her wild cries. The golden light surrounded them both, piercing Eleanor's mind like the unshielded sun.

Her body shuddered and twitched, warm liquid coursing down the inside of her thighs, but Eleanor was less aware of this than of a flood of emotions for which she had no words. When they drew their mouths apart, the golden light lingered inside her. She did not try to identify it but took a deep sobbing breath and accepted it as something she might never understand. Then she blushed at her nakedness and the intimacy the lady's kiss had brought her.

Sal chuckled. "Silly goose. You just experienced the most perfect thing in the cosmos and you're embarrassed. Still, you are the product of thousands of years of guilt, which is a forerunner of the Darkness itself. And you did kiss me first, which I had not anticipated.

"No, I am not angry. You gave me such a token of love as I have not had in many years. All that joy, bottled up inside you! I am only surprised you never found a release for it, as human beings have been doing forever. Yes, I know your father overshadowed any rivals. Conceited man. Well, men all are, since they conceived the notion they were the Lords of Creation. Poor Electra. A father is only a suitable love object before one is ten. Ah, you shiver. Come, let us get some garments on you. One of the great mysteries is how such puny creatures as you humans can yet be so strong and enduring, while we, who need not food or shelter or clothing, dwindle. Perhaps it is the love you bear each other that sustains you. I feel positively juvenile, having tasted your love, child. 'Tis a fair, sweet thing, and I hope the brawny bastard who will take your maidenhead appreciates what he is getting. He probably won't, being male and Irish in the bargain. But he has dark hair, and that's a hopeful sign."

As she spoke, Sally helped Eleanor to her feet and handed her a gown of deep blue wool and a shift of rosy linen. Eleanor dressed silently. Then the lady handed her a knotted cincture of glossy white stuff, which she tied around her waist.

"Why is black hair a hopeful sign?"

"Dark men are the most considerate lovers. Never bed a flaxen-haired man unless you have no choice, or wish to get something from him. As for redheads, look at their hands. Good, square workman's hands are an indication of a caring nature, while fine, soft, elegant ones belong to a man who would dissect your nature in order to destroy you or try to reconstruct you in his own image."

"Like my father?"

"Yes. Now we will drink tea together, and I shall instruct you."

Eleanor remembered nothing after her first sip of bitter willowbark tea. It seemed to her she raised the earthenware cup to her lips, and when she lowered it, she was very tired. Her eyelids closed in sleep as she sat.

VII

Something warm and wet lapped her face. Eleanor reached out and felt Wrolf's shaggy mane. She pried her eyes open and looked around. She was lying on the ground, wrapped in her blanket, in a small stand of willow trees. The dark bulk of Silbury stood over her. She sat up, pushed the blanket aside, and stood up.

The air was warmer, and the willow trees were beginning to show swellings of green along their drooping branches. The ground was damp, but she could see no trace of snow in any direction. She could not guess how long she had spent with the Lady of the Willows, but from the appearance of the trees, it had been at least a month. She had a moment's thought for the stick she had begged from Sam, planning to notch it to keep track of the days. Now she would never know.

Eleanor looked at her things heaped on the ground. Bridget's cloak and sword, bound with the patterned belt, lay on the ground where her head had rested. The leather bag Ambrosius had given her bulged lumpily. There was another bag beside it, a dyed and worked leather sack, vermilion with golden suns, and a short strap.

She sat down again and went through everything. In the first bag she found a tunic, shift and hose, the mead, the book, and the knitting pins. The ball of wool Sarah had given her was gone, replaced with another of finer stuff, pure white and almost as smooth as silk. And there was the dowel Sam had given her. There were nicks in it. She counted them. Thirty slashes. So, it must be March the third or fourth.

Then Eleanor opened the other bag. There was a bowl and cup, of light-colored wood with a fine grain. It was carved around the outside with a braided pattern, and she paused over it, thinking of the embroidered bands on the robe of the cleric and on the tunics she had found at Gretry Hall. She kept meaning to ask about them and kept forgetting. There was also a small, carved spoon. She rubbed the wood with her fingers, feeling comforted. There was a bottle of almost clear stuff, which might be water. Then, in the bottom of the bag, a large napkin was tied around a beautiful loaf of bread, smelling slightly of honey, some white cheese, a roasted fowl, and some pieces of bark. She repacked the bag and tried to remember anything beyond the bitter taste of willow tea.

There was a nickering sound behind her. Eleanor turned around and saw a horse, a veritable monarch of his kind, as black as night but with a silvery mane, tail, and hooves. He pawed the ground and whinnied softly.

"Hello, big fellow," she said, standing up, all thoughts of willow tea forgotten. She raised her hand to stroke the quivering muscles along the neck. The horse snorted and tossed its head. "Where did you spring from? You are a steed fit for an emperor, at least."

There was a fine leather bridle around his neck, just a hackamore with no bit. The leather was silvery gray, as supple as willow but very strong. He wore no saddle or other trappings.

"Well, I *did* wish for a horse, but you are quite beyond my dreams. Will you bear my body upon your back?" The horse nickered and nodded its great head.

"Mounting you is going to be a real challenge. Hmm. The rock over there is a pretty good height." She bent over and picked up the cloak-bound sword. She tied it across her shoulders, then put on her cape. She shook out the blanket vigorously, folded it, and laid it over the broad back of the horse, moving slowly and doing nothing that might spook him. He stood there as if having soiled and tatty blankets put on him was an everyday occurrence. "This isn't nearly nice enough for you, but I hope you won't mind too much. There's a good fellow." She picked up her two bags, slipped them over her shoulder, and sighed.

She looked at herself, seeing the rosy shift and wool tunic that Sally had dressed her in what seemed like a moment before. The silky white cord lay in her hands, and she had a fugitive memory that the knots in it meant something. She had a brief flash of visions, like single frames of a hundred different movies spliced together, words, touches, smells and sounds, all blurred, then gone.

Eleanor turned to the mound and bowed. "I thank you, oh Lady of the Willows, for all your gifts and your many kindnesses. I go to try to accomplish the tasks set for me by your sister Bridget with a glad heart and the hope that the harmony between my people and yours, which you have taught me, will someday be realizable. I shall not forget the sweetness of our voices together, nor the love you gave to me." She found her face was wet with tears and that she had a sense of loss as great as that which followed her father's death. A sound, like a stag at bay, seemed to echo from the earth before her, a noise so filled with pain that Eleanor wanted to clap her hands to her ears. Wrolf howled and scrabbled his paws over his flattened ears.

She bowed her head and let the tears fall for several minutes. She felt her own sorrow, but even worse, she sensed Sal's loss. The goddess had not released her gladly or willingly. "I'll come back. I promise." Then she straightened her shoulders, feeling the bite of the hilt of the sword in her right scapula, and turned to the horse. She led him to the stone she had chosen for a mounting block.

On her first try, Eleanor caught her foot in her skirts and slid off the horse onto the other side, landing in a tumble of legs and baggage. Eleanor giggled at her clumsiness, got up, and brushed the dirt off her bottom, then kilted the bottoms of her robe and shift up into the knotted cincture. She replaced the blanket, and her second mounting was more successful and more graceful. The horse stood with the quiet patience of his kind while she tugged her cloak into place, shifting the two bags into the least uncomfortable position she could find. She patted his neck and took the bridle lightly in her hand.

Wrolf was on his feet, barking. He dashed back and forth while she tried to figure out what she had done wrong. Finally, he grasped the rowan staff in his huge teeth and dragged it over toward her, growling. He put his forepaws on the mounting block and raised it enough so that Eleanor could bend down and grasp it without slipping off the horse. She took it in her left hand.

"Thank you, Wrolf. I don't know what I'd do without you. Shall we go?" He barked his reply, and the horse began a slow walk through the willow trees. Eleanor, unfamiliar with near bareback riding, though she was a good enough horsewoman with a saddle and a bitted horse, let him choose the pace. She had her hands full, literally, with the reins and stave, concentrating on pressing her knees in to grip the horse. Wrolf wove along before them, bouncing in and out of the trees like a puppy.

They went south around the mound and came out into a flat field. The horse increased its pace a little, moving faster than Eleanor could have walked but not so fast that Wrolf couldn't keep up.

The sky was an unbroken gray. They went south, as best as Eleanor could guess, and a little west. The terrain was rough with stands of trees here and there. By the time the sun was making a pale patch almost overhead, they came to the edge of the Salisbury Plain, the land falling away flatly, the ground damp and marshy. She could not judge the distance to the famous circle at Stonehenge, but in any case, it was too far away to see.

The horse turned west now, skirting the edge of the plain. Eleanor's legs began to ache, and the blanket chafed her calves through her hose. She gritted her teeth and hung on, ignoring her shoulders, cut by the straps of her bags and the constant rubbing of the sword on her left hip. The land grew hillier, and she was considering walking when they came to the castle.

Since it was the first intact stone structure she had seen since St. Bridget's Priory, Eleanor stared at it in mild disbelief. She had almost forgotten such things existed.

It was not particularly large or impressive in any way, just thick stone walls around some buildings, a tower rising over the tops of the walls. She was glad for this sign of human habitation but nervous, too. The horse drew to a halt before the drawbridge while Eleanor wondered whether to dismount or urge him onward.

"Well, Wrolf, how does this place feel to you?" The wolf raised his hackles and whined at the same time. The whine she had come to know as a signal of pleasure, but the ruffled fur about his neck puzzled her. "Good and bad, huh?" He answered with his sharp bark.

Two men came out from under the portcullis. One was tall and fair, walking with a strong stride, the chain mail he wore making a tiny jingling noise. His companion was bent with age, leaning heavily on a thorny black stick, his eyes running with rheum and his steps halting. In the pale, fading half-light of day, she could hardly see their auras. Since she could make no judgment about them, she mistrusted them both.

The younger man spoke after looking at her and the horse. "What a fine gift this is, a horse and a good, strapping wench." He moved toward her while Eleanor fumed slightly over his words.

"Clovis, stop it!" That was the old man.

"Quiet, dodderer, or I'll kill you where you stand. I might do it, anyway. You are sooo boring."

"Don't be a fool." The old man hurried forward, wheezing and coughing to stand beside the younger man. "Milady, he is young and im—" A sharp smack in the mouth stopped the quavering flow of words from the old man. A trickle of blood ran from the corner of his mouth. Wrolf gave his low growl but did not move.

Eleanor watched the little scene, thinking furiously. Rape was not an alternative she had previously considered. She decided quickly that while she was not mesmerized by any snake or virginity, neither was she inclined to submit to the inevitable. The sword tied to her back would have made short work of Clovis, but it wasn't available, and besides, she knew her knowledge of swordsmanship was clumsy, too awkward to try on horseback with no saddle to steady her. She was pretty sure *he* knew how to handle the great thing clanging at his side.

Clovis came up to the horse's head and reached for the bridle. Eleanor dropped the reins and grasped the rowan staff in both hands. Then she brought the end up and rammed it into the man's chest with all her weight and energy, barely managing not to unseat herself. She squeezed her legs against the horse, and he took a step forward.

Clovis made an *oof*ing noise and staggered backward. Eleanor brought the carved end of the staff down on his head with a sharp crack, and he slumped to the ground in a half-conscious heap. He put a hand to his brow and struggled up, but his knees sagged under him again.

"I will . . . kill . . . you for this," he muttered, and vomited on the ground. He retched horribly and grabbed for her foot.

"Stubborn bastard, aren't you?" she shouted, kicking the hand away and almost unseating herself. "Coward! Keep your filthy hands on the ground where they belong, or I'll break them off. Down, dog of night! Grovel! You are a breath away from death." The words startled her, and she sensed that they came not from her, but from the cloak pressing against her back.

Clovis cowered on the ground, almost whimpering and bringing up thick, dark vomit. The old man moaned helplessly.

"Don't kill him, milady. He meant no harm."

"No harm! Have your wits left you? Of course he meant me harm. He's as full of sin as an egg's full of meat," she said, falling back on an expression of her mother's. "My wolf has better manners."

The old man struggled forward but stopped well out of her reach. "Yes, milady. Whatever you say, milady. What should I do? Blessed Mary, what should I do? If only he were not so spoilt!" He twisted his hands together, and his stick fell to the ground.

"Spoiled?" She glanced down at the golden hair and the nape of the man on the ground. "He's rotten, which is a different matter altogether."

"Yes, milady. Oh, dear, oh, dear. And it is his birthday, too."

Eleanor was reminded so forcibly of the White Rabbit that she almost expected the old man to pull a watch from under his robes. "Stop fussing, old one. I never kick a man when he can't fight back. Get someone to help carry him into the keep, or do the two of you dwell here alone?"

"No, milady. Hoy! Will! Gowan! Master's ill. Come quick." The old man's voice was reedy but carried surprisingly well.

Two men emerged from the shadow of the portcullis. They wore leather tunics and rough leggings, and neither of them looked very friendly. Eleanor reined the horse back from the fallen body of Clovis, and the men picked him up, shoulders and feet, and carried him away.

"Who are you, old man?" she asked.

"Some days I hardly know myself," he answered. "But I am called Roderick. This is Nunnally Castle. Milady, night comes. Will you enter, for I must close the gates quickly. There are *things* that howl around our walls after day. Still, your brightness may keep them away. My lord's sister would no doubt be pleased in your company."

Eleanor considered. The horse and Wrolf had brought her here, and she did not doubt there was some purpose in the visit. It annoyed her that her animal companions knew more about what was going on than she did, in one way, but she trusted Wrolf utterly. She was inclined to trust the unnamed horse as well.

A night in the open did not appeal to her, not with the memory of the Black Beast as fresh as yesterday, though more time had passed than that. She urged the horse forward and dismounted on the drawbridge when she had passed Clovis's vile mess. She swung her right leg over the horse's back and slid to the ground with a thump. The blanket fell to the ground and she picked it up, shaking the dust out of it, then tossed it around her shoulders over her cloak. Then she pulled her skirts out of her belt, covering her legs.

The old man took her dismount for acquiescence and bent to recover his bumpy cane. She scooped it up for him, fearing he would fall flat on his face. He grunted and began to hobble toward the gates. She peered over the edge of the drawbridge as she followed him and saw the water in the moat. It was so murky that it offered her no hint of reflection.

They crossed the drawbridge and came to an open court beyond the portcullis. "Where is your stable?" Eleanor asked.

"There, milady. But, the men will—"

"I prefer to see to my horse's needs myself." She went into the stable, a large, dank hall with a few stalls in a dilapidated state. "Oh, what a mess. Whew! Ah, a shovel." She picked up the tool and scooped out the least dirty stall as Roderick watched helplessly. Then she found some fairly clean straw and scattered it about, keeping back a handful or two for rubbing down the horse's coat. When she was satisfied with her arrangements, she led the horse into the stall and gave him a good rubdown, although he had barely worked up a sweat. Still, it was a gesture of affection she could hardly deny her new friend. She found some rather wormy grain in a damp barrel and carried several handfuls over to the manger, tossing anelids on the filthy floor and hoping he wouldn't get sick. Then she stroked his great neck and murmured foolish pleasantries, reluctant to depart. The horse snorted and blew and gave her a nudge, clearly indicating that the audience was ended.

When Eleanor, Wrolf, and Roderick crossed the court, night had come. The drawbridge was pulled up and several men loitered in the court, more visible by their muddy brown auras than by the single torch flickering against the wall. They huddled together, eying her, muttering ominously. As she approached, they sorted themselves into a hostile mob, nervous and spoiling for a fight.

"No wench can hit our master!"

"What's she here for, anyhow?"

"Here, now, Roderick, what call had yew to bring her in here!"

"Let's grab her."

"Break her jaw so she can't bite."

"Let's have a bit o' fun before we kill her."

Eleanor was tired from a long day on horseback. She was hungry, and she found she had neither the patience nor the energy to deal with a pack of suspicious yokels bent on rape and murder. The cloak across her back was hot and heavy, and again she felt as she had when she had spoken to Clovis, that she was an empty cup into which someone had just poured some fearfully potent liquor. She brought the end of her staff down on the stones with a ringing smack.

"Silence!" The men hesitated. "Your master is a coward and a thief!" They rumbled angrily. "Oh? Then would you see me as I really am?" Eleanor pushed back her cloak and lifted the staff, feeling the power of the elements themselves flow through her booted feet.

Light coursed around her, throwing great shadows on the flagstones. A huge ball of silvery light seemed to emanate from the head of the stave. The men stared at her and seemed to shrink back. Sticks and stones fell from nerveless hands, and they scattered into the darkness like a covey of quail. In a few moments, the courtyard was empty.

Eleanor felt the strange power leave her. She wondered who or what it was, and the answer came into her mind, that it was Bridefire, the essence of Bridget. Sally would not have let the men off so quickly or so lightly. Now, with the deity withdrawn, Eleanor was scared, though she did not show it. I am going to have to keep a good grip on my Irish temper from now on, she thought. I might have killed someone. She got a response to that thought from the sword. It had no scruples about killing. Killing was what it was for. She was distracted by her thoughts of an amoral weapon by Roderick's fluttering apology.

"Milady, I beg your forgiveness for the men. They did not know...who you were. As, indeed, I do not. Oh, if only *he* were not so foolhardy. Who *are* you?"

Her name rose to her lips and died there. Sally's voice touched her mind. "Never give your name to strangers." And she knew her basic magic well enough to know that made good sense. "You may call me...Esperanza," she answered, amused at herself. Still, the Spanish word for hope was as good a name as any, and her last name in the bargain.

Roderick shuffled his feet and nodded his head. "Oh? Esperanza. It is a foreign name."

"I have traveled across the sea." That was true enough. If one did not say which sea.

"Welcome to thee, Lady Esperanza. These are dark nights."

"Yes, for strangers to travel," she answered, using the passwords from Sir Arthur Conan Doyle's *The Valley of Fear* without thinking. Then she realized that her

response had confused the old man, and she was furious
with herself. "Forgive me, Roderick, but I am tired. I
am glad to be here and sorry that I had to punish Clovis."

"Ah, if only the old master had done so, before his
death, we might not have come to this. But he pampered
Master Clovis, yes, and spoilt him. And paid no mind
to poor Lady Iseult, though he is the elder. Here is the
hall, milady."

A few half-starved dogs stood up and wagged hopefully, then took one look at Wrolf and fled ignomini-
ously to a dark corner, yelping piteously. The hall was
long and dark, a fire dying in the enormous fireplace,
the dogs and people giving off faint nimbuses in the
gloom.

Before the fire, Clovis lay on a pallet, a woman bend-
ing over him and placing wet cloths on his brow. Eleanor
looked at the woman while Roderick shuffled forward
to lay a small log on the grate. The fire licked at the
log like a hungry beast.

The woman was fair, though darker than Clovis, her
long braids like streams of honey over her shoulders.
Her tunic was worn and patched, and the hem of her
shift was dark with dirt. But the likeness between the
unconscious man and the woman left no doubt in Elean-
or's mind that they were closely related and that this
was almost certainly the Lady Iseult.

She measured them in the radiance of their beings,
as had become almost instinctive in her few meetings
with people since Ambrosius had told her what the glow
was. She knew, too, from the reactions of people, that
her own was very bright, though she had no idea why.
And the story was plain enough. Clovis flickered, his
light fading in and out like a wavering candle. The
woman glowed with a steady brightness that the added
fire did nothing to diminish. This, at least, confirmed
Eleanor's suspicion that it was Clovis who was suc-
cumbing to the Darkness, not the entire castle.

"Lady Iseult, here is milady Esperanza. Oh, the fire
burns the wood so quickly! How is Master Clovis?" He
put another log in the hearth.

"He sleeps and does not wake. Lady, why did you
strike my brother?"

"He threatened to rape me and steal my horse. It seemed just cause at the time."

"But your body is his by right."

"Nonsense. My body is mine, and I give it where *I* please, not to any cock-a-hoop petty lordling with more balls than brains. Certainly I don't lie with cowards. Stop defending him out of duty, as he goes to the Darkness, and look to yourself. Stand up and look to the light, Lady."

Iseult staggered to her feet, jerked by an invisible chain. She turned and stared at Eleanor, then stumbled forward and knelt, clutching the hem of Eleanor's gown and sobbing. Eleanor took the trembling hands and held them, smiling.

"Here, now, none of that. Oh, you poor dear. It's all right now." She bent down and hugged the woman and kissed her cheek. "No, no, I am not She to whom you pray. Shh, that's almost sacrilege. I am but the youngest of her servants. There, now. Dry your eyes. I am only hope, not deliverance. Why, woman, you are skin and bones. Why is Lady Iseult dressed in rags and half-starved?" She patted the bony back and addressed her question to Roderick. Several servants in the hall looked away, and the old man shuffled and hummed and coughed.

"'Twas by his order."

"Why?"

"I know not."

"He...wished to lie with me," Iseult whispered. "I could not."

"Of course you couldn't," Eleanor whispered back. She looked at the sleeping cause of all the problems and was half-tempted to leave him where he was. But those forces that had invested themselves in her, Bridget and Sally, would not tolerate that. She felt their command: "Heal, always heal."

"Roderick, is there a large barrel or cauldron in the keep?"

"Yes, milady."

"Good. Have it brought before the fire. Heat water and fill it. And meanwhile, I require food, and so does Lady Iseult." *The problem with having a couple of goddesses inside you is you get a little bossy.* Eleanor was not used to asserting herself, and it made her acutely uncomfortable.

The next half hour was a bustle of activity. Nervous women in kerchiefs and aprons brought out roasted fowls and the cooked haunch of some animal while some of the men Eleanor had confronted in the courtyard dragged a barrel before the fire. Pots of water were heated and the barrel slowly filled.

Eleanor, feeling that charge of the keep had obscurely passed to her for the moment, forced meat and a mealy bread on the still stunned Iseult. The lady ate like a wolf. In fact, Wrolf's approach to the scraps Eleanor tossed him was more elegant. There was a boiled fowl as well, and Eleanor hacked a leg off it and chewed at it messily, ignoring the lack of seasonings and trying not to recall Sarah's savory stew. She was not about to send her compliments to the cook. She realized with a start that she had some assumptions about the food of the Middle Ages, mainly gathered from old movies, which had nothing to do with the reality.

The meal was silent. Various servants and liege men took places at the far end of the table, gobbling up bowls of a stew that looked nasty and smelled worse. The bread they got was worse than that which she and Iseult shared, for she could see the animal life that had been baked into it. Roderick sat down by her and hacked off a slab of cooling meat. The fat was congealing, and Eleanor was glad she had stuck to boiled bird.

"The water is as hot as it will get, milady," he muttered, dribbling juices from the corners of his mouth.

Eleanor rose from the table, causing some confusion below the salt, for the servants were undecided if they should go on eating or stand. She waved a calm hand at them, and they stayed where they were.

Since she had entered the cold, drafty hall, there had been a voice inside her that she recognized as Sally's. "Wherever you can, child, heal. Bring light and joy. Always joy. Remember our two voices raised in love and know that you can give that harmony to others. You have given me back my own laughter. I had forgot. Let your light shine in the joy of life, and heal!"

Somehow, in the month of which she had no memory, only fragments, Eleanor had accepted that task as well as the ones Bridget had set her. In truth, she felt more confident about healing than about killing beasts and driving out the Darkness. And she found that she had made a discovery in that lost month. She was a joyous person, and she had never known it before. She knew, too, that she took more pleasure in solitude than in the company of others, and in that, she was like the Lady of the Willows, but Eleanor felt now that she understood both of the goddesses better.

The water in the barrel was tepid to the touch. Eleanor rubbed her greasy fingers in the stuff, then closed her eyes and thought of fire. Her right hand became a glowing member, which she could "see" even with her eyes shut. She thrust it into the water, and the water churned and bubbled. When she was satisfied that the water was hot, she withdrew her hand and watched it turn back into its normal self. She went to the table.

"I want Clovis put into the water."

Roderick got up sputtering. "But—"

"Remove his boots and mail and stand him in the tub." She used a voice that was neither Sally's nor Bridget's nor her own, but a curious combination, which nonetheless carried command. A couple of men got up from the end of the table and came to the sleeping Clovis. They took off his boots, and Eleanor wished her nose were less fussy. Then they sat him up and dragged off the mail. One took Clovis under the arms and stood him up, and the other lifted his legs into the water.

With some difficulty, they got him into the barrel, for Clovis was both flaccid and awkward. Water splashed over the sides and onto the filthy floor. Eleanor opened the vermilion bag and unwrapped the tied napkin. She took a piece of willow bark out and dropped it into the water. Clovis sank down until the liquid was up to his shoulders. Eleanor got out the little wooden cup and poured it over his head as the bitter scent of willow pervaded the hall. It seemed to sweep out all the dank and musty odors that had accumulated there, and Eleanor paused a moment, feeling the poignant memories and the terrible sense of loss the scent brought back to her.

Then she filled the little cup with the water and

poured it over Clovis's head. Speaking very softly, she said, "In the name of the Light, I bless you. In the name of Joy, I bless you. Be thou reborn in the hope of life. You will wake and be whole and clean and strong. In the faith of life everlasting, I christen thee... Lewis of Nunnally. May you turn your face ever from the Shadow. Come now, Lewis, and cast off the Darkness and look only to the Light." Eleanor leaned down and kissed the damp brow.

His eyes snapped open. He looked at her blankly for a second. "What a comely girl you are, indeed. What is this? Am I a pickle? Or are the stores so scarce you must boil me for dinner in my clothes? No, I see some meat upon the board. What is all this, dark maiden? No, you are not dark. I don't think I've ever seen so much light. It's quite blinding and it's giving me a headache. Iseult, Roderick, what is happening?" The men helped him, dripping, from the barrel while they tried very hard not to laugh in his face.

Iseult rose, smiled, and hugged her brother. "You've been ill, Lewis, and this wise woman has healed you. Now come and eat. Go get him some dry clothes," she directed a servant.

He sat in the great chair at the head of the board. "Ill? I don't remember being ill. And why are you wearing those old clothes, Iseult? Are we poor, sister? I can't seem to remember anything."

"No, no. But you have been ill a long time. Have some meat."

"I'm not hungry. Who is *she*?" Eleanor was putting her cup back in her bag.

"The wise woman is Esperanza. She came a great distance to make you well."

"Sperance? Does that not mean *hope* in the common tongue? I thought you were locked up in a box somewhere. No, that is another story. I suppose I should be thankful, milady, but since I have no memory of being ill, it is difficult to be grateful. Still, from the look on my sister's face... it must have been awful, and I am glad to be spared the memory. Turn away from me, will you not, for I am quite dazzled."

Eleanor drew her cloak about her and pulled up the hood. She was relieved that by renaming Clovis she had not apparently changed his personality. He seemed to be the same obnoxious, egotistical kind of fellow she had met before the gates. He still had reacted first to her sexually, just as he had outside. But she wondered why her light bothered him. Iseult had not complained of it. Where will I ever find a man with enough light of his own? she wondered.

"There is no box large enough to hold hope," she said.

"Perhaps." He clearly wasn't philosophical. "But why is there no music?"

VIII

The stunned silence that followed his question indicated to Eleanor that whatever had happened to the household musicians, it was a very bad thing. The people at the far end of the table hung their heads, and Iseult and Roderick turned very pale in the firelight.

"They are *gone,* my lord," Roderick said in a strangled voice.

"But I want music!" the young man said petulantly. He pouted and frowned.

Eleanor's palm itched to slap his pretty face, but she resisted the impulse. Instead, she fumbled in her mind for a tune, for there were many there, jostling each other. One cannot spend a dozen and more summers in Ireland without acquiring at least a nodding acquaintance with the rich musical heritage of the island, and indeed Eleanor had virtually been nursed to the sound of the Rovers and the Chieftains. She rarely sang herself, having a soft voice and a limited range, unlike her father's bari-tenor and her mother's hefty alto; song was the one place where Daniel and Elizabeth ever displayed the spirit that had led them to wed, back before the sadness of all the lost babies corrupted their love into a kind of coldness.

The song that rose to her lips was not a typical drinking song or a tale of love betrayed, both subjects so dear to the Gaelic heart, but an odd tune in a minor key Eleanor had always thought had come back from Syria or Greece with some Crusader, so Eastern were its rhythms and progressions. But it swelled out of her throat with a will of its own, the words still in Gaelic, for she had no intention of trying to translate and sing at the same time. But it was a song of roses, and like its subject, the song had a certain fragile fragrance of its own.

Lewis stared at her, his mouth in a slack smile, and then closed his eyes. He was asleep, snoring gently, before she was done, leaving Eleanor to reflect on music to soothe the savage beast and sleep to knit up the raveled sleeve of care. He was ridiculously young and vulnerable-looking in his slumber. The serving folk muttered uneasily. Wrolf, asprawl by the fire, growled them into silence.

Iseult looked at her brother. "He is only sleeping. 'Tis quite normal. Carry him to bed. What was that you sang, lady?"

"Just a tune from far away. Just a song of roses, nothing more. What...happened to your musician?"

Iseult looked ill. "There were two. He hacked them up in a fury one night, then...ate them."

Eleanor decided she did not want any further details. Besides, she could hear something far away on the Plain, a sound that made her blood run cold, and sweat run down her body. It was a horrible, keening scream, and the others heard it, too, for they shifted nervously in their places.

"What was that?"

"A great animal that stalks the Plain, a sort of...wolf. We have tried to kill it, but—"

"Does it attack the keep?"

"It tried, but the very stones seem to have some virtue to keep it at bay. My mother told me the castle was built from stones set in a circle and that the circle was a temple of the moon."

Eleanor looked at the stones around her and heard a faint echo of the song she had heard at Avebury. The voices of the stones were weak, and she grieved a little for them. Still, there was light and energy in them yet. Her "hearing" seemed to expand, and she felt the suffering of the earth as the creature moved across it and heard the voice of the ancient spring somewhere beneath the castle. It was Sally's music, that spring, and it spoke to her quite clearly.

"Heal, always heal. Kill the wolf! Restore me. Kill the wolf!"

Eleanor was tired after a day on horseback, but she

was obedient to the wishes of her mentor. She did not pause to wonder if she had the strength to do what she was asked. Then she heard Bridget's voice, too. "Be careful. Circle to the right, always right, as you attack."

"Give me a garment... here, you, take off your tunic. I'll be damned if I'm going to be hampered by skirts." She picked the coat of mail off the floor where someone had left it when they'd put Lewis in the barrel. The man gaped at her, then slowly undid his belt. Eleanor weighed the chain mail in her hands, wondering if it was worth using. The man handed her his tunic. It smelled of earth and sweat and beer, but Eleanor didn't care. Those were good, clean, real scents, and they reassured her.

She moved to a dark corner and untied the sword and cloak from her back. Then she removed the blue tunic and rosy undergarment and put the man's tunic on. It hung to her knees. She tied a belt around it with nervous fingers. The mail she left behind. She folded her robes carefully into a neat pile.

Eleanor unrolled Bridget's cloak and sword. Whispering a litany in words she did not understand, she picked up the sword. After a moment's pause, she put the wonderful blue cloak around her for the first time. The chill that the lack of undergarments had left on her skin departed.

The sword lay in her hand as if it had always sat there. This time there was no shock but only a feeling of strength and warmth. Deciding she was as ready as she would ever be, Eleanor turned to face the people at the table.

"Milady..." Roderick began.

"Just open the gate. We'll talk about it later. Listen, he's almost here."

"Open the gates," Iseult said slowly. "God go with you, Esperanza."

When they came into the courtyard, the horse was standing there, his silver mane and tail twinkling in the darkness, and soft puffs of ruddy mist coming from his nostrils. He screamed his horsey challenge and stamped his feet on the stones, sending out little sparks of light.

"Sorry, old fellow, but I can't ride you without a

saddle, not for this. But you can come along for the fun, if you like." She caressed his soft nose.

"Fun? Is she mad?" someone muttered near her.

"No, only Irish," Eleanor answered irrelevantly. The crowd around her was a glow of pale souls in the darkness. She could see fear and anxiety on the faces, but a few looked a little hopeful. She could hear the whisper of prayers from some of the women.

The moon had risen, but its slender light was just a sliver of white in the sky. Still, Eleanor felt a faint flicker of power from it.

The creaking of wood and metal told her the portcullis was being drawn up. She walked into the dark arch and out onto the drawbridge. When she got across, she looked back for a second and saw a slight glimmer upon the battlements, which indicated that a few hardy souls had decided to watch.

Wrolf and the horse stood on either side of her. She waited, listening to the terrible howling of the animal as it came closer. It loped forward, then stopped about fifty feet away from her and gave a growl that sent shivers over her body.

It was indeed a wolf, or something of that nature, and it was enormous. She guessed its height to be about twelve feet at the shoulder, and she wondered how she was going to reach it.

"Oh, Bridget, if only I were as tall as you. But if I can get under his belly . . . He's so black." She trembled a little, then threw her shoulders back and took a deep breath. "Away with you, son of Night! Go back to the pit that spawned you."

The wolf bounded toward her, a dark mist flowing from its slavering jaws. Eleanor stepped to the right and almost slipped in Clovis's dreadful vomit. Wrolf howled, and the horse raced at the beast, running past its side, then rearing and striking its hooves at the rear flank. Wrolf leapt under the belly and closed his jaws on the other's rear leg.

The huge animal howled in rage and surprise. It turned its great head to snap at the horse, but the horse danced away. Eleanor brought the sword down on the undefended foreleg. Dark blood gushed out. She danced around to the right as the great head came around to snap at her.

An enormous blast of lightning struck the ground nearby. The wolf howled and screamed at the light. The stink of ozone reached her over even the rotting smell of the beast. There was more lightning, until the four combatants were almost in a corral of bright bolts.

Wrolf worried at the hind legs of the beast while the horse seemed to be wherever the head of the wolf was not, running in a circle around the animal. Eleanor darted around, cutting at whatever limb of the animal she could reach. Finally, she hacked through the sinew of one hind leg. The blood gushed out and hit her in the face, almost blinding her. She stumbled back and wiped her face on a sticky sleeve.

The head of the beast loomed over her, his icy breath filling Eleanor's nostrils. A terrible darkness covered her mind, but she raised the sword and hacked at the snout. The sword of Bridget flamed where it touched the muzzle, and the wolf screamed. The mental blackness passed, but the lightning almost blinded her.

Eleanor stepped back and blinked. The rear end of the beast sagged slowly to earth. The horse drove its hooves into the backbone as the wolf twisted to try to reach it. Eleanor leapt forward and drove the sword into the exposed throat of the wolf with all her might. She pulled the sword out and stepped away.

The wolf gave a gurgling shudder, and its head fell forward. A gasping breath was exhaled from its collapsing lungs. Eleanor felt the icy blackness cover her face. Then she knew nothing.

There were voices nearby, but she could not reach them. They called her, but she was unable to answer. There was nothing but icy cold and darkness, except a distant rippling noise that meant nothing.

"Lady Iseult, she hardly breathes."

"I can see that, Roderick! Bring me her things. Perhaps there is some virtuous herb or magic medicine within them. It has been a day and a night since she fell, and there is no wound. This is bread and fine cheese and some pieces of bark. A bottle. Nothing but water or wine. No, see how her tongue presses at her teeth.

Lift up her head—gently, you old fool! It does not smell like water or wine, does it? Her tongue is so swollen...hold her higher. I don't want to choke her."

Something hard and cold touched her lips. There was a smell she could remember but not name, then a taste on her tongue, a bitter, acrid, green flavor. Some liquid flowed back into her throat and she swallowed.

The rippling sound seemed to flow through her, and words without meaning echoed in her darkness. *River, stream, brook, pond, spring. Green, green, green grow the rushes.*

Eleanor gave a choking gasp and opened her eyes. She clawed at the bottle Iseult held to her mouth and gulped a huge mouthful. The bitter taste of willow seemed to course over her whole being. The blackness dwindled and faded as she remembered the fight and the wolf's dark breath.

She lay before the fireplace in the hall, dressed in a shift and piled deep in blankets. Wrolf was panting at her feet, and he gave one of his sharp barks. Iseult knelt beside her, and the old man cradled her shoulders in his trembling arms. Warmth returned to her and she began to sweat.

"Thank you," she croaked. Her voice sounded like a rusty hinge.

"Shh. Don't speak."

"Thirsty."

Iseult held out the bottle of water, and Eleanor shook her head. Iseult closed it up and went to the fireplace. She poured something from a pot hanging there into a cup and brought it back. She held the cup to Eleanor's mouth.

It was wine, hot and redolent of spices. It smelled better than it tasted, but Eleanor gulped it down. The dregs almost choked her. Then she pushed some of the coverings aside weakly.

"Hot," she muttered. Her throat ached as if she had screamed for hours. "Hungry."

Roderick released her and dragged away some of the blankets. Eleanor leaned back and let Wrolf lick her face. Iseult came with a bowl of sticky porridge and fed Eleanor despite her slight protests. She fell asleep almost in the middle of a mouthful.

She awoke as suddenly. There were more people in the hall now, moving quietly about, bringing food to the big table. She pushed away her covering and stood up shakily.

"No, no, my lady. You are still weak." It was one of the women.

"No, I'm all right." But she sat down quickly at the table. The woman scurried away and returned with Iseult. The fair woman looked at Eleanor closely but seemed satisfied with what she saw.

"What day is this?"

"'Tis the seventh day of March, my lady," Iseult answered.

I've been in Albion more than a month, and I only remember a week. I wonder if the wolf melted like the Black Beast did? How am I going to get to Ireland? I have to go. I'm running out of time.

But Eleanor was too tired to move. Iseult put food before her and she ate slowly and painfully. Her jaws hurt and her head throbbed slightly. The meal passed in near silence, and it was only at the end that Eleanor became aware of the absence of the master of the household.

"Where is your brother?"

"Gone."

"Gone? Where?"

"I don't know. At first light yesterday, he put on his clothes and said he was going to Jerusalem. Then he tried to take your horse and nearly got himself killed. The last I saw of him he was walking east."

"You've had your hands full, haven't you? What with me doing a Sleeping Beauty pastiche—or maybe it was Snow White—I can see I am not making any sense to you. But you don't appear unduly distressed by your brother's departure."

Iseult offered her grave smile. "Distressed? More relieved than anything. I know you took . . . you drove the demons out of my brother, and for that I am grateful. But he was not a good man to begin with. It is difficult to explain. Clovis could never bear to be wrong in any matter, nor to lose any contest. I will not be surprised if someday word reaches me that he has conquered the City of Jerusalem and set himself up as king. But I

would as soon have him far away from me, for I can
never trust him. Yet I think he will change his mind
and return, which I wish he would not, or worse, that
he will be recaptured by this force that casts its shadow
on us, completely, this time, and then come back."

"Was there any reason for this sudden need for pil-
grimage?"

"He said he had remembered that he killed the musicians and wished to be absolved from his sin."

"Only that he had killed them?" Eleanor asked.

"Yes."

"I sincerely hope he will not return, Lady Iseult."

The two women fell silent across the table from each
other. Eleanor wished she knew precisely what had
happened after she had destroyed the wolf but decided
she did not want to ask questions at night. In the morning, she would leave and go on. Now she needed nothing
more than rest.

The day was surprisingly bright. Eleanor blinked a
little at the unaccustomed light as she came into the
courtyard the following morning. The sky was no longer
gunmetal, but a paler gray, and the sun above the eastern horizon was a hazy peach instead of the blot of
amber she had learned to accept for light. As she looked
toward the west, she saw the sky darkened again.

Iseult had given her food—though the loaf and cheese
from Sal were as fresh as they had been four days earlier—some wine, and a couple of Clovis's outfits, plus
new boots. Her old ones had been beyond recovery. The
blood of the wolf had stiffened into slatelike hardness
even before they cut them off her sleeping body.

The clothes she had received from Sal were folded
carefully away along with her older tunic and shift in
the roll of her blanket. Iseult had offered her a saddle,
a remnant of days when she had ridden herself, so
Eleanor was dressed as a man, in cross-gartered trousers and high boots a little long in the toe, a knee-length
tunic, and leather jerkin. The knotted white cincture
held the tunic at the waist, bearing the little belt pouch
with her knife and the holy water.

Wrolf darted ahead across the stones into the stable,
barking. The horse came out after him a few seconds

later, trailed by an anxious-looking man carrying a saddle and blanket. He approached the horse with his burden, but the horse stepped smartly away.

"Here, let me," Eleanor said, setting her gear on the stones. "Good morning, big fellow." She stroked his velvet nose. "Have they been feeding you well?" He submitted to her caresses with nickering responses.

Eleanor took the blanket from the fingers of the man. He protested faintly. Roderick had told him to saddle the horse, and saddle it he would, if the pesky creature would just stand still. Saddling horses was no occupation for a female, however many wolves she might have killed, which he doubted, having missed the event for a romantic tussle with one of the kitchen girls whose screams of excitement at his ministrations had quite drowned out howls and lightning bolts alike. Eleanor ignored him and got the blanket across her steed's back.

She continued her aimless chatter to the horse while she threw the saddle across him, then put the belly strap around him. He bore it all with equine patience, accepting Eleanor's apologies for the shabby blanket and worn saddle with great dignity. The man had finally decided she knew what she was doing and had stopped driving her mad with his directions and interference. She checked all the cinches twice, then tied the blanket roll on behind the saddle and looped her bags over the pommel.

It was time to go. She overcame her reluctance to leave, which seemed to her to increase with each leave-taking, though none, she thought, would ever be so shattering as her departure from Sal. Roderick and Lady Iseult came out to see her off, and Eleanor could sense their relief at being rid of so troublesome a guest. But Lady Iseult kissed her graciously and expressed a proper regret at her departure.

They went through the tunnel, under the portcullis, gate, and out to the beginning of the drawbridge, Eleanor leading the horse lightly by the reins. Here she mounted, and Roderick handed her up the rowan-wood stave. The sword and cloak were in their now accustomed place across her shoulders, covered by the woolen cloak, which was beginning to look terribly shabby.

Eleanor looked out at the place before the castle gates

where she had battled a creature of the Darkness and almost succumbed. The ground was scorched in a circle perhaps a hundred feet across. Near the center of the circle lay a tumble of stones she did not remember.

"What is that?" she asked, pointing with her stave.

"Why, milady, that is the remains of the beast," answered Roderick in his quavering voice.

IX

They moved across the rumpled landscape at moderate speed. Eleanor thought about the Stone Wolf and his icy breath. She now knew more about the Creatures of Darkness, or at least some of them, than most of the people in her world, but she did not find the knowledge in any way comforting. But she spent much of the gray morning thinking about the melted Black Beast and the Stone Wolf, wondering why the two creatures had ended so differently.

The sky grew steadily darker as they moved south and west. "I hope you know where you are going, because I have only the vaguest idea. I would swear it was going to rain, but it's just the light. I'd give a lot for some honest sunshine."

A little past the noon hour, they stopped in a small circle of standing stones. Eleanor ate her bread and cheese while Wrolf rested and the horse cropped the grass inside the circle. She sensed the odd virtue of the place, for not only was the grass greener and higher than outside, but the circle seemed welcoming, though these stones had no voices that she could hear.

They went on, the silent landscape darkening until it felt like early evening. Eleanor found the total absence of people very disquieting, but the lack of birds bothered her more. And whatever place they were traveling toward was very bad indeed.

The horse seemed to sense her unease. He nickered softly to reassure her and, curiously, she was. They swung west abruptly, bringing the area of darkness to their right. Eleanor could see nothing distinct within the shadowed place but guessed it might be the Glass Castle Ambrosius had warned her of. The notion of returning there and driving the Darkness away did not seem in any way appealing, but then neither did the other tasks she had been given.

Eleanor was looking for some place they might camp when she saw the man. He appeared to be nothing more than a fellow traveler, but her experience at Nunnally made her wary. He was a tall man, but he was so thin that his clothes hung on him. He saw her and quickened his pace toward her, moving with a shambling gait.

Wrolf bristled and growled, which was all the warning Eleanor needed to alert her. The man paused about ten feet from her, and she took a good look at him. His eyes were two dark pools with very little white around them, and she was reminded of the expression of a drugged girl she had seen in Greenwich Village. He had big teeth, which seemed even larger in his thin face. The half-dead look she had seen in Clovis's eyes was much stronger in the stranger, and she assumed that he was a person who belonged wholly to the Darkness.

He appeared to be listening to something she didn't hear. Suddenly, he leapt forward like an ungainly avian, his ragged clothes flapping about him. She cracked her rowan stave down sharply on his skull. Bright sparks showered his head and body, and a shimmer of silvery light chased up and down his body.

The man opened his mouth and howled silently, leaping about and slapping at himself like he was on fire. He danced around like a demented crow, then charged again.

Eleanor struck the head of the stave down on his shoulder. He staggered but grabbed for the head and caught it for a second. Then he snatched his hand away, and she could see the thin flesh of the palm smoking. The silent scream rose in his throat as pale fire traveled up his arm. It raced up the muscles and across his shoulder, then up the scrawny neck.

The scream became audible, which seemed to surprise the man as much as it did her. He hopped around in a circle, holding the smoking hand away from him and plucking at his body with the other hand, as if he were fighting unseen insects. He slapped and screamed and finally tumbled into a heap of whimpering misery some feet away from her.

The fire died upon his body, and he struggled to regain his feet. Eleanor took the tiny vial of holy water from her pouch and removed the stopper. She splashed some drops on his face as he rose, saying, *"In nomine Sanctus Spiritus, benedicte,"* remembering her childhood, when Latin was still the tongue of the Church.

He sobbed and clutched his brow where the water touched it. "Naw, naw, stop. Hurt. Aargh! Kill! Eat! Kill! Aargh." He bunched himself for another attack, but Eleanor touched the stave to his chest and he collapsed, hugging himself.

Wrolf sat down and watched the man with an air of disinterested curiosity. The horse stamped his hooves and tossed his head a little. The stave-fire made a flickering ball of light over the man's heart, shining through his hands as he beat his chest.

"Naw! Hate, kill. Eat, eat." He gurgled words out and finally curled into a ball, pulling his bony knees up to his shoulders, moaning terribly.

Eleanor hated to see a fellow creature in pain, but she was terrified to dismount and get closer. The horse gave her an advantage she was reluctant to lose. The goddess's admonition to heal was less strong than her need to survive.

After a few minutes, he sat up and looked at her. One eye was now a quite normal brown-and-white orb, but the other was still an unreflective pit. There were red weals along the flesh where the fire had touched, and spots like drops of blood where the holy water had fallen.

"Filthy bitch! I'll follow you to the ends of the earth. I'll give you fire. Cook you slow, very slow, till you beg for death, and eat your flesh."

"Silence!" She was puzzled for a second, because she thought the holy water should have worked some curative power on the man. The condition of the eye told her either the water or the stave had effected some change. Then she realized that the man did not wish to be healed and resented her interference fiercely. It had not previously occurred to her that anyone might *like* the Darkness. Clovis had still been near human, human enough to want food and sex, even if only in terms of rape. But this poor creature was too far gone for her to reach with her limited knowledge. Whatever lessons she had learned in Sal's Mound, they were buried too deeply to offer any counsel.

Lady of Light, Lady of the Willows, what should I do?

Go! You have done what you could. Go now!

The horse began moving almost before the thought was complete. He broke into a bone-jarring trot as the man started to get up, then fell back.

"I'll tell Master! Eat you! Oh, the warmth. It hurts! Curse you, Servant of Light. I was happy, and you ruined it. I was fine! Find Master. Tell Master! Eat you...aahh..." He picked up a stone and shied it weakly at them. It fell a few feet from him, and the last view Eleanor had of him was that of a scrabbling crab, crawling over the ground, weeping and tossing stones.

The horse stretched its legs into a canter, Wrolf racing alongside, over the broken ground. Eleanor hung on to the silky mane and thought of nothing at all.

After a distance, the horse slackened its pace back to a walk. They appeared to be following a road of some kind, and Eleanor wondered where it would take them. Wrolf trotted along, panting.

It was nearing the dreary sunset when they came to the church. The horse stopped and indicated that they would go no farther, so Eleanor dismounted and entered the shattered building cautiously. Wrolf came with her, sniffing but showing no signs of danger.

The roof of the building sagged inward at the center, as if smashed by an enormous fist. It made great patches of shadow even in the dim light. Something skittered nearby, and Eleanor gave a shrill squeak in her fright. Wrolf leapt into the darkness, and she heard a short scream and the sound of crunching bone. She decided that whatever it was, it was quite normal, and Wrolf's dinner in the bargain. She hoped it was a rabbit or a squirrel, for rats were not among her favorite beasts, not even the cute ones in laboratories.

One corner of the church was less damaged than the rest. She kicked the litter aside and unloaded the horse, then she wiped him down with the saddle blanket.

The rowan staff cast a slight silvery light when she took it into the corner. She spread her bedroll out and put the shrouded sword at one end. Then she sat with her back against the wall and ate. The nasty twilight faded into starless darkness and silence, broken only by the click of Wrolf's nails on the stones and occasional squeaks as he hunted dinner through the ruin.

Then, far away, she heard a keening wail. Something very like the Stone Wolf was out there, and she hoped it would find other sport. Eleanor undid the sword just in case.

Wrolf came and sprawled next to her, and the horse wandered in, smelling of cropped grass on his breath. She lay down and slept almost immediately.

The sharp bark of her wolf awakened her instantly. The horrid keening was closer. The wolf bounded around in the faint light, whining and scrabbling at the flagstones. It was still full night, for the horse and wolf shone completely. She knew something was hunting her, and she decided not to wait around to see what it was.

She got the horse saddled and packed, retied the sword across her aching shoulders, and led him outside the little church. She managed to mount with the stave in one hand.

"Okay, big fellow. Show your silver heels." As she spoke the last words, she knew she had named the great black horse. He whinnied his response, and they sped into the night.

X

The next two days were always a blur in Eleanor's mind. They rested twice, for a few hours each time, once in a circle of stones and once in an abandoned farmhouse. The few people they saw gaped at them, but Eleanor was gratified by a wave from a shy toddler. The sound of wailing was always behind them, and she got a crick in her neck from looking back. She learned she could nap, after a fashion, on horseback, and that it was possible for all seven hundred plus muscles in her body to hurt. She discovered that willow water rubbed on aching thighs numbed the pain. She longingly remembered Sal's sacred pool, despite the still frightening memory of her rough baptism therein. There were fogs and mizzling rains, but Eleanor just hugged her cloak around her and rode.

Sometime after noon on the second day, the smell of the air changed. Eleanor breathed the clean tang of salt and knew she was somewhere near the sea, though just where she was, she was not sure. Silver Heels had brought them vaguely south and west, and the mountainous terrain told her she was in Cornwall, but she knew there was a lot of coastline between Lynmouth on the Bay of Bristol and Penzance at the tip of Britain. She had tried to guess how far they had traveled, but she had no idea how fast the horse went in his different gaits or how to count the distance when a great deal of it was vertical. But the smell of the sea revived her, and she began to look around her with more interest.

Silver Heels picked his way along a trail that came out onto a cliff overlooking the ocean. Eleanor could hear the sea more than she could view it, for there was a modest fog. The slap of waves against rock offered her no clue as to how high she was above the water. The path wound upward to end in a crumbling tower.

She dismounted and looked at the building. It looked somewhat familiar, but her interest in fortifications merely allowed her to distinguish between Norman castles and Tudor ones. As this structure was neither, she was puzzled, but decided it must be very old. She was so tired, she was not thinking very clearly, so she pulled out the last of the food from Nunnally and ate it. Wrolf sprawled on the ground, and Silver Heels hung his proud head.

Eleanor got up and unsaddled the horse.

He moved off a little to crop the thin grass.

"Well, Wrolf, now what?" He whined a little and pointed to the ocean. Then he trotted around the base of the tower and vanished from view.

She followed him to the mouth of a cave. When she saw it, she was fairly certain where she was, for she had seen photographs of it hundreds of times. Wrolf stood just inside the entrance and barked at her. This was Tintagel, and the cave led to another, called Merlin's Grotto by a twentieth century that sincerely wished that Arthur lived, down at sea level.

Eleanor went into the cave cautiously, but Wrolf stood in her way and gave his "no" bark, then led her back out and over to the pile of gear. He whined and took the worn strap of Ambrosius's bag in his jaws and pushed it at her hand.

After a moment, she took the sack and then the other, her bedroll and the staff. Wrolf trotted toward the cave. Eleanor looked at the horse. He stopped eating and blew an equine kiss in her direction. She went over and stroked his soft nose and fine neck.

"So long, Silver Heels. Thank you for everything. I hope you'll be all right, but you're probably better off without me." The terrible keening that had pursued them for two days sounded nearby, so she planted a hasty kiss on the horse's nose and hurried to the cave.

The path beyond the entrance was wet and slippery. It was dark except for Wrolf's glimmer and the faint light from the staff, but Eleanor found her eyes were much better in the gloom than they had ever been in her own time. She assumed it was accommodation, forgetting that like her companion, she gave off a light, too.

The tunnel curved slightly and went down. She could hear the whisper of the sea below her and the screaming of the hunter behind. She moved as quickly as she could, envying Wrolf his extra legs a little, and wondered if she was going to swim to Ireland or hail a passing whale.

When she reached the grotto below and saw the toy of a boat bobbling in the water, she was both relieved and terrified. Swimming seemed almost preferable to entrusting herself to this fragile craft. On the other hand, she was not about to deny a gift of the Lady, not with an unknown pursuer hot on her heels.

She pulled off her boots and waded into the icy water to pull the little craft closer to the rocks. It was almost round, made of leather, and on a wooden framework. She dropped her bags and bedroll in it, then clambered in, using her staff to balance on. Wrolf hit the water with a large splash and paddled over to the craft. He got his forequarters over the side but could get no farther and almost overturned the bobbing boat in his efforts. Eleanor climbed out and heaved his hindquarters over the side again. She was soaked and freezing, but she grabbed the staff and pushed it against the nearest rock.

A gibbering howl echoed down the tunnel. Something came into the grotto, but she didn't pause, poling at the rocks and floor frantically. As she passed under the arched entrance of the cave, she caught a glimpse of something like an enormous wolverine, a nightmare of teeth and eyes, straining after her on the rocks. A splash of seawater hit the great clawed paws, and the flesh hissed. She didn't wait to see if it could swim but bent her back to get across the small tidepool at the mouth of the grotto.

The current caught them and swept them around and around, spinning the boat farther and farther from the jagged shore. Eleanor collapsed on the bottom of the boat and gasped for breath.

After several minutes, she was recovered enough to look at her craft. There was a sort of bench dividing the boat in two. Wrolf was in the foresection, dripping seawater and giving her his wolfly grin. The bench was made of wicker, and she found the seat lifted. Inside there was a flat oar. She got it out and put her bags into the space. She opened the bedroll, which was remarkably dry, and got out her old tunic and the tattered hose. She slithered out of her wet leggings and tunic and, balancing carefully, managed to redress. Eleanor put Bridget's sword on top of the bags and draped her soaking cloak over one part of the boat, hoping it would dry.

Finally, she positioned herself carefully in the middle of the bench and began to use the oar. After ten minutes, she was exhausted, but she had the satisfaction of seeing that the shore was more distant and was, in fact, fading into a fog bank. She was warmer now, but the breeze off the sea was fairly brisk, so she wrapped the blanket around her. The ocean jostled them back and forth, and she hoped she could decide on some form of navigation.

"You are one helluva fine wolf, Wrolf. You don't by any chance have a knowledge of celestial navigation, do you? What am I saying? For that you need stars. We haven't seen any stars for ages. Let me think. Do storms blow from the east or the west? From the west, I think. Yes, the Atlantic Ocean makes a big weather front. I think that means I have to go against the current. Except there is probably also a northerly current in the Irish Channel. If we were up in Scotland, it would be easy. We could island-hop across. Ireland is a big island, Wrolf, but we could miss it altogether. That's a cheery thought. The Lady has been good to us so far, so I will have to trust to that. But I'd give a lot for a compass." She fell into thought and finally began paddling in the general direction in which she had last seen the sun. When her arms began to ache, she stopped.

Eleanor decided she had to rest. She curled up miserably in the rear of the boat, but sleep refused to come. Finally, she opened the bench and got out the wine Iseult had given her.

She removed the stopper, and the boat bobbed a little more. Eleanor smelled the slightly acrid scent of wine no Frenchman would put on his table. But it brought back memories of the fire in the hall at Nunnally and a fine Beaujolais her father had served on her eighteenth birthday. It reminded her of the golden sunlight of the vineyards of California and the almost eye-aching sun in the south of France. The boat jostled sharply.

She leaned carefully to one side of the boat, knowing she was giddy with exhaustion, and clumsy as well. "Are you thirsty, Mother of Oceans? I thank you for bearing me upon your bosom. Here is wine," she said as she shakily poured a large amount into the sea, "in gratitude of my salvation. I wish it were a better vintage, but three days on horseback would ruin anything." Then she took a large swallow herself, thinking of Homer's "wine-dark sea" and a choral piece by Frederick Delius. The boat settled into the waves and became like the music in her mind, a setting for Whitman's "Out of the Cradle, Endlessly Rocking." Eleanor stoppered the bottle and slipped into a state between trance and sleep.

A woman rose from the waters, sweet and majestic all at once. The moon bound her fair hair and silvered her unclad body, outlined in the cloak of starry sky behind her. She smiled, and the gesture was a benediction.

Eleanor knew her by many names, though her mind recalled none now. But her heart was glad, and the little slivers of doubt and fear that pierced it melted away and vanished under the Lady's calm gaze. Then she knew nothing until a splash of water smacked her face.

The wind had risen, for the waves were higher now. The boat was bouncing between troughs and crests like a piece of cork, and she was surprised they hadn't been swamped already. She got on the bench and started paddling, trying to steer the little vessel between the waves. The boat wallowed, and Eleanor prayed and tried to keep it afloat. It seemed to be going in *some* direction, but whether it was away from Britain or back to it, she had no idea.

When her arms could paddle no longer, she paused. There was something she should remember, but it eluded her. Something about Bridget. She knelt down by the bench and shoved the plank aside. With cramped fingers, she untied the cloak from the sword. Obeying some inner voice, she clasped the cloak around her throat.

It felt as if the four winds were battling in her face. Sea spray stung her cheeks like slaps, and she was almost blinded. She turned slowly and carefully in place, trying to keep her balance against the pitching of the boat.

Suddenly, the wind caught the folds of the cloak and billowed them out. She spread her arms out under it. The little craft bobbled and wavered, then steadied and began to skim across the waves. Wrolf crouched in the bows, his forepaws resting on the edge, and became a figurehead, a ghostly, silver wolf upon the prow.

Her arms ached and her eyes stung with saltwater, but Eleanor gritted her teeth and kept her arms out. They raced *across* the waves, with Eleanor as the sail and the wolf as a dim beacon. It took her awhile to realize that what they were doing was probably impossible, because they were moving *against* the wind, but by the time she noticed, she was too tired to care and could only sympathize with Moses keeping his arms up to hold off the Amalekites. She only wished she had an Aaron to help out.

The wind faded finally and died. Eleanor let her arms drop to her sides and flopped bonelessly into the bottom of the boat. It was ankle-deep in water, and she bailed with her icy fingers until she remembered she had a bowl that would serve her better.

She twisted her neck and rubbed her shoulders to ease the cramps. "First, straighten this mess up. Then rest." She crouched down and opened the bench and removed the contents. The two leather bags had repelled most of the water, and the sword was unharmed. She got out her bowl and rewrapped the sword carefully. Her blanket and old cloak lay in the aft section, fairly wet. She sat on the bench and shoved them into the water in the boat with her soaking feet. They absorbed an astonishing amount of water, and after she had wrung them out as much as she could, there was not a great deal of bailing left to do. Eleanor crawled around carefully and spread the two things out as much as possible. Her movements kept her fairly warm, and she was too tired for the effort of redressing in the tiny boat. Instead, she drank some water and followed it with some mead.

Dawn was rising, and to her surprise, the sun seemed more like its old self. It wasn't quite the golden solar body she was accustomed to, but it was more than the sullen spot that lightened Albion's slate gray skies. It rose out of the sea in a blush of pinky grays and violets, and Eleanor felt her heart rise. She toasted the sun in honey wine, then realized that it was behind her. The boat was pointing west, and if the wind had not driven her too far in that direction, Ireland should be somewhere before her. Eleanor curled up in the aft section and dozed.

When she woke, stiff and aching, the sun had climbed up but had not reached its midpoint. Eleanor was damp and clammy, so she took the oar and started to paddle. The waves were small, green touched with gold, and the sun seemed to warm her back. She paddled and rested several times. The sun crossed its high point and began to curve down the bowl of the sky.

A dark line sat on the horizon. She shaded her eyes and looked at it for a while. Then she resumed her paddling. It got closer and soon became a discernible shoreline. Finally, she paddled into a good-sized bay and found a fairly smooth beach.

Eleanor stumbled onto dry land, or rather, damp sand, fell on her face, and kissed the earth. She murmured the sweet words "Erin, I am home" and then just lay there. After a time, she got up and emptied the boat, putting the oar back under the bench. Wrolf was nowhere to be seen, but a set of tracks in the sand marked his trail. She dumped her things down, spread the half-dry blanket and her damp clothing out on the shore, and surrendered herself to sleep.

XI

The sun was almost down when she awoke. Wrolf had returned, his chest showing the evidence of a hearty meal. He greeted her arousal, as was his wont, and watched as she opened her bags and sorted through the contents.

The napkin with Sal's bread and cheese was as clean as the first day she had seen it. The bread was still soft and fresh, and she ate some with swigs of water and pieces of the cheese. She thanked the Lady of Willows again and tied up the rest of the food.

The clothes Iseult had given her were still damp as were the ones she was wearing, so she took out the rosy shift and blue gown Sal had given her and put them on. The cloak was damp but not dripping, so she left it off.

"Next time, let's take Aer Lingus, Wrolf. I wonder where we are. Somewhere between Cork and Dublin, I'll bet. I don't recognize this bay, but there's no reason I should. Look, the Evening Star. Hail to thee, bright Venus." The twilight deepened, and the sky began to cloud up. She studied it, Irish weatherwise, and began picking up her things. "It's going to rain," she told the wolf as she tied the sword across her shoulders. "I don't know why I'm surprised. I've just seen enough wet for a while. Let's see if we can find some cover. People who say it's always raining in Ireland are wrong. It only rains when you are there. I wonder if I am ever going to be dry and well rested again. I hope Silver Heels is all right. And where am I going to find the sheath for Bridget's sword? Ireland is a big country. Oh, well, I shouldn't expect a neat itinerary. But I wish I had one. This is like a scavenger hunt with no clues. Do you know where we are going, Wrolf? Yes, of course you do. You are my guide. *I* want to know where, though, and you can't tell me."

She was babbling and she knew it. She halted the flow of words, aware that she was lonely for the sound of a human voice, and somewhat afraid. This was no friendly Ireland of her childhood, but a gloomy, mist-cloaked *terra incognita*. She was filled with doubts, suddenly, as if she sensed some faintly distasteful event lay before her. What had Sal said? Something about a dark-haired lover. The idea chilled her in a way the sea had not. Realizing the danger of reflection, of anticipation, she turned back to Wrolf. "Lead on, MacDuff."

He barked his answer and trotted into the trees. Eleanor trudged after him, glad in the pale green of spring leaf. The smells of earth and mulch under her feet were reassuring.

A fine rain began to fall, but Wrolf led her on. The trees were crowded close together and caught most of the wetness, but Eleanor was very damp by the time they came to the hall. She stared at it in mild disbelief, for it was a fine building to find in the middle of the forest.

Wrolf padded up and scratched at the great door. It was carved and painted with the wonderful interlaces so characteristic of Hibernian art, but she was sure she had never seen anything like it before, for the building was round, not rectangular, and looked as if a stand of oak had grown into a house. The exterior walls were like the trunks of trees with their bark stripped away, decorated with pattern and color.

Eleanor found she was shivering, not from cold but from an excitement that was part fear and part joy. There was a face carved in the center of the door, a beast's face, neither cat nor dog but a blend of the two. It had a wolf's muzzle and a cat's pricked and tufted ears. The eyes were two smooth stones, as rounded as moonstones, but golden, not white. They seemed to look at her.

"Do stop scratching, Wrolf. You'll mar the paint. Are you sure there's not a motel in the neighborhood? Damn! I never wanted to have adventures." The wolf whined and butted her hand. "Yes, yes. I'll knock. Don't be pushy."

She lifted her hand and tapped softly. Then she lowered it and clung to Wrolf's mane, sinking her fingers into the rough hair and feeling the warmth of his body beneath it.

The door was yanked open with great force. A large man with reddish hair and golden eyes loomed over her, his face twisted in a sullen snarl. He looked at Eleanor in her streaming clothes and hair plastered to her wet face, and he pursed his lips.

"What did you do, swim?" he barked. His voice was harsh. "Some princess. Come in, come in. You're making a draft," he added, as if the cold and wet were her fault. He stepped aside. "I can't see you're worth all the fuss."

Eleanor found his mutterings a complete puzzle and was sure he had mistaken her for someone else. Still, Wrolf had brought her there, and she trusted her companion as guide and friend.

"Thank you, kind sir," she said, and entered. He started to shut the door in Wrolf's face and got a deep growl.

"No one said anything to me about letting a muddy beast track up the floor."

"Oh. Well, in that case, I'll just leave," she snapped. Eleanor wasn't sure if he was master or servant, but his rudeness annoyed her.

"Don't be such a dog-in-the-manger, Baird," said a woman's voice. "She'd singe you to ashes in a month. If it took that long. Close the door, you great oaf. I'll take a chill."

The red man closed the door, appearing to take the criticism in good part. Eleanor looked at him and found he was eyeing her in a way she didn't care for. "I don't see why Doyle should have all the fun. He isn't even here to greet his ladylove. Why shouldn't I just take her and the sword? I'm a better man than he is, any day."

Baird reached out two large hands, golden with hair along the backs, and clasped Eleanor to his chest before she could protest. Close up, he smelled of cat, a kind of acrid pungency that filled her nostrils. Wrolf hackled and growled but made no move.

"Let me go!" Eleanor commanded, her voice muffled

in the soft wool of his tunic. She pushed her hands against his chest, then shoved the rowan stave at him ineffectually.

"I'm glad to see you have a little fight for a drowned rat," he chuckled. "I like a girl with a bit of spirit. Really, I'm much nicer than Doyle. He's dark and ugly and morose. Tell Mother you like me."

Eleanor felt a prickle of fear, like the sense she had of Clovis on their first meeting but less strong. She squirmed to get away. A large, hairy hand clamped over her face, pinching her nose and covering her mouth.

"Tell Mother you want me, or I'll take you right here," he hissed. "A bed would be better, don't you agree?"

Eleanor's head was spinning from lack of air, and she had a vagrant thought that every man she met either wished to bed her or eat her. Then she formed Bridget's name in her mind and found herself sitting on the floor some feet from the now howling Baird. He flopped his hands and licked them piteously, and she knew the fire had come to her again.

"I told you not to touch her, Baird," came the woman's voice again. "Why are all my sons so stubborn? And willful? I've tried to teach them manners," the voice went on, aggrieved, "but I might as well try to teach a worm to dance."

Eleanor looked around for the speaker. At first she saw nothing but the painted walls of the hall and the tiled floor, an eye-wearying confusion of interweaving patterns. The ceiling was an interlace of branches, stylized and natural at the same time.

Finally her eyes came to rest on a circular fire pit in the center of the room. Curled beside it was a woman whose clothing seemed to be a continuation of the floor patterns, so that she was almost invisible, except for a pale face set in braided hair. Even the plaits seemed to follow the interlace of the tiles, the colors shifting as the woman moved her head.

The woman was tiny, ageless, and elfin, and Eleanor wondered how so small a female could have birthed the hulking Baird. Eleanor got to her feet, her boots making a squeaking sound, and curtsied toward the little figure.

"You are a cunning one, to see me so quickly. Come to the fire, child. I won't hurt you. Leave your cloak by the door. See, your wolf is already making himself quite at home. Take off your boots, too. Stop blubbering, Baird. Anyone would think you were dying. Go find a dry garment for her. You'll excuse me for not getting up. I can't disrupt the pattern just yet. Oh, I could, but even such a guest as you doesn't seem worth an earthquake."

"I should think not," Eleanor answered, shedding the cloak and tugging off the boots. Her teeth started to chatter when her feet rested unshod on the tiles. She moved toward the fire pit and found herself circling it. The patterns of the room were confusing, dizzying, and she peered at the myriad colors, seeking some clue to proceed upon. She made another try, setting her foot upon a wide red band, and found herself moving back toward the snivelling Baird. She closed her eyes for a second and tried to *feel* the patterns, but all she found was an overwhelming sense of energies. It took her two more tries to find a line that led her to the fire pit. She walked along it cautiously until she came to the pit. Then she sank gratefully down, feeling the energy of the various patterns strumming up her body. Eleanor shifted her weight around until she was nearly comfortable, though she still had a sense of being in two other places at once, besides sitting by the fire.

The tiny woman watched all this with interest, her eyes bright in her pale face. Eleanor was puzzled by the whole place, for she could not think of anything quite like it in folklore or myth. She realized that to some extent she had been guided by unconscious assessments drawn from her rather extensive background in legend. But this strange chamber was disturbing because she did not know what it meant. What kind of person was the coiled woman across the fire pit—a goddess or a lady?

The fire was pitifully small, and yet the heat it gave off was enormous. Eleanor felt the clothing begin to dry on her body. She rubbed the blue tunic Sal had given her between her fingers, feeling the good wool and remembering the Lady of the Willows with great affection and some nostalgia. Then she remembered the knitting pins and the ball of yarn in her bag and got them out, eager to keep her hands busy. She cast on for a stole, a simple rectangle, knowing she would unravel it later, and began to work.

The large size of the needles made the work go fast, and the ball of stuff with which Sal had replaced Sarah's wool was as smooth as satin and had a dull sheen. Eleanor didn't know if it was silk or linen or some fiber she had never heard of. She only knew the knitting soothed away her uneasiness.

The woman's voice brought her back to her surroundings with a start. "Well, you aren't one for idle chatter, I see. Now, me, I chatter quite a bit. It passes the time for me, which hangs heavy on my hands. My sons are *not* entertaining companions, whatever their other virtues."

"I beg your pardon," Eleanor said, blushing furiously. "I didn't mean to be rude. It's just been a long time since I had a minute to think, what with Black Beasts and Stone Wolves, and other things."

"I understand entirely. I have nothing to do but think. So, you are come on an errand from Bridget. Pushy female. You mustn't be in awe of her, girl. I knew her when she was only an egg. Always arranging things to suit herself. Like this whole matter of the sheath. Did she ask me nicely, would I give it up? She did not. She yanks you out of bed and says, 'Go get it.' Still, I can see you're a good girl." The woman shifted, and the patterns on her gown blurred and flowed. The many tiny braids of her hair seemed to rearrange themselves like tiny serpents into a new pattern.

Eleanor's fingers continued knitting by feel as she watched. She was struck by the contention that Bridget was younger than her companion. What was older than a goddess? The universe, or the earth itself. "The young are often thoughtless of the...prerogatives of others, my...Lady Eldest." Eleanor stumbled over the words, feeling them form like a silky thread in her mind, only to slip away from her.

"True, true. She rushes off one night to impress a bunch of dirty priests, for she was ever one to need adulation, even at the price of altering her nature, and leaves the sheath and hasn't even the kindness to come and get it herself. Never mind that I've been crippled by the separation of sword and sheath, for the greater power lies in my portion, but it is useless without the blade. Never mind that she hasn't sent so much as a daffodil in centuries or inquired as to my health. Oh, no! She just sends you over here to remove *my* treasures, without a by-your-leave. Impertinent hussy!"

Eleanor wasn't sure what to make of this catalog of grievances. "I . . . didn't know."

"Of course you didn't! That girl glories in being cryptic! I've never had a straight answer from her, never. She thinks her purposes are the cosmos. Conceit, that's what it is." The words were hard, but the voice was still sweet. "No, child. I know it's not *your* fault. Pawns just go where they are pushed. And I must admit, the need is very great. But if she'd paid attention to her business, instead of letting herself be limited by her worshipers, none of this might have come to pass. Going off to Albion to dwindle into a saint. Self-serving pride, that's what it was."

"I cannot argue with you, because I don't really know what you are talking about," Eleanor said quietly.

The little woman gave a chuckle. "Sharp as a pin under all that politeness, aren't you? Here is a riddle, then. What has no beginning or middle or end, is eternal and dies, eats itself and is never consumed?"

Eleanor stared at the woman and let her mind play with the images as her fingers flew across the needles. She could think of an answer for each part, but not one for the whole. She saw a moebius strip first, but it did not eat or die. The patterns on the woman's dress dazzled her and seemed to color her mental image until the moebius was a rainbow interlace. She stopped thinking of literal objects then and let herself manipulate symbols freely.

Finally she said, "A serpent, bowed and nowed," using the heraldic term for knotted. She thought of the Midgard Serpent and the Worm Ouroboros as she spoke.

"Remind me not to play knucklebones with you, child. Your mind at play is a charming thing, full of light and color. Like your name. Perhaps Bridget was wiser than I thought. Do you know me now?"

"I . . . think you are . . . the Earth Serpent, girdling the world. Except that all the stories I know...uh, change your gender."

Another chuckle. "Of course they do. That dangle on a man is very like a snake sometimes. I've had my prerogatives altered so many times, it doesn't even annoy me anymore. I'll still be here when the cosmos winks out, ready to make a new one. Men have been trying to steal eternity since life began. Before time was invented. They never have, but they keep at it. You have no idea how often I've had my head hacked off with that very blade you carry, or one of its mates, by my envious offspring and lovers. Baird would be doing it now if I hadn't sent him into the pattern so we could talk. Men are such a nuisance sometimes. I'm glad they aren't my creation."

"They aren't?"

"Goodness, child, did you think I was the Creative? What a sweet compliment. No, that's much too energetic a job for me. I know my place. I don't aspire to the High Seat. It's a cold chair, that one, and I like my comforts. Except my sons—and they can't hurt me—no one tries to take my place. But the High Seat is ever in contention. There is *always* war in Heaven. Dreadful, bickering place, and cold as mischief. Take my advice and avoid it."

Eleanor smiled. "I hardly think I will have any reason to make the choice." She looked down at her knitting, and her jaw dropped. She had done about twelve inches, and there was a pattern, a complex interlace that would have required a third needle and much counting and concentration. Nor was the ball of yarn any smaller than when she began.

"You've already made your choice, Eleanor. That's Albion hanging from your needles. Not the island you just left but the lines of force that make it up. All the world is here in this chamber, woven into bands of color. You are part of the war for the High Seat, but all mortals are, no matter if they serve the Light or the Dark. Listen! Doyle comes."

Somewhere, far away, there was the sound of a horn bellowing brazenly. Then the noise of a pack of some canine creatures, though Eleanor could not guess if they were hounds or wolves. The door was flung back, and a huge figure stood outlined in the dying light, a man with snarling animals roiling at his knees.

XII

"Shut the door, Doyle. You know I hate the draft. And keep those beasts quiet. We have guests."

He did as he was bid and slammed the door. The animals stopped their snapping and yelping at a gesture. There were seven of them, wolves, with silvery coats and russet ears. They stiffened and pointed at Wrolf, who rose from his place beside Eleanor. He gave a single sharp bark, and the largest of the pack trotted across the tiles toward him, apparently unhampered by the patterns. The two great animals touched noses, and Wrolf wagged his tail and fawned.

Eleanor barely noticed. She was too busy staring at the huge man, as dark as his brother was fair, wet with rain and covered with gore along his arms and chest. He had black hair, unkempt and flowing over his shoulders, and a great fountain of a beard, braided below the chin and tied back over his shoulders. His eyes were blue, hard, and unwelcoming, and his mouth below his long mustache seemed never to have smiled. Steam began to rise from his body even before he approached the fire pit.

He hunkered down and stretched huge, bloody hands toward the fire. Eleanor stared, because he was like her father in a way, but seemed wholly lacking in any of Daniel Hope's urbanity. The sword across her shoulders seemed to hum, and she understood that he was somehow the proper wielder of the bright weapon. She also knew that he was himself a sword, and she a scabbard. The idea of surrendering to whatever passions lay locked in the bloody chest was absolutely chilling. Her first impulse was to hand him the sword and run into the woods.

The serpent woman stirred a little by the fire. Eleanor

set her hands to knitting and stared at the flames. Baird had been right. She would have preferred the fair brother to the dark. But when she thought of him with the sword, his golden greatness shrank, and she knew that Baird could not wield the thing. So she shrugged about her doubts, swallowed her rage, and tried not to think of the great hands on her body. The stiff-necked pride that was a portion of the Darlington heritage from her mother rose in her throat like bitter bile, and she bit her lip in vexation. The acrid taste of Sal's mouth on hers brought confused memories of love and instruction, and she banished the pride to look at the man again.

Eleanor saw that not all the blood on him was from whatever beast he had slain. There was a deep slash in the dark leather of his jerkin, and blood oozed from the cut in the flesh beneath. There were long scratches on his arms as well, and she had an empathetic surge of pain. She hated the cuts as she hated his silent endurance of them.

She cleared her throat. "If there is water, I...would clean your wounds for you...if you wish."

The blue eyes seemed to bore into her mind. "No need," he finally said. He had a deep voice, like the growl of the north wind in winter.

Eleanor was annoyed by this rejection. "Does he always hug his pain to him like something precious?" she asked his mother.

"Five minutes and I'm already mediating your first fight," clucked the woman. "Of course he does. Didn't Baird tell you he was morose?"

"Yes, but no one mentioned he was spoilt in the bargain," Eleanor snapped. "But perhaps you've had other matters on your mind than teaching good manners and polite behavior."

"Aren't you a brave one, sweet serpent's tooth," the woman crooned. "Yes, you must be, or you wouldn't be here at all. But a little foolhardy, too. Your argument is with him, not me."

"Then keep out of it, Orphiana," said the man. Doyle shifted his weight a little. "My mother would dice with the Devil, if she only had hands." He fell silent again for a moment. "She enjoys games, too much, sometimes. Where's Baird?"

"I sent him away. He was being very annoying," Orphiana replied. "He tried to take what is yours, just like he always does. He's the grabbiest, greediest child."

"You stopped him, I suppose. Why didn't you let him have his way? I don't want the wench, not with all those lines attached."

Eleanor was piqued at first by this cold rejection. Then her sense of humor caught her, and she realized that Doyle was as unwilling to enter her adventure as she was to have it. The perversity of chaining the two of them, stubborn and reluctant, to one yoke seemed to her the epitome of Olympian meddling.

She laughed in spite of herself. "Believe me, the feeling is mutual."

"I didn't interfere. She's quite able to look out for herself. Baird got his hands burnt for his presumption. She let him off lightly. That's a fault in her. She forgives quite easily."

"Bring him out," Doyle said. "He'll be a hornet's nest if you don't."

"What? So he can try to slay you? You know he will. And you'll mess up the patterns, and it will take me months to set them right again." She turned her head to Eleanor. "Take my advice, child, and don't have sons. Daughters are more biddable."

Doyle seemed deep in thought. His head lowered into his massive shoulders until his chin almost rested on his chest. His hands clenched and flexed as if two forces warred in him.

Suddenly, he rose and stepped around the fire pit, yanking Eleanor to her feet and pulling her head back by the hair. He was cold where his body pressed against her, colder than the breath of Darkness from the Stone Wolf. She struggled against that cold, calling on Bridget's fire, as she scratched his face and tried to free herself. The flame did not come as he covered her mouth with his.

His chill breath seemed to fill her lungs, and she tasted blood in his kiss. The Eleanor who had killed two beasts of Darkness, who had grown and changed, was swept aside like a tiny leaf in the wind. She could feel nothing, think nothing, but empty blackness. With an agonizing wrench, she let her body go. Let him have the shell, if that was his desire.

But the cold taste of his tongue and the press of his lips brought Sal's kiss to her, and with it the endless play of green water and golden light. The endless instant of love she had shared with the goddess played in her like a bubbling spring. Eleanor felt her bones turn to cool water, bitter and quickening.

The hard hands slackened their grip, and Doyle pulled away his mouth. He held her shoulders and looked into her face for a long time. Then he drew her head to his chest and stroked her face with clumsy gestures. He trembled and made a groaning growl deep in his throat.

She could hear the thunder of his heart under her cheek, the labored moan of his breathing. Eleanor turned her face up and saw that his blue eyes were brimmed with tears. An icy crystal slid down his cheek and splashed on her nose. It tickled, and she gulped to keep from giggling.

"Just look what you've done to the pattern," screamed Orphiana. "Have you no sense? Selfish beast. You could at least have dragged her outside before you—"

"Mother, be quiet," he said. "I'll help you set it right in a moment." For once, the snake mother held her peace. "I am not accustomed to doing things I do not wish to do," he told Eleanor.

"You didn't want to...kiss me?"

He pulled a long face. "Was ever a man more misunderstood than I? Of course I wanted to kiss you, Lady Innocence. Curse all women! The world would be in less trouble if they had never been created."

Doyle released her suddenly and bent down, examining the tiles on the floor. The interlaces where their feet had stood were a jumble of broken lines and colors. He traced one with a broad hand. A band of green seemed to thicken like a serpent undulating, and he grasped it and drew it down, manipulating another of blue at the same time. There was a hollow groan from somewhere underground. Eleanor felt a deep shaking under her feet, distant and thunderous. She moved carefully out of his way as he repaired the disrupted pattern.

"Why does everyone get to play with a full deck but

me?" she asked, addressing her question to no one in particular.

"There, there, my wriggler"—Orphiana chuckled—"your fangs are showing. What fun is a game if you know the outcome? Don't glare at me like that. You're as stern as Doyle. What serious children you will make, solemn little prunes of virtue. Don't you see any humor in Greenland nearly sinking in the power of your passion? Of course you don't. Trust Bridget to send a dull stick. She's almost as tedious as a Valkyrie herself."

Eleanor understood the apparent passionlessness of her hostess, remembering how the very earth suffered under the tread of the Black Beast. Orphiana was tied to her task of nurturing the world, and Eleanor was sure that it wasn't a pleasant job. The snake mother felt every grain of sand on the shore and every shoot of grass pushing its way from darkness into light. It was an occupation that bred cynicism, and Orphiana was no more resigned to it than Eleanor was truly resigned to the tasks Bridget had set her.

She closed her eyes to shut out the play of pattern around her, aware of a slight headache. Resisting an impulse to say "Tell me everything," she attempted to form logical questions, knowing that if a little learning was a dangerous thing, ignorance could be deadly. Eleanor realized she had not had the time and leisure to examine the problem properly. At first, she had moved from a sense of duty, and later she had just run to keep away from the bogies. Whatever the Darkness was, it clearly did not regard her with any great concern. She was just a nuisance, a gnat to be swatted at will.

The headache, she decided, was part hunger. She looked around for where she had set her pack. Eleanor was tired of bread and cheese and sour wine and would happily have traded the whole lot for a sight of the Golden Arches. She was weary of rain and cold, of damp clothes and soggy hose, of the sword across her shoulders and the constant ache it made in her back. *If I'm not careful, I'll have a proper fit of Irish doldrums.*

Eleanor pushed her hunger and her fatigue aside and went back to her place by the fire. She picked up her knitting and stared at it, then rolled it up. Doyle rose from his work on the floor and came over to sit next to her.

After a long silence he asked, "Are you angry with me?"

"Angry? Of course not! I am getting quite accustomed to being nearly raped by every Tom, Dick, and Harry I meet. It's so flattering to know I arouse lust in the heart of every fellow I come across. That's every woman's dream! No, that's not quite true. There was a scarecrow of Darkness who wanted to cook me over a slow fire. And Sam was very courteous, but his wife was watching. The goddess only knows how he would have behaved without Sarah's eye upon him. Why should I be angry?"

"Will you let me explain?"

"And spoil all the fun?" she snapped. "Can't you realize I just adore blundering around with cryptic instructions? Go here, do this, go there, find that! It's worse than a package tour of Greece—sixteen islands in thirteen days. Why should you tell me anything?"

"Are you always this unreasonable?"

"No. Only when I'm hungry and tired and dirty and mad as hell!" Eleanor found that venting her frustration did not make her feel any better, and she tried to stop. Her skin itched with dried salt, and her hose were still damp, though the rest of her clothing was nearly dry. But the anger was a hard knot under her chest, a sickening lump of cold frustration.

"Why didn't you say so?" he asked. Eleanor balled a fist and punched him on the arm as hard as she could. Doyle smiled at her maddeningly, took the hand, and kissed it. Shivers of some emotion she had no name for raced through her at his touch. "You're a proper firebrand, *macushla*. Food, then."

Doyle got up and crossed the chamber, vanishing into one of the pillars. He reappeared a moment later carrying a tray with two steaming bowls and wooden tankards on it. He set it on the floor between them and handed her a bowl. Eleanor ate the hot stew, mutton with carrots and onions, and felt the tension in her body begin to ease. The cups were filled with dark ale, and there was bread, a sturdy loaf of peasant bread, to mop up the last of the stew with. After three days on horseback and a chilly trip across the sea, it seemed ambrosial to her. She licked her fingers and watched him finish his food.

"Baird is quite irritated," he said conversationally, "but that's his normal state. I can't help wishing you were his. I'd find the conflagration very amusing."

"Well, I'm not, nor yours, either!" He reminded her forcibly of her father with his cool arrogance. She hated his confidence, his laughing sureness that he could dominate her. That was like Daniel Hope, too, and Eleanor found it more than a little frightening. The memory of his cold breath in her lungs returned, and she shifted her body uneasily.

"That's true enough. What is it like, belonging to yourself?"

The question stunned her, for she could tell he was quite serious. She wondered what kind of mind lay beneath that black hair. His eyes told her nothing. Eleanor drank the last of her ale before she tried to answer. "Everyone belongs to themselves. It isn't *like* anything. It just is."

He shook his head and held his hand over her tankard. When he drew it away, it was filled again with ale. "No. Men don't. First they belong to their mothers and later to their wives and daughters."

"I...would say you had it the wrong way around," she answered thoughtfully.

"That's what you have been taught. It is a thing men have been trying to peddle for centuries. But a lie doesn't become true by repetition. False is false. Every man knows in his heart that he is chattel. It gnaws at his vitals like worms. I don't have any wish to leave my mother's house and take on a new rider, but I haven't any choice in the matter. I thought I did, but no, I do not."

Eleanor was very disturbed by his words. Her last expectation in the world was to find a "liberated" male in thirteenth-century Hibernia. She herself found the stridency of the women's movement disquieting, for she could not quite believe that being equal in a man's world was a desirable thing. But this wasn't her time or her place at all, and she did not know what to make of Doyle.

"I didn't choose to come on this quest, either."

"No one made you bring that sword to us, did they?"

"No, no one *made* me."

"Then you did choose."

"I . . . suppose. It truly just never crossed my mind to say, 'Bridget, find another suck—ah, servant.' You could say I have the habit of obedience."

"And you never chafe under it?"

"Of course I do. Everyone does things they don't wish to. All I want is . . . less mysterious directions. It's like being ridden out of town on a rail—if it wasn't for the honor of the thing, I'd rather not. Yes, I was terribly flattered. I never thought I'd be chosen to do anything important. I still wonder when I am going to wake up in my bed and find it was all a dream. Being a nobody is much simpler than being somebody."

"Then you do this out of pride?" He frowned over his ale.

"I don't know. I haven't given it much thought. Sure, why not? Everything comes from pride, doesn't it? Or fear. Will you please tell me about the sword?"

"Yes, I will. Back at the beginning, before time was thought of, when the gods were still squalling brats, my mother had a lover. I do not know what sort of man . . . or being he was, but he was a craftsman, a smith. He was the father of all smiths, first of his craft. Hephestus is but a dim shadow of what he was, and Vulcan a buffoon. Being a male, he desired to release himself from my mother's . . . tutelage. In pride and imitation of himself, he made that sword and three others. I believe it was the first thing ever made in reflection of the male, so, of course, it was a weapon. He used it to cut off Orphiana's head—used each of those swords in turn to slay her. And each time she made a sheath for the blades, from her sloughing skin, as she herself was a sheath—as women are. And much of the power of the blade was . . . absorbed by the scabbard. The sword is a very weak thing, separate from its sheath."

"Weak!" Eleanor remembered the terrible shock her first handling had given her and how difficult the two subsequent uses had been. She wasn't at all sure she wanted to know the full capacity of the weapon. "I'll take your word for it. How did Bridget get it?"

"The tale goes, she diced it away from Llyr. She is fire, and so is the sword. She got Llyr drunk and gamed with him. He was too hotheaded to handle it—like Baird."

Eleanor had great difficulty imagining the dignified figure at the priory on her knees, shaking a set of bones and muttering for Little Joe, like some back-alley crapshooter. "And the sheath?"

"Was in Orphiana's care. For a time, Bridget had both, but she and Mother had a falling out."

"Noisy, pushy wench," hissed Orphiana. "No manners, no courtesy. She needs to be beaten with a stick."

"I...assume," Eleanor began, as the old woman stopped speaking, "that if the sword and sheath are brought together, the wielder is very...powerful."

Doyle laughed, his deep rumble bouncing off the walls. "Yes, he is. There's a madness in it."

"And I'm supposed to hand it over to you? Why don't you just take it?"

"I tried. Have you forgotten?"

"Was *that* what you were doing? I must have a dirtier mind than I thought. So much for lust. I take it you'll be master of the world, once you get your hands on it."

"Yes, unless I am contained."

Eleanor shied away from the meaning of his words violently. "And you don't want to be...restrained."

"Slaves rarely like changing masters."

"All this superior-inferior nonsense is stupid! It's sickening. Why don't you think better of yourself! I don't want...a mouse!" Eleanor did not understand her feelings. She tried to force her emotions into a semblance of order, but they squirmed into knots of conflicting ideas. Equality and dominance seemed to have started a war inside her, with a lifetime of being "Daddy's girl" battling both the notion of sexual equality and the idea of holding dominion over this great, dark man. For a second she wished she could just hand him the sword, and with it the responsibility to finish Bridget's tasks. Let the Devil take the hindmost.

The realization that she hadn't really accepted this quest was like Sal's hard hands holding her head down in the well. Eleanor came face-to-face with her great fear of failure and her anger at having the job thrust

upon her. She did not curse the gods or the war in
Heaven; she cursed her own blind pride and obedience.

She didn't want the responsibilities. Eleanor looked
herself squarely in her inner eye and admitted she had
avoided actual responsibility, rather successfully, all
her life. She'd even managed not to choose a career,
letting Daniel guide her instead. And then he had died
that slow, painful death, and she had known betrayal.
Her father had not loved her enough to continue living.
She mistrusted love now and felt almost relieved that
Doyle did not appear to possess a single romantic bone
in his large, scarred body. He didn't want her, just the
sword. It seemed to confirm her sense of lovelessness.

Then Sal's white face rose in her mind, and the memory of their shared emotions, and she realized the problem lay within her. Eleanor hated the idea of a marriage
of convenience. It fairly sickened her. She wanted to be
able to care about the man who took her body, not out
of any reverence for virginity but simply from self-
respect. To lie with a man toward some mutual end
beyond passion or begetting was disgusting. She was
unsure of where those emotions were within her, or
even if she possessed them, for the love she carried for
the Lady of the Willows seemed remote from this great,
dark man.

"A mouse!" he growled suddenly. "No, only a man."

"But...you are more than that. You fixed the pattern where our...feet disrupted it. I couldn't do that."

"No, you couldn't. But I only did it by my mother's
leave. That's the problem, you see. I shall ever be some
woman's thrall."

That felt very upside-down to Eleanor, though she
did not doubt Doyle's sincerity, at least no more than
she mistrusted any Irishman. "But women feel the same
way. Everyone wants to be on top"—she blushed furiously as she spoke—"and everyone can't be at once."

He smiled a little. "The color rises up your throat to
your face like a sunrise. Pure and innocent and virginal.
My mother has no talent for blushing, and she was
never virginal."

"Almost a virgin," Eleanor said, thinking of Sal. "I
have known love." The words were a whisper, almost
lost in the hiss of the fire.

"And honest to a fault."

Eleanor shrugged, exhausted from days of running, warmed with ale and stew, her eyelids heavy suddenly. It would be so nice to just tumble into Doyle's strong arms and sleep. Just give him the sword and forget everything. She hovered in that dream for a few moments. Then her eyes snapped open and she stared into Doyle's dark face.

He was watching her with a kind of tenderness that made her heart pound. The expression was unexpected and disconcerting, and she longed for the simple companionship of Wrolf and Silver Heels. Doyle was, what? A man? Demigod? God? Elemental. There was no clear-cut answer to her question, and she knew that whatever the answer was, it was not simple. One moment he was an arrogant boor she could dismiss with ease, the next a charming storyteller who was nearly irresistible.

"Why should you have the sword?" she asked.

"To fight the Shadow."

"A good answer, if I can believe you."

Strangely, this questioning of his veracity did not seem to disturb Doyle. "That is why I want it now. What I'll do with it when I get it is another matter. Those swords—the four of them, or five—are a terrible thing. They arouse no more bloodlust in a woman than an ax, yet I can hear yours singing to me, and no ax on earth can still the sirens in it for me. If I had the strength, I'd wrest it from you. But I cannot. It is the first time I have been powerless in my life."

His candor was disarming, but Eleanor was too accustomed to Irish charm to rise to the bait completely. Instead, like an ancient trout of wisdom, she eyed it suspiciously, suspecting the tempting morsel of having a hook hidden within it. "You don't look feeble to me."

"You really don't understand, do you? You aren't some ignorant mortal any longer. You keep seeing yourself as a child or a girl. But that isn't meaningful. You have power that could change the face of the world, literally, and you act like...a dairy maid. Where is your pride?"

"I am not blessed with the kind of pride I think you mean."

"Then...you don't love yourself."

Eleanor felt a chord echo within her, a faint ring of memory like the murmur of water over stones. She did love herself now, but it was new knowledge, unassessed and unknown. She realized that of all that had happened to her, her meeting with Sal was the most important. "Why is it we must go contrary to our natures?"

"What?"

"I *never* wanted adventures, and I still don't. And I don't want a black, morose, sober-sides of a husband or a magic sword or anything. And you don't want a woman you can't control, and you don't want responsibility and would probably prefer to stay here and hunt with your pack. Where is Wrolf, by the way? He seems to have vanished."

"He's with the pack."

"Now, Baird would just adore running amok with the Sword of Bridget in his great, hammy hand, and of the two of you, I'd probably enjoy his company more in the long run. You and I are both so serious. Why can't things be logical and tidy?"

"The Cosmos is not a logical thing. It's...perverse."

"Almost Irish," she muttered.

"We could *learn* to laugh together, Eleanor."

Her heart betrayed her, leaping into her throat like a roebuck. It was such a foolish thing, her need for the sound of merriment. But his offer was like water to the thirsty—irresistible. The cold, unlaughing silences of her childhood were a desert she had marched through to Sal's oasis of water and laughter. Now he knew or shared her need, and she was tempted almost beyond anything. Caught, in truth.

"I suppose we ought to try for the sake of the world and all."

He roared with laughter, the huge sound rising to the interlaced roof to echo back to them. "Come along, you little minx. For the sake of the world, indeed."

Then Doyle swung her up in his arms, sword and all, and carried her across the room of colors into the walls beyond the world.

The plain stretched away on all sides, unfeatured but by low-growing shrubs and a single dolmen silhouetted against the sky. The air was crisp with the smell of heather and the land a crumpled violet coverlet, the bees humming in their work. The sky was the blue of Bridget's cloak, unmarked by sun or moon, and Eleanor was almost afraid to ask where they were.

Doyle carried her to the dolmen and set her on the springy turf. To her surprise it was as soft as a feather bed, not scratchy at all, and smelled of strange spices. The lintel of the dolmen loomed over them, several tons of dressed rock, weathered by time yet ageless. She hugged her knees to her chest and tried not to think about the stone above her head or the Irish lovers, Greine and Diarmat, who fled across the land, sleeping each night in a new dolmen.

He stood over her a moment, his bulk blotting out the sky, and Eleanor yearned for counsel. Sal, or even her mother, would have been a welcome intrusion, for she realized that in her sexual education, she had only gotten to where you put the noses when you kiss. Gooseflesh crawled along her skin, though it was not cold. The air, in fact, was warm and clean and it was the most pleasant thing she could remember since Sal's mountain. Somewhere out on the plain, a lark and a nightingale raised their voices in an unearthly counterpoint of melody.

Doyle sat beside her and put an arm around her shoulder, then drew it back, for Bridget's sword still rested across her back. She untied the cords that bound it and lay it to one side.

He shook his head. "I think it will always lie between us."

"Typical fatalistic Celt," she snapped.

"Have you ever been spanked?"

"No, and I don't suggest you try it."

He ran a broad forefinger along her face from brow to jaw, sending shivers of excitement through her. "Too late. You're spoilt already."

"I had no idea you were so knowledgable." Eleanor was frightened, not of sex, though that was there, but of the emotions that rose out of physical intimacy. She considered herself too well educated to be scared by cautionary tales from old wives of pain, humiliation, and disgust, but she wished she had something in the way of experience to reassure her.

"Heather cat," he rumbled, stroking the nape of her neck. "Admit it, you want everything in neat bundles."

"Yes, I suppose I do. And a real bed, too."

Doyle ignored her remark, taking her face in both his huge hands. "I am going to kiss you now. I would like it if you could kiss me back." His blue eyes seemed to bore into her.

This kiss was not cold and stifling, as the first had been. Instead, it seemed to warm her bones like the rays of the sun. Eleanor did her best to kiss him back and found her pulses moving from walk to trot, then to a slow canter. It was not unpleasant, and she began to relax.

They undressed, spreading their clothing beneath them on the ground, and Eleanor was gripped with panic. Naked, Doyle seemed a great bear in a man-suit. She could not for the life of her remember why "Snow White and Rose Red" had been her favorite childhood fairy tale.

He touched her body in the places of passion, and memory dimmed. Eleanor saw in his eyes a hunger, a demand, a need that frightened her. Had her father looked at her mother like that? Was that why her mother always looked burdened and resigned?

Eleanor did not push him away when he mounted her, tenderly and without much discomfort after the initial shock, the tearing thrust that terminated her maidenhood, but she retreated in mind from the whole matter. The sword, Bridget, the Darkness, all could go hang themselves. She had been tricked into surrendering her body, betrayed by a mess of chemicals, but she was suddenly determined never to surrender her self. There was such a need in him that she could never fill, and she decided not to try. He didn't want her, just the damn sword. She was damned if she was going to take responsibility for seeing he was a good boy with it. After all, she hadn't asked for any of this, had she?

Doyle seemed to fill the cosmos, his dark hair brushing her face, his soft lips touching her mouth, his hands pressing her body against him. All the empty places in her were filled with him, like black velvet, so she began to slip into a dark void torn with scarlet lightning. He was going to tear her to pieces.

Something in her rose to meet the threat. The burning brand in her body must be contained and quenched. Eleanor felt her "self" meld with her body, matching him in passion until they crested almost as one, the dam smashed to pieces, and they huddled together, weeping like tired children.

Doyle rested his head on her breast, fingers idly plucking the damp hair between her limbs, while Eleanor stroked his head and cursed herself for containing him. Now there was no way out. She was committed, as Sal and Bridget had probably known she would be, to the tasks, not out of duty, but from some other need she had no name for. As the postcoital depression caught her in its toils, she wondered how anyone could mistake passion for love. There must be some mystery in it. Doyle was right. She wanted all her answers in neat packages. Then she slept.

"Doyle, where is this place?" They were curled up together, warmly awake and beginning to be hungry, if the rumble from his abdomen was anything to judge by.

"In my mother's house, of course. Don't claw me, little cat. This plain...is a favorite place of mine, but I do not know a name for it. I just like it."

"Oh. What happened to the other swords that got made?"

"Are you always so curious after coupling? No, you would not know. One lies, they say, in a heart of stone, another in the sea. One is now a tree, and the last invisible. Only the sword of flames is...accessible. Why?"

"Because I don't know the story." She sat up and drew her shift on. "How old are you?"

"I have no idea. The years don't make much matter in my mother's house."

They crossed the plain and returned to the strange room of interlaces to find Baird in noisy argument with his mother. "That sword and the woman are rightfully mine. I will get them, too. Doyle is a boring dullard. You didn't even give me a chance to show her how cunning I am. And Doyle cheated. He got born first. He always gets born first."

"If you were the only man on earth, I doubt she would have you," Orphiana snapped, shifting her body and sending ripples through the pattern.

"That doesn't matter. She could use frequent beatings."

"She would be no easier to control than I, dear son."

"Why not? She's mortal. Please, Mother, just let me kill Doyle and have her. She'd learn to like me better than Doyle. Other Bairds have gotten to."

"How many times have I told you not to gossip with the water devils? Of all the Bairds I have ever borne, you are the worst. Get it into your impenetrable skull, Eleanor is not for you, never was, and never could be."

"You hidebound old snake! Why does everything always have to be the same every single time? Why should I sit here and wait for that whey-faced sourpuss of a girl to appear, the one I always get. Doyle is going off with the sword and the woman while I have to stay here and listen to you. No, no, no."

The great golden man swung around quickly, leapt the interlaced floor in a huge bound, and seized Eleanor in his arms. Baird slapped her smartly across the head, so that her ears rang, then closed his hands around her throat, pressing his thumbs against her windpipe. "Tell Doyle you want me, or I'll snap your neck like a splinter."

Eleanor was cold with terror, and Doyle made no move to aid her. She did not understand the rivalry between the brothers, but she hated it intensely. She sagged in Baird's grasp, weak with surprise. Oddly, no anger came to her, none of Bridget's fire. Instead, she felt a great sadness because she knew that she could never care for Baird, that although she did not yet love Doyle, she might in time. But Baird was too much like a graduate student of her father's, a charming, handsome young man who quite literally stole his thesis from another girl, and who had been petulantly irritated, not repentant, when caught. His opinion was that the girl should have been happy to give up her academic future for him; hadn't he paid attention to her? Daniel had been livid, of course.

She wished Baird would just wash away, for he contaminated the earth in a way. Like the lord of Nunnally Castle, he would always be spoiled and irresponsible, and that made her sad.

Huge, wet drops began to fall from the interlaced ceiling, splattering down on Baird's golden arms and vaporizing with an angry hiss. Wounds opened where the drops fell, and he released her with a huge howl. He raised a ham-fist, Eleanor ducked, and his punch slammed into the wall behind her.

"Bitch! I will not be denied. You will be mine if I have to tear the house apart to have you."

"If you ever touch me again, I'll tear your heart out through your throat, hack it into pieces, and feed it to my wolf." Eleanor felt her face flush with a sudden rage, fury at Doyle for not raising a hand to protect her, and at Baird for being a conceited brat. "You are a coward. I despise you." She turned her back on him as the strange moisture continued to fall on Baird, making fresh stigmata on his arms and face. She glared at Doyle. "Is this the kind of partnership I get to look forward to? Wrolf would have been more useful." Then she picked her way across the room to the fire. "You are a dreadful mother," she told Orphiana, determined not to omit any of the odd family.

Baird howled and ran into one of the interlaced walls, pursued by the strange cloud of moisture that dripped on him. Eleanor hunkered down, puzzled over the cloud, and picked up her personal belongings which he had scattered—the cup and spoon, the precious book, her knitting. Doyle again did his vanishing act and reappeared with two steaming bowls of porridge, sweet with honey and dotted with plump raisins.

They ate in thoughtful, if somewhat grumpy, silence, with only the hissing of the fire to break it. Finally Doyle said, "You really must learn to control your magicks, Eleanor."

"What?"

"That rain you made on Baird—"

"*I* made? Me?" She stared at him in amazement, then burst into giggles. "I have always wanted to rain on someone's parade."

"It is not funny," Doyle replied solemnly. "You can't

kill Baird or me, but you could damage him, and then what would happen?"

"I have no idea. *You* have the script. I am just ad-libbing as best I can." She gave him a sour look. "What should I have done, let him hit me? Or maybe you enjoy watching him beat up women."

"Stop it! I should have put more honey in your breakfast to sweeten your disposition. Of course I don't like it. But I can't touch Baird in this house."

"And he knew that and took advantage of it. What is this 'magicks' stuff?"

"You have powers, Eleanor, unexpected ones. The Bride Fire I understand, for the holder of that sword would hardly be without it. But I beg you, be careful of it now. You are changed, and it is much more potent. But you have other gifts, it seems, including the power to command water into this house. This is a place of earth, girl. You did not get that power from Bridget."

Eleanor leaned back, clasping her hands on one bent knee and balancing on her buttocks. She thought about everything that had happened and had been said and realized that somehow her sojourn with the Goddess of the Willows had escaped the notice of Orphiana. This was odd, for the old snake commanded earth, and Sal's holding under Silbury appeared to be on earth.

Either Sal was somehow hidden from Orphiana or the snake woman was pretending to ignorance for her own reasons. Galloping paranoia seemed imminent, so Eleanor tried to quell it, aware that everyone's motives but her own were suspect. Doyle and Baird wanted the sword, Orphiana wanted peace, and Sal and Bridget wanted—what?—worshipers perhaps.

The gifts, like Bridget's fire and the acid rain she had showered on Baird, puzzled her. They appeared without warning when she was threatened, but she seemed to have no control over them. How could she know her "magicks" if they popped up only under stress?

As a child, Eleanor had exhibited a violent temper. When she was ten, she had broken a playmate's collarbone in a fit of fury, and after that she had trained herself to be passive and cool. She thought a great many sharp remarks, but she rarely spoke them.

Now it felt as if the unruly and headstrong child had

reemerged with horns and a tail. The sense of being shoved around, used, and manipulated returned, for Eleanor was fully aware that Sal had buried messages in her mind that arose at need. Of all those she had met, the Willow Goddess was the one she least resented. Perhaps it was an illusion, but she felt that Sal had seen her as a person, not a tool. She agreed with Orphiana's assessment of Bridget as a hasty person.

What she wanted most at that moment was to be back in her silly, frilly, adolescent bedroom with no fabulous sword, no great dark man, no quest. Let someone else be invested with strange powers, and let sleeping demons lie. She remembered Frodo promising to go to Mordor, though he did not know the way, and thought him a fool. And failing all of those things, she wanted a hot bath, a cup of coffee, and a real bed.

Reducing her needs from the impossible to the ridiculous restored her sense of humor a little. "I don't know what you mean, as usual. In fact, I am heartily sick of this whole mess. Everyone talks in riddles and looks at me with a sneer when I ask for a straight answer. You can play your little games to your heart's content. Just bring Wrolf out from where you've hidden him and I'll leave."

"Leave?"

"Yes, you know, put one foot in front of the other."

"But why? Do you not wish to free Albion from bondage?"

"Sure, as soon as I figure out how not to rain on poor fellows like Baird. I think five or six years in meditation on Mt. Conavalla will do the trick. If it was good enough for St. Kevin, it ought to suit me fine."

"You jest."

"Yes, I do. I doubt I can master my demons in under a decade."

"There is a great temptation to . . . spank you, Eleanor."

"And I would like to box your ears so hard you couldn't hear for a month. Look, this is just not going to work at all. You bring out the very worst in me. You want the sword. Take it. It's yours, or Baird's or anyone's but mine. I don't want all this power—and I don't think I'm up to the job. Bridget should have picked someone else. Here, take it."

Eleanor shoved the cloak-wrapped bundle toward him. He did not move to take it. "No. Without you, it is just dead metal. Eleanor, I *need* you."

The siren call of Daniel Hope played in her mind. She tried desperately to form words of denial, but none came. Those fetters of obligation, so recently dissolved, returned, so she almost felt chains around her. Why should three small and probably insincere words have the power to reduce her to a cringing child?

Then she looked at his face, the ice-blue eyes, the sensuous mouth hidden in the beard, and knew he meant it, and that the admission had cost him greatly. The tears brimmed in her eyes as she acknowledged her own defeat. "Damn you to freezing hell, Doyle."

He drew her against him, stroking her tangled hair and murmuring comforting nonsense. He did not understand why she wept, only that it was from pain, not joy. He remembered the light in her eyes under the dolmen and the way her firm jaw softened in sleep, and he could hardly bear her tears. Doyle felt weak and inadequate, yet filled with a kind of warmth he had never experienced. There was no name for it yet, for the thing was too new and young. So he tucked Eleanor into his lap and rocked her like a child until the sobs faded and only the hissing of the fire pit broke the silence.

XIII

Eleanor slept fitfully. It was her usual pre-travel anxiety, a thing she got before every trip with her father, or even such a trivial event as spending the night with a school friend. She had mentally gone over the list of her few possessions, each one precious to her, especially those gifts of Sal's, a dozen times, and the litany had lulled her into a frowning doze. Doyle lay beside her enjoying the undisturbed slumber of those who are not given to worry about forgotten socks or toothbrushes.

Three days—or what seemed that amount of time—since Eleanor's arrival at the House of Orphiana, and the next morning they would start their return to beleaguered Albion. Yet something was not right. She mumbled her list in her sleep again.

Finally, she said, "Wrolf!" And a great hand covered her mouth while another yanked her head back by the long, dark hair. Eleanor stared into Baird's grinning face as he dragged her away from her bed. She slapped at him futilely, bit at his hand, but he clipped her smartly under the jaw and everything went gray in her head.

When she regained consciousness, Eleanor found herself in what appeared to be a seraglio. The room was huge and colorful, the walls bright with graceful gazelles and leopards against smooth limestone, the ceiling upheld by columns decorated with arabesques of red or blue against luminescent white, the floor a rippling stream made of blue and white tiles. A fountain played in the center of the room, not of water but of light, the colors changing and flashing with each cascade.

Eleanor moved and heard a faint jingle. She found she was chained, wrist and ankle, to a curious bed, a contraption of posters and pillows she would have found amusing if she had not been confined to it. The posters were carved with a series of explicit and unlikely figures engaged in sexual acrobatics, while the pillows appeared to have escaped from a work of Japanese pornography. She almost laughed and noticed the gag.

Baird appeared, garbed like a caliph, grinning and gloating. "I always get my way," he began with simple smugness. "Do not struggle. It is quite useless. You are mine now. Doyle will never find you, and if he does, I will kill you. It was very stupid of you to think you could defeat me."

Eleanor knew with a stomach-wrenching certainty that he was going to rape her. Or try to. Her "magicks" were too new and untrained to be effective yet, and Baird was alert to Bridget's fire and Sal's acid dew.

Then she remembered Moria Kerry, a half-mad old woman with a wealth of tales tucked away in a fading mind. She had lived in a cottage redolent of onions and goats, and resembled nothing so much as a classic witch with white wispy hair, a face of seams and wrinkles, a back bent with spinal arthritis. For some reason, she had taken an aversion to Daniel, so Eleanor had gone to gather the stories before the old woman died and took them into her soddy grave. Nothing irritated Daniel more than folk slipping off before he'd vacuumed their minds!

Moria had larded her adventures with the fairies, for she claimed to have been born in 1689 and spent three hundred years dancing with the Sidhe under Tara—with advice on such diverse matters as how to treat a scald and how to avoid rape.

Eleanor had never previously had occasion to try Moria's method—invented, she claimed, by a Sidhe named Maeve when trapped by saucy Jack Paggett up at Rafter's Glen—but she decided she really didn't have any other available options.

Eleanor closed her eyes and tried the "spell," attempting not to recall the blurred figure of a woman in stone, which stood in that glen and which was the result of Maeve's solution. Moria had never felt the need to tidy up any inconsistencies in her tales. Turning Baird into a rock seemed a nicer solution than some she had, but Eleanor was adamantly determined not to let him win.

Cold. Her bones felt like iron, her flesh was flint. Heavy. Leaden. Crack! One of the posts she was chained to snapped, and Eleanor yanked her arm free.

Baird goggled, then leapt on her as she tore at the gag. Her movements were slow, her fingers stiff, but she drew her arm back to flail at him with the dangling chain. It landed harmlessly on his back.

Baird ripped at her clothing as she tried to get the gag away. Eleanor wondered what effect stone teeth would have on his immortal flesh. He tore her filmy trousers away and stared in horror.

"You...bitch!" he screamed.

Eleanor looked down and discovered her legs were green, swirly stone, and her privates were as smooth as a Greek Venus. The girl with malachite pussy, she thought irreverently.

The bed collapsed under their weights, and Baird rolled off onto the tiled floor. Eleanor pulled her chains free and rose with slow majesty. *"Ah, that this too, too solid flesh would melt." How do I reverse this process? I can always get a job in a horror movie, I suppose. I wish I were in Cleveland!*

"Baird, go hump a dolmen." Her voice was like a gravel fall, rough and grating.

He stood up blazing, literally. The brilliance of his body was like the noon sun, and he advanced again. "I will have you, woman, and you will wish you had come to me willingly."

Baird was dazzling, and it was painful to look at him, even through eyes of stone. She longed to freeze his torrid essence out of existence, then realized that this was as impossible as falling up. For an instant, she knew who he was, who Doyle was, then it was gone, and she faced a man with the sun inside him, determined to rule her or destroy her in the bargain.

Eleanor turned her eyes away from him, seeking some exit. The pillars! Interlaced with arabesques! She stepped back, seeking some familiar pattern that might bring her to the house of the Earth Serpent. Doyle had shown her enough for her to know that the ways of that multidimensional place were not simple.

Moving with ponderous strides, Eleanor backed away, leaving huge holes in the floor. Then she saw a twist of decoration, a vinelike motif she recognized. She hurried to it, as much as a living statue could, and thrust herself into the pattern as Baird howled behind her. "No!"

Then she dropped onto the interlaced floor of Orphiana's room with a thump, and sprawled there, too heavy to stir. Doyle rose from his place by the fire and came toward her.

"You've just caused a dozen earthquakes, falling on my pattern that way," snarled the Earth Serpent.

"It isn't my fault Baird is an idiot, Mother-in-law."

"Be still! Your voice hurts! Doyle, change her back."

"Gladly, Mother." He crouched beside her, a strange expression, which might have been tenderness, in his eyes, and placed his hand upon her breast. "What a curious mixture you have made yourself. Onyx breasts and moonstone nipples. I liked you better as you were before. Ah, but you did not change so much. Your heart is not of stone."

Eleanor felt the terrible heaviness fade from her bones. She sat up wearily, glanced at Doyle, and shrugged. "I guess you couldn't . . . have come after me."

"That does not mean I did not wish to."

They were sitting together, their departure delayed by Baird's abduction, in a sort of mellow silence. Eleanor clicked at her knitting and Doyle cleaned the leather of his jerkin. It was domestic and companionable.

"Doyle," she asked, "are we married, or just sleeping together?"

"Is it important?"

"I don't know. I think, if I ever thought about marriage, I sort of had my heart set on a long white dress and a veil and all. Or at least a judge reading the words. Though I don't think I would have promised to obey."

Doyle looked bemused and stroked his beard. "No, you wouldn't say that, I guess. Still, I see the need of a ceremony to dignify the matter. I cannot conjure you a gown or judge, but perhaps Orphiana could be convinced to say a few words."

The Earth Serpent seemed to drouse by the fire, and

her head jerked up at the sound of her name. She fixed her son and daughter-in-law with a glittering gaze. "This is a new turn."

"Would you, ma'am?" Eleanor was respectful.

"My words will bind and seal you, you know."

"You mean I can't divorce the lout if I change my mind?"

"Such loverlike words," Doyle muttered. "First she says let's marry, then she calls me names."

"It would be for as long as you live," Orphiana continued. Eleanor caught an odd note in the old snake's voice, one she could not identify.

"Yes, I know. But I think I want it anyhow."

"And you, Doyle?"

"Yes. I think it would comfort me to know that my fractious woman here would give me such a vow."

"Very well." Orphiana shifted her body. "Vow then that you shall be true to one another as long as life runs in your veins, that you will aid each the other, and that you will take no other partners except by mutual consent."

Eleanor was a little startled by that last, but if Doyle agreed, she would at least be sure he wouldn't dally with some farm girl. "I promise," she answered slowly.

"And so I vow, as long as breath remains in my lungs."

The morning they left the house of the Earth Serpent was cold and windy. Eleanor stepped out smartly, almost eagerly, to be away from her contentious in-laws, and Wrolf frolicked beside her. His days of dalliance with Doyle's pack had done him no apparent damage, and their reunion had been joyous. She wondered a little, remembering wolves to be monogamous and life mates at that, at what had transpired between Wrolf and the silver-pelted sirens who had accompanied Doyle on his hunts, for he had once told her he kept no males in his pack. Wrolf remained the soul of discretion.

It was almost as if they were beginning their adventures again, except for the somewhat disturbing presence of Doyle. Eleanor realized as she glanced at her companion that she mistrusted everything—her own emotions, this stranger/spouse, and even the mach-

inations of the goddess. It must be something about the
air, she decided, recalling her father's oft-repeated saying: "There's nuthin' like the clime of Erin to make a
skeptic a' you."

The rain began, a steady sprinkle that hardly impeded
progress but eventually soaked through clothing. Doyle
seemed to be heedless of it, but Eleanor was less than
happy with the situation. There was also the fact that
she was somewhat uncomfortable traveling with him,
for it suddenly seemed to be his adventure, and she
appeared relegated to the role of spear carrier. It did
not matter that she had never desired the quest and
had undertaken it from a sense of duty. Eleanor had
come to value her newfound independence and almost
resented the reality that they must work together, for
she had little doubt that he would make all the decisions and that she would agree out of a kind of reflex.
So, having worked herself into a black mood, aided by
the now increasing precipitation, she silently cursed
her late father, Doyle, males in general, and the un-
heeding cosmos for inventing such troublesome beasts
as men.

Eleanor pressed the point of her rowan-wood stave
into the peaty ground with more vigor than was needed,
and pits of sod spattered on her cloak. Doyle walked
ahead of her, his back as straight as a plank, the sword
of Bridget in its sheath carried across his broad shoulders, with only the hilt with its large jewel sticking up
under the neck opening of his red cloak. She realized
that this meant he must have a steady trickle of cold
rain down his back, and grinned. Doyle was right. The
sword would always lie between them. She included the
unnamed smith who had forged the weapon to slay Orphiana in her litany of spleen, then made an effort to
cast off her doldrums.

"May one ask where we are going?"

"To Albion," Doyle grunted.

"I know that. But . . . how?"

"You'll see."

Eleanor kicked him firmly in the bottom with a
mucky boot. "Listen, you overgrown ape, I didn't walk
across half of England and brave the Irish Sea in winter
to tag along after you saying 'Yes, Master, no, Master.'"

Doyle swung around and caught her by the shoulders. "Listen, minx, you'll do it my way or no way at all."

They glared at each other, and Wrolf growled and raised his hackles. "You don't like me very much, do you?" Eleanor asked her question while tracing the square line of his jaw with her fingertips. His look turned her bones to water, but she was not going to let him know it.

"No, I don't. I told you in the beginning, I had no joy in exchanging one distaff for another."

"Then we might as well turn back right now and get a divorce—only we cannot, can we—because it isn't going to work. You resent me because without me that sword is just dead metal, and I resent you because I *had* to surrender it to you. Let's toss the thing into the sea or stick it into Queen Mab's tomb and let Albion die. I can meet you halfway, Doyle, but I can't do the accommodating for both of us."

"Damn you for an iron mistress!" Doyle gave her a look compounded of lust and chagrin. "I have no gift for cooperation, child."

"Then you had damned well learn!"

Doyle put his arm over her shoulders, and they began to walk again. "Do you know, it is impossible to truly defeat a woman? Just when you think you have her neatly fenced up, she changes shape and pops up outside your enclosure. It isn't fair."

"No one ever promised you fair," Eleanor answered, struck by his comment as it related to her parents. The truth of it gave her a new insight into her mother, and she had another twist of guilt. Had she simply vanished, or was that other Alianora taking her place? She sincerely hoped that the hasty Bridget had not caused her mother any worry, but she had no confidence in that hope.

"No, they did not. I just keep hoping. And I hate it when you are right. I... well, Baird is surely going to try to stop us, and I didn't wish to worry you."

"Don't be considerate when my ignorance could be fatal," she snapped.

"He would not hurt you, not really."

"Baird said he would kill me if he could not have me."

"You really don't know, or understand, do you, Eleanor?"

"Know what? If I had tuppence for everything I don't know, or even don't know about this quest, I could buy a magic carpet to fly us out of this rain. The Bahamas, now, or Tahiti. We've never had a honeymoon."

"Your mind is full of such fair irrelevancies. The fate of the world hangs in the balance, and you are dreaming."

"Oh, pooh! The world is always on the edge of disaster. Yes, I know this world is different because I have it in my hands—sort of. But to return to your question, no, I don't know or understand. Every fact I gather just raises more questions. And I never seem to get a straight answer. I am trying very hard not to sit down and fold my arms and refuse to move until I understand the situation, believe me. I keep telling myself that tomorrow, or the day after, I will understand. I never do. Even Sal didn't tell me what I wanted to know."

"And what do you wish to know?"

"Everything," Eleanor replied with maddening simplicity.

"Then I cannot help you. *I* don't know everything. And besides, there isn't time." He sounded a little sad under his light tone, and she gave him a sharp look.

"No, there is never enough time," she agreed. "All right, where are we headed?"

"That I will not tell you, for Baird has overlong ears."

"Is that why he's so short of brains?"

"You've a tongue dipped in venom, woman."

"And you wanted a sweet, fair-headed lass who would never gainsay you."

"Perhaps. You have a bit too much of my mother in you for comfort."

"And you remind me of my father in all the less desirable ways. Do we ever get to be ourselves instead of a...reflection of the other person's experiences?"

"In time, we might." Again, the slight melancholy of his tone made her look at him. His profile gave her no clues to his thoughts, so she admired the clean line of wide brow and long nose above the sensuous mouth hidden by beard and mustache. "I would have wanted a more restful woman, I think, for I am a man who likes his comforts."

"Oh? Am I that...uncomfortable?"

"Challenging more than uncomfortable," he answered. "I wondered, when I took you, that you were still a virgin. You are...like trumpets and tocsin ringing in the night. An invitation to rape and violence."

"Me?" Eleanor gave a nervous laugh, remembering the lord of Nunnally Castle, and Baird. "How? Why? I don't mean...to be a tease or...anything."

He laughed his rumbling laugh. "No, you are not. It's the power in you, in all females. Do you think Apollo pursued Daphne because she was a pretty girl?"

"I suppose. All those Greek gods were always running after mortal women, which I have never understood. I mean, why, when there were all those goddesses? Even the ones like Artemis who were supposedly virgins went around bathing in fountains, renewing themselves, so they must have been...fooling around."

"There is a kind of power that is born in every woman. Virginity is prized because it is a guarantee that the woman has never shared that power with a man before. A woman who never shares it is as much a traitor as one who gives some to every fellow she meets."

"'Hoggamus, pogamus, woman monogamous, Higgamus, pigamus, men are polygamous.'"

"What was that?"

"A silly poetic form called a double dactyl. Is all this a subtle way of telling me to be faithful, Doyle?"

"No. Women share their power where they will, and a man must just do the best that he can. It is why fathers guard their daughters while their sons rut with milkmaids."

"But, don't men have power, too?" Eleanor thought for a moment about how effectively Daniel had kept her out of circulation.

"Certainly. But never enough. It must needs be enhanced...by the love of a good woman."

"Or several good women?"

"Umm, yes."

"I think this is one of the silliest things I've ever heard. It makes me feel like a nuclear power plant or something. If I have any power, which I rather doubt, then I can't transfer it to you or anyone else. It isn't a bank draft."

"No, it isn't. And a woman never gives it up. Shares, occasionally. But men pursue women in the blind hope that they will find one who will ... surrender. They are often fooled by the illusion of surrender, too."

"It all sounds very antagonistic, but it does explain Baird's lunatic determination to possess me. How uncomplimentary. I am not even a sex object, just a power tool."

"Don't be so hard on yourself. And, yes, it is antagonistic—and resentful. The man is angry because he can't get what he wants, and the woman is furious because she senses she is being used."

"It is a good thing women don't know about this theory, or the race would have died out long ago. Do you really believe what you are saying?"

"Yes."

"Does this mean we are going to fight to a draw every time we have a disagreement? Isn't there any room for compromise?"

"There would be, if I would meet you halfway."

"And will you?"

"Perhaps." He kissed her on the forehead and hugged her against his chest. "Your generosity may shame me into it." With that, Eleanor chose to be content.

At nightfall they came to a curious structure, a sort of yurt made by drawing supple lengths of willow together to form a round hut and covering it with bark. Eleanor looked at it with some amusement, for she recognized it as a native American building called a wickiup, used by the Plains Indians for both temporary and more enduring edifices. It had as little business in thirteenth-century Ireland, even *this* thirteenth-century Ireland, as she did. She was also wary of anomalies.

"We sleep here tonight," Doyle announced, thrusting his shoulders through the narrow opening. Eleanor followed him and found him shaking his great cloak out and hanging it across the doorway to prevent a draft. There was a fire pit with wood laid out, as yet unlit, and a fat coney, unskinned but fresh, lying beside it. "Light the fire, will you?"

Eleanor removed her cloak and hung it on the wall, shook out her damp skirts, and automatically looked around for matches, a cigarette lighter, or even flint and steel. She was about to query her husband if he would have her make bricks without straw as well, for she was cold, wet, tired, and hungry, and inclined to be irritable. Wrolf came in and lolled at her feet, and she could not remain too dour in the face of his lupine good humor.

Then she remembered her first encounter with Baird and crouched down to see if she could make Bridget's fire her servant as well as her protector. Eleanor focused her mind on the idea of fire and was rewarded by the pleasant sight of flames dancing on her skin without heat or burn. The fantasy flames even cast shadows on the wall of the hut but remained illusion.

Grunting, she knelt beside the fire pit and tried a different tack—supplication. The result was entirely unsatisfactory, though Eleanor was not sure if she had not asked correctly or if that was just not the way to go. She rested back on her heels, frowning, and abstractedly watched Doyle begin skinning and cleaning the dead rabbit. She mentally ran through all the poems and incantations she knew from folklore for conjuring fire, and found none to her liking. Magic was harder than it looked.

Eleanor pursed her lips, thinking now about the nature of combustion, which she understood in only the vaguest way, then extended her hands above the wood. She rubbed them together, and a shower of sparks cascaded down into the pit, a few smoldering among the curls of kindling for a second before fading away.

"Damn!" Eleanor muttered, clapping her palms together in an angry gesture. A flash that might have been a minor lightning bolt leapt from her hands, ignited the kindling, and almost singed her sleeves in the process. "Yeow!" she cried, snatching her hands back from the now blazing wood.

Doyle finished cleaning the rabbit, spitted it, and thrust it into the flames. "Why didn't you ask for help?"

"Of all the stupid, arrogant...because no one gives

me a straight answer! Bridget says go here and do this. You've made it very plain you would prefer *not* to be... under my tutelage. Everyone uses me. But no one ever really explains anything to me. Even Sal."

Hot tears pricked her eyes, and she swung around to face the wall, furious with herself for losing control, aching for Sal, who had loved her, and hurting because Doyle would always regard her as simply a means to power. Eleanor had never defined what she wanted for herself, choosing instead to let Daniel make those decisions for her, and now it appeared that the one thing she did want was impossible to attain. After several minutes of fighting off tears and a general feeling of melancholy, she thought about the question posed by Eleanor of Aquitaine in the Courts of Love—"Is love possible after marriage?" The court had never arrived at a satisfactory answer, and Eleanor found a perverse pleasure in the knowledge that everyone else was as confused as she was. Her sense of humor tickled, she turned back to Doyle and the fireplace.

"I will say this," he began, "you don't sulk long, and you don't carry on much."

"I was *not* sulking; I was thinking."

"Thinkin' you'd like to roast my liver an' lights."

"No, I was hardly thinking of you at all. I was really thinking about Sal and Eleanor of Aquitaine."

"A fitting pair of harpies, I suppose. Consider my withers wrung and my vanity pricked. I keep forgetting you are honest to a fault. How fierce you are when you glare at me. My brother should be grateful you aren't his, for he'd have a blazing headache all the time, from your eyes."

"And you don't?" Eleanor kept her temper in with great difficulty. She recognized his jocularity as a way of avoiding some subject that upset him, and decided not to be too provoking.

"No, it gets me more in my guts," he replied with a droll expression.

"Wait until you eat my cooking," she said.

"I suspected as much, which is why I am burning the coney."

"Doyle, who made this... wickiup?"

"Withyfay, I expect."

"Willow fairies? I have never heard of them—not specifically. I hate to say anything about it—"

"That's never stopped you before," he cut in.

"Because it sounds like it's raining worse," she continued, as if he had not spoken, "but this place feels... wrong, vaguely wrong. Please don't tell me I am a hysterical female."

"To my great regret, it is the one thing you never are."

"Why regret? Do you *like* hysterics?"

"Because if you were, I would never have to take you seriously. Yes, I feel it, too, the wrongness. I can't put a finger to it, so I think we should take our chances."

Eleanor nodded and rose to sort out their blankets and spread them beside the fire. She found the room warm enough to remove her tunic and go about in her shift.

"You have beautiful breasts," Doyle said quietly. "Your nipples are like roses."

Eleanor felt her face redden and drew her arms across her chest with reflexive modesty. "No one has ever said anything like that to me before," she said in a choked voice.

"I know, and I can't decide if I am angrier at the waste or gladder at my good fortune. You've been ready for bedding for years, I think. Still, I don't have to exceed the feats of previous men, for which I rejoice. But if I go on looking at you, I'll burn dinner."

Part of Eleanor wanted to say dinner be damned, but it wasn't that simple. She didn't know how to be sexually aggressive, and she had no idea how Doyle would react. Coquetry seemed beyond her capacity, and so she was frozen in place, trapped between desire and decorum. She felt as if she couldn't breathe from her frustration, so she sat beside him and rubbed her head against his shoulder, like a cat demanding attention.

Doyle turned his dark head and regarded the top of hers with the dispassionate eye of a hunter looking upon his prey. He watched the way her hands clasped her upper arms, noting tension, the careful joining of her knees, so her mysteries were hidden, despite the sheerness of her shift, and cursed himself for a stiff-necked, arrogant fool. They had so little time together

that he feared to love her, even a bit, to stem the pain
of loss. He added selfish to his catalog of faults, con-
fessing to himself that he liked her well enough for
such a brief acquaintance, that she was brave, smart,
resourceful, and didn't whine. He enjoyed her bouts of
temper, her flashes of fire, but especially the way her
body felt beneath his. No woman, not even his mother,
could ever have been so alive before. Of course, he was
not besotted by a square jaw with too much mulishness
about it for beauty, or a pair of eyes like sunlight through
leaves, or even a courageous spirit. No, he was immune
to any tender feelings where females were concerned.
For which he was grateful, for it meant the lump in his
throat must be a bit of a cold from walking in the rain
all day.

Then the wench lifted her head to give him a shy
smile, a tentative look like a dog who has been kicked
too often, and he felt as if he had been poleaxed, silently
cursing his late father-in-law for a brute, that this
splendid woman should be grateful for such bits of love
as he had grudgingly parceled out. The mouth was so
inviting, the gold-flecked eyes so tender, that his heart
felt ready to burst in his chest. He bent to kiss the still
smiling lips and wondered for the first time in his life
where lust ceased and love began.

"Doyle, please, take me now." It was a whisper in
his mind, like a breeze across water, a siren song, an
aching longing that would not be denied.

He drew the shift up over her head and threw it
aside, rabbit and fire forgotten. His tunic and breeches
removed hastily, he drew her atop him, setting her riding him, watching the play of firelight across breast
and flesh, feeling the wildness rise within her to meet
his own, pleasuring in cries of passion that rang around
the little hut, and finally shouting his own response;
then they lay, still coupled, sweaty and entangled like
two battlefield casualties until the hissing of the fire
reminded them of dinner.

"I think you've made me ruin our meal," he said in
his deep voice.

"I'm sorry. I always did prefer dessert to the main
course."

Doyle roared with laughter, glad that the Fates had

dealt him this fierce and lusty creature instead of some milk-and-water maiden. For a moment, he did not care that their time was so short, that when he had left, she would bestow her gifts elsewhere. Or would she? Eleanor possessed a kind of fierce loyalty that might linger past the grave, and he wondered if any would pass this place again without feeling an echo of their sharing. *She is worthy of me, but am I worthy of her?*

At this moment, the object of his speculations rolled off him and bent over the fire. Doyle watched the shadow of her body on the wall of the hut, the smooth curve of breast, and the long fall of night-dark hair, bemused and content. Then he sneered at his smugness, knowing that no man has ever truly won a contest on the couch of Venus, though many have lost. He decided they had at least fought to a draw, and sat up.

"I think it is still edible," Eleanor said, holding out the charred rabbit.

"Good."

They ate, naked, in companionable silence, tossing Wrolf the bones. Then they curled up together on the blanket, covered with Eleanor's rather shabby cloak, Eleanor pillowing her head against his shoulder, the fire smoldering in the pit.

"Doyle, why are you so sad?"

"Sad?"

"When we...make love, I always sense a terrible sadness."

"Just my nature, I think."

"Please, don't lie to me."

"If you wanted a cheerful fellow, you should have taken Baird." He did not want her to know what lay ahead, as he wished he did not know himself.

Eleanor sighed. "Someday I'll get a straight answer out of someone, and the shock will probably kill me." She touched his shoulder with light fingertips. "I...tried to share my power, Doyle."

It was a whiplash across his heart, a simple testament of a love he did not feel he merited, and it somehow hurt almost more than he could bear. "You are a sweet woman, Eleanor," he said, and kissed her so she would not see the tears that threatened to overflow his cold blue eyes.

XIV

Eleanor was drowning in a river of blood. It was boiling, roiling, bubbling across her face, and she clawed her way up to free her aching lungs. Her head broke the waves, and she screamed for air, smelling the iron reek of the liquid as it began to suck her down again.

There was something on her wrist, something wet and sharp. A mouth! Some dreadful creature that lived in blood. Eleanor struggled to get free, slopping and scratching, until a sound, a remembered and unnamed noise, came to her ears. A growl.

Wrolf! A word, a picture, then the feel of rough fur under her hand. Eleanor tried to get her eyes open, eyes gummy with some foreign substance, a line of pain across her forehead. It was slow, clumsy work, like swimming in glue, but at least she could breathe. Finally, she peered blurrily around the hut, very dim now as the fire died.

The floor was covered with something that looked like a flock of thumbs wearing tiny red hats. Eleanor blinked her eyes several times to clear her vision, but the hats on thumbs persisted. There was a sound, too, a kind of high, squeaky hiss, like a castrati teakettle on the boil, which filled the room. She looked around for Doyle and discovered him a few feet away, his lower body being towed underground while the horrible little creatures swarmed across his chest and face. They were dragging her down as well while Wrolf barked and scattered them with great paws, smashing squeaking bodies with a blood-foamed mouth.

Eleanor struggled to free her legs from the relentless undertow that seemed to be sucking her into the earth, wondering if her mother-in-law felt her movements along the patterns while she tried to think of some way to combat the things. She had something of two elements at her command, fire and water, and little practical capacity to use them yet. As Doyle said, so far her magicks were a function of her temper.

As fast as she brushed the red caps off her legs, new battalions attacked. The tide of funny hats was a nightmare of every image she had of brownies and leprechauns, and she loathed them helplessly. Doyle seemed dead, and she was afraid. What to do? The sword was useless against the attack unless she amputated a few limbs. The cloak, if she could have reached it, resting in a silky blue heap a few feet away, seemed to have some defensive capacity, for the red hats flowed around it. Doyle was underground almost to his slim hips now, and Wrolf was shaking, sending showers of plump little worms flying through the air to splat disgustingly against wall and floor.

The sight of Doyle's fast-vanishing body infuriated her, and with a great shout, she clapped her hands together in an actinic flash. The red hats seemed to pause. The hiss became more shrill.

Eleanor raised her hands above her head and cast a fireball the size of a cantaloupe into the walls of the hut. It spread across the dry willow branches like a flaming carpet unrolling down the walls. When it touched the floor, it flowed like blazing honey across the tiny creatures. There was a scream of rage or terror—one voice or many, she could not tell—but her legs were no longer frozen in earth.

Scrambling up, Eleanor rushed to her husband, grabbing him under the arms and dragging him away from the rising tide of flame. He was heavy, and her strength was barely equal to the task; she coughed and gasped in the acrid willow smoke. He grunted suddenly, opened his eyes, and struggled to his feet. They burst through the doorway of the hut. A moment later, Wrolf appeared, his plumed tail alight, and then the whole structure collapsed in a flaming whoosh, the scream of the red hats rising eerily above the fire.

They crouched together, Eleanor slapping out the fire on Wrolf's tail with her bare hands, careless of herself. The hut burned merrily as the chill, misty dawn rose. At first they were both too busy coughing to speak, and clinging to one another in wordless affirmation of the other's continued existence. But as the fire died and the stench of burned flesh warred with the sweet scents of morning, they spoke, or rather croaked, at each other like a pair of jackdaws.

"So much for a good night's sleep," muttered Eleanor.

Doyle chuckled a little. "If they cut off your head, will you complain the knife was dull?"

"Probably. What were those...things?"

"I do not know. My mother has many strange creatures in her, some I have never seen, and the Shadow too has minions. You're shivering."

He put a strong arm around her shoulders and drew her against his chest. Doyle was warm, almost hot, in the chill of the morning, and he smelled of sweat and blood and smoke.

"I did not bargain for being mother-naked in an Irish spring morn," she snapped, and coughed again. "The next time a goddess tells me to save the world, I am going to say no." She coughed so hard she bent over double, gasping for air and clinging to his strong hand.

"You wouldn't, you know." Doyle stroked her long black hair. "Like me, you're much too duty-bound."

"Then I'll demand an instruction manual. Doyle, I could have killed us. I don't know how to handle my powers...and who is going to teach me?" She sighed. "I liked that hut. It made me think of Sal."

"What a pass to come to. My only rival is a droopy creature of wells and moonlight. Why do you love her so much? I should have thought bright Bridget would be more to your taste, my spitfire."

Eleanor did not answer for a long time, thinking of his words, sensing the seriousness beneath the faint teasing. Why did she love the cool lady of the willows, who reminded her in curious ways of a mother she had never cared for? There was no answer in her, except a kind of music, the sweet sound of rushing water across rock, two voices raised in wordless song. "Maybe because she cared enough to come down off her high seat and tell me things instead of speaking in riddles."

"Do you think that was love? Goddesses rarely give gifts without...attachments."

"It's more than I've gotten from anyone else. You won't even tell me how we're going to return to Albion."

"You mean she didn't show you how to walk on water?"

Several replies rose to her lips, but she only said, "Teasing Irishmen are a dead bore."

"Ouch! Next you'll be boxing my ears."

"Maybe. I've already singed your beard," she answered, tugging at a few crisped wisps. "Everything is burned up, isn't it?"

"Not the sword, for it was made in fire."

"Damn the sword! I wonder you bother to sleep with me when you love it so much!"

"Nay, I wouldn't. Think of my manhood."

Eleanor giggled. "I can hardly think of anything else when it's staring me in the face."

"Lusty wench! For a lass who was a maiden not long ago, you're remarkably...healthy."

"I don't know any other way to be. Should I act embarrassed or shy?"

"No. It's just a bit unexpected, though why I should imagine I could predict a woman, I don't know. One second you're a sulking termagant, the next a nymph. And here comes some Irish weather to make our day perfect."

The overcast sky released its burden of moisture in a drenching downpour, which soaked them and made the dying fire hiss and steam. In ten minutes it stopped, or passed over them to some other place, and they rose to explore the ashes of the hut.

As Doyle had predicted, the sword and its scabbard were unharmed, the interlace patterns still bright with color. Bridget's cloak, too, was intact, and to Eleanor's surprise, her rowan-wood staff with the quarters of the moon carved in the top was unmarred. Everything else was destroyed, and she had a pang for the precious impedimentia of her journey, the knitting pins and yarn, the cup and bowl from Sal, the clothes, and the beautiful book of Bridget that Brother Ambrosius had given her.

Eleanor clasped the blue cloak around her throat, and it fluttered and billowed slightly in the faint breeze. She looked at her staff, unaware that she appeared to Doyle a bright figure garbed in starry night, for a moment displaying the unnamed deity of which she was a reflection, a servant, and an aspect. The staff was a rod of power, tying earth and sky together an instant.

Doyle was awed, shriveled by the limitations of himself, man and nearly immortal, giant and yet dwarfed by a mere slip of a girl. For a second, she was the most beautiful and terrible of women, a thing to make a worm of his mother, and then she was just a naked girl with sooty feet and smears of ashes on her face. He shrugged and remembered that in the end they were only mortals and that the gods within them were less important than the fragile, tenuous partnership they had begun. She did not know her power yet, might never know it completely, but he was sure that if he told her, she would probably laugh and call him foolish. The strength was not diminished by being unacknowledged, but it would not be enhanced by premature disclosure.

For the first time in his very long existence, Doyle was aware of the briefness of what remained. Soon he must surrender to his ritual fate, a fate long delayed by the needs of time itself, and he found a deep regret. The earth he had taken for granted would swallow him up soon, and he wished it might be different, though once he took a wife and left his mother's house, the die was cast. He wanted to see her come into her own, her full glory, and there was no time. Then she spoke, and he let loose of the heaviness in his heart, wishing now to make their time together sweetly memorable.

"Doyle, why didn't the staff burn, too? It isn't magic— at least no more than rowan is. But Sam told me it was carved by human hands, and I seem to remember rowan burns well, not the reverse."

"Because you've put some of your own power in it."

"How?" Her eyes were bright with interest.

"There you stand, turning blue with cold and begging for instruction. Come along. Let's move to get warm, and I will tell you what little I know."

They reached a small cove in midafternoon. Eleanor's bare feet were bruised and cut with stones, her calves scratched with brambles, and she was cold, for a brisk wind blew up from the chilly sea. She was hungry as well, for their midday meal had been some nuts and bitter windfall from a crab apple tree. But she was well content, for Doyle had spoken of magic and power, and she had learned something of the possibilities, if not her own capacities.

Naked, Doyle was even more bearlike than clothed, and he seemed unaffected by the cold or hunger. But he, too, seemed pleased with their talking. And Wrolf padded beside them, occasionally racing off through the underbrush to strike terror into the hearts of rabbits and squirrels, though his actions appeared more playful than serious.

They climbed down a path of sorts, to the cove, and Eleanor glanced around, half expecting a coracle to float in on the foam-flecked waves. There was nothing but sea and sky. She drew the starry cloak closer around her and regarded Doyle hopefully.

"Are we going to fly?"

"You might but not me. And I fear you will not like the mode of transport I have in mind."

Eleanor looked out at the choppy sea. "Unless it's the Queen Mary, you're probably right. Could I really fly?"

"Yes, but not yet. We must go out to the end of that spit." He pointed to a rocky projection on the left.

"Oh, my aching feet." But she trudged beside him through the gravelly sand, onto lichen-covered rocks, and out to the point. The water curled against battered stones. There was nothing else. "Doyle, I'm not a strong swimmer."

He did not answer but bent over the churning sea and made a sound like a scream. Then he sat down and folded his arms over his knees to wait. Eleanor shrugged and sat next to him.

After ten or fifteen minutes, a spout of water broke the sea, followed by a sleek, dark head with gaping teeth. Eleanor stared in horror at the grinning monster, then at two. They cried a sharp note and capered in the waves.

"Doyle," she whispered, "those are killer whales."

"Yes, I know." He rose and walked to the water. "Come along."

"You're right. I don't like it at all. How does one...
ride...mount...hold on?"

Doyle had stepped into the sea and vanished, for it
was very deep beyond the rocks. His dark head broke
the water a few feet offshore, and he stroked strongly
toward one of the orcas. Wrolf barked and leapt into
the ocean, and Eleanor took a deep breath, said a mental prayer to the capricious lady who had gotten her
into the mess, and followed suit, clutching her staff
awkwardly in one hand.

The icy waters closed over her head, and she almost
panicked, remembering Sal's iron hands holding her
down in the bath. She kicked hard and felt herself rise
until she came to the surface, coughing. The salt stung
her cuts and scratches, and the cold seemed to freeze
her lungs, but she put her arms forward, holding the
staff with both hands, and flutter-kicked away from the
rocks. Something sleek and smooth slid under her belly
and lifted her above the waves. The great intelligent
eye of a killer whale regarded her curiously as she
choked and gasped. Something rough brushed her
knuckles, and she saw there was a kind of harness, a
thing of silvery stuff, around its shoulders. Eleanor
grabbed it with her right hand, held the staff in her
left, and clenched her jaws to keep them from chattering.

A rough head broke the water beside her, and large
brown eyes looked at her. It was Wrolf, but a Wrolf so
changed, she would never have known him but for the
now familiar aura of light that glowed from the silvery
pelt. A seal? she wondered, then saw the webbed paws
and realized that her companion was now, somehow,
an otter, the biggest otter, perhaps, the world had ever
known.

Doyle, atop the other whale, gave his strange cry,
and they raced off into the Irish Sea. The journey was
a nightmare of cold and eye-stinging spray, of aching
hands and cramped muscles, of screaming lungs when
the beast submerged and gasping breath when it came
up. Eleanor discovered after a time that she could gauge
when the whale was about to go down, and it took all
her concentration to manage that.

The world darkened as the sun set, and the dreadful

trip continued. Twice she was sure she was going to drown in the chilly waters when it seemed the orca would never come up, and once she was certain she had seen the kelp-crowned lady of the deep, whose face she found more terrible than Sal's or Bridget's or any other she might imagine, for the face smiled and beckoned, the bony hands reached out and clutched. But the orca sped past, and there was air and starlight, and finally the faint, warm, earthy scent of vegetation that meant land.

The orca ceased its headlong rush, and Eleanor released her death grip in the harness, slipping into the waters as the beast swam away. She forced her legs to move, a bicycling movement that got her head above the sea, then dog-paddled with one hand and two cramped legs until her chilled toes struck bottom. She half waded, half crawled onto the shore and crouched there, retching and coughing with the sodden cloak across her.

Doyle picked her up and carried her up across the rocky beach and into some sandy dunes that lay beyond. There was some sweet-smelling stuff growing crouched across the dunes, and he laid her down on it. Wrolf sprawled nearby, his normal wolfish self, and set about grooming his paw pads. Eleanor huddled and tried to think warm, dry thoughts, but the chatter of her teeth distracted her. Doyle chafed her hands with his, rubbing screaming muscles with strong fingers, until she began to feel the tingle of blood in them.

Eleanor looked up and saw that the sky was starless now. Albion still lay under the terrible Darkness, and she wondered how, even with Doyle, she could defeat such a presence. Then she slipped into a fitful doze that blotted out cold and hunger and a task she was too tired to contemplate.

XV

She woke pillowed against his bare shoulder, with Wrolf pressed against her other side. It was a warm nest of flesh and fur, with the sky cloak lying lightly across her body. Eleanor ignored a call of nature, reluctant to move, aching in every bone and muscle, hungry, thirsty, yet filled with a sense of serenity that even the grim morning of Albion could not depress. Then Wrolf stirred and padded off in search of breakfast, and she dragged herself up and some distance away, rather surprised her body had any fluids to remove.

When she came back, Doyle was sitting up, his black hair snarled and matted with salt, looking more beast than man. He gave her a partial smile, for his lips were cracked and bleeding, giving his friendly gesture an ogrelike flavor.

"Next time, let's walk," she croaked.

"Or fly." His voice was a creaky hinge. "Let's find some water."

Eleanor wrapped the cloak around her, took up the staff, and they went inland until they found a trickling stream. She thought no liquid had ever tasted so sweet. When her thirst was quenched, she splashed the chilly stuff on her salt-rimed face, shivering and flinching at the stings, suppressing visions of steaming baths, scented soaps, and odorous oils. Then she dabbled her feet in the icy waters and wiggled them in the air to dry.

"I'm hungry," she said with the air of making a great revelation.

Doyle, rinsing his black mane in the stream, chuckled. "What, no fit of fury over our journey? Has the sea damped my spitfire?"

"After I eat."

"A practical woman."

"Doyle, can you call animals like you called the whales?"

"I can, but I won't. When I hunt, I am as other men."

"Oops. Sorry. It's hard to think when I'm hungry. Where are we?"

"In the country of the Cymry, I believe."

"Wales!" She was dismayed for a moment, thinking of her torn feet and the miles to Glastonbury. Then her sense of the ridiculous bubbled up like a spring. "Why should I be surprised? Where else could they have brought us?"

Wrolf bounded up, gave his follow-me bark, and leapt away. They got up and went in the direction he indicated, and came eventually to a drousing farmstead with a pen of sheep complaining in ovine voices, and chickens scratching at the ground for grain or worms. Three largish dogs lolled in the shadow of the house, but they leapt to their feet when they saw the strangers, barking furiously and bounding forward. Wrolf growled and raised his hackles, and two of the canines paused in their attack. The third, a younger and less experienced animal, flew at Wrolf's throat, but the wolf just swung his great head, knocked the dog onto its flank, and it fled, yelping.

A man emerged from the shadow of the doorway and stood gaping at them. The other dogs decided discretion was the better part of valor and continued barking from a distance until Doyle said a single word, at which point they groveled and whimpered. The man eyed them cautiously, clearly unsure what to make of two naked people in his farmyard, and Eleanor wondered where she had misplaced her modesty.

"Good day!" Doyle shouted.

The farmer considered this a moment. "Aye, but fairin' up fur rayne."

"Could we get some breakfast?" It was such a foolish request from such a savage-looking man.

"Porridge," answered the farmer, as if wild men and women were an everyday occurrence on his doorstep. "Come in."

Doyle had to crouch his head to get under the lintel, and Eleanor's brow was a mere inch from it. Inside,

they found a large room, low and claustrophobic for
them, warmed by a huge fireplace and reeking of cooking, sweat, animals, and damp babies. Two toddlers
staggered around their mother's skirts, and several older
children regarded the intruders with round eyes. They
were all small and dark but neatly dressed in homespun
wool, if the loom in one corner was any indication. The
trestle table was scrubbed and clean, set with wooden
bowls and spoons.

The farmer's wife turned from her stirring, saw Doyle,
and gave a shriek. Eleanor didn't blame her in the least
and hoped sincerely that Wrolf would stay outside. Then
the wolf stuffed his head through the door and lolled
his rosy tongue at the solemn youngsters. One little
fellow burst into tears, but the others were too bemused
to respond.

The farmer was clearly well out of his social depth,
and Doyle oblivious to the overwhelming effect of his
size and manhood, so Eleanor stepped discreetly in front
of him, shielding her own body with the cloak, and
forced a sincere smile across her face. "Good morning."

Apparently relieved by this simple greeting, the wife
nodded and bobbled a curtsy of sorts. "More bowls," she
said to one of the older children, a pretty girl about
twelve. They were clearly not a very gabby family.

The young girl goggled at Eleanor, mouth open, and
refused to turn her eyes away as she took bowls off a
clumsy shelf and dusted them out with the sleeve of
her shift. The wife clanked the pot of porridge down on
the wooden table and began serving. The children held
out their bowls, and Doyle and Eleanor sat down,
Eleanor excising her mind to think of some garment
for her companion. Even if the farmer had any extra
clothing, it would hardly fit her large husband, who
clearly had no modesty at all and wore clothing only
for warmth.

They ate the rather sticky cereal, unsweetened but
nutty-flavored, in the silence that seemed to suit the
family. The children gave Eleanor an occasional shy
smile but eyed Doyle with some awe. The meal was
done before a quarter of an hour had passed, and Eleanor
was pleasantly warmed by the fire and a full belly.

She turned on the bench and saw two of the children,

the girl and a slightly younger brother, shielding their siblings from Wrolf's benign interest. Eleanor reflected that none of the males in her life ever seemed aware of their impact on the world, including her father, in this mild criticism. "He will not hurt you. He likes children."

The girl gave her a look, as if to say, "raw or cooked?" Then she asked a question that clearly had been trying her mind during breakfast: "Art thou merry merry?"

Eleanor nearly said she was happy but not that happy, then realized that the child was saying Mary *maré*, a common epithet of the Virgin for those who lived near the sea, as well as being an easy pun in tongues derived from Latin. She shook her head and smiled, then chose a name in Welsh, which had the same context as her own, though a slightly different meaning: "Guinevere." She knew she was safe with these simple folk, but she could not overcome her reluctance to reveal her own name, knowing that the innocent could serve the Darkness as well as the committed.

The girl's mouth made an O, and Eleanor immediately wondered whether she was being mistaken for Arthur's wife or the local goddess of the same name who predated him. The scholar in her stirred, and she wished she could just be a simple folklorist, collecting adventures instead of having them. He wistful reverie was broken by a sound like brazen trumpets outside.

Eleanor rose in a flutter of cloak and said, "Silver Heels!"

Doyle gripped her arm and yanked her back so hard, her neck snapped. "Not yet," he hissed.

Wrolf turned around and crouched across the door, growling. Eleanor turned to Doyle. "I know his whinny."

"He has a new rider," Doyle answered.

Eleanor felt ill, the mush suddenly lead in her middle. What could have captured her marvelous steed? The possibilities were not pleasant to contemplate.

Wrolf's growl increased, and the children huddled back. Eleanor rose and walked to the door, taking the rowan staff from where she had leaned it against the wall. She turned and looked at Doyle, whose blue eyes seemed almost black now. "This fight is yours alone," he said.

Eleanor knew the sword of Bridget lay between them again, for it was no longer hers to wield. The power that had been hers had passed to him on their first bedding, at least where the sword was concerned. But Doyle's instruction had not been in vain. She experienced a moment's pause, that he might let her die to gain complete control over that blasted bit of magic metal, then shrugged. "Come watch."

Doyle stared at her, concealing from Eleanor his overwhelming fear that she might die, and his rage at the Lords of Destiny that he was forced to stand by impotent. They had very little time left together, unless she won all the way through, but until this moment, he had not realized that he might survive *her*. He silently cursed all swords, all women, especially his mother and Bridget, and the patterns of the fates. Then he forced a grin and said "Surely," as if it were no more than a cockfight. The only aid he could give her was not to let her see his worry.

They stepped into the murky sunlight, and she suppressed a gasp of horror. The horse still carried the saddle she had gotten from the Lady Iseult at Nunnally Castle, and by that and that alone she knew him. The aura had diminished to a sooty miasma, but worse, the steed was now a thing of rotting flesh and exposed bone that stank all the way across the compound. The eyes once fiery with light were smoldering coals.

Eleanor had a moment of pity for her horse, a tiny sorrow that even this gift of Sal's was no more, and a fountain of rage at the force that could pervert the living into the travesty before her. Something indistinct slouched in the moldering saddle, a shadow, or was it the shadow of a shadow?

At first it appeared to be a smutty sack, slung like a bag of spuds across the seat, but as she studied it, she saw a faint head with bulging eyes above a triangular jaw. The head seemed covered with a shiny black substance like melted glass or some odd black jewel, the horrible eyes like dark opals. The body was a squat, lumpy shape with long, floppy feet dangling above the decaying stirrups.

The opaline eyes focused on her, and something like a smile seemed to flicker on the strange face. It shifted its body in the saddle with supreme confidence and urged the horse forward. Wrolf growled but gave ground. The Thing gave a clucking noise and said, "Mine."

Eleanor felt herself moving forward, as if her feet belonged to someone else. She resisted, but they stepped forward. Her body felt cold, colder than it had the night before, except her hand around the rowan staff. That was flame, and painful. She wanted to drop the staff, but she couldn't do that.

A long tongue flickered out from the triangular jaw of the thing on the horse. It brushed the tips of her pubic hair before it snapped back into the horrible mouth. "Mine," it repeated.

A wave of utter cold seemed to grow in her loins. Eleanor, helpless and outraged, moved one step closer, understanding something of the obscene rider. Then she froze in place, watching in horror as the tongue flipped out again to continue its rape.

With a great effort, she moved her still hot hand an inch. Eleanor ignored the strange sensations in her genitals and swung the rowan staff around to smash it down upon the half-bare skull of the horse. She could not speak to cry for help, but she thought of flame and cleansing fire. A blinding flash sparked against the bone and raced across decaying flesh.

Silver Heels began to burn, one foreleg falling off at the shoulder. The stench was awful, and Eleanor gagged as the steed collapsed, spilling its misshapen burden to the ground. The beast rolled over, landed on its floppy feet, and shot its tongue out again.

Eleanor hated the sensation in her body, and like a spear, she brought the head of her staff down on the dripping member. It flickered into the gaping mouth with a tiny spark creeping along the unwholesome flesh. The beast gave her a look of near astonishment with his bulging eyes, and exploded. The black, shiny skull burst into sharp, glassy fragments, one of which flew past her eye so close she flinched and fell backward onto the ground.

The cold in her body vanished to be replaced by a nausea so violent she could hardly breathe. Breakfast departed in a noisome mess, and she crouched on the earth, retching and choking while the rowan fire consumed the white bones of her horse and the black substance of its rider.

Eleanor crawled away from battle, cutting knees and palms on bits of black glass until strong hands hauled her up. She stared unrecognizingly into blue eyes and tried to pull away.

"Don't touch me!"

He clutched her by the wrists until they hurt. "It's over!"

For a second, the great, dark man seemed to be a part of the black thing she had destroyed. Then she knew him again. Recognition brought no lessening of her repulsion. No one would ever touch her again! "No! Dirty hands away!"

The wolf pushed his great head in between them, and she could feel his warm, moist breath against her ribs. A cold nose touched her stomach, and she felt the earth murmur under her bare feet. The green voices of hidden waters swelled, and she turned her head to find their source.

The household well was perhaps fifty feet away, but it seemed to Eleanor to be a distance farther than the stars. She was too dirty, too soiled. All the waters of the world were insufficient to cleanse her. She felt frozen in an agony of yearning and disgust.

Somehow she was free of the great hands, and she took a step forward toward the battered wooden structure. Each forward movement was a wrenching torment, and she fell and crept, whimpering and crying out a word she did not understand. "Sal! Sal! Sal!" It echoed in her mind, meaningless and wonderful at once. Finally, she crouched against the splintery well housing, clawing to get upright and reach the green-and-golden music that seemed just beyond her grasp.

Then she looked into a silvery mirror and saw a ghastly face that wept red tears. The long, weedy hair was the color of starless night, the skin as white as the moon's face, eyes like green glass and thin mouth with lips as red as blood. Eleanor found the reflection terrifying and inviting all at once.

She bent toward the mirror, closer and closer, until the tips of the noses almost met. There was a scent she could not name, a pleasant smell full of vague remembrance. Then she plunged her face into the mirror, which shattered into icy liquid and covered her. The voices seemed to grow more intense, and her still open eyes saw golden lights within the waters.

Eleanor reached for the lights and the music and found they eluded her grasp. Then she was being hauled up, sputtering, to see Doyle's dark face above hers, his expression almost unreadable except that it might contain concern. She coughed and knew who she was and what she was again. There was a second's longing for the Lady of Willows, then it was gone. "I feel awful," she muttered.

Doyle put an arm over her shoulders, still encloaked, and hugged her to his chest. "I am sure you do." He wiped moisture off her forehead with one hand. "You are very brave."

"Was I? I don't feel brave, just tired. Poor Silver Heels. How did he get caught?"

"We are all vulnerable."

Eleanor looked at the smoldering remains of steed and rider. The ground around the beast was a scatter of black glass, so clearly obsidian that she almost grinned. Some future geologist was going to have a fit. "Even you?"

"Yes."

His answer gave Eleanor a chill that had nothing to do with her exhaustion or her unclothed state. She leaned closer to him as if she could dispel her fear by simple contact. Then she said, "I'm still hungry."

PART II

Beltane

XVI

It was all very well, Eleanor reflected, for Bridget to say, "Go here or there and do this or that," and a great deal more difficult to actually implement her instructions. It must have been simpler in archetypal times, when goddesses popped in and out of people's lives like jack-in-the-boxes, and no one was troubled by self-doubts. Ulysses didn't say to Athena, "What do you think I am, a bloody carpenter?" Hercules hadn't said, "To hell with my labors; I'd rather get drunk with the centaurs." And Psyche hadn't told her mother-in-law, "Take your tasks and your son and shove off."

Since her encounter with the toad thing and what had once been her horse, Eleanor had been morose and fearful. If Wrolf was gone overlong on his foraging, she was gripped with icy panic until he returned with messy, blood-spattered chops and the heavy scent of carnivore breath. If Doyle was hidden from view by underbrush or trees, she had to choke back whimpers, and when he went hunting, she cut moon-shaped scratches in her palms with chipped nails.

And she was never warm anymore. They had found clothing of sorts in a shattered keep four days' walking from their landfall, a battered leather jerkin big enough to cover Doyle's shoulders and broad chest, and a red wool gown that had been a rich garment before the moths had feasted upon it. Doyle had cobbled them footwear out of odd bits of leather, and she'd asked him if he'd studied with the leprechauns. He had only replied that shoemaking was something he'd always known, and she remembered the tale of how Gwydion tricked Arianrhod into giving a name to her son with some shoes of fine cordovan leather. But the land they passed through was rich in those tales, and where they found folk huddled in careful solitude like the farmer's family, they were friendly enough after the initial suspicion had passed, and she occasionally heard unrecorded variants to make her scholar's heart glad. It was about her only comfort.

Eleanor knew it wasn't the tiny holes in her gown that made her cold but only fear. Even Doyle's touch could not warm her, and that, too, she suffered uneasily, always terrified it might be the last time. It gave an ardor to their loving, a dreadful grasping eagerness, which was anything but tender, as if he, too, were infected by the possibility of loss.

For five weeks they had wandered south toward Glastonbury, each growing more silent until sometimes a day passed with hardly a word. The Shadow had touched her, but it seemed to Eleanor that somehow it had touched him as well. Often she would have curled up by the side of the trail and waited for starvation to take her but for her sense of responsibility. Instead, she nurtured harsh thoughts of Bridget and forced one foot to follow another.

Albion struggled into a sickly spring, and Eleanor reflected that this was one April old Robert Browning would cheerfully have missed. Each day was gray with frequent rain squalls that stung and dried the skin. The few wild flowers that pushed their heads above the ground looked as if they wished they hadn't, and she grew to hate the sight of leprous daffodils dropping amid the weedy remains of scabrous Queen Anne's lace and skeletal nettle. Each night was starless and chill, and the moon made no impact on the darkness except a ghostly nimbus at its full.

Twice they encountered small packs of Shadow folk, tattered, lightless people like the victims of some hideous disease. At these times, Eleanor woke to life, casting off her despondency and wading in with her rowan staff with a fury worthy of some Nordic berserker. It did not cross her mind that she was being foolhardy. She just knew she wanted to rid the earth of them. And afterward, she always spewed up the contents of her stomach until she was empty. She felt faintly queasy most of the time anyhow but blamed it on the dreary landscape and her depression.

Well before nightfall, they were encamped, if a wolf, a man, a woman, no fire, and no shelter could be termed a camp. Actually, Eleanor knew they were hiding, that Doyle had chosen this stony shelf both for its vantage over the vale and to keep them out of the Shadow traffic, which was arriving in increasing numbers.

Eleanor crouched under the still unmarred perfection of Bridget's cloak and watched the churning gutter of beings pouring into the valley like a dark flood. They all came from the west, from Bath or Bristol, and they were a silent mob. Their quiet disturbed her, for all her experience said that many people together should be singing or gossiping or something! She guessed it was a group of between five and six thousand, and she wondered what call drew them here. And why none came from the south or the east.

She spoke that question aloud. Doyle, sucking a stem of grass, considered it a long time. Then he said, "Something prevents them." He pointed southwest. "There's a...channel from down that way I get glimpses of, and if we were still in my mother's house, we could see it plainer. It's fair straight, and it goes away that direction," he continued, hooking a thumb northeast. "I been puzzlin' over it, trying to remember the pattern, but it's right hard because I've never paid much mind to the old snake's business except not to muck it up too much."

Eleanor stared south where he had pointed, trying to penetrate the distance with her mind. Finally, her memory responded, and she said, "The Old, Straight Track."

"What?"

"No, that's not right either. Something about a dragon. And St. Michael. Got it!"

She felt pleased with herself out of all proportion to the meager bit of information her tired mind had given her, because it had been so long since she had really been able to think of more than setting one foot before the other. And it wasn't even real information, just the half-baked theory of some mystical amateur named Ley. Eleanor still carried the academic's contempt for the uncredentialed around with her. Still, it amused her that there might be some substance in the farfetched notions of the crackpots of her own century.

She gave a slight smile. Doyle reached out a hand and traced her mouth with broad, square fingers. "I was almost afraid you had forgotten how to do that."

"What?"

"Smile. You have been as solemn as a bear for days."

"Oh. Are bears...solemn?"

"Very serious fellows, always trundling on their business and never stopping to chat."

Eleanor's experience with ursine animals was from zoos and circuses, and she had difficulty reconciling either the bored and listless inhabitants of a zoo, or the memory of a ball-tossing Asian bear with his picture.

"They dance very well," she said.

"Dance?" Doyle sounded scandalized. "It would be beneath his dignity."

Eleanor couldn't help laughing at the expression of horror on her spouse's face. She laughed until tears dripped from her eyes and until the laughter died and she wept against his chest, silent, sobless crying. Doyle stroked her hair and said nothing until she was done. Eleanor rubbed her face with the rough sleeve of her garment and snuffled noisily. She would cheerfully have gone hungry for a box of tissues.

"Doyle, what are we going to do about *that?*" She pointed at the straggling column of Shadow folk. "There are so many."

"Kill them."

"How?"

"I do not know."

She suppressed an angry retort and stared at the sullen skyline. Glastonbury Tor, topped with its old stone church, seemed to beckon her. She noticed that the Shadow folk gave it a wide berth and that the line of them swerved away to what had been the town.

It didn't much look like Arthur's Avalon, for the many apple trees in the vale had been hacked and burned. A few tormented branches still put forth fragile leaves and blossoms, as if to rebuke their passing tormentors. There was, she reflected, no spot in all England so legend-laden as this place, from Joseph of Arimathea bringing the thornbush, the chalice of the

Last Supper, and the Veil of Veronica there in a miraculous seven-day passage from the Holy Land, to the monks' perhaps spurious discovery of an oaken coffin containing the mortal remains of the fabled hero Arthur and his wife Guinevere. This, in spite of the contradictory tale that the unfaithful spouse had entered a convent after Arthur's death. The chalice had become the Holy Grail, the thornbush mysteriously flowered at Christmas, and only the veil had disappeared without a trace. No doubt that touch had been added by some troubadour who knew that magical things travel in threes for companionship. The well, the Chalice Well, hard by the foot of the tor, had reputed healing powers even in Eleanor's technology-stricken world.

It suddenly struck her as odd that there were two churches so close together, since the construction of a stone building was no small undertaking. The one on the tor was older, she recalled, and dedicated to that ever-popular flaming angel, St. Michael, dragon slayer and all-around superhero. She recalled the Beast of Avebury she had fought what seemed like a lifetime before and reflected that he must have missed a few.

But there was something niggling at her, something about St. Michael and dragons, about the well, which eluded her. Until Avebury she had rather liked dragons, at least the benevolent Eastern ones who were always chasing after mystic pearls. Their Western cousins were a slothful, greedy race except in heraldry, always gobbling up the sun during eclipses and eating virgins in between. Odd dietary habit, she thought, leaning back onto the chilly ground to stare at the leaden sky.

She searched for the sun, for it was just past midday, and found the vague amber orb that gave little light and less warmth here. High places, like the tor, were usually sacred to the sun, and St. Michael certainly fit the mold of a solar figure. Why was that important? She wanted to smash away the shadowy sky and let the sun touch her. Too much legend and not enough light, she decided.

Eleanor sat up abruptly and studied the tor again. The sun and the moon, for wells and water were always part of the lunar cycle, were married on this spot, as she and Doyle were, though it was difficult to cast her dark husband in the role. Baird, his brother, looked the part better.

"Doyle, can we get up on the tor?"

"I been wondering that myself. If we could fly or were invisible, 'twould be simple. You might but not me."

"You keep telling me I can fly, but I can't...yet." She pursed her lips. "Shape change." The words came out without any conscious formation.

Doyle gave a long, slow grin and nodded. "Perhaps that would serve. But...what?"

"Well, what can you do?" It was not a matter they had ever discussed.

"Like Wrolf, anything of earth or water."

The answer surprised her, both halves of it, and she twisted a strand of hair around one finger thoughtfully. There *was* something the wolf and the man held in common. "I saw Wrolf turn into an otter. Is that what you mean by water?"

"It's one possibility."

"Why won't you give me real answers?" She was tired and irritable, and she had a craving for turkey sandwiches smeared in mayonnaise. The closest turkey was halfway around the world and wouldn't come to England for several hundred years. And coffee and some cigarettes, she added to her wish list. *Everything I want is in America.*

"Because it is more interesting to watch your mind work—and better for you, too."

"Sure. Everyone is always doing me favors for my own good!" She twisted another strand of hair almost viciously into a curl.

"It is not my place to instruct you. I have probably told you more than I should already."

"I thought..."

"You thought you could depend on me, and you were wrong. Never depend on anyone, Eleanor. Or anything. You have to work this out on your own."

"Then why are you here?" She smothered the hurt of his words.

"It's my destiny, not my task. I am only a player in *your* tale."

"No! I won't have it! I know you were reluctant to

begin, and I suppose perhaps you only did it because you wanted the damned sword. Well, you have it. But things are different now, aren't they?"

"No. It's still your tale, not mine."

"That really must irk the hell out of you, playing second fiddle to a woman."

"'Tisn't new."

"So why don't you just take the sword and leave? I won't stop you." She was livid.

"Nay. I can use this hunk of metal, but it still belongs to you. The sword only functions properly... well, it needs a woman's touch."

"But I used it."

"When you were yet a maiden."

Eleanor considered that statement, thinking of Artemis and Diana and Athena and Bridget in their bloody nymph aspects, and understood what he meant. She didn't want that power back, and yet she admitted she missed it. Until this moment, she'd thought Doyle was a fair trade for her virginity. She was tired of challenges and wished she could curl up in a nice quiet hut somewhere and raise sheep and knit. She reached a hand out to caress the rowan-wood staff, remembering Sam and Sarah and their baby, regretting all the small comforts that had vanished in the fire. Then she shook herself and turned a glare on him.

"If I had wanted to do this alone, I could have skipped two very wet journeys."

"You look a proper Medusa with all those snaky curls round your face, and I'd turn to stone if I knew how."

Irishmen always tease when they want to hide their feelings. Her father's presence was almost tangible for a second as she recalled those words. So she used her mother's time-honored method of dealing with Celtic jocularity. She changed the subject.

"Why can't you? Stone is of earth, isn't it?" She noticed that her words and voice mimicked her mother's, which made her frown, then shrug.

"I canna' decide if I care less for yur bark or yur bite, vixen."

"Yes, I know you would prefer me to be a die-away miss who never lifted anything heavier than a kerchief. What can't you turn to stone?"

"You'd be useless if you were. Stone is not of earth, it *is* earth. A faint and philosophical distinction but real. I cannot explain it better."

She thought about that, then said, "You mean, if you could be a thing of fire, you could be...a phoenix but not a flame?"

"Yes."

"All right. Could you change to a dragon? Your mother *is* a serpent, after all."

"I might, but I still could not fly. Or breathe fire."

"No, I see that. You'd be...more of a great worm."

"If I wasn't afraid you'd break, I'd beat you."

Her green eyes glittered. "No, you wouldn't. I'd probably enjoy it and spoil all your fun."

He smiled slowly. "I think my mother got a daughter-in-law worthy of her. Vixen is too mild for you. Shrew."

Eleanor remembered the terrible beast that had pursued her into Merlin's Grotto and shook her head. "Try wolverine."

"Cooked or raw? Now, tell me, lady, why you would wish me to be...a great worm, to use your infelicitous phrase."

"See that tor? The church on it was dedicated to St. Michael, the dragonslayer. My...educated guess is that perhaps that means that there is some energy in the hill that is anti-dragon. I want to wake it up, if it exists, and send it against the Shadow here at Glastonbury. And if there's nothing there, we will have at least gotten to the top of the hill. Those Shadow folk would assume, I think, that a dragon would be one of their own and give it a wide berth. But somehow we must get to the tor."

"An interesting plan. A good plan, if fraught with a number of unknown qualities. If you are right, what will stop this energy you sense from rising up and killing me?" He didn't sound worried by the possibility, just curious.

"Your light, I hope. Or turning back into yourself!"

"Your mind is like a roebuck pursued by hunters, graceful and swift."

Eleanor found her face was hot under this unexpected compliment, and her heart raced unruly in her chest. She forced calm into herself. "Doyle, what day is it? I have lost all track of time."

"May Eve."

She did not ask how he knew, but thought instead of Beltane, the pagan fire festival the church had turned into May Day or Lady Day, changing whatever goddess was honored to the Virgin Mary. Frazier, she remembered, had commented that it was a time for hunting witches in Germany. *Walpurgisnacht*. She could not recall if Hieronymus Bosch had ever painted that event in his twisted, hellish vision of the cosmos, but if he had, she was sure the faces in his painting must look like those empty people flooding into Glastonbury in answer to some dreadful summons. Eleanor spent a moment pitying her future victims, then turned her mind to the task at hand.

XVII

Doyle made an impressive dragon, she decided, studying the completed change with a director's eye. He was about a dozen feet long, elephant-high, and covered with a scaled hide of bronzy leather. His jaw was crocodilian, toothed and fanged fearsomely, and only his eyes remained their natural blue. A nightmare creature with six limbs, four walking and two clawed arms at his "shoulders," and a tail ending in a barbed point. He carried the sword, ensheathed, in one clawed hand, and he was decidedly male.

Eleanor found herself blushing for the second time in an hour. Then she allowed him to lift her with his other claw and settled onto a sort of natural saddle between his arms and the first set of legs. Wrolf had watched the entire proceeding with lupine superiority, and now he got to his feet with a grin that said he was glad to be moving again. Eleanor clutched her staff and pressed her knees into the leathery hide.

As they moved down the hill, she found her thoughts drifting to a friend of her father's, an American writer who lived in Ireland in a farm called Dragonhold, and wondering what she would think of Doyle's form. She certainly didn't feel like one of the writer's dragon riders. She only wished she was as gutsy as Lessa of Pern.

I don't care for scrawny redheads.

The thought startled her, and Eleanor realized it had come from Doyle. "What? Did you . . . read my mind?"

How else could I speak in this bloody body! I never would have expected such a prim and proper female to have such a shocking imagination.

Eleanor mastered her sense of personal violation after a few minutes. There was no portion of her body he did not know, so why worry about her mind? Except she did. Finally she answered, "Not shocking. Just boringly Freudian."

She had the mental sense of a snort, then his thought, *He must have been a sad fellow, if those were his ideas. My, I had no idea you had so much knowledge stuffed into your head. No wonder you wanted to hear all those tales. Would you have gotten renowned in your world, for your knowledge?*

"I don't think so. I would always have been compared to Daddy."

Not thy dame? She seems to have worn her own face.

"I'm not as strong as my mother."

Again the snort. *You don't know how strong you are.*

They reached the bottom of the incline, moved through a stand of blighted apple trees, and out into the sight of the straggling mob. Eleanor leaned forward against the dragon's back, making herself as flat as possible and praying the Shadow pilgrims wouldn't look too closely. She could hear uneasy murmurs in the crowd, but apparently there wasn't much initiative left in the human husks. Despite the coolness of the day, sweat dripped down her sides. Wrolf trotted beside Doyle so he was hidden from the mob's view.

An exhausting hour later, they reached the base of the tor as the crowd veered away toward the remains of the town. The dragon clambered up the fairly steep incline with the wolf loping ahead, and they finally reached the battered stone tower, all that remained of the church of St. Michael. Eleanor slipped off to the ground and found her knees shaking. Without volition, she lay facedown upon the earth and kissed it, though whether she homaged her mother-in-law or some other spirit she could not have said.

She could hear, as she had at Avebury, the murmurs of earth under the feet of Darkness. There were other sounds as well: the choked rattle of water stifled in its course, and something like the distant rumble of thunder. How long she lay crucified upon the ground she never knew, but when she rose, the bloody globe of the solar body was sinking in the west.

Eleanor leaned on her staff, trying to sort the voices of earth and their tales. She looked around for storm clouds, for the thunder still echoed in her mind, but there was nothing. Still, she had her clues, if she could only interpret them.

Twilight fell as she thought, and she looked at the faint silhouettes of the many mounds that surrounded the vale. An image forced its way up through the clutter of her mind. *The witch-fires of Arnor.* For a long time it had no meaning. The starless shadow of the Darkness crept onward.

Eleanor walked around the base of the tower, and she heard a gabble of shouts from below. Looking down, she saw a pack of shadow people staring up at her. From the positions of their hands, she knew they had been defiling the well at the bottom of the hill with their bodily wastes.

Something snapped inside her, some cord of kindness and pity. She hated them and what they served. Eleanor lifted her arms and shouted, "Bridget, come to me." For a second, she was horrified at her abrupt presumption.

Then the tip of her staff sparked, and she pointed it at a distant mound. The hill burst into cheery flame at its top. Grimly, she continued her circuit of the tower, widdershins, bringing each rounded hill into fiery life.

She returned to the still draconian Doyle, and Wrolf. *Wife, you make a fine bonfire!* He had never called her that, and it shocked her and steadied her simultaneously. *Now what?*

"I haven't the faintest idea," she replied sharply. "I'm making this up as I go." Eleanor paused. "But I think I wait for moonrise."

Yes, you'll need to draw down the moon.

Why this old phrase frightened her she did not know, but something was stirring in the bones of the earth that was more pressing. The thunder was closer, a rumbling noise that penetrated the soles of her feet.

"I think I'm about to make a mess of your mother's floor," she commented.

Serves her right for being so tidy.

Eleanor would have laughed if the tower had not suddenly sprouted an apparition of eye-searing magnificence. It was blue, the blue of flame, and winged, but it was more harpy than angel—naked, winged and talonged, sad-faced and angry. It rose a hundred feet around the building, dripping globules like molten gold and screaming.

"Doyle, change!"

I hate missing a good fight was his answer. He galloped down the tor to swing Bridget's fiery sword against a mob of Shadow people, who had finally found the impetus to attack. The blue flame-thing seemed to hover above the tower for a second, as if disoriented, then swooped down on the chaos that the dragon and the mob were creating between them. Eleanor was too stunned by the scene to take any action at first, the blue glow of the creature illuminating the players with something not unlike the glare of lightning while the Beltane fires she had raised on the hilltops seemed to gouge at the Shadow-sky with ruddy fingers. The people rushed back and forth, attempting to evade their various adversaries.

Doyle seemed possessed by an unseemly bloodlust, even for an Irishman, trampling, hacking, and smashing the folk aside with his tail. The angel-thing alternately attacked the dragon and the mob, as if it could not choose between enemies, and Wrolf had apparently decided the whole thing was a frolic, for though he tore out throats of the Shadow folk efficiently enough, he had a playful air about him.

Eleanor decided his draconian body must have affected Doyle's mind. The worst part was that there was no way she could conceive to direct the angel, and as she watched, she became afraid that it would damage her spouse as badly as the Shadow people. The golden drops from its body clung and burned to every surface they touched, and the hands seared actinically when they made contact.

The Shadow folk were not completely ineffectual, if only by their sheer numbers. They hated the light, but it seemed to drive them into frenzies of action, and Eleanor realized that if she didn't enter into the battle, Doyle and the wolf would almost certainly die. If only she could think of what to do, for she knew that charging into the fray with her staff would only be a little more than no use.

Draw down the moon. The command rang inside her head, and she stood bewildered. Despite all that had happened, Eleanor felt ignorant and inadequate. And afraid. Studying the activities of the blue angel, she was not confident of her capacity to make independent judgments. Still, she could not just stand there!

She moved around the tower again until she stood above the well. The cries of the combatants faded as Eleanor searched for the newborn moon above the shadow of Albion. It was difficult, for she was tired, the moon was young, and the mindless malevolence of the Darkness was strong. For a time it seemed impossible.

There was then in her mind a ripple of silvery green waters, with laughter, and the Lady of the Willows was almost tangible within her. It was at once a lover's embrace and a mother's comfort. Eleanor remembered her discussion about the relationship between the symbol and the reality and suddenly knew she did not need the real lunar orb to give her power.

She felt a flush of affection for Sal and her acerbic sense of humor, turned the face of her rowan staff so the new-moon carving stood away from her, and sent her thoughts down into the earth, to the waters that fed the sacred well of Glastonbury. An argent glow came from the staff, and far away she "heard" a gurgle that rose to a chorus, then became a roar, as if all the waters of the world were rushing to this single point.

The Chalice Well fountained like a geyser, straight up in a silvery column a hundred feet or more above the earth, scattering the choking debris in its throat all about. The waters fell back to ground like quicksilver, rushing floodlike toward the mass of Shadow people surrounding Doyle. It swept and swirled, rising higher and higher, and a kind of mist enveloped the people, a fireless smoke that coiled from their mouths and eyes in the lightning-blue glow cast by the angel-thing.

They screamed and slapped at their bodies as if they were being eaten by driver ants. The waters gushed onward, sheeting out around the foot of the tor and inundating the remains of the town. A few Shadow folk tried to outrun the flood, but the argentine stuff stretched out curling tentacles to lay them by the heels and send them howling into cleansing death.

The silence was as sudden as a shout in the night, and Eleanor stared down at a surface as smooth as the face of a telescope's mirror. It reflected the witch fires she had called on the low hills, the anguished countenance of the angel, and a sliver of white that was the moon of her staff. The only sound was a faint paddling sound and an occasional lupine grunt as Wrolf dispatched those few creatures who had survived.

The angel-thing surveyed the mirror of water for a long moment, then shot up into the sky as if it wished to rend the veil of Darkness and dived back into the tower to vanish. Eleanor blinked and strained her eyes against the sudden absence of blue light and ran down the tor. The waters shimmered for a second, then sank into the earth as if they had never been.

The mud Eleanor encountered was her only evidence that the waters had been real. She picked her way between the blackened skeletons of the dead, searching for Doyle by the now faint glow of her staff. The bones crumbled to ash around her.

The flicker of Bridget's sword drew her to him. His draconian form was gone, and he lay on the muddy earth as still as his slain foes. There were many slashes on his arms and legs, which bled feebly, and burns where the angel had touched him.

Eleanor knelt beside him and touched his throat, seeking a pulse and suppressing the panic that he might be dead. A faint throb reassured her, and she stroked his broad brow and tried to rouse him.

"Doyle, Doyle, wake up." He did not move.

Wrolf lumbered up, tongue lolling, and giving every evidence of having had a high old time in his fashion. He flopped wetly down beside Doyle's unconscious form and began grooming his paw pads. Eleanor wished she had his simple confidence. She sat on the sodden earth and pillowed Doyle's head in her lap, too weary to do more.

The dim light of dawn found her stiff and aching, and Doyle still unmoving. Eleanor had slept fitfully, and her neck hurt from slumping forward. She rubbed the muscles with icy fingers and tried to ignore a growling stomach, a parched throat, and a full bladder. The latter finally made its demands so strident that she set Doyle's head down and stepped away to relieve herself.

She went to the well, now bubbling gently in its course, and cupped a handful of water to her lips. A wooden cup floated up into view, and Eleanor just stared at it blankly for a moment. Then she caught it in chilled fingers and turned it around. It was carved from willow wood and identical, as far as she could tell, to the one that had perished in the fire she had made in Ireland.

"Thank you, Sal," she whispered, once more comforted by the presence of her cool mentor. She dipped a little water into it and drank again. It tasted acid, clean and bitter, and she was refreshed.

Eleanor paused, thinking about the Grail, and wondered if she should return the cup to the gurgling waters. That legendary artifact so vital to Arthurian tales, whether the Chalice of the Last Supper or the Cornucopia of earlier stories, was too potent to treat casually. But after some consideration, she decided it was her personal grail, both within and without the greater tale, and filled it again to take to Doyle.

He lay very still, breathing shallowly, his pale skin as gray as the dawn except where it puckered around the angel burns or was a sullen red beside scabbing wounds. Eleanor lifted his head and pressed the cup against his lips. Liquid trickled down into his blood- and mud-spattered beard.

"Wake up, you black-hearted misbegotten son of a serpent!" she hissed, caught between her exhaustion and her fear.

Doyle grunted, groaned, opened blue eyes, and stared at her for a second, then sat up abruptly, knocking the cup aside. "Such loverlike language," he muttered, lowering his head into his great hands.

Eleanor repressed the urge to kick him for worrying her, to kiss him for being alive, and to burst into tears simultaneously. Instead, she reclaimed the cup to cover her conflicting emotions. "No one forced you to go berserk," she said.

"Shh! My head hurts."

"Good. I told you to turn—"

"Silence!" he roared, them moaned. "I feel as if I had tried to outdrink Dionysus."

Eleanor bit back another sharp remark, realizing that they were both too tired and hungry to be civil. She had a passing wish that her magic was the kind that could conjure up a good hotel, complete with an unending supply of hot water and steaming cups of coffee. She spent a pleasant moment imagining the Plaza suddenly materializing on the muddy earth before her, dwelling luxuriously on the thought of a real bed, clean sheets, and plush carpets. I'd even settle for a Howard Johnson's, she decided. Or Nunnally Castle.

With a bit of a shock Eleanor realized she was twenty-five or perhaps thirty miles from the Lady Iseult's keep, as the crow flies. A day's ride on horseback, two on foot, but with her current weariness and Doyle weakened, three or four. So near, yet almost unreachable. And who knew what had happened there in two months?

Still, her heart longed for the sight of the hall, for Iseult's flaxen beauty and sweetness, for the quavering voice of old Roderick and the wary yet human faces of the servants. She wanted to go there and sleep for about a week. *Could I but fly or conjure horses,* she thought, and knew herself too tired to magic a butterfly.

Doyle seemed to sense her despair, for he reached a hand out to cover hers. He brushed her unbound hair away from her face, caught her jaw between his fingers, and said, "Have I told you how brave and beautiful you are?"

"Not recently."

"Well, you've mud on your face and smuts in your hair. There's blood, probably mine, dried on your gown, and I cannot think of a finer sight."

"Blarney-gabble," she replied, grinning a little. "Does shape-changing always give you a hangover?"

"Always. Except when I am a bear, and then there's no difference."

"No, there wouldn't be. You're a bear in a man-suit most of the time anyhow. Can you walk?"

"I expect I can, but slowly. Why?"

"Because there's a keep, Nunnally, where we might find shelter, about thirty miles from here."

"Where you bested Wrolf's stone cousin?"

"Yes."

"We won't get there sitting in the mud." He got up

slowly and picked up the sword as if it weighed a great deal. Eleanor rose and took her staff, looking curiously at the new-moon face to see if it bore any evidence of the magic it had made the night before. There was nothing. She tucked the willow cup into her bodice and tied her girdle tighter so it would not slip out and turned toward the north. "You look like many-breasted Erda," he commented.

Eleanor looked around at the vale, the bones of Shadowfolk crumbling into dust, great scorches charring the earth, and recalled Sal's admonition to heal. A tiny breeze brushed her cheek, bearing on it the scent of apple blossoms and the faint hum of honeybees, and she was refreshed. She could do no more here. Relieved that she need not cure every ill in Albion, Eleanor set forth with a lighter heart than she had felt in days.

XVIII

In all it took them five days to reach Nunnally, and they returned to their habit of silence, for the Battle of the Tor lay between them like a raw sore. Eleanor could not bring herself to abuse Doyle for endangering his life by not returning to human form, and he could not admit to his error. Only Wrolf was unaffected.

Mercifully, they met no one except a few nervous farmers disinclined to offer either hospitality or conversation. It was midday when they came to the stone remains of the Shadow Wolf before the keep. The drawbridge was up, but a slight haze above the chimneys indicated the place was still habited. A head bobbed above the battlements, then vanished. Eleanor looked at the walls, which had somehow become grown over with creeping roses, so that the place resembled the castle of "The Sleeping Beauty," and wondered what had happened.

"They don't seem glad to see us," Doyle said dryly.

"We are pretty raggle-taggle, except Wrolf. He is dressed for any occasion."

"Sometimes I think you care more for him than you do for me."

"I've known him longer," she replied. "I can't believe I actually fought that thing. I wonder how long it will take for the earth to green again." She studied the burn marks left from her battle.

"There is none so foolhardy as a Hibernian in battle lust."

"I know," she answered with a quick grin, realizing it was the most apology she would ever get. Her father had once said, "There would be no Irish problem if we could only admit that anyone else on earth was right."

The drawbridge creaked into life and began to descend. Roderick tottered out, looking even older and more frail than two months before. He leaned on his blackthorn staff and moved at a snail's pace, and from the expression on his face, they would find no welcome at Nunnally. The old man stopped a good ten feet away, peered at them with rheumy eyes, and straightened himself up.

"We wish no more of your magicks here, Lady Esperanza."

"I only wish a meal and a place to sleep."

"No. We will give you food, ill though we can spare it, but you may not enter."

"What happened?"

"The Lady Iseult was ill repaid for her kindness to you, for she goes about the keep having congress with stones. Waters well up in the court, between the flags, and strange things grow." He shuddered. "She garlands herself in flowers and sings strange words."

At this, the lady herself stepped out onto the drawbridge, looking like a Hawaiian Ophelia. Huge leis of orchids were wound around her neck, and a wreath of ferns rested on her golden hair. She was naked beneath her garlands, and Eleanor could not blame the old man for being deeply disturbed. One could not rear a girl from childhood and see her turn into an avatar of the goddess Flora without qualms. Iseult was a bit too pagan for the canons of good taste, even in this time and place.

Still, she seemed very cheerful in her divine madness, and Eleanor was glad to see a face, any face, with an expression of joy. Iseult stepped off the drawbridge, flung her arms apart, and capered gaily. Roderick stumbled to restrain her, but she danced away, leaving a path of golden primroses, the faery flower, wherever her unshod foot touched the earth. The still air freshened with smells of sun-drenched ground, and vegetation and the walls of the keep seemed to glow.

"I knew you would return," Iseult called, continuing her dance. "See how well I recall your lesson. I shall turn the world green again, if the sun will only show its face. Oh, your dress is so worn. Dear Roderick, give her all my garments. They are of no use to me. And that battered bear beside her. He, too, must have raiment. I go to clothe the earth in beauty."

"Lady Iseult, you cannot desert your castle," Eleanor cried.

"But there isn't room for another blossom," the woman replied. "Now I am free." Then she sped away toward the south with a speed worthy of the fabled Atalanta, who only lost her famous foot race because she paused to pick up the golden apples of Aphrodite.

Roderick wrung his gnarled hands and moaned. "Now, see what you have done."

"*I* didn't do anything," Eleanor replied, too tired to be polite. She had a nagging doubt that she might be responsible for Iseult's transformation, too, like a pebble that begins a landslide. Roderick did not listen and tottered back into the keep.

The drawbridge remained lowered, and about half an hour later, two defiant and nervous men scurried out with bundles of garments. They dropped them and loped back across the span. It began creaking up as soon as they were within the shadow of the portcullis.

Doyle and Eleanor examined the offerings, a couple of shabby robes, and a heavy cloak for her, a large and clearly unworn tunic that actually fit him, plus a moldy rectangle of wool too long for a blanket and an odd shape for a garment. There was also a mealy half-loaf, some grayish meat, and an onion. Eleanor picked up the onion, stared at it a long time, then began to laugh. She laughed so hard, she sat down in a patch of primroses and tears ran down her cheeks.

He looked alarmed at her sudden merriment and sat down beside her, draping one huge arm across her shoulders. Eleanor leaned against the comforting firmness of his chest. "What is it, *macushla?*"

"I'm...tired, that's all. And I feel funny. What am I supposed to do with one onion?"

"Keep it till I bring you a nice, fat coney."

To her surprise, the thought of rabbit brought an attack of nausea, and she retched miserably. For several moments, she would cheerfully have lain down in the flowers and died. Then it passed, and she said to Doyle, "No rabbit, please. What I want is a bowl of my mother's north country porridge with honey and raisins in it. Let's get away from here."

A mist lay along the ground as Eleanor and Doyle came to the ruins of a keep. The day's journey from Nunnally had been silent except for Wrolf's occasional bark when he coursed some bird or beast from the underbrush. He was not seriously hunting but engaging in wolfish play by stirring up the local wildlife.

"I do not like the feel of this place," Doyle said slowly, turning his head from side to side to study the broken walls.

"I am sure you are right, but I'm so tired I can barely move, and I think it's going to rain soon." As if in agreement, there was a boom of thunder in the graying sky.

"Yes. There seems to be some shelter in that corner." Part of a wooden roof jutted out crazily from the remains of two walls, and they crawled under it as the heavens opened up in a clamorous downpour. In a few minutes, the roof was leaking merrily.

Eleanor was suddenly furious at the weather and the adventure and her own fatigue. She stood up, gripped her staff for the light it would provide, and charged out into the ruins to see if there was not some drier place. It was either that or scream at Doyle. None of this was his fault, but unreasonably she felt he ought to do *something*.

She returned some minutes later, drenched but triumphant. "I found a little room. Come on."

It was just that, a little room in one wall by the gate, barely eight feet in any direction. At the base of one wall, the earth was disturbed as if by some large, burrowing animal, but Eleanor was too intent on sleeping on a relatively dry floor to notice. Wrolf trotted in, sniffed at the hole, raised his hackles, and growled softly.

Eleanor and Doyle spread out their cloaks to dry. There were a few bits of old lumber scattered around, and he piled them up and she set them alight. They left the door open a crack for the smoke and settled down to enjoy the relative comfort of damp stone and a pitiful blaze. Doyle got out their food, but she refused any. The sight of the meat made her stomach knot.

After a time, Eleanor took her willow cup out of her

tunic, held it out the door until it was half-full of rain-
water, then used the magic fire of her hands to heat it.
The slightly acrid smell of willow tea mingled with the
smoke, and she sipped it and thought of Sal. It warmed
her.

"Would you like some willow tea?" she asked.

"I do not care for witches' brews," he replied sharply.

Her control snapped. "Then why don't you just go
home to your mother! Take the sword and go. I'm sick
to death of you. And your bellyful of pride. And your
stupid jealousy. I don't see why you came at all. All you
ever cared about was that damned piece of iron. Well,
go sleep with it if you love it so much!"

"You are an ungrateful bitch, Eleanor."

"Ungrateful, am I! Of course I am. You would not
have touched me except you wanted my ... dowry. What
kind of whore does that make you, Doyle? I did not ask
for your help."

"You took it quick enough, shrew."

"Yes, I did. I cannot imagine what possessed me.
Lust, I suppose. Only I mistook it for something else.
How incredibly stupid of me to think I was worthy of
a great man like you—or of Bridget's trust. I wasn't
cut out to be a heroine or a wife or even a very good
woman." She blinked back angry tears. "It is not my
fault."

"But it is. No one held a knife to your throat and
made you undertake the saving of Albion. And you
never asked if it was your task. You just blundered
around and into my life. You never asked if it was my
quest."

"Oh, no, you don't. You made a choice, too. You
wanted the sword. Not me. I wish I could say I'm sorry
you made a bad bargain. But no one forced you, either."

"The Fates have not been kind to you. Or me. And
like my mother, you have a rare talent for speaking
the truth. The fire's almost gone. I'll see if I can find
more wood."

Eleanor watched him leave and wondered if he would
return. She was ashamed of her outburst but too exhausted to berate herself further. Instead, she curled
up in a miserable huddle and slipped into an uneasy
slumber.

At first she dreamed of bright stars against a darkened sky, but the stars fell, and the blackness grew until it filled her. Even her mouth seemed stifled. There were damp hands in the darkness, soft, fleshy hands, pawing her body.

She screamed and found her mouth filled with dirt. Eleanor could feel moist earth on her eyes, and knew she was not dreaming. The hands were real. And there were voices, deep whispers like the thud of crumbling clods.

"Eat."

"No, too bright to eat."

"Hurt eyes."

"Kill bright."

Soft hands pushed damp earth over her body. Eleanor struggled and forced herself to move, to sit up. She spat the dirt from her mouth and shook her head. The dirt slid away from her face.

There was a tunnel around her, and several small misshapen men. The roof of the tunnel touched her head. The little men cowered for a second, covering their eyes against her light, then blundered over her, pushing her back to the ground. Three sat on her chest while the others started burying her again. She fought them and her rising panic, but their numbers overwhelmed her. The earth pressed down on her, and she gasped for air. Then there was nothing.

Doyle had paced the tumbled courtyard in the rain for an hour, fighting his own anger at the truth. Eleanor was right and wrong at once. He was committed to her but not to her task. His own mortality lay ahead of him like some huge wall of stone she could pass through. He cursed his foreknowledge and the fact that he could not bear to leave her, even for a season. Then he found some sodden wood and went back to the room.

It was vacant. Eleanor's staff and starry cloak lay on the stone floor, the fragile willow cup overturned beside the ashes of their fire. He peered around and saw a faint trail of dirt leading to the hole in the wall. The earth looked as if something heavy had been dragged across it. He sniffed at the hole, wondering what lived in it, and raged at himself for not investigating sooner.

Then he stripped off his soaking tunic and transformed himself into a monstrous badger. The earth flew away under the great clawed paws. A small tunnel opened before him.

Doyle widened it with furious swipes. He heard the whispers before he saw the speakers. One moment there was nothing but dark tunnel; the next, a dozen startled faces gaped at him. He smashed a little man against the wall of the tunnel with a clumsy gesture, and the others scrambled away.

All that was visible of Eleanor was her toes sticking up above the dirt. Doyle scraped away at her body, growling. He got her face clear, and she opened her eyes, stared at him a moment, then screamed. He tried to tell her she was safe, but her mind was locked in panic. She clawed at the walls of the tunnel frantically with her bound hands. In desperation, he flipped her onto her stomach, grasped the back of her gown in his teeth, and dragged her along the tunnel floor beneath him. She was an awkward burden under his furred belly, fighting him and the earth.

Finally, she stopped struggling, and in a few minutes they emerged into the room. Doyle returned to his normal shape and cut Eleanor's hands free while she sobbed and gasped. She was utterly filthy and cut in several places where his claws had raked her.

Doyle pulled her to her feet, took her gown off, and dragged her outside into the pouring rain. The water washed the dirt and blood away until she was a slim, white figure glimmering in the darkness.

Eleanor turned and looked at him. Then she touched his cheek with a tender gesture. She kissed his lips lightly, and he grinned and pulled her in out of the rain.

Neither of them noticed their wet bodies or the chill of the room as they came together. As she fell asleep, he heard her murmur, "You make a very handsome badger."

XIX

Eleanor looked sadly at the muddy wreck of her garment on the stone floor. "Adventures sure do play hell with a woman's wardrobe," she commented.

"Poor Lady Vanity," he answered, patting her playfully on the bottom.

"Well, I can't shape-change into a bear or a badger. Thank goodness for these things we got at Nunnally, even if they are a bit damp and air-conditioned. Or thank Iseult, I should say. Go ahead. Laugh at me. I don't like traipsing around in my altogether."

"Why not? 'Tis splendid. Last night, in the rain, you would have put fair Aphrodite to shame."

Eleanor blushed and giggled. Then she shook out one of the tired robes that old Roderick had grudgingly offered and pulled it over her head. It was a faded green and must have been a garment for a younger Iseult, for it came barely to Eleanor's ankles. She tied her belt around it and tucked the willow cup into her bosom, then began braiding her long black hair. Doyle dressed himself and gathered up the remaining garments.

"You could have stopped those little dirt men if you had wanted, you know."

Eleanor stopped in mid-plait and stared at him white-faced. "How?"

"By pushing them back to their essence, which is earth."

She continued her braiding more slowly. "I never thought of 'ashes to ashes, dust to dust' as a magic formula. Besides, I was...too scared. I couldn't breathe."

"You are afraid of yourself."

"What!"

"You are very brave, Eleanor, but you fear your strength, your power. No one is stopping you but you."

"Let me see if I have this straight. I'm a bitch and a shrew and a weakling. Have I forgotten anything?"

"Trust a woman to hear only what suits her. No, you are no weakling."

Balked of argument and aware that she really did not want another brangle with the man, Eleanor changed the subject. "How could I have forced those ...gnomes, I guess, back into earth?"

"You had the answer, as you just said: 'Ashes to ashes, dust to dust.'"

"But those are just words."

"No. All words have magic in them. You...empower them."

"With what?"

"Yourself."

Eleanor shivered all over. "That is much too heavy a matter to face on an empty stomach."

"There's meat."

"No, thank you. I am considering becoming a strict vegetarian. I don't know why, but I get a little queasy at the thought of meat. In fact, I feel like I have the flu."

He made no reply, which Eleanor took as faint rebuff. Illness, she knew, made her father uneasy, and she assumed Doyle felt the same. "Shall we go?"

They headed north as Albion sulked under a dismal May. The occasional farmstead provided a relief from their own company as well as a few hot meals, but those were few and far between. Eleanor began to dread Doyle's talkativeness as she had once disliked his silence. There was something behind his sudden eagerness to instruct her in the avenues of magic that she mistrusted.

One evening, just at dusk, they came upon a sturdy wall she recognized as that bulwark Hadrian had built to hold back the fearsome Picts. The remains of a long-abandoned guardpost offered them shelter, and some coarse meal begged from a farmer provided dinner. Eleanor had found a small iron pot in an empty building and carried it along, despite its awkwardness and her uneasiness that it might be lead and might poison them. She cooked the meal into porridge and wolfed down the gluey mess while Doyle charred a plucked grouse over the flames of their small fire.

Dusk, as they had journeyed north and the days lengthened, lasted longer and longer. Eleanor rose and explored the remains of the wall fort, amazed at the furious industry of the Romans. She climbed to the flat parapet and looked first south, then north. Some white blobs that might have been sheep moved on a hillside about a mile away, but otherwise the land seemed empty. Finally she climbed down and returned to her husband.

Doyle brooded over the fire, more bear than man in the shadows. Wrolf sprawled asleep on one side of the flames, twitching in some lupine dream. She crouched down and stared into the bright flower of light.

"What were you thinking of, up there on the wall?"

"Oh, nothing much. Just how the Romans tried to keep back their Darkness with this wall, and another one farther north. They could not conquer the tribes up there. It must have been a terrible blow to their pride, because they had conquered the world, and yet they could not defeat a bunch of what they thought of as howling savages. And finally they got tired and went home. Thousands of men have marched these walls, and nothing remains but a bunch of stone and some graffiti. Just seems a bit futile."

"Nothing lasts forever. But you mustn't let that stop you, ever."

"How splendidly morose." Eleanor tried to ignore the prickle of apprehension that jangled along her nerves.

"No, not morose. The effort, the attempt, is what is important, not the outcome."

"Why do I feel like I've suddenly gone deaf or lost my reason? No, don't tell me. I really don't want to know."

"Yes, you do. But I won't plague you with it if you'll play the word game with me."

"What a choice," she muttered. For the past few weeks, Doyle had been egging her to a strange play. At first, it had seemed mildly amusing, to think of all the things a given word might mean, and it served to pass the time. Until one evening when she had been so intent on *snake* that she materialized a very annoyed and spitting cobra over the fire. It had fallen into the flames while Eleanor and Doyle scrambled away and Wrolf barked madly from a few feet away. Writhing out, it had reared its hood and spat, missing Eleanor's face by a breath. In a panic, she brought the fire out to consume it, and a few minutes later stared down at the charred vertebrae. Even as the venom had passed before her, she had not believed it was real. The bones would not be denied. She picked up the flat skull and held it at arm's length in the flickering firelight. A milky drop of fluid oozed along one elegant fang. Eleanor wrapped the skull in a tattered piece of her steadily deteriorating clothing and carried it in her pouch to remind her not to play any more games. And until now, Doyle had not asked her to engage in it again.

"Doyle, tell me, where did that snake come from? Did I transport it from its swampy home in India?"

"No, though you could have. But you let down the doorways in your mind and made it. You created it. It was the essence of 'snake' to you."

"How do you know that?"

"When we were at the tor, I saw your mind. It's very tidy, all the little bits of knowledge folded up in pretty bundles and locked away. And you are very good at matching up odd pieces—what you call motifs. And there you stop. You know, and refuse understanding. Until you are tricked into letting go."

"Why?"

"Because you are afraid of your own essence. And you should not be. It's quite good." He smiled at her complacently.

"If I'm so good, why a cobra?"

"Who troubles that beast?"

"No one in their right mind."

"That is part of you."

"Oh. 'Don't tread on me.' I see, I guess."

"Does it frighten you to know how strong you are?"

"No, because I don't know—and I don't want to!"

"What do you mean when you think of strength?"

Eleanor was silent a long time, mesmerized by the dancing flames. "A kind of careless arrogance," she answered finally. "Which isn't strength at all, is it? Only a noisy weakness. My father was the strongest man I ever knew. He made himself the sun, and we all re-

volved around him. I've seen him arm-wrestle men half
his age and win. He made everyone else seem small."

"Tell me, did it make him happy?"

"I don't believe so. The year before he got sick was
a kind of nightmare. He was finishing a book—or rather,
I was finishing it. There was a young man, Dennis,
whom I rather liked, but he couldn't stand up to Daniel.
No one ever did, except maybe my mother. And several
pretty graduate students. He'd favor one for a month,
then discard her for another. One day he was a big
laughing man and the next he was a shriveled husk.
Whatever it was in him ate him up. But for all his loud
laughter, I don't think he was happy."

"Did you ever rebuke him?"

Eleanor laughed. "Not on your life. Before I came to
Albion, I barely said boo to a goose. He would have
squashed me like a bug."

"So you had the strength of forebearance."

"Is that what it was? It seems more like cowardice
to me."

"A coward is a man who *always* runs away. You fight
when you must, which is real strength. And you do not
let sentiment weaken you, which is rare in a woman.
What is the strongest thing you can think of?"

"Sequoia gigantus."

"Who is he?"

"Not he. It's a tree, a great, mucking, four-thousand-
year-old tree."

"And how is it strong?"

"I don't know. It—they—endure. Snow, drought,
wind—anything but fire. They just stand there. They
don't do anything. They just are. One year my father
did a guest professorship in California, and we went to
Muir Woods. It's so quiet there. Like the beginning of
the world." Eleanor did not add her youthful fantasy
of elves and ents, for her visit to the redwoods had come
close upon her discovery of Tolkien. "I did not want to
leave."

"Power?"

"Yes. Like the energy under the tor but older and
more silent."

"That is earth, Eleanor. Earth of which my mother
is but an echo. Take it."

His voice was a whisper above the crackle of the fire. Eleanor hugged her knees to her chin and remembered the many voices of earth she had heard—the singing stones at Avebury, the groaning ground beneath the Black Beast's feet, the murmur of Nunnally's foundation, and the hum of Muir Woods. There were other sounds as well. The faint, slithering noise of Orphiana's house, the song of Sal's mound, the scream of the tunnels of the gnomes. She felt herself turn to dirt, to dust, to stone. It welled up and over her, turning her to molten rock, and she forgot for an eternity any name or presence. There was no air, no water, no fire.

She fell, past stars, past wars and loves, into a silence that promised nothing and gave all. It swallowed her into darkness. There was a dance in that blackness. She did not see it, nor hear the music. She felt it in bone and sinew. And then the void retreated, and she found herself lying pillowed in Doyle's lap.

"I must have fallen asleep," she croaked. Her voice sounded like a rusty hinge. "What a strange dream I had."

Doyle stroked her hair and forehead. Then he lifted her shoulders and held the willow cup to her lips. Eleanor gulped down the bitter contents. She was hungry and thirsty and weak as a baby. Doyle handed her a piece of cooked bird, and she tore the flesh off the fragile bones with her teeth.

Halfway through the meat, she started to shiver uncontrollably. Eleanor dropped the food and clung to him miserably. Doyle wound her in cloaks and blankets, then held her against his body. "Am I sick?" she gasped.

"No, just weary, dear one. You have journeyed far and no doubt disturbed my mother at her virtuous rest. There, there. Go ahead and cry."

Eleanor struggled with tears, because she could think of no reason why she should be crying, except she was tired and she ached all over, even the soles of her feet, and she was cold and the ground was hard and rocky. Suddenly, she said, "I'm pregnant."

"Yes, I know." She stared at him, for he sounded a little sad. Eleanor touched his face with a trembling hand. Then her eyelids felt like lead, and she slipped into a healing slumber usually reserved for the very young or the very old.

Dawn tinted the gray stones of the wall a sickly yellow. Eleanor stared at them a long time, then became aware of Doyle on one side of her and the wolf on the other. A faint bleat of sheep broke the morning's stillness.

Doyle sat up and stretched beside her. "How are you?"

"I think I have a hangover without the drunk before."

"Well, at least you didn't lose your tongue. Hungry?"

"Ravenous. Oh, lord! I'm pregnant."

"You never called me that before."

"Don't give yourself airs."

"Ah, my sweet-mouthed vixen. So gentle. So tender." But he held out another piece of cooked bird as he spoke, so Eleanor decided to forgive his teasing.

As she ate, she surveyed the campsite. The depth of the ash and the cleaned bones of several grouse bore witness that she had been there more than a night. "How long?"

"Four nights."

"I slept for four days!"

"No, not slept; traveled, perhaps."

"I've done nothing else since I got here! A Cook's Tour of the Cosmos on five dollars a day! Lousy accommodations. Next time I want first class." Eleanor rubbed her forehead. "I have a terrible headache."

He handed her the willow cup, and she drank from it. "Poor Eleanor."

"No, just confused. Doyle, how long have you known I was pregnant?"

"A while."

"Why didn't you tell me?"

"Because you did not wish to know."

"Oh." She pouted a little. "I hate it when you are right. Four days! It must be nearly the middle of June."

"Only the sixth."

"Yes, but there's still the small problem of finding the Heir. You know, I never imagined the goddess was subject to a schedule."

"Time is the ultimate master."

Eleanor caught the tinge of sadness in his voice again and wondered why. Then Wrolf leapt up barking, and a rather slovenly shepherd drove his flock through the gate. The phalanx of ovine imbecility flowed around them, baaing and butting, and the moment was gone.

XX

"My heart may be in the highlands," Eleanor said, "but I wish my feet weren't." She felt as if they had been climbing for days, and despite hardened muscles, it was still rough going. It was not merely the yet slight burden of the child in her womb rearranging her bodily chemicals and giving her strange appetites, nor Doyle's odd insistence on making her practice her growing command of fire and water, but the vague presence in her mind of what she had learned while she slept in the shadow of Hadrian's Wall. She remembered little of it, but vague bits would bobble into her thoughts at odd times and, distracted, she would stumble clumsily, so her forearms were a mosaic of tiny scratches. "You don't think I could talk Bridget into letting it go for a year, until the baby is born, do you?"

"I have never heard of anyone talking her into anything. My mother's charges of stubborn and capricious are not without reason. And don't tell me again the pregnant woman doesn't go on adventures. I know nothing would please you more than a nice cottage...."

"Yes, with roses growing round the door."

"Do not interrupt. You would be bored in a week."

"Doyle, what's that?" A sound echoed over the hills, a hollow noise like the striking of a great gong.

"A horn, I think. A hunter's horn."

"I wonder who it is."

They had journeyed from Hadrian's Wall, northward past the smaller wall of Antonius Pius at the Clyde River, and in that time had seen little more than sheep and stags so fearless of humans that they stared at the travelers in surprise. There had been a castle or two crouched on rises of land, but they had both felt a reluctance to enter them. Despite an almost continual

mild state of disagreement, Doyle and Eleanor preferred their own fractious company to that of strangers.
A case, Eleanor had told him teasingly, of the Devil I
know.

The horn was an uneasy sound, faintly discordant
and challenging. Doyle stopped and stood listening. "I
don't know, but I think we are their quarry. Yes, there's
something on our scent."

Under the horn came a clamor of other sounds, some
canine barks, beast snarls, and a kind of murky voice
that might be human.

"They aren't very subtle about it, are they?"

"No. They prefer to course their prey."

"How do you know?"

"They...smell of a running hunt."

Eleanor did not question this, for while three months
in the wild had taught her much woodcraft, Doyle had
a lifetime of experience. So she peered through the trees
and tried to see the hunters. Something stirred in the
recesses of her mind then, and the trees became trans-
parent to her eyes. She "saw" the pack.

"There are about twenty of them, Doyle. About a
dozen men in beast helms—bears and pigs and a bunch
of doggy things that aren't, somehow. The men are very,
very hairy."

"A pack of Reavers."

"Friends of yours?"

"Hardly. They are shape-changers that have taken
on some of the nature of the beasts they are. With each
change, they become more beastlike, until they lose
their humanness completely. So, they hunt humans.
We can't outrun them, and this is not a good place to
fight so many. Eleanor, you must shape-change...into
something swift."

"Doyle, I can't. We've argued that over and over."

"Yes, you can. You *must*."

Eleanor swallowed and stared at him. He had shown
her how and she understood the technique, but something in her was afraid of the transformation. Some
part of her clung fiercely to "Eleanor," to form and
shape, to identity. "Why can't I...just set the woods
afire?"

"Because it will not stop them. We must outrun them, and these bodies are not enough."

A trickle of sweat ran down her back, and her throat went dry. A beast was too real. She might never be Eleanor again. Something swift, he said. She thought of deer and horses, swift but vulnerable, and the fierce, feral quickness of wolves and leopards. None struck a chord she could respond to.

Her finger touched the little belt pouch that contained the burned skull of a cobra. No serpent was swift compared to that which ran on four legs, but she had a curious desire to fight. Perhaps to redeem herself from her miserable showing with the puny gnomes.

Eleanor shed her tunic, laid her hands along her sides, and remembered the "essence" of snake, which had allowed her to create a cobra. She "felt" it, and struggled, until a kind of acceptance touched her. Her body seemed to melt, and she could feel it reshape. The bough of a pine tree brushed her face—no, her hood.

Lidlessly staring at a world through eyes that saw movement but no color, she reared above the trees. A man gaped at her. She flicked out a long tongue and "heard" the ugly noise of the man-beast pack and leaned her head toward it.

Eleanor, that was not what I had in mind.

The words inside her head made her turn, and there, where the man had been, was a familiar beast of armored sides and crocodilian head. *It was all I could manage.*

If Mother could only see you now! the dragon replied, pulling the fire sword from its brightly colored sheath. *You are a surprising woman, dear one.*

She had no time to savor the words, for the canine companions of the Reavers burst through the trees. They huddled into a snarling, cowering bunch in the face of their strange opponents. Doyle swung the sword into the dogs, and a severed head made a bloody arc as it parted company with its owner.

Then the Reavers appeared, bears and boars, and Eleanor spat her venom into the snouts of the first arrivals. There was a scream, half-beast, half-human, as they collapsed, losing their animal forms and becoming writhing men trampled under the hooves and claws of their fellows. The dogs apparently decided the fight was not to their liking, for several darted away into the trees, only to confront Wrolf. Doyle hacked at a pair of bears as she slid her sinuous body around them to strike again at the piggy eyes of a tusked beast.

Slither, strike, slither, strike. Eleanor felt nothing but the power of death in her. Around her were screams; under her scaled body the warm, wet gush of blood from broken arteries. Then, suddenly, they were gone, and there was silence.

She swayed, tongue flicking, seeking some forgotten thing. All her mind contained was a fearless pride. *Eleanor.*

She turned the hooded head and peered down into a face. It had a name she could not recall. *Change back, Eleanor.* The words had no meaning. *Damn the woman, and damn me for a fool. How am I going to get her back?*

Eleanor "saw" a woman in her serpentine mind— naked and clothed in stars, bearing the moon on a staff, beautiful and powerful. She had never seen this light-clad female before, and yet there was something about her. Swaying, vision blurred. The earth rushed up to meet her.

Eleanor opened her eyes and found Wrolf's pink tongue lapping her cheek. She hugged his rough mane and sat up. "What happened?" She glanced around at the carnage in the glade and shuddered.

Doyle, cleaning the sword, replied, "I suppose you are the first cobra in history to faint. Next time will you please try for something with a better brain?"

"There won't be any next time." Then she remembered the lovely woman she had seen just before she collapsed. "Who was that, Doyle?"

"What?"

"I saw—"

"That, my silly, was you. The way I remember you after the Red Hats." He paused and rubbed his hands on some dried pine needles. "Why won't there be a next time? You act as if shape-changing were indecent."

Eleanor gestured at the remains of the Reavers. "It is." She didn't add how lost she felt inside and how she feared losing herself, as the folk of the beast hunt did.

"No, it is not. It is just a thing one can do. You never

really stop being what you are. It's a disguise to wear over the disguise of the body. The spirit always remains the same."

She glared at him and put her clothes back on. Doyle returned a bland look, which made her long to hit him, put the sword in its sheath, and prepared to move on.

They crossed the Grampion Mountains and entered the Highlands proper, and found a land that seemed even more empty of people than the lowlands. Eleanor, who had been to Scotland several times in her own time, thought she had never seen so beautiful, or so peaceful, a place. Where, she wondered, were the squabbling clans in their muted plaids, so much lovelier than the harsh color combinations of modern tartan, with the strident cry of war pipes echoing from hill to hill? But there were only hills, more hills, and the azure beauty of the lochs. Salmon and trout almost bounded out of rippling streams to provide them a change from grouse and woodcock, and prickly gooseberries hung on their bushes like bunches of grapes.

For a time, she managed to forget the quest and the Darkness over Albion, to ignore the constant presence of the rowan-wood staff in her hand with the moon's faces on its head and the bright blue cloak that hung from her shoulders, for it was too warm in the day for the wool one, and a bit cool to go without. Bridget, Sal, and Orphiana became an uneasy dream, the lost Heir a fugitive shade. All that was real was Doyle, silent for the most part, and the lupine good humor of the wolf.

But finally the land turned harsh and rocky, and the wind had a salty tang to it. They stood on high cliffs, and the ocean churned as it continued its relentless attempt to eat the land. Huge waves burst against the rocks, and the wind sent the foam into their faces.

Eleanor sank down and turned her back to the sea, pulling the wool cloak around her. Bridget had said, "Go to the North Wind to find the Heir," and she knew that while the Land of the North Wind had several locations, depending on which mythology one dealt with, the British one was the islands above Scotland: the Orkneys and the Shetlands. Hyperboria, home of Conan the Barbarian, was one she rather liked, but her mind went back to a favorite book of her youth, George MacDonald's *At the Back of the North Wind*. Why she had cherished that particular piece of Victorian morbidity had never been clear to her, and she thought perhaps it was the wonderful illustrations, especially the one of the young hero, Diamond, nestled in the black tresses of the beautiful North Wind as they flew above the spires of London. Sal, she realized, might have posed for the paintings.

But the North Wind was death, and Eleanor felt all the fears she had suppressed for the past week come rushing back like a flight of ravens, black wings brushing her mind. She looked at Doyle, who was building a fire of driftwood in the meager shelter of some protruding rocks, and Wrolf, nosing at the burrow of some subterranean animal, and she suppressed an insane desire to scream. If anything happened to them— She pressed the thought away, got up and joined Doyle, lighting the twisted wood into a cheerful blaze with the fire of her hands.

"Do you have any clever ideas about where we go from here?" she asked.

"Ask Wrolf. He's the guide." Doyle spitted a couple of pigeons on a stick and held them over the fire.

"Well, Wrolf," she said with a cheerfulness she was far from feeling, "how do you feel about a lovely tour of the scenic Orkney Islands? There can't be more than twenty of them, and we should be able to complete the search in, oh, a year or two." Eleanor knew quite well she had perhaps five days to find the Heir, but she felt as if it would be simpler to find a needle in a haystack.

Wrolf whined and shook his great head. "He means yes to the Orkneys, and no to the rest," Doyle said.

"I know. And how should we get there? A boat would help, but there don't seem to be any growing around here, or wings. Actually, I wouldn't really want to take a boat out on that."

"No, I thought we would swim."

"Swim!" Eleanor's voice squeaked.

"Of course. I think you'd make a very pretty dolphin." Doyle had on his teasing but serious face.

Eleanor was torn by his suggestion, for she had a tremendous affection for those playful sea mammals and had often wished, when she had visited marine parks, that she could climb in and frolic with them. But it meant shape-changing, and while their march across the Highlands had given her some time to become more comfortable with the idea, the idea of being a dolphin was too attractive. *I'm not sure I'd want to come back.*

She rubbed the back of her neck with a chilled hand. "I think an orca would be better," she said finally.

Doyle roared his hearty laugh. "There is such a fierce heart under that sweet chest. Cobras and killer whales. I wonder you haven't become a she-wolf and run off with Wrolf there."

She ruffled the wolf's mane and smiled at him.

"No. I'm already mated for life."

Doyle caught her against his chest with such vigor, he nearly knocked the breath out of her, and he kissed her as if he had just invented the gesture. Food, fire, and the damp wind forgotten, they came together on the hard sands. Her cries blew away like the call of some strange seabird, and they clung to one another for a long time after the passion was past. Later they supped on almost-burned pigeon and fell into exhausted sleep under the pale summer sky.

XXI

They stood naked in the roiling sea, their garments tied in bundles across their backs. The water was untouched by the warmth of summer, but Eleanor was chilled by more than that.

"Doyle, what the devil do I do with my staff?" Eleanor wondered why she hadn't thought of that sooner.

"Make a wand of it. Or cut off the head and take that. You *can* make a new body for it." He was impatient.

Eleanor stared at the object that had been given her by Sam, and which had come to mean so much. She remembered Gandalf arguing with the doorkeeper at Rohan to keep his staff and understood the reluctance to part with such a thing. Then she closed her eyes, ignored the rude hands of the sea lapping at her thighs, and tried to apply the many lessons Doyle had forced on her over the months. When she opened them, the staff was a baton perhaps eighteen inches long.

"Put it in my bundle," she said, teeth chattering.

Doyle stared at her a second, took it gingerly between two fingers, and slipped it into her burden. "It carries quite a charge," he commented.

"I know. I am a baggage and an inconvenience." Her heart seemed to squeeze in her chest as she realized the lines she was misquoting and those that followed them:

> You are a baggage and an inconvenience
> And I shall be loath to forego one
> Day of you
> Even to my ultimate friendly death.

Eleanor silently cursed her excellent memory, the as yet unborn playwright, and her overactive imagination. She forced her feet off the stony seabed and waded out behind the bulk of Doyle's broad shoulders.

The change was less difficult than she expected. Her body just seemed to streamline, and suddenly she was cutting through the waves. The power of her form was incredible, and she snapped the great jaws with their cruel teeth at a bit of flotsam. It crunched, and she pushed it away with the round tongue.

Something butted her side, and she turned a great walleye to observe the now otter-form Wrolf. *Come on.* Doyle, a dolphin, leapt along and chattered. She followed the flat shape of her wolf-otter into the icy waters of the sea.

Eleanor found, as she moved along, she heard the thoughts of both her companions. Wrolf's were focused on an image of a shoreline, and Doyle's were mildly scatological. This amused her, remembering that before the dolphin had become sacred to the rationalist Apollo, he had been favored by the loving Aphrodite. But for the most part, she ignored the vagrant mental whispers and concentrated on getting the most out of being a killer whale. She dove and watched shoals of herring scurry away and, rising to the surface, honked her laughter.

But occasionally she caught a sense of sadness in the thoughts of her companions, and she wondered if they had noticed her own fears and feeling of doom. The images grew more frequent, until she was almost glad when she spotted the shoreline Wrolf carried in his mind. She was a little reluctant to shed her wondrous shape but relieved to be unable to "hear" any further thoughts.

The long day was fading as they waded onto a rocky shore, and the cold hit her like a blow. Eleanor loosed the soaking bundle from her back and ran in place, mindless of sharp stones under bare feet until the blood rushed in her head and she was a little warmer. Then she unfastened the dripping mess of cloth and pulled out the starry cape, which was dry. She hugged it to her shivering body.

"I think I hate adventures," she told Doyle.

"But think of the wonderful stories you will have to tell the child."

"He probably won't believe me, even if Wrolf stands up as godfather." She felt a sudden panic. "Doyle—shape-changing! What if the baby—"

"Comes out with a cobra's body and a whale's head? Goose! He had his essence the moment he was conceived." He gave her a rough hug and patted her head. "Such a one for borrowing trouble. Don't imagine problems. The cosmos will provide all you need."

"I can always depend on you for comfort," she said, rubbing her head against his chest.

They found shelter and laid out their clothes. Doyle gathered wood, and Eleanor lit a fire and warmed herself while he found a rabbit too stupid or trusting to know its peril. It screamed when it died, and Eleanor wondered at herself, that a few short months had shorn away any sentimentality about soft, furry animals. She no longer regarded regular baths as a necessity, the bitter climate of Albion having given her a few too many chilly and undesired ones, and clean clothes and the splendor of warm blankets now seemed a vague dream. Coffee, however, still lingered in her mind like a boozer's memory of alcohol.

"Essence," she whispered. Eleanor grinned, got out the willow cup, and went looking for a source of water. She finally found a trickling stream and filled the cup.

She returned from the stream and settled down next to the fire. Doyle had skinned the rabbit and was spitting it. Eleanor heated the water with a flaming finger, then concentrated on coffee. She conjured the rich smell, the bitter-kind taste, the dark richness of it. She opened her eyes and looked at a swirling bowl of blackness. The scent of it curled up on fingers of steam.

Tentatively, she sipped. Yes, it was coffee, though not the pleasant bitterness she had hoped for. It was strong, very strong, and had the taste of boiled java from a greasy spoon. Eleanor did not care and drank with the pleasure of a true caffeine addict.

"Smells nice. What is it?"

"Coffee. Want to taste?" She held it out.

Doyle sipped, made a face, and spat it out. "Gah! You actually like that?"

"Well, it is a trifle strong," she replied, extending her hand. "But I've never magicked coffee before. Give me a few days, and I'll make a drink fit for the gods."

"You can take all eternity for all I care. Why couldn't you turn your gift to something fit—like beer?"

"Because I didn't think of it." The bitter brew had warmed her and lifted her spirits. "Besides, it's cold for beer. I have an idea."

She grabbed her cooking pot and trotted off into the pale night. Wrolf looked after her, then turned his face to Doyle. "I know. I don't understand women, either," the man said, and turned his attention to the rabbit.

Eleanor returned with a pot of water and, realizing that her mistake on the coffee had been to begin with boiling water, first set herself the task of duplicating the feat of the Wedding Feast at Cana. Several minutes of hard work got her a raw burgundy, so young it was almost in diapers. Doyle watched curiously while she muttered over the pot. "Allspice, cinnamon, cloves." Then she heated it a little, tasting carefully, and finally produced a mulled wine that was drinkable if not an oenophile's delight. She offered Doyle some and was rewarded with a smile. "Now, that's tasty," he said.

They drank together and ate the rabbit, becoming first a little silly, then amorous. Eleanor felt her nipples harden under his touch and drew him into her with joy. Their coupling was first gentle, then frantic, and when she opened her eyes to look into his face, the aurora borealis shimmered in the pale sky like a ghostly crown above his head. Then they slept, drunken and love-sated, through the brief night of Midsummer's Eve.

Dawn was chill and rosy across the island as Eleanor woke. She pulled on a still damp tunic and collected more driftwood, allowing Doyle to continue sleeping. He was, she noticed, a tidy sleeper, neither sprawling nor allowing his mouth to gap. She washed the dregs of mulled wine out of her pot and wondered if she could conjure oatmeal.

Doyle woke suddenly, as if from some snatch of dark dreaming, gave a grunt, and stumbled away to relieve himself. She stared fondly at the broad, furred back and gave her yet flat stomach a small self-satisfied pat. It was going to be a glorious day, and she felt she was the happiest woman alive.

Breakfasted and gear repacked, they headed for the interior of the island, following Wrolf, still a bit ruddy about the chops from his repast. The rocky shore gave way to stony terrain where meager topsoil supported the brief season of a few straggling heather plants and a tough, aggressive grass with knife-sharp blades. The ground rose steeply toward a spine of hills, which seemed to bisect the island.

Wrolf brought them to what seemed to be a natural amphitheater, a shallow bowl shadowed by small cliffs. A hole gaped in one wall, but Eleanor hardly noticed it. Beside the opening was a pillar of light, and within it stood a long-boned man of perhaps twenty, with the beaky features and red-gold hair that characterized many of the Plantagenet line. He seemed frozen in sleep.

Eleanor approached the pillar and touched it. It resisted penetration despite its fragile appearance, and she turned to ask Doyle what to do. A cough made her look at the cave mouth, and she saw a pair of gleaming and unfriendly eyes. A moment later, a huge boar ambled out and glared disdainfully at her.

It was so enormous, she could hardly take it in, for her five feet seven inches barely came to the top of one stubby leg. The curving tusks were as thick as a man's body at their base, and she backed away quickly, although the beast showed no inclination to do more than snort and paw the sterile earth a little.

Doyle removed the sword from its gay sheath and walked toward the boar as she retreated. His face had no expression, and Eleanor felt herself chill. She knew that look, though she could not say why, and it frightened her.

The boar gave a contemptuous grunt and lowered its great head. Doyle moved to one side with a mobile grace strange in so large a man and brought the sword down on one shoulder. The beast screamed in rage and turned on stubby legs, but Doyle kept moving around, leading it in a tight circle that kept him out of range of the terrible tusks. The thick hide broached under repeated slashes, and blood began to color the leg and the earth. Eleanor raised her staff to summon some aid and found Wrolf's mouth firmly around her wrist. He clamped sharp teeth until she loosed her grip. "This is his fight?" The wolf gave a yelp she interpreted in the affirmative. She glared at the animal a second, then turned her attention back to the strange, unequal battle.

The boar was fast for all its size, but Doyle was quicker, and one side of the beast was a mass of wounds. The ground was red with blood, and Doyle's legs were spattered as well. There was a scream from the boar, and Doyle slipped in the muck. A huge tusk gored his body.

Eleanor watched the great head rise with her husband impaled on it. Doyle's huge arms lifted and drove Bridget's sword deep into a piggy eye. The boar quivered all over, tossed its head to free itself, and sent Doyle's body flying to earth. The stubby legs splayed out under the porcine body, and it sank into twitching death throes.

She ran to Doyle and found his face as pain-free and untroubled as she had seen it in sleep. The hole where his belly had been leaked fluids, but he looked so tranquil that for a moment she was not frightened. She reached out to heal the dreadful wound and found his strong hand over hers.

"No, beloved."

"Doyle, I can—"

"No. My time is done. It is the way of these things."

"Don't leave me! Let me—"

"Sweet, sweet Eleanor. The light of my life. I did not think it would be this hard to leave you. I never said how much I loved you—because there are no words for it." He smiled. "I do. But you must go on without me. You can, you know. You always could. Farewell." The blue eyes closed, and he was still.

The ground shivered and began to open beneath his body. Eleanor watched a fleshy gullet engulf him, a serpent's mouth, and then he was gone, and all that remained was the bright sheath and smeared sword. She was too stunned to move, to even weep, for a long moment.

Then, with chilled fingers, she clawed the ground where he had lain and screamed. She tore away, mindless of ripping fingernails and palms cut by sharpened stones. She cried words, cursing the goddess in her many guises, until the tears fell and her rage was swept away in grief.

A hand touched her shoulder, a warm, real human hand. She felt herself dragged up from where she had lain pressing herself to earth, and was leaned against a narrow chest. There was a voice, too, speaking gentle words, though their meaning was incomprehensible. Long, spatulate fingers brushed her cheek.

Eleanor looked up into the rather homely countenance of the Heir of Albion, a boy's face on a man's body as yet unmarred by cruel experience. *For this I lost my Doyle.* Then she felt a slight stirring in her womb, the first real sign of the new life she carried within her, and drew away from this comforting stranger's embrace.

"I am Eleanor," she said. *The light of my life.*

XXII

Arthur searched her face, seeking some clue to her identity beyond her name. "That is a good name," he said finally, "but surely you are not my grandmother made young once more by some great sorcery. She was dark like you in her youth, though her hair was argented when I knew her. And my sister was quite fair, though—"

"No, no. I am no relation of yours—at least, I don't believe I am. None of my people ever claimed to have come down from the Conqueror. No, I am just Eleanor who...came to rescue you. It's rather complicated." She slipped out of the light grasp he still had about her shoulders and stood up. Her legs trembled, but she tottered across the bloody arena and clambered up the carcass of the boar to pull the sword from where it still stuck out of a dead eye. Ichorous fluids gushed out and flooded her boots and the hem of her gown.

The young man waited to assist her down from the gruesome corpse. Eleanor held the sword aloft and glared at its unmarred blade. "I wish you had never been forged," she whispered. Then she retrieved the sheath and joined them, trying not to think how she would never again unsheath the sword of love within her.

"'Tis a fair weapon, lady," Arthur said, extending his hand toward the grip.

"I would not touch it if I were—"

There was a flash of white light, and he snatched his hand back and yelled. Then he stared in amazement at the palm, where no mark showed. Eleanor sighed and shook her head. "I see you are as headstrong and impetuous as the rest of your family." She suddenly felt very old, though their ages were about the same. "Come on. Let's get out of this charnel pit."

She looked at the meager bundle of Doyle's gear—
tattered cloak, weary spare tunic, and a set of snares
all wrapped in the blanket—and decided that she did
not have the energy to be sentimental. "You carry that."
Then she got her staff and her bundle and led him away
until they found a sluggish brook.

Eleanor stopped, too weary to progress a step farther,
knelt down, and washed the ruin of her hands and a
face smeared with dirt, blood, and tears. Then she sat
on a rock and dangled her boots and lowered her gown
in the water until they were free of the filth.

"Gather some wood for a fire," she told him, quite
forgetting that he was Arthur of Brittany, Heir of Albion. Then she bit her lower lip and fought back a fresh
flood of tears. Wrolf, who had shadowed them on their
walk, appeared and put a huge head across her lap,
whining. She patted him between the ears, and a hot
tear rolled down her cheek despite her effort to resist
it. "I guess it's just the two of us again, old friend." The
wolf gave her a glance of such infinite compassion,
Eleanor was certain her heart would break in two.

Arthur came noisily back, his arms loaded with
branches of twisted heather, some dead and some still
lavender with blossoms. He piled it clumsily on the
ground, and Eleanor wondered how she was going to
survive with such an inept woodsman. Still, he seemed
willing and cheerful, and she decided to settle for that.

She rose wearily, sorted out the deadwood, and created a fire. Arthur watched her with a kind of wary
astonishment as she removed her boots to dry beside
it, then folded her cloak to sit on. Wrolf curled up beside
her, pressing his warmth against her thigh, and the
young man sat across the fire from them, nervously
pleating the hem of his knee-length tunic.

Finally she pulled the pot out of the bundle and held
it out. "Will you get some water, please." She sat stiff
and still while he did her bidding, trying to order her
thoughts. "No, not on the fire. Give it to me."

*If ever a woman deserved the pleasure of a good Irish
wake, it is me.* With that thought, she set about making
the contents of her cooking pot as alcoholic as possible.
The result, to her surprise, was a passable Calvados,
the wonderful apple brandy of Northern France. The

act heartened her in some strange fashion she could not discern, and she muttered, "Eat your heart out, Harold O'Shea." Then she filled her willow cup and, taking the Queen's advice to Alice, began at the beginning of her tale. Instinctively, she used the storyteller's mode, the roll and rhythm of country folk since time began. And, like the storyteller, she omitted a great deal of rain, cold, and hunger.

The day was fading before she was done, and the level of the liquor in the pot considerably diminished, until she was in that muzzy, anesthetized state where the true toper goes to forget her sorrows. Like her mother, Eleanor was a cheerful drunk.

"A most amazing tale, Lady Eleanor. One I could not believe but for the evidence of that terrible sword and that strange wine you have made. I remember nothing but a great banquet to celebrate my birthday and the end of my regency. I drank wine my cousin John poured for me and awoke by the carcass of that dead boar. No troubadour ever sang such a song as this. And I'm very sorry about your man, Doyle."

"I am, too. I should have remembered my folklore better. Then I should have known his days were numbered." She swallowed convulsively. "He was both a man and something besides. But I have been loved. And for the moment, that will have to do."

"But you are young, and surely—"

"No, Doyle was my life-mate." She ruffled Wrolf's mane. "Anyone else would suffer by comparison."

The twilight of midsummer covered them, and Arthur laid a still green bough of heather on the fire. The sparks rose up in a cheerful column. It seemed to thicken into a pillar of fire, and Bridget materialized in its midst with her Si'monetta half-smile and her starry cloak mirroring the sky.

"You have done well, daughter."

Eleanor glared at the vision. "Yes, I'm a good little girl."

"Do not be angry."

"Angry? Me? Why, of course not, you meddling anachronism. You drag me out of my life and tell me to do six impossible things before breakfast. Go here, go there. Do this, do that. Love a man and watch him die. Why me?"

"It is your task, child."

"Perhaps. But Sal is twice the goddess you are, and I'd cheerfully swap you both for my mother-in-law." Eleanor found her throat parched and gulped a little more brandy. "All right, Lady, now what?"

Bridget shook her lovely head slowly. "The only mortals worthy to be our hands are spirited, so I shall overlook that disrespect. You have served us well and faithfully, and I know you grieve for your beloved. And I shall ignore the strange use you have made of *my* sacred apples."

"Gracious of you."

"The Harp lies where you cannot see Hibernia any longer. The Pipes sing upon Lothean's Plain. Find them and go to London City. Drive out the Darkness, Daughter of Great Light. I am always with you, though you rebuke me in your anguish and will again. But by the moon's sweet light, you will always have a guide. And you will be well rewarded for your efforts."

"I don't want any reward. I want Doyle back." Eleanor spoke to empty air, for Bridget had vanished. "Orphiana said she was flighty. Rotten sense of humor, too." Her eyelids sagged. She pulled her cloak out from under her clumsily and wrapped it around her. "Good night, sweet prince," she muttered, pillowing her head on her elbow, and drifted off into a dream of Doyle crowned in light.

"I wonder if sorcery cures a hangover," Eleanor said, as Arthur arrived with a fresh load of firewood. *"Her* sacred apples, indeed. Conceited bitch. I wonder if goddesses have annual conventions, like Elks. Aphrodite will set her straight." She dragged herself to her feet and tottered to the brackish stream to gulp down water and bathe her face. Her headache subsided to a dull roar.

Arthur was huddled in Doyle's worn cloak, looking pinched and anxious. "I tried to find something to eat, but—"

"Not much around, unless you're Wrolf. And he never shares. Well, lets see if I can do something besides rotgut in my pot." Eleanor washed it out in the stream, then tried for porridge. She was rewarded with a gluey, tasteless mess that filled her stomach but nothing more. "I wish I had paid more attention in the kitchen," she said.

Arthur gave her a wobbly smile. "I wish I knew what was happening. I mean, I think I saw you speak to a woman in the fire last night, but I might have been dreaming. She looked so like my sister, Eleanor, I almost thought I was mad. But I cannot recall her owning such a cloak. I wonder how she is."

"No one knows. She vanished off the earth. At least, as I know her story. Perhaps it is different here." She spoke in response to the undisguised anguish of his bony face. With his sharp cheekbones and long nose, he resembled a very young Charlton Heston. "What is she like?"

The lopsided grin again. "She is wonderful. Full of song and light. And very gentle. Not like grandmother at all, though they share the same name. She would go into the courtyard at Anjou and lift her voice, and birds would flutter in and sit on her arms and on the sunlit stones at her feet. And like my grandmother did in her youth, she called the unicorns from the forest. Perhaps she, too, is trapped in some sorcery by my cousin John."

Eleanor didn't have the heart to dash his hope and nodded. Her longing for Doyle's bearlike presence was almost a physical ache, and she knew her grief was less than a breath away, if she let it come. But there was no time for that luxury, as there had been when her father had died. So she swallowed and tried to make some plan.

The Harp must be her next task. Bridget's clue was clear enough to her—Iona, the island where the arrogant and contentious St. Columba had exiled himself after some disagreement, which, being Irish, was both religious and political. Her father's folk never seemed to have discovered any way to separate the two. She thought of the war-wracked Belfast of her own time and shook her head. Columba had sailed east until he could no longer see Ireland and made a monastery where beautiful illuminations sprang up in sharp contrast to the barren bit of land the establishment stood on.

The first problem was to cross the North Sea and get back to Scotland. She could shape-change and so could Wrolf, but Arthur was another matter. Doyle had not instructed her in the transformation of others, and with his ruddy coloring, the young prince seemed like a lion cub to her. That would hardly answer. Could she bear him on her back?

The idea was a mistake, for it brought back memories of her last day with Doyle. Tears welled in her green eyes and rolled down her face until she brushed them away angrily. She wiped her sleeve across her face and forced herself to be calm again. *I wonder if I can conjure a cabin cruiser,* she thought irrelevantly, and found that the foolishness of her idea lessened her sense of despair. *I need a boat, for certain. A shame they don't grow on trees.*

For a long time, she stared off at a sky so blue it was almost painful, until her mind recalled those lessons of Doyle's around the fire. Essence of boat. What the devil was that? Her abysmal ignorance of what constituted a seaworthy vessel depressed her momentarily, and her head was full of images of the Butcher, the Baker, and the Candlestick Maker in their famous tub. Instead, she searched her memory for every scrap of information she possessed about the art of ship building. A raft she and Arthur could build if they could find some wood on the island, but she dismissed that quickly. The North Sea, even in its gentle summer guise, was no place for a flatboat.

Eleanor rose, took her willow cup, and went to the stream. She drank several cups of water and found the pounding of her headache subsiding. Then she looked at the cup for a long time, turning it in her hands, and finally nodding to herself.

"I think we should get going, young Arthur."

"Certainly, my lady. But where?"

"Back to Scotland, if the winds are kind. Gather the gear. And remind me never to touch Calvados again." In her head, she heard a faint laugh, and she felt the cool affection of the Lady of the Willows. For an instant, she was paralyzed with longing for Sal. But the memory was like a benediction that strengthened and reassured her.

* * *

The wind was running from the west when they came to the rocky shore, and the waves that rose and fell seemed huge. Eleanor felt her confidence evaporate. Suddenly, she was tired, weary of struggling to reach goals that never turned out to be quite worthwhile, somehow. She would not dare that sea in anything less than the *QEII*, and certainly not a willow cup. Her shoulders sagged under the weight of her burden, and the unaccustomed rigidity of the sword seemed to cut into them. She felt tempted to fly away, as Doyle had often assured her she could, and leave Arthur to fend for himself, except she could not think where she would fly to. Somehow, as sure as she was of the love of the goddess, to return to Sal with the job unfinished seemed wrong. Then she felt the faint stirring of the life within her, and she took a deep breath and straighened her body. It was all she had left of Doyle, but it was worth fighting for.

The sea went flat when I commanded it to.
I didn't think to ask for more.

The quote floated to the surface of her mind, and for a moment she was puzzled as to its source. Then she realized it was from *The Lion In Winter,* words spoken by another Eleanor, a more redoubtable woman than herself, and she turned to young Arthur.

"Could your grandmother really command the sea to her bidding?"

"I never heard of it, but she was a powerful woman, so I should not be surprised. Why?"

"Curious, just curious. You said she could call unicorns, which I had never heard before. I thought only virgins had that talent."

"No—at least I don't think so. My aunt Johanna could do it when her sons were grown to manhood. It is a gift of the daughters of my house, I think." He seemed amused by the question.

"This is not getting us anywhere. I don't suppose you have any idea how to tack across the wind, do you?"

"No. I do not know what you mean."

"I don't either, except it's a seaman's trick for getting

where he wants to go when the wind is against him."
She took out the willow cup and turned it in her hands
awhile. A fragile craft.

Eleanor knelt on the rocky beach and put the cup
before her. The strange, undigested information she
had gotten during her journey beside Hadrian's Wall
bobbled in her mind like flotsam. Finally, she decided
it was simply a problem in shape-changing. If a five-
foot-seven-inch woman could become a fifteen-foot cobra,
then a cup could become a boat. She "told" the vessel
to change.

It expanded with alarming rapidity, the lip catching
Eleanor across the chest, sending her reeling, and leaving her breathless, weak, and ravenous. She lay on the
beach gasping for several minutes, her head spinning.
Then she staggered up to study her handiwork.

The cup had retained its round shape but was now
large enough to contain two people and a wolf, if they
were friendly. It was thick wood, seamless and sturdy,
and while she had misgivings about its seaworthiness,
she was pretty sure it would float. She wondered if she
could alter its shape into something less tublike and
realized she lacked the energy to try.

"We'll leave tomorrow. See if you can get something
for a fire. I must rest." With those words, she curled up
on the tepid beach and fell into a deep sleep.

When she awoke, the sun was sinking into the sea,
and the tide had crept up almost to the boat. Arthur
had piled driftwood and dried heather in a heap and
was studying a dead coney. She sat up.

"Where did you get that?"

"It came up to me when I was getting wood, and I
hit it over the head with a stick."

"Good for you. Here, give it to me." She skinned and
gutted the animal, started the fire, spitted the meat,
and began cooking it. Wrolf was not visible, so she assumed he was off hunting his own supper. The smell
of roasting meat was tantalizing, and Eleanor has hard-
pressed to keep from eating it half-raw. They ate in
silence in the long twilight.

"My lady, I do not think the sea will let us wait for
the morrow."

"What?" She looked at the encroaching tide. *"Merde.*

Well, I suppose it's for the best. I don't know if we could
have launched it between the two of us." She stood and
shook the sand from her garments and shouted for the
wolf. Then she began tossing her gear into the ship.

Wrolf, a bit bloody, appeared in a spatter of gritty
blood, eyed the boat with suspicion, and barked loudly.
Eleanor interpreted this to mean he did not care for
their craft.

She shrugged. "Suit yourself, old fellow. A paddle.
How the . . . ah, my staff." She paused for a second, amazed
at herself, then transformed one end of the rowan-wood
staff into an oar of sorts.

The sea lapped under the boat, and she and Arthur
pushed it farther out into the water. It was lighter than
it looked, but it was still heavy work, and they were
both sweating by the time it was afloat, up to their
thighs in chill ocean. Arthur leapt in first, then reached
for Eleanor.

For all his slenderness, he was strong. He put his
arms under hers and lifted her across the lip of the
boat, which tilted wildly. She thrust her legs over and
clung to him a second, feeling hard muscles and the
musky smell of sweaty man. It was good to touch him,
and she wanted to continue. Horrified at herself, and
shamed by disloyalty to Doyle, she drew back hastily.
Arthur seemed unaware of her reaction and set about
stowing their gear.

"What about the wolf?" he asked.

"Oh, he can take care of himself. Watch."

Wrolf jumped into the waves and took on his otterine
form as Eleanor began to paddle. The wolf swam around,
pressed its great head against one side of the boat, and
swam strongly, pushing them out away from the shore
currents.

Beyond the eddies of the shore, the boat still wallowed like a pig. Eleanor went to the side of it, which
she thought of as the front, because it pointed where
she wished to go, or at least where she sincerely hoped
Scotland lay. Yes, there was the otter's great, sleek
shape breasting the waves. She leaned her body against
the wood and felt it mold sinuously against her chest.

"Good old Salacious Sal," she muttered. An echo of
laughter trilled through her mind. *Lean out.* Eleanor

could not tell if the command was from her own mind or from the Lady of the Willows, but she leaned. The wind whipped her face and blew her hair out behind, and the spray stung her eyes, but suddenly she was the prow of some proud sailing vessel. The little boat shuddered, then seemed to spring across the waves. She heard a faint gasp from Arthur, behind her, and then she was aware of nothing but sea and sky. She held her arms before her, using Wrolf's aura as her guide, and willed the vessel across the waters.

Eleanor thought it a glorious experience, until she realized that she was soaked, her legs shaking, and her arms trembling. After that, it became a grim contest of mind over flesh until, at last, as the sun began to tint the sky a pale lavender, she saw the silhouette of a rocky coast. The sight renewed her a little, and she gritted her teeth and urged the boat onward.

Huge cliffs loomed up, and a rocky shore, which offered no easy landing place. Eleanor pulled herself back for fear she would send them onto the rocks and slid down into the depression in the middle, an exhausted, sodden mess. The boat whirled like a top.

She wiped the spray from her face and discovered Arthur bailing with her cooking pot. He gave her a broad grin and continued. The shore lay out of reach but tantalizingly close. Eleanor flexed her aching shoulders, rubbed her numbed hands together, then picked up the oar and stood up again. The power in her staff seemed to penetrate her chill and exhaustion, and she found she somehow had the strength to paddle.

But it was nearly two hours before she found a cove they could land in, navigated its waters, and waded onto a stone-strewn beach. Then she lay there, too tired and cold to move or care if she ever moved again. She was faintly aware of the young man struggling with something, but it didn't seem very important as she drifted off to a light doze that deepened into sleep.

Something was chasing her. It was hot and bright and terrible. The light blinded her, so she stumbled. Great hands grasped her shoulders, and a mouth covered hers.

Eleanor sat up screaming. She stared blank-eyed at the waves, and cry after cry ripped out of her throat.

Arthur put clumsy arms around her and held her against him.

"Sh, shh. It was only a dream. You are quite safe. There, there."

Eleanor sagged against a comforting shoulder and wiped tears away from her cheeks. "It was awful. I couldn't...get away," she mumbled. "I'm so tired. Cold."

"Yes. We both are. I've gathered some wood. If you could manage to start a fire, we could get warm and dry our clothes."

"I don't think I could make a spark," she answered as she gently disengaged herself from his embrace. She crawled to the pile of driftwood and begged for fire. To her surprise, it appeared, and in a few minutes, a cheery blaze crackled on the beach. It was, she realized, dark again. "Have I slept the day away?"

"Indeed, you have. I spread out the cloaks to dry, but the sun doesn't get in this cove much, and everything is still damp. I pulled off your boots, though. I was afraid the leather would shrink and hurt your feet."

Eleanor wiggled her toes toward the fire. "It's all right. I have resigned myself. I'll never be warm, dry, and well fed again."

Arthur gave her a toothy grin. "When I am restored to my throne, you will have anything you wish."

She gave him a shrug. "I don't think you can give me what I really want. But it doesn't matter. Really, I've become quite accustomed to being soaked to the skin. But the salt has dried, and I itch terribly. That's the worst part. I wonder where we are. There are times when I wish Wrolf could speak, though I don't think map-reading is one of his talents."

The wolf, resting on one side of the fire, lifted his head at the sound of his name and lolled his tongue out. Then he flopped back down and returned to his slumbers. Eleanor envied his cheerful disposition. Her stomach rumbled, but she knew she had no strength left for magic, so she curled up and closed her eyes.

Dawn found her refreshed and itchy. Arthur was feeding the dying fire with bits of wood and singing softly to himself. "Did you sleep?" she asked, standing up and shaking sand and rimed salt from her now dry garments.

"A bit. I do not seem to need very much."

"Well, you were sort of asleep for twenty years. And your grandfather apparently didn't need much, either."

"Really. I never knew him or my father. Lots of stories, though. And tales of my Uncle Richard. I have often felt that they were giants and that I would never be able to follow in their footsteps. And my grandmother! She is more alive than other women. Like a comet or a falling star. My mother used to get a terrible rash all up and down her arms whenever Grandmother came to visit. I almost expected Eleanor to have wings like a dragon, but she was always bright and kind."

"I had never thought much about it, but I guess they must be fairly formidable as a family. My father was, too, but hardly in the same class. We'd better do something about breakfast."

"I . . . found these. Do you think they are good to eat?" He displayed three slightly speckled eggs beside him on the sand. "There was another one, but it broke." He reminded her of an overlarge and anxious Irish setter.

"I have no idea, but if there isn't a baby bird inside, I guess it won't kill us. Actually, I think there are people who eat unborn baby birds. I'm just not ready to become one." She took the cooking pot, filled it with seawater, and set the eggs into it. Twenty minutes later, they were eating hard-boiled and slightly salty eggs with the enthusiasm of the ravenous.

They packed up the gear, the willow cup having returned to its normal state, and the staff as well, and started searching for some way up to the cliffs above. It took an hour, and Eleanor was wet to the knees again before a path revealed itself. It was rocky and so narrow at one point that they could barely squeeze through, and Arthur tore his tunic, but eventually they reached the top.

XXIII

By midday, the sea was well behind them, and Eleanor found a small stream. The desire to get dried salt off her body was irresistible, so they decided to stop there. Arthur went off to see if he could discover another stupid rabbit, and she happily discarded her clothing and washed her body, scrubbing until she was pink, then sitting on a rock to let the sun dry her.

A large hand covered her mouth and another pulled her hair, dragging her off the rock, cutting her legs in the process. Baird grinned down at her, his bright hair glinting in the sunlight. He covered both her mouth and nose as she clawed at him, then laughed as she ceased to struggle.

"That's better. Much better. Glare at me all you like. You are going to be mine. I'm much nicer than Doyle, a better lover. You'll see."

She bit his hand as hard as she could, and he slapped her until her head rang. Then he grabbed one breast and twisted it until she cried in pain. Eleanor clawed at him, but his longer arms gave him an unfair advantage. All she could reach was his shoulders, encased in soft leather.

Baird put one hand around her throat and the other between her legs, manipulating the flesh. She gasped and fought her body's responses, trying to think of some way to defeat him. There was nothing. She was still too weak from the sea voyage.

The grip on her throat tightened. "Stop fighting me. I am going to have you and the sword. Surrender, little slave." The blue sky overhead seemed to darken, and she knew that she must not lose consciousness, whatever happened. Instead, she fluttered her eyelids and feigned a faint. He loosened his grip on her throat and pushed her legs farther apart. Then he was inside her.

Her body responded a little, and she felt betrayed. No one but Doyle should make her feel like this. Remembering her husband was a mistake. Her muscles quivered at the thought. She must not think of anything remotely sexual. It was amazing, she discovered, how little was free of sexual connotation. The sea was like waves of pleasure. Fire was full of passion. Music was languorous and sensual. Earth was hard, like a man. Animals, plants, they all brought images.

She could reach his face now, his eyes, but it was hard to wish to. Her body desired release, and it wasn't particular how it achieved it. But Eleanor knew if she allowed herself to climax with the grunting brute atop her, he would indeed win the sword and be her master. She gouged at his eyes halfheartedly, and he slapped her again and again. She cried out to Bridget and Sal but heard no answer.

Eleanor forced herself to one more effort. She slowly quelled her body, denying each response, until the image of a still pool of water rose in her mind. Sal was there! Nothing ruffled the smooth surface of the pool, no breeze, no emotion. She felt herself become part of the glassy waters. Faintly, far away, she heard his roar of triumph, and she felt his moisture enter her, but she knew it to be a hollow victory for him.

Then Wrolf landed on his back and sank great teeth into the exposed throat of the man. For an instant, she was almost crushed beneath their combined weights, then Baird rolled off with a bellow. He yanked a knife from his belt and tore into the wolf's belly.

Eleanor staggered up on trembling legs as they rolled into the stream, locked in mortal combat. She gasped for a moment, then got her staff and waded into the pinkish water to smash Baird across the skull.

Wrolf's coat was bright with blood, but he continued to rip at the man. Baird sank the knife into the wolf's throat just as Eleanor brought her staff down a third time.

There was silence. Wolf and man lay in the shallow stream, unmoving. One side of Baird's face was ruined, and the eye was gone, but she gave him no more than a glance. She tugged his flaccid arms from around the animal and felt the wet coat at the chest. Nothing.

Eleanor sat down in the stream and took the dead head of her companion into her lap. The waters swirled around them, carrying the gore downstream as she wept.

Arthur found her there, stroking the head of a dead wolf with the huge body of a man beside her. He goggled at the carnage, then waded into the water and drew her away to the shore.

Eleanor stared down at them, the man still alive by the rise and fall of his chest. She wanted to go over and stab Baird in the throat, as he had killed Wrolf, with the same knife. A cool voice in her mind said, "No. It is not his time to die."

Her tears ceased, and she removed herself from Arthur's light embrace, suddenly aware that however young he was, he was perfectly healthy about having a naked woman in his grasp. Ignoring her bloody legs, she pulled her salty tunic on.

Baird sat up and groaned. He lowered his head to his hands, then vomited violently into the stream. Eleanor watched icily as he heaved and retched. I hope I gave him a terrific concussion, she thought. He tried to stand up, but his legs gave way, and he fell back into the stream. Finally, he crawled to shore moaning. Baird flopped on one side and lay panting. She could see a line of red seeping from his scalp where she had struck him. There was a slight feeling of pleasure that she had marked him, though Wrolf had done the greatest damage.

"Help me get Wrolf to shore," she told Arthur. It was an awkward burden, but they carried the wolf onto the earth, and Eleanor removed the knife that remained buried in his throat. She washed it off, dried it on her tunic, and stuck it into her belt.

Baird gave a bellow that rang through the vale. "My eye! My eye!"

"It should have been your throat, you bastard," Eleanor answered. "Count yourself lucky I don't cut off your balls!"

"You...bitch! I'll make you pay. No one can treat me—"

"Silence, churl," roared Arthur, kicking Baird with

a damp boot. "Should I kill him for you, my lady?" He had an expression that left no doubt in Eleanor's mind that he meant it.

"No. It isn't his time to die yet. Let's gather stones for Wrolf." She bent and picked up two hefty rocks and began to place them around the carcass. It was mid-afternoon before the cairn was completed, and Baird seemed to have fallen asleep. Eleanor heaped the last stone into place, then turned and gathered her staff. She walked away from the grave and the man without a backward glance.

By sunset, they had walked south a few miles, and Eleanor felt the anger and adrenaline that sustained her fade as quickly as ice in a fire. Her feet suddenly refused to progress another step, and she sat down on a nearby rock.

Arthur looked at her, nodded, and broke some dead-wood off nearby bushes. Then he removed the rather battered rabbit he had caught from his belt and began skinning it clumsily. Eleanor made a tiny fire and sat back again. The fire sword lay across her back like a yoke, and she released it. She took it onto her lap and stared down at the bright sheath. Fingering the inter-lace patterns in the twilight, she wondered if it was worth the lives of her husband and Wrolf. Bridget, she decided, had a great deal to answer for, but who could call the gods to task? A faint Sal echo in her mind said, "Only themselves," and she felt some content in that.

Eleanor fell into a light doze after they had eaten, sitting up against the rock, tense for any sound that might herald Baird pursuing them. He would follow them, she was certain. She woke suddenly from a dream of a banquet table groaning with her favorite foods— salmon mousse, tacos, bloody beef, and German choc-olate cake.

Two coals seemed to glow beyond the fading fire. She stared at them until she realized it was a cat with an aura darker than night. It lay sphinxlike and regarded her with feline insolence. Was it some creature of Dark-ness, to have so somber a light?

As if it caught her question, the animal stood, stretching gracefully, and she saw it was much larger than she had assumed. It moved slowly around the fire, and she realized it was a panther. It came and sat Bast-like before her and stared at her with golden eyes. She returned the look until the animal gave a slow blink.

Carefully, Eleanor extended a hand slowly. The panther sniffed at it indifferently, then stretched out on its stomach until its front paws almost touched Eleanor's hem. It made a low noise in its throat, which she took for a purr, though it was very like a soft growl. "Hullo." She wondered if Elliot's instructions on greeting felines included black panthers. "How do you do?" It gave a low grunt, which Eleanor took to mean, "Well enough, thank you."

It inched closer, until its sleek head was beside Eleanor's lap. Then it leaned its chin against her thigh and gave a slight sigh, as if it derived some obscure pleasure from human contact. Eleanor slowly lifted her hand and gave the beast a tentative stroke behind the ears. It snuggled closer.

"You are overlarge for a lapcat," she said very quietly. The panther just gave her a blink of golden eyes. "I suppose you are my guide now." She leaned back against the rock, thinking sadly of Wrolf, and continued to pet the animal while she stared into the fire. Her mind was a tumble of odd bits of memory, the story of the Great Cat of Pulag that had held terrible sway over a portion of Wales in some misty past, her meeting of Wrolf in the woods, the avatars of the Goddess Diana as bear, wolf, and cat. The wolf was winter, and the cat summer, just as Doyle and Baird were tied to those seasons. Bridget had said she would find helpers along the way, and she supposed this must be one.

The grief she had walled up behind some invisible barrier in her mind flowed out. She longed for Doyle's touch and Wrolf's cheerful disposition. Tears dripped down her cheeks.

The panther turned and raised its head, putting one paw on Eleanor's breast. It regarded her steadily, and there was comfort in its touch, so she rubbed the tears away. "You realize you have absolutely no business in Scotland," she told it. The cat yawned, as if matters of geography were quite irrelevant. "I shall call you Sable, if you have no objections. I never was very clever with names. I had three dogs, all called Prince, even though one was a princess, but that was in another country, and a white cat called Fluffy. I guess we are both strangers in a strange land, because this is very unlike Africa, isn't it? Were you sitting on a tree limb, contemplating the sunset, when you were whisked to my fireside? Or were you prowling the halls of Olympus?" The panther gave her a playful butt of head against chest, as if to say it did not matter.

Eleanor had an overwhelming desire for a cigarette and a cup of coffee, a hot shower and a real bed. She shifted her shoulders a little, trying to find a better position against the rock, aware of an enormous fatigue. Where am I going to find the strength to continue? she wondered. The warmth of the panther seemed to ease the tiredness a little, and she slid her body down to the earth, turning onto one side and pillowing her head on one arm. Sable sort of flowed to stretch alongside her, feline spine pressing on leg and belly.

Despite exhaustion, sleep eluded her. Eleanor tried to discover why, and found that she was angry. It was not the bright, clear rage of her father but instead the colder Northern fury of her mother's people, with their mixture of Viking and Celtic blood. First it seemed to be anger at Bridget, for yanking her from her time and place and setting her a task too great for her feeble strengths. Then she realized she was furious with herself for getting involved with the task. No one told me that no was an answer, too. Why did I take the sword and cloak? Who the hell did I think I was, anyhow? If I had left well enough alone, Doyle would be alive now.

Guilt flooded through her. Everything was all her fault. She had felt that way after her father died, that somehow she was to blame for the cancer that turned him from a lusty man into an empty husk. It was an icy, tearless guilt, dark as the void. I had the free will not to choose this job, and saying I didn't know doesn't change anything. I am being punished for my vanity. I can't do it.

Eleanor untucked her arm from under her head because it was going to sleep, and rested against the bare ground. The murmurs of earth touched her. She heard the constant creak of Orphiana's serpentine body shifting, the distant singing of the stones at Avebury, and the answering chorus of other circles, and the ripple of the waters at Sal's pool. They seemed to laugh at her. *Silly goose*, she heard the Willow Lady's acerbic voice whisper, *you cannot blame yourself for other people's choices. Only your own, and you have done well. Do not corrupt your love with fear and doubt.*

It slowly dawned on the woman that she had not forced Doyle into their too-brief marriage. He had wanted the sword and the freedom that went with it. Later, she knew, he had come to love her, and he had cared enough to force her into continued independence. The unborn child stirred within her, reminding her of their passion. I should have castrated Baird, she thought as a dreamless sleep overtook her.

XXIV

Arthur eyed the panther with great suspicion as it sat beside the fire. Eleanor had managed to conjure up another mess of tasteless, gluey porridge, which now lay in her belly like lead. She was tranquil, despite an aching jaw and the beginnings of a black eye where Baird had struck her.

"Are you sure that animal is friendly?" he asked.

"Believe me, if he wasn't, neither of us would be here to worry about it. I think a herd of antelope could have overrun the camp without waking you. You snore."

"Do I?"

"Very softly." She gave him a grin and winced. Eleanor rubbed her jaw tenderly. For a moment, she wondered why Baird's rape had not disturbed her more, then realized she had simply inundated her feelings with her own rage, so she could not partake of the depression and guilt that dwelled there also. When I'm finished with all this, I am going to have a rip-roaring nervous breakdown. I've earned it, she thought.

They gathered their gear, and Eleanor strapped the sword across her shoulders, wishing she was tall enough to wear it from her waist. It chafed against unhealed scratches and into her back and rubbed one bruised hip. She felt filthy, and she would cheerfully have cast her shabby garments onto the dying fire if she had had replacements. The wool of her tunic seemed itchy, and she realized it was still salty, for she had not washed it.

The panther stood up and walked off purposefully in a vaguely southerly direction. They followed and soon came to a moor so thick with heather it seemed a sea of lavender. There was a constant murmur of bees and the occasional squawk of grouse startled in their avian

236

pursuits. The sun beat down with almost tropical fierceness, and Eleanor found her throat parched for water.

It was slow going, for the vegetation clutched at the hem of her gown and scratched arms and face. There was no path Eleanor could discern, though Sable seemed quite confident of the way. The bushes got larger and larger, until they came to a hut made of wattle and daub, which looked like a bird's nest turned upside down. A pale whisp of smoke eddied out of the top, but it appeared empty.

Sable sat down on his haunches and regarded the hut with feline disinterest. Eleanor studied it, and after a moment, she saw that there was an old woman sitting outside the hut. Her wrinkled face blended perfectly with the building, and her clothing was covered with twigs and bits of heather. Eleanor thought she could have played all three witches in *Macbeth* with no problem at all, for she had never seen a face more ruined by age. Arthur, beside her, gave a sharp intake of breath, then made a courtly bow.

Eleanor followed with a clumsy curtsy and wondered at the bemused expression on her companion's face. "Good day to thee, fair lady," he said. She gave him a hard look and discovered him preening the rusty stubble of beard he was growing.

The woman rose slowly, and for a second, she shimmered. Eleanor caught a glimpse of an exquisitely beautiful woman dressed in shining white robes and understood Arthur's odd behavior.

"Welcome, young sir and lady." The voice was like honey, and Eleanor felt the flesh on the back of her neck prickle. She had an impulse to run from the clearing. Only the panther's cool assurance stopped her. "Won't you come inside out of the sun?"

They entered, Arthur eagerly, Eleanor with some reluctance. The interior was as smooth as glass and black. She caught a reflection of herself, a pale face with a bruised eye, hair tangled with leaves and twigs, and a garment almost as tattered as her hostess's. I look like death warmed over, she thought.

There was a fire pit surrounded by white stones and a couple of benches. Over the fire hung a cauldron that smelled of stew. The floor was hard-packed dirt.

"Pray, be seated." Like a conjurer, the woman produced two wooden cups filled with a foamy brew. She handed them to Arthur and Eleanor with a toothless grin. "Heather ale," she explained. Eleanor tasted it cautiously and found it a robust beer that banished her thirst almost instantly. Arthur gulped his down, and the woman refilled his cup from an earthenware pitcher.

To break the silence, Eleanor said, "It's delicious."

"Thank you, my dear. I brew it myself. Would you like to use my comb?" The object appeared in a wrinkled claw of a hand.

Eleanor took it gingerly and set to work getting the tangles out. Arthur just stared at the woman like a man bewitched and drank his ale. The only sounds in the hut were the popping of the fire and an occasional grunt from Eleanor when she discovered a bad snarl.

Finally the woman spoke. "Do not be afraid, child. I am no enemy of yours. It is not as if you were unfamiliar with my face." The seamed countenance changed, and Eleanor looked into her father's face as he breathed his last, then Doyle's, and finally the blood-smeared head of the wolf. Her throat thickened with unshed tears, and her hands came to rest in her lap, comb and hair forgotten.

"Yes," she said finally. "But I don't *know* you."

"No, no mortal does, until the end. And yours is many years away."

"I suppose I should be gratified."

"Poor child. It is so hard to live, isn't it?"

"Yes, ma'am. I keep having to make decisions, and I always worry I'm not doing the right thing. I feel I'm not really up to everything."

"That is the burden of mortals—doubt. The deities do not suffer from it, so their failures are more crushing. There is, for instance, one fellow I have been pursuing for over a millenium. He keeps eluding me, and I wonder if I'll ever catch him. Oh, I will, for all flesh comes to me eventually. Our successes count less, and yours more, because you can overcome your fears. We have none and thus are robbed of achievement. We must content ourselves with toying with the fragile existences of those who no longer even acknowledge our presence."

Eleanor found herself smiling. "I never thought of it in that light."

"Certainly not. Being self-involved is one way man and the gods are similar."

"You can say that again," Eleanor answered, thinking of Bridget. "What now?" She picked the comb up from her lap and went back to work on her hair.

"Now you will eat and rest."

"And what will that cost me?"

"Ah, you know my nature better than I thought."

"I think I could even put a name to you, lady."

"How polite of you not to do so. You may, if you wish, then."

"Bera, perhaps."

"My sister Sal told me you were clever. She holds you in great affection."

"It is very mutual. What do you ask from me?"

"Just a little blood."

Eleanor blanched, though she knew Bera the Hag was a vampire. "That seems a stiff price for hospitality."

"I will also give you a charm that will...discourage, shall we say, that brother-in-law of yours."

"Baird?" She raised her fingers to her swollen cheek and felt a quiver of fear. "Yes, I'll do it for that."

The bright eyes within the wrinkled face regarded her thoughtfully. "You aren't afraid of me, are you?"

"Yes, some."

"You hide it well. As for the lad, I will not take more than a year or two, which he can well spare. Besides, he's eager for my touch."

Eleanor almost protested. Instead, she said, "What will he get out of it?"

"He will never be afraid of me again."

"That, I think, is a great gift."

Bera just smiled and said, "I know."

They ate, and Eleanor found herself very sleepy after the meal. She stretched out on the floor on her tired cloak and slid into a dark dream. Some great weight oppressed her, and there was a sharp moment of pain in her throat. Then there was pleasure, a deep, black pleasure that coursed through veins and mind, followed by nothing.

A gray dawn was coloring the heath when she looked

out the hut door. Arthur was still asleep, a faint smile on his lips. He looked different somehow, and she realized his beard had thickened and darkened. He was more a man and less a boy. Bera sat on a bench, twirling a spindle and humming softly.

"Did you sleep well?" the Hag asked.

"Yes, thank you. I feel... wonderful." That imp which made her speak before thinking possessed her. "Was I tasty?"

The Hag laughed, and Arthur woke up. "Delicious," she said.

The man stretched, yawned, and scratched his face. He regarded Bera affectionately, rose, and placed a gentle kiss on the withered cheek. "Good morning, milady."

Eleanor wondered what he would do if he could see the beldam as she really was, then decided that was not her concern. He obviously had gotten a fair trade for his life's blood, and that was all that mattered.

They breakfasted on stew and ale. Then Bera rose and opened her hands. A violet tunic lay across her outstretched palms. "I think you will find this more suitable than what you are wearing, Eleanor."

Eleanor took it and rubbed the soft linen between her fingers. A pattern of white blossoms was embroidered around the neck and cuffs. "It is beautiful. Thank you."

"And this." Bera held out a sprig of white heather. "Baird won't like it at all." She gave a tooth-rotted grin and a cackle, which made Eleanor's blood chill in her veins. "Not at all."

She tucked the sprig into her belt pouch. "I thank you for your gifts, lady."

Bera reached out a clawed hand and patted Eleanor's cheek. "Such a polite, solemn little one. So brave. But you should laugh more. That hero's heart that throbs within your chest would be better for some gaiety."

A protest rose and died unspoken. Eleanor could not speak the pain inside her, the unspent grief and the rage beyond it, and Bera knew all that in any case. *What do I have to laugh about? I think my Irish blood must be very anemic.* And, with Celtic perversity that made her smile, both for the sudden notion of Cuchulain or Finian with an iron deficiency, and a realization that after a brief time in Bera's arms, she possibly was, a little.

The loneliness she bore swept across her, and she felt the pang of separation she had experienced the morning she woke up outside Sal's mound. I am beloved of the goddess, she thought, and was both humbled and furious at the distinction. Some need lay within her to return that affection, the love she had never shown her mother, which could only be pressed by touch and feel, the press of flesh on flesh.

Eleanor embraced Bera, kissing the withered cheek and stroking the weedy locks of hair. She stared unafraid into eyes like ponds of dead water and smiled. To her astonishment, two huge tears rolled down the Hag's face, rilling into the canyons of skin that ran from nose to mouth and dripping from the pointed chin. She felt bony hands tremble upon her shoulder blades.

"I am repaid tenfold by thy grace, Eleanor." The voice shook and sounded old. "You have put me in thy debt."

"Huh?"

"We are never...spontaneous. Our gifts are all a calculation, to buy that which is called by the paltry term *love*. Only men can give that thing freely and with joy." Another tear swelled from an ancient eye.

"Don't cry, Mother," Eleanor said quietly.

"Why not? I had almost forgotten how. I see now why Sal holds you so dear. I feel quite young again, and I wish you might abide here with me forever."

"No doubt I will return to you someday."

"No. The willows have marked you as their own, and Sal will claim you when your body fades, but it is a sweet thought. Now, you must go." Bera slipped out of her embrace.

They took their leave of the Hag, and Sable led them across the heath. Arthur was quiet in a thoughtful way for some time. Finally, he spoke.

"Who was our fair hostess, Lady Eleanor?"

"Death," she replied without thought.

Arthur gave a grunt. "I suspected she was not as she appeared. I feel very strange. Are you angry that she came to me...in the night?"

"No. I'm not the jealous sort, and who you bed is your business, in any case. You aren't afraid to have lain with the Hag?"

"She is very beautiful," he replied, as if that settled the matter. "No, I am not afraid of anything this morn."

"I wish I could say the same."

XXV

The southerly route the panther led them along clung to the coast, so they skirted lochs of great grandeur and were never more than a few miles from the sea. The days became blurred, each like the one before, though Eleanor noted a difference in her companion. He was stronger, more assured and confident. His hunting skills improved, and they ate better, for which she was grateful. She carried a nagging horror of the effects of malnutrition upon the unborn child in her womb, though in truth she was not sure just what diet was best for a healthy baby. Fresh fruits and vegetables seemed logical, so she gathered berries whenever they found them and learned to recognize the leaves of wild onions and the feathery fronds of carrots. Milk, which she loathed, she conjured each evening and drank as a kind of penance.

Sometimes her loneliness was nearly insupportable, and she would dream of Doyle's body covering hers, raising her arms in sleep to clutch a phantom. Then she would awake weary, bruised from her tossing, and unrefreshed. His name lay on her lips each dawn, and her hair would be a mass of snarls she yanked out with rough fingers, as if the pain would ease her grief.

Five or six days after they left Bera, she knelt by a still pool beside a brook to wash her face and found a haggard reflection staring back at her. Baird's bruise had faded, but dark circles under both eyes had replaced it. Her mouth was a thin line, and she could see her jaw muscles taut with tension. The eyes seemed to stare back at her like grapes, lackluster and emotionless. I look starved, she thought, studying her cheekbones, or shell-shocked. The hilt of the fire sword over one shoul-

der glowed like a flame, heightening the pallor of her
skin.

Eleanor thrust her hands into the water to dash the
reflection into shards and splashed chill water on her
skin. The sword seemed to press down on her, and she
was so weary of its weight, she would cheerfully have
consigned it to a watery grave. The water seemed to
have no power to refresh her, so she stood up, filled her
cooking pot, and walked back to the campsite.

Arthur knelt beside their fire, plucking the feathers
off a plump grouse. She stood for a moment behind him,
studying the line of his back and the jut of his jaw
adorned with an auburn beard full of golden glints. His
hands were big and strong, and she liked the purposeful
way they moved across the plumage. Her mind made
a picture of those hands upon her breasts, and she pushed
the image away in horror. Doyle was not even two weeks
dead. A blush of shame rose in her cheeks and traveled
downward to her thighs.

What am I thinking of, came the angry words in her
mind. There was a terrible impulse to hug him, to put
her head upon his chest just to feel the steady lub-dub
of another heart. I'm so lonely I could kiss the Devil,
she thought.

Eleanor remembered the day of her father's funeral,
and the college chapel filled with faculty and students,
past and current. It had been a warm May day, and the
damp smell of floral tributes had mingled with the
slightly musky odor of too many bodies crowded together in a confined space. She had thought the sunlight streaming through the stained-glass windows
heartless, as if nature should have wept for Daniel
Hope's departure.

But afterward, at the home of the department chair-
man, who was hosting a very civilized wake, at least
for an Irishman, people she barely knew had hugged
her and kissed her. Her mother had sat in splendid
isolation in a wing chair, dry-eyed and hard-mouthed,
putting back neat Scotch as if she were trying to single-
handedly cancel Britain's trade deficit. Eleanor had been
almost blind with grief, her eyes ever full of unspent
tears. And something in those awkward gestures of
comfort had eased her pain a little.

The most vivid memory of all was of Letitia Hayward, the striking redhead who had been Daniel's last lover before he got ill. Eleanor had always been uncomfortable around her father's ladies, and Letty acutely so, for she was always perfectly turned out in silk dresses or linen suits, hair coiled into fantastic knots, nails gleaming with enamel. A cloud of gardenias surrounded her person, so she announced her presence in a room even before she was seen.

She had come to the hospital several times, until Eleanor had made it quite clear she was not welcome. Now she lurched across the room in a discreetly dove-gray suit, which showed a mournful respect but no more. Her glass-green eyes had the glazed look of alcoholic anesthetic. Putting her drink on a table with exaggerated caution, Letty had gripped Eleanor's wrists with amazing strength for one so slender.

"Tell me how he died," she hissed.

Eleanor, embarrassed and angry, had tried to break free, but Letty had hung on. Finally, she had used her tongue to try to wound her tormentor, detailing the ghastly end of a vigorous man in vivid detail and barely noticing the steady trickle of tears upon her cheek until a wisp of gardenia-scented lace and linen dabbed her face.

"Your mascara is running," Letty said, slipping an arm around Eleanor's shoulders and pillowing her head on the gray silk. "Do you know how lucky we were to have loved him? Those others remember him as a brilliant scholar, but we knew the man. He made everyone else pale by comparison, Eleanor, but don't fall into the trap I did."

"Trap?"

"Don't let him blind you."

The memory of that cryptic statement brought her back to the here and now of Sable sprawling beside the fire and Arthur removing the entrails of the grouse. Eleanor sat down, stilled the cacophony of conflicts in her mind, and concentrated on getting pilaf and not rice gruel in her pot. She was getting better in her culinary conjurings, but she still had disasters and found the task demanded her undivided attention. *I can cross the sea in a willow cup, but I still mess up supper.*

Arthur had spitted the two halves of the bird onto sticks and thrust them into the fire when she raised her head from her task. He had been looking at her and shifted his eyes away uneasily. It wasn't a guilty look, but something was bothering him.

"What is it?" she asked.

"You are so tired, and I am worried about you."

"It has been a long six months. Hell, it's been a lifetime. And I'm not sleeping well."

"I know. Are you afraid of Baird?"

"Of course. I would be a fool not to be. I mean, no one warned me I would get to play Isis to his Set and Doyle's Osiris, and I really don't know my lines."

"Who?"

"It is a long story," she said, setting the pot upon the fire. After a moment of watching the flames, she began. "Once upon a time in the land of Egypt," and plunged into a tale three thousand years old, as much to pass the time as to shift the subject away from her own health. She told of how Set had murdered his brother Osiris and cut his body into pieces and cast them into the Nile and how Isis had spent a year gathering them up to be reborn as the god Horus, coloring the tale a little with her own experiences, and drawing the incidents from her vast background in myth. It eased some hurt to dwell for a time in that ancient world, though she did not know if Doyle had become the judge of the dead. It was both real and unreal, for she lacked the vanity to see herself as an object worthy of fraternal rivalry.

As they ate charred bird and scooped saffron rice out of the pot like a pair of bedouins, Arthur asked, "You said she had a cloak of blue with stars. Is it the same one you have?"

Eleanor looked at the object in question, folded up atop the rest of her belongings. "I am not certain. It is a magical garment, for sure, because it never gets dirty or anything. Bridget is a lot like Isis, though I cannot recall Isis ever waving a mucking great sword around. The cloak of stars goes with a lot of goddesses—Aphrodite or Venus, and even Mary, Jesus's mother, wears one. They say that the blossoms of the rosemary bush were originally white, but the Virgin hung her cloak over a rosemary bush, and the flowers turned blue in her honor. I suppose it would be safe to say that this cloak is a reflection of the original."

He brought his bushy eyebrows together in thought. "Does it trouble you to know all these tales of gods and heroes and bear some part of them at the same time?"

"Yes, it does. In my own time, these stories were studied as curiosities from the childhood of man. To believe in them was to mark yourself as a superstitious fool. I remember once my father gave a lecture in a town called Berkeley, not part of his class but as a seminar. Never mind, I'm confusing you. Anyhow, these people showed up, about a dozen of them, in long white robes embroidered with flowers and moons. They said they were Druids, and I thought he was going to explode. They were terribly sincere and intense and invited him to a ritual they were planning. He was quite rude about it, and they looked at him with such disappointment. They really believed, and he didn't."

"Did he go?"

Eleanor smiled slowly. "As a matter of fact, he did, purely as a matter of academic curiosity. Actually, my mother convinced him it would be useful to see in what manner modern people used archaic material. We all went. There were, oh, fifty people, most of them in their twenties or thirties, dressed in all sorts of fanciful garments. We gathered in a grove of trees near the sea, and they sang songs and did circle dances as the moon rose over the hills and was reflected in the ocean. And afterward we ate honey cakes and drank terrible red wine, and a lot of people went off into the trees for loving. Father got cornered by a dark-haired woman a little older than the rest who told him she could trace her origins back to the witches of Thessaly. I think he almost believed her. I think part of him wanted to believe in the gods, and he couldn't quite make the leap. I didn't have that choice. But sometimes I wonder if this isn't some dream I have blundered into."

Arthur nodded. "When I saw you clawing the earth by the body of that boar, I thought I was dreaming. But then, the last thing I remembered was the banquet hall and a goblet with a dragon coiled round its stem."

"Tell me about your cousin John."

"I hardly know him, for he was ever busy with the ordering of the kingdom. Until I was sixteen, I only met him a dozen times, for I lived at Brittany with my mother and my sister. I had two tutors, Père Jean and Père Gerard, and Master Guillaume to teach me sword craft.

"I would say that he is clever. His eyes dart here and there, watching all. A serious, thoughtful man, I would judge him, though I have heard some tales—servants' gossip—that he is a great lover of wine and women. My mother hated him, and my sister avoided him."

"And Master Guillaume?"

Arthur smiled fondly. "As much father as I have ever known. I was perhaps eight when he came to us, having had some falling-out with my Uncle Richard. He had a son with him, also called Guillaume, a year my younger. He offered his services to my mother, which I think she was glad of, and lived with us, off and on, for the next ten years. He told me tales of my grandfather and the exploits of my Uncle Richard and my father as boys and men. He was killed in an ambush a few months before I was eighteen."

"How very convenient for your cousin John," Eleanor answered with some asperity.

"My mother felt the same, but she sees plots in every bush. She used to say I was a changeling, for I do not rush headlong into every fray, as she does. And Master Guillaume pounded it into me with his strong right arm that a worthy knight uses his brains as well as his muscles. My father had a name for deviousness and guile, but my sister contends that was from being squeezed between Grandfather, Uncle Henry, his son John, and my Uncle Richard. Not to mention Grandmother."

"So William Marshall actually found an Angevin he could beat some sense into. Amazing. Are you pious as well?"

Arthur shook his head. "Père Gerard forced the catechism down my gullet, but I cannot say it stayed. Père Jean was content if I learned my letters. Poor Gerard. He was the family confessor, but we brought him little traffic, and he always went about with a fierce scowl, muttering gloom and doom."

Eleanor reviewed her knowledge of the domestic lives

of the Plantagenets, a tapestry of violence and betrayal run through with the single thread of William Marshall, who served them loyally until he outlived even wicked King John and served as regent for his young son Henry, the third of that name. He had refused to kill Richard, in rebellion against his father, and had slain his horse instead, and had been lettered enough to pen an autobiography, a remarkable achievement for a man of his time and profession. And here, in this other Albion, he had chosen to serve Arthur of Brittany in his later years.

It seemed a strange choice until she realized that Richard fathered no children and that the legitimacy of this King John was doubtful at best. Arthur was simply the only certain male issue of the line. John wasn't the first bastard to sit in Westminster, but the Conqueror was not remembered with any affection, and Stephen of Blois was surely a blot upon the escutcheon.

Eleanor stretched out, pillowing her head on Bridget's cloak, the fire sword beside her and Sable curled at her feet. Their talk had relaxed her somewhat, involved her mind with what was still to some degree history to her. The rolls of kings and bastards, queens and consorts, soothed her, easing away nagging questions, except the figure of William Marshall seemed to stand like a pivot point between them. Why was that important?

Then it hit her that it was because he had chosen to serve, to serve one family through wars and rebellions, crusades and marriages. She had made a choice, too, months before, in a chilly chapel. No one had forced her to accept the sword and the task, but she had pretended to herself that by some alchemy, it was all Bridget's fault. The weight of her many burdens seemed to press on her chest, like the weight of Baird's body. She had entered into the adventure with a light heart and had never asked the pivotal question, "Is this my task?" until it was much too late. Doyle's fate was sealed by her choice, and she knew that in one way she was as much to blame for his death as the tusk of the boar that had killed him. And she knew the dreadful tale of her arrogance and ignorance. Doyle and Wrolf dead, Baird maimed, all because she had said yes without thinking.

Tears slid out of her eyes and puddled in her ears as she stared up at the summer stars. It had been Doyle's choice to take the sword, even knowing it would cost him his life. He could have lived forever in his mother's house, but he chose love and death. Was that why the gods were concerned with the ways of men, to experience that which they had invented but could not actually understand, the final severing of flesh and spirit?

The mystery was too great for her weary mind, and Somnos covered her with his grace, sleep. It was an uneasy repose, full of whimperings and restless tossing, until the nightmare caught her, the grinning presence of Baird's unmarred countenance above her face, the musky scent of sweat and leather crowding her nostrils. The weight of cruel hands pressed her shoulders, and she struck out with taloned hands and screamed.

"Ouch! Stop that!" Strong hands gripped her wrists. "Mercy, you are strong. Wake up, milady. Come on, wake up!"

Arthur's ruddy face was silhouetted by the stars, making a coronet above the curling hair. She stared blankly at him for a moment, then noticed a long scratch on one cheek. He slipped one arm around her shoulders and patted her awkwardly. Eleanor leaned her head against his chest, reveling in the comfort of his touch. She lifted a shaking hand to touch the scratch.

"I'm sorry."

"'Tis nothing. My sister has done much worse."

"What? The gentle Eleanor who calls the unicorns?" It felt so good to hear the steady thumping of his heart upon her cheek, the rise and fall of air from his chest. She wanted to clutch at him.

Arthur gave a crack of laughter. "What a milky maiden your history has made of her. My sister is gentle only by comparison to my mother and the rest of the family. She has a rare temper, like rain falling in sunshine, for she gives no warning. One moment still as a lake, the next a stormy sea. The only gentle Eleanor I know is you, dear lady." His voice deepened, and he lifted his hand to stroke her tangled hair.

It seemed the most natural thing in the world to lift her face to his, to find lips brushing in a tentative kiss. The memory of grouse and saffron rice lingered on his mouth, mingled with the smell of sweat. It was a scent she had previously found unpleasant, the tense, acrid odor of a classroom full of students taking an exam, the sour smell of old beer and tobacco after a party, or the way her father smelled after a night with Letitia, a cloying mixture of gardenia, deodorant, and sex. And here was wool too long unwashed upon a body still rich with the flavors of exertion, and she found it comforting. Like the feel of his shoulders under her hands, it was simple and real.

A large, long-fingered hand cupped her breast as he kissed her more deeply. Eleanor made a halfhearted gesture of protest, a muffled moan. Her mind and body went to war for a moment as visions of her dark-haired Doyle danced behind her closed eyes. How could a few stupid chemicals make nonsense of love and loyalty? Then came the faint laughter of the willows and the deeper chuckle of the man, and she knew she betrayed nothing, that indeed Doyle would expect her to bestow her affections as she saw fit.

Instead, she opened her eyes and searched the face above hers. Arthur paused under her gaze, as if aware of her conflict. The boy she had helped rescue was gone, and the stranger. The days had made them friends, and Bera had brought him into manhood. Eleanor found she liked him and knew that she could, if she chose, love him. *If I choose. No act is free of consequences.* She could not tell if the thought was her own or some memory of Sal. *This time I will not rush into anything thoughtlessly.* A faint tension in her loins told her how foolish this was.

> "'So subtly is the fume of life designed
>   to clarify the blood and cloud the mind.'"

Eleanor spoke the words without realizing it. "What?"
"Part of a poem, which ends,

> 'I find this frenzy insufficient reason
>   for conversation when we meet again.'

Nasty bit of verse to remember at the moment."

Arthur laughed. "The twists of your mind no longer surprise me. Frenzy, indeed." He kissed her again, leaving no doubt of his desire. A strong hand slipped under her gown and caressed aching thighs.

The skeins of tomorrows unrolled before her eyes. Eleanor saw a splendid altar, and herself garbed in cloth of silver, shimmering in the colored light of stained-glass windows. Arthur, crowned and dressed in blue, stood beside her, facing a slender man in the robes of a bishop. Then there was a hard-faced woman, her countenance riddled with rage and passion, handing her a goblet of wine. Poison, no doubt. A chill chamber with a white-faced, exhausted Eleanor murmuring over a small, dark head upon her breast, staring in horror as the stones of the floor erupted, and finally, Arthur, facing some unseen adversary with the fire sword bright in his hands.

Eleanor pulled her head away, breathing raggedly. The jumbled images chased in her mind. "Bring your bedding next to mine, I think." He released his grasp reluctantly and returned in haste. She reclined on the starry cloak, looking at the pale night and trying to shake herself into some semblance of sense. The moon had just risen, silvering the rocks and bushes and turning Sable to argentine.

She turned and laid her head upon his chest, feeling a firm hand in the small of her back. They kissed, and she realized that he was lonely, too. Her body sang to have its emptiness filled. Soon there was nothing but the press of his weight upon her, until the final flood of release, the sharp cries of passion, brought her back to rocky ground and tangled garments. Eleanor laughed shakily, and he joined her after a second. They hugged and cuddled, all peril forgotten for a moment. Then she thought of nothing as pleasure turned to dreamless sleep against his warmth.

XXVI

Eleanor was aware of a strange buzzing beside her ear. It came and went, and she pried open sleep-clogged eyes to seek its origin. Arthur was snoring gently, one arm pillowing her head, the other across her chest, his hand grasping her biceps tenderly, as if he was afraid to release his hold. The young face was handsome in repose, the strong jaw softened by the beard, the hooklike nose shadowing the generous mouth.

She was stiff from lying too long in one position, so she turned to face him, flexing her muscles. His head rested on the cloak as Doyle's had so often, and she searched her soul for shame or guilt. There was nothing but a sense that she was no longer alone. A person of any real sensitivity, she scolded herself, would feel awful. The question isn't whether he will respect me in the morning but whether I will. That made her chuckle, and the sound stirred the sleeper.

Arthur peered at her, a bit bemused for a moment, then kissed her lips. They clung together as if aware of how tender a thing now lay between them, then drew apart a little. "Good morning, dear lady." He touched her cheek with one finger, tracing the muscles down to her long throat.

"Good morning to thee." She found she could not say "milord." The bond was too new for her submission.

The wedge-shaped face of the panther looked over his shoulder, as if to say, "Are you two going to dally the day away?" and Eleanor realized the sun was well up. She wondered if she would ever lie with a man on a real bed with sheets and blankets, then sat up. Her body immediately informed her of a need to remove its waste, and she staggered away for the semiprivacy of a bush, astonished that the same flesh that scaled the battlements of passion should yet have such earthy insistences.

When she returned, Arthur was laying fresh bits of wood on the ashes of the previous night's fire. The panther was nowhere in sight, and the blankets and cloaks of their bed had been folded neatly, removing all traces of intimacy but memory. Eleanor stood for a second, watching the sunlight gleam on the golden hair along his forearms, filled with postcoital affection and the cold doubt that it would not be returned. Then he glanced up and grinned at her, and it was suddenly a glorious day.

She walked forward and picked up the fire sword and held it out to him. "This...is yours now, I think."

"Mine?" He gasped. "I don't understand."

"Well," Eleanor replied, crouching on her haunches with the sword across her knees, "I'm not sure I do, either. *This* is why Baird raped me. You remember how it hurt you when you touched it, back on the island? It would have done the same to him, for it can only be wielded by a man who has...brought me to rest." She touched the interlaced sheath. "This is me, this gaudy bit of Orphiana's hide. The sword isn't very good without both parts—I mean, it is not as strong. I used it when I was still a maiden, but I think that was because I was untouched. When Doyle took me, it became his. Baird wanted it—wants it—and the only way he could get it was to master me. Now, I regret to say, he would also have to kill you. I thought I had taken all the risks of what we did last night into account, but...I was not thinking very clearly. Also," she added a little bitterly, "I was not given real good instructions about the nature of the thing—just a bunch of vague directions. Magical appliances just don't come with a user's manual, dammit. If they did, Aladdin would never have left his old lamp hanging about on the wall, and perhaps there would be no stories."

Arthur was staring at her, clearly confused. "But you just said...that it is Doyle's," he said, fastening on the single point he had completely grasped.

"No, it is mine—at least it is mine to bestow, in a way. Perhaps it is a remnant of those times when men got their names and arms from their mothers. I do not know. I just know that for a moment last night I saw you use it—in my mind—and since I believe such visions have meaning, I think then that I may offer it to you without reservation. Are you afraid?"

"Only a little, for I see it binds us together in a terrible way. I must always seek your grace to wield it, and light as that fetter is, my blood bears no restraint well. We chafe at any limitation. My master often said that I would be the best of the family, could I but learn to yoke my passions to the correct cart. Then he would add that, even counting Uncle Richard, there was not a lot to choose from. I find I am loath to accept the gift." His blue eyes sparkled, and she saw for the first time the unbending pride that several generations of strong men and haughty women had created. His mother, Constance of Brittany, had an intemperate reputation; his grandmother, Eleanor of Aquitaine, was so strong-willed, her husband had jailed her, though not in this Albion; and his great-grandmother, Matilda, had brought England to civil war to satisfy her craving for power.

She felt somewhat intimidated by those fierce female ancestors of his, and chuckled inwardly as she remembered the words Henry had uttered in the dungeon in Goldman's play, *The Lion in Winter,* "I could have conquered Europe, all of it, but I had women in my life." Perhaps the playwright had simply spoken a universal truth about the battle of the sexes, which like the war in heaven, went on forever.

Eleanor sighed and reached her hand forward to the dry sticks, setting them ablaze and thinking of the struggle she had had that night so long ago, it seemed, to manage a task she found commonplace now. Her mind went back to the conversation she had had with Doyle on that occasion, remembering his healthy resentment at an existence bounded by women. As if, somehow, it was all her fault. The wood popped and crackled, and the sound brought her back to the present. Perhaps she had been wrong.

"I can hardly force you to take it. Very well, I shall continue to bear it, though it is a burden to me." She smiled, to take the sting of her words away.

"You make me feel like an ungrateful boor."

"No, only a cautious fellow. If the Trojans had had you in their councils, they would never have let the wooden horse inside their walls, and the world might be poorer by an epic. But tell me, have there not been gifts given by your ancestors?"

"Exchanged, if you mean the unicorns and the elf-stone."

"Now, that is a story I do not know. Tell me." She laid the sword aside and stirred the remains of last night's rice in the pot. She scooped a bit into her mouth and found that even cold it tasted of sunlight.

"My grandmother wished to have back an heirloom of her own mother's folk, a great green beryl, and she in turn said that if Henry would bring it to her, she would gift him with a fabulous beast, the unicorn, to be a supporter of his house for all time. Since she had borne two daughters to her husband, Louis, and was no longer a maiden, Henry, though besotted, must have been doubtful of her promise. But she made it very clear she would not marry him without the stone, which had passed from her grandmother, Dangereuse, to Aenor, her daughter. But it was lost upon her death. I have never heard the full tale of how he got it—perhaps no man living knows it. But it is said he went to the caverns of the fée and got it back. And Eleanor called the unicorns from the sea, and they came, a great herd of them, a stallion and many mares, and these now live in the forests of France and perhaps other lands. They are very shy and are rarely seen except when someone calls them, as my sister could. She also has that stone, a gift upon her thirteenth year, unless it has been reclaimed by the cavern folk. If they have it, she must be dead, for she wore it round her throat and none could remove it."

"How charming. Here, eat some rice—it's good." They munched in silence, and Sable ambled into the campsite. "So, since you have nothing to give me, you can't take the sword. *And* you don't want to be beholden."

He nodded, but he looked at the sword a bit sadly. Eleanor simply reflected that if he was as thoughtful in his kingship as he was in refusing it, he would probably be an admirable monarch. Then she stood up and began packing her gear.

* * *

As they trudged along, Eleanor nursed several harsh thoughts about men in general, and the men in her life in specific. If ever there was such a pack of ornery, contrary, inconsistent, stiff-necked, prideful bastards, she had no wish to know. Then she mentally scratched inconsistent off her catalog of faults and chuckled at her need for precision. What was it her friend Cora Reed was wont to say—"Men and women don't understand each other because they are two different races that happen to be mutually fertile"? Good old down-to-earth Cora.

It was, she reflected, the matter of an awkward dowry, and indeed the rub of the sword against one shoulder and the opposite hip was uncomfortable, more so even today. Doyle and Arthur did not appreciate the bride price it cost. That made her grin, for *bride* was a common corruption of Bridget, as in Brideswell or Brideshead. She found herself escaping into the safe, sure world of myth and folklore, playing word games and humming a little as she walked. At least Arthur did not covet the sword, per se.

"What is that tune, Lady Eleanor?"

"Huh?" She had to think, for she had been humming mindlessly. "'The Gypsy Rover,' I think. I was sort of skipping around."

"Has it words as well?"

"Oh, yes." She cleared her throat and began. When she was done, she glanced at her companion, curious at his reaction.

"I like that, though the melody seems odd."

"Well, music changes over the centuries. Church music, for instance, is not plain chant but hymns, some rousing, mostly doleful." She thought of Bach masses and the Verdi or Mozart requiem and decided that they were beyond her talents. "And there is rock 'n' roll, which is the contemporary music of my time, although several other kinds exist as well." She decided that a brief history of jazz, blues, and American folk music would not be useful. "Like 'The Yellow Submarine.'" Eleanor sang with the mental accompaniment of the Beatles in her mind.

"That is a happy song, though I do not understand the words in some parts."

"Well, the men who wrote it enjoyed being a bit confusing. They were four poor kids from an industrial town called Liverpool. For a time they were the voice of the youth of their era. You could hardly turn on a radio without hearing their tunes. They became wealthy, very wealthy, and grew apart to make their music separately."

"What is a radio?"

Eleanor had to think hard before she said, "A device that transmits sound over great distances, across the world, even." She was not about to get into any attempt to describe electricity, which despite managing to get through high school physics with a passing grade, she regarded as a kind of magic that came out of sockets in the wall. "There is also television, which provides a picture as well as sound, so that people in France can see an event in England at the moment it happens."

"What a wondrous time you come from."

"In some ways." She thought of the constant threat of global war she had grown up with and was sad. "Here is a song they say your Uncle Richard wrote." She groped in her mind for the fugitive melody.

"I have never heard it before, but I know he had some repute as a poet. Are you angry with me for refusing the sword?"

Eleanor was nonplussed by the sudden change in topic. "No, not angry. Disappointed, perhaps. I—"

The bushes errupted with short, dark men, naked and armed with spears. Their skins were stained blue with woad. With a smooth movement, Arthur wrested the sword from its sheath across her back, and the panther sprang upon the throat of a surprised-looking tribesman. Arthur charged a group of three men, swinging the bright blade in an arc around his head as a spear missed his back by inches. A moment later, a severed head flew through the air as Eleanor turned and raised her staff toward the attackers on the other side of the circle. Fire leapt from the carved head and caught one man in the chest. He screamed as he seemed to explode and his nearby companions turned tail and scurried away into the underbrush.

A bowlegged fellow leapt forward to wrest the staff from her hand, and Eleanor kicked him in the crotch, then brought her staff down into his skull with both hands. Another spear whizzed by her as the crack of wood on bone sounded sickeningly. She raised the staff in the direction the weapon had come from, only to see the backs of several warriors in hasty retreat.

It was over almost as quickly as it had begun, and there was no sound but the moans of the two men who had not finished dying. Arthur's face was spattered with blood, and his hands were gory. About a dozen man lay around, some with their throats ripped out, some hacked with the sword.

Arthur seemed a little dazed, though she could see no wound upon him. He looked at the sword in his hands, the blade wet with blood, and gave a sort of sigh. Sable sat and licked a rusty spatter off one dark flank. Then he stood, gave Eleanor a look that said, "This way," and led them away from the ambush.

They did not stop until they came to a small stream. No word had passed between them, and Eleanor wondered what Arthur was thinking as he knelt and washed his hands and face. He wiped the blade clean with grass and then sat on a rock, staring at the cloudless sky.

Finally, he spoke. "They say that at the hour of my birth, a strange beast was seen flying around the keep. It had in its claw a flaming brand; great, leathery wings, and a head like a serpent. My mother took it for a portent and named me Arthur, after the dragon-king of Albion. It was a name that pleased no one but her, certainly not my grandmother, who wrote her sharply for her presumption.

"I have never put much stock in the tale, for none saw the beast but some ignorant servants and superstitious peasants. The mantle of that fabled king was nothing I desired, nor do I desire it now. But when I grasped the hilt of the sword, a strange sense touched me. It felt... correct. As if that burning brand and the sword were one. My master often told me that if you are destined to do great deeds, they will seek you out and find you, however you hide in the bowels of the earth.

"But he gave me, too, a sense of disgust at ambition.

He taught me it was better to serve well and with a good heart than to seek for glory. Indeed, he said the glory came from good service, and he warned me of the dangers of my heritage. He pointed out there was no honor in son warring with father, as Henry did with his, all because he would not wait for the throne. He said it was a judgment upon my uncle that he snatched what was not his and died leaving the kingdom in disarray, with John's legitimacy so much in question.

"My mother burns with such ambition, and wished, upon Richard's death, to rush me to the throne and place herself as regent. She envied Grandmother her kingly sons, I think. I was just frightened, though I cannot say what I was afraid of. I think I knew somehow it was not time. It was not yet my time.

"But always I have borne the burden of other people's desires for me, so I had little room for seeing my own. My grandmother did not like my father, and though she wished me no ill, neither did she wish me well. She would prefer that I did not exist at all. My mother wants me to be the dragon-king of my birth omen, that she may glory in bringing me to life. Master William wished that I would be a perfect knight, a flower of chivalry, and Père Gerard that I would be pious. My sister alone desired nothing of me but my affection. She knew I was no hero but just a man.

"That *thing*," he continued, pointing at the sword beside him on the damp grass, "makes me more than a man. Its power, even that first day when I touched it before it was my time, called the dragon in me. I had so willfully banished that portion of myself that I believed it exorcised and let it become the faint memory of a distant dream. I chose to believe that the great destiny predicted for me was a mistake, the issue of my mother's ambition. Am I not the greatest fool ever made?"

Eleanor, hearing the torment of doubt and confession in his every word, shook her head. The depth of his introspection seemed remarkable in one so young, but he had had good teachers, and bad ones as well. "No, you are not a fool. You are just very human, and you are afraid that you will displease, that you will fail to live up to the great expectations thrust down your throat like a pelican feeding its young. I think it is easy to choke to death on other people's regurgitated needs. And no matter how you twist and turn, it never seems to be enough to satisfy them.

"But it comforts me a little that you do not want the sword because of me. I have had enough of that, though I think Doyle and I had reached some compromise before he died. I understand that you are afraid of what you might become."

"No, no. I am afraid of what I am, of the bright madness that fills my blood when that power courses through my veins. All in me that is good and just is swept away on a tide of fury."

Eleanor was silent a long while, remembering Doyle at Glastonbury, so filled with berserk madness that he continued to fight in dragon-shape, that he did not recognize his peril from the angel-thing. Doyle had known his fate, down perhaps to the moment of his death. He had had years to prepare his mind to face his destiny, centuries even. The sword awakened no sleeping demons, though his love for her had perhaps roused a few. Arthur had spent his brief lifetime avoiding an unwanted destiny, only to have it shoved into his hands. She saw, too, that the rather pleasant, cooperative young man she had taken to be Arthur was a careful pose he had made to avoid both his mother's ambitions and his cousin's enmity. He had, she suspected, masked the famous Plantagenet temperament with geniality, so much so that he had begun to believe the disguise was real. That dragon within him must seem a ravenous beast, threatening to gobble up his fragile virtues and leave him with nothing but pride and fury. What a loveless upbringing he must have had, to be regarded as nothing more than a path to power or an obstacle to it. Now, why did I think that people were less complex in ancient days than in my time? she wondered as she searched her mind for some counsel that would ease his distress.

"Tell me what you are."

"A beast."

Eleanor laughed, and he glared at her. "I'm sorry, Arthur, but that is one of the silliest things I ever heard. We are all beasts, sometimes, or the Darkness that shadows Albion would never find a foothold. But we are more than that as well, because...we can make choices. A true beast cannot. It is driven entirely by instinct. Put a mouse in a box with even a well-fed cat, and the cat will toy with it until it dies. The cat has no will in the matter. Upon seeing the mouse, its brain says, 'Pounce.' There is no man who is completely virtuous or evil. There was a great tyrant in my time who put to death millions of people but who ate no meat. In fact, being a vegetarian is considered an act of virtue and is supposed to promote a placid, cowlike disposition. There was nothing bovine about this fellow, believe me. But he made a choice to slaughter innocent people and thought it right. And if you don't choose to surrender to your fate and become a great man, no one can force you to it. No thing can, either. That hunk of metal will not change a thing about you except by your will."

Then she paused, caught in the classic problem of predetermination versus free will. Did I exercise free will when I took the sword, or was it some plan of Bridget's that reached forward in time to the moment of my conception, or even before, to the unlikely marriage of my parents? Does it matter? Eleanor, after several moments of staring down at the sunlight dappling the little stream, decided it did not, and that all that really mattered was the choices themselves, and their consequences. She heard Sal's voice whisper, *You are a most delightful and satisfactory daughter*. A wash of affection, warmer than sunlight, filled her.

Arthur sighed and chuckled. "You could split hairs with a cleric."

"That's the Irish in me, I suppose. We are great exponents of irrational logic."

The man leaned back and stretched out on the grass, putting his arms above his head. "I would like to stay here forever and just be quiet."

Eleanor shared his wish but only if Doyle was beside her. "Well, you can't," she said a little sharply.

"No." He snaked out a long arm and pulled her down onto his chest. His hand stroked her hair. "But the world will not end if I take a moment to hold you, to tell you how strong and good you are."

She giggled at the words out of a slight sense of

embarrassment. "No, no. I am just an ordinary woman in an extraordinary situation, and I have the good fortune to have had a very wise teacher in the Lady of the Willows. Doyle sometimes said she was his only rival for my affections."

"You do yourself less credit than you deserve, then, for while the gods may direct, you are the one out here killing ugly little savages and trying to recover the heirlooms of my house. They aren't out here, pregnant and with a reluctant hero on their hands, are they?"

"Are you reluctant?" she asked, ignoring the faint slur on Bridget and Sal.

"Very. I have no assurance that I will do it correctly."

"I knew I forgot something. My 'Hero's Handbook.' It is full of useful advice on how to slay dragons and what to do with unwanted princesses, the care and feeding of magical swords, and how to lay siege to a castle. But I do not recall a single word about how to judge the rightness of an action. It is the nature of dragons, I suppose, to gather up treasure and desire an occasional virgin in their diet of sheep and goats, just as it is Sable's nature to kill birds. And it is the hero's to slay such beasts, but that has nothing to do with right or wrong."

"And what, dear lady, do you do with a hero who is also a dragon?"

"Keep him away from Glastonbury, and feed him milk and honey to sweeten his disposition, I suppose." They both laughed, sat up, and prepared to continue their journey.

XXVII

A week later they stood at the end of a long peninsula and looked across blue waters toward the isle of Iona, mist-shrouded home of the quarrelsome St. Columba and his monks, though the saint was centuries dead and the monastery abandoned. Their journey had been marked by two more attacks by the natives and once by the sounds of the Reavers pursuing some other prey. Not for the first time, Eleanor wished that Britain was not an island, for she sometimes felt she had spent the better part of her adult life cold and rimed with salt.

Iona was tantalizingly close, yet far enough away that it would entail another voyage. She had little desire to repeat her performance in changing the willow cup into a vessel, for she lacked the energy for such magicks. Alone she could cross as an orca, and Sable no doubt shared Wrolf's ability to become some aquatic animal, but that did not solve the problem of transporting Arthur.

"You frown, my lady."

"Hmm. Just trying to decide how to get there from here. I would prefer to travel on a fast wish, but I am fresh out of them. No one warned me that magic was so full of decisions. It is a shame we can't just...call the Harp to us. Not to mention the fun it is going to be trundling a fragile musical instrument around in the wild. But I guess a harmonica would not be nearly so pretty on the arms of England."

It was, she realized, another onset of what she had come to call "the blacks," that deep despair that made the blues seem frivolous. They descended upon her like some recurrent fever, unannounced and unwanted, in bright daylight or the dark of night. One moment she was fine, the next her face was wet with tears and

Doyle's name lay across her lips. She made stupid jokes in an effort to allay her sense of loss and her resentment at having no leisure for grief. Sometimes she wished to pick an argument with Arthur, just to relieve her frustrations, but she was afraid of his anger and even more of her own.

The burden of the sword no longer weighed her shoulders, but little else had changed. The child in her belly grew heavier each day, and so did her sense of weariness. She had grown to respect her companion, to find some healing in the pleasure of his body, but the fact remained that he was not Doyle and never would be.

She knelt down on the sandy soil and abstractedly scratched the panther between its ears. Fond as she was of felines, she had not yet developed any of the kind of closeness she had had with the wolf, and she realized it as an instinctive reluctance to risk love again, on even so remote a creature as the big cat. Some illogical, primitive part of her had made a causal connection between love and death, and it did not matter that her father would have perished if she had not adored him, or that Doyle would die in some midsummer, if not this one. She still felt it was her fault. It was not a Gordian knot she could hack through with any sword of her mind. The ropes renewed themselves after each severing.

Eleanor, you have to ask. She went still at the words in her mind. Ask for what? From whom? *Mother, I can do it myself.* That was her own voice, a piping child's voice, over the matter of some shoelaces. I wonder what has always seemed so terrible about asking for help. She remembered her father hunched over his huge desk, pawing through piles of books, desperately struggling to complete his last work, snarling like a cur at any interruption or offer of assistance. His rejection had hurt, and she decided that that kind of pigheaded independence was not an admirable quality. Doyle had had it, too, so she had every expectation of the child within her being willful to a fault.

Sable leaned his head into her lap and regarded Eleanor with great golden eyes. Arthur was piling dried wood for a fire, whistling what she realized was the tune for "Michelle," for it had become a habit between them to sing as they walked, and he had learned both melody and words to several songs that had no business in the thirteenth century. He possessed a fine, clear, baritone range, and she realized with a pang that she had never sung with Doyle. And what, her scholar's mind wondered, would be the effect, if any, of songs out of time? She let that thought distract her from memories of Doyle. A vagrant fragment of a tune floated in her mind, a voice like blown smoke she could not identify, singing all of the songs never sung for one man before, full of infinite joy and sadness, and she had to fight off tears.

A rough wet tongue touched her wrist, and she looked at Sable. Eleanor stroked the smooth head and neck, feeling the incredible muscles underneath the skin. Its face seemed to shimmer for a second, the black muzzle fading into dead-white skin and berry red lips. Sal's face smiled at her a moment, then was gone.

Okay, I have to ask for help. Dear Goddess, will you please give me a boat, a raft, a log and paddle, for I am weary, otherwise I wouldn't bother you. The ungracious tone of her supplication struck her, and she felt a little ashamed. That was hardly the two voices singing in harmony that Sal had proposed as the proper relationship between the gods and men. But she heard the tinkle of laughter and saw the reflection of sunlight on willow-shaded waters, which reassured her that no offense had been taken. With a faint sense of shock, Eleanor realized that despite the importance of her task, she did not regard herself as worthy to petition the deities for aid. It was an odd mixture of pride and humility, a vanity of self-reliance and independence, as if she needed no one. She knew it for a lie and a delusion.

"What is it, milady?" Arthur's words broke into her thoughts. "You have the strangest expression on your face, as if you had just swallowed sour wine."

"Submission has a bitter taste."

"Yes, but my master ofttimes told me that no man can be ruler of himself unless he is willing to bend the will of another. That the strong are ever at the mercy of the weak."

Eleanor stared at him blankly for a second, trying

to make some sense of the words. She thought then of Bridget, trapping herself in a chilly priory so that she might continue to receive the reverence of a handful of monks, becoming less the queen of Heaven with each year as they forgot her true nature. Bridget could draw her over the centuries, but she must put her fate and that of Albion in the hands of a slender slip of a girl who never touched a sword before. She had imprisoned herself in a statue, so the knowledge of her might not vanish entirely and was at the mercy of frail men with brief attention spans. How mortifying. Or Sal, immured in her hill, because she was too proud to call men to adore her. It was a splendid isolation but isolation all the same. Was that the sole purpose of creation? To be adored?

Eleanor decided that was much too great a matter for her and set about getting the fire alight. As she watched the spark leap from her hand, she wondered why she served Bridget and yet loved Sal the better. They were but two aspects of the same force, as Wrolf and Sable were two faces of a single thing. Perhaps it was that Bridget demanded, and Sal, with watery grace, had suggested. Or perhaps it was that for all her fiery nature, Bridget was something of a cold fish. Then she dismissed the problem firmly and started to prepare dinner.

A dinghy bobbed on the waves the following morning. It was painted bright blue with white trim, and two real oars lay across the seat. Eleanor looked at it and wondered if some wealthy boatman in Newport was suddenly raising hell over the disappearance of it. She would have been content with an inflatable raft.

Arthur raised an eyebrow at it, then began stowing their gear. Sable viewed the operation with feline remoteness. Eleanor and Arthur got aboard, and she looked expectantly at the panther, curious to see if it would turn into a seal or some other ocean creature. Sable gave her a look of mild disdain and stretched. A moment later, wings sprang from its shoulders, and the cat's head took on an avian shape. The forepaws became eagle's claws. The hindquarters bunched and sprang into the air, the gold-feathered wings beating and sending a flurry of sand. The sunlight reflected off the gleaming feathers as it flapped away toward the island.

"A griffin. Of course. I should have known Sable would do something like that."

"Why?" Arthur asked, as he began to row in the glassy sea.

"Because... he's summer, as Wrolf was winter. I guess he is fire and air, as Wrolf was earth and water. Elemental, my dear..." She grinned at her own foolishness. Arthur gave her a half-shrug and went on rowing.

Perhaps an hour later, they reached the island, a barren hump of land with the ruins of a monastery sitting on a rise like a set of broken teeth. Sable sat above the shore, placidly grooming his paws. They dragged the boat above the tide line, and Eleanor took her rowan staff but left everything else behind.

Sable led them inland, startling several families of coney and grouse into hysterics by his passage. Eleanor felt uneasy, and the feeling increased as they got farther from the shore. It became a stab of pain behind her eyes, almost like a migraine headache, by the time they came to the ruins of the monastery, so she felt dizzy and weak and slightly nauseous.

The stones of the building had been tossed around, as if a giant had played tiddledywinks there, and in the center of what had been a courtyard there was a gaping hole. Torn and rain-battered, broken-backed volumes of illumination lay around the mouth of the hole, along with several golden sacramental vessels. Whatever had happened here, loot had not been the object. A kind of cold fear began to creep into her, though Eleanor could not name what she was afraid of. The sun shone brightly onto her shoulders, and there seemed nothing extraordinary about the hole in the ground. Except her experience was that nothing good lurked in the dark places of the earth. Eleanor told herself not to be silly.

Sable advanced to the edge of the hole, sniffed delicately, and made a hissing noise that brought his black whiskers bristling forward. Obviously, it didn't smell right to him. Then he placed a dainty, if deadly, paw on the sloping dirt and put his head into the tunnel. A moment later, the panther had vanished from view.

Eleanor and Arthur looked at each other. She

shrugged, and they moved cautiously toward the opening. It was indeed a tunnel, high enough for a panther to walk upright or a man to move bent forward. The earth was hard-packed, as if something heavy had pressed upon it. They crept in, and Eleanor was fairly certain Arthur shared her apprehension.

The tunnel widened and broadened as it spiraled downward, so that they could finally walk erect, though the roof of it almost brushed Arthur's head. Their auras glowed in the darkness, making odd near-shadows against the smooth walls. Eleanor realized the walls were glassy, as if the sand in them had been fused. She wasn't sure what kind of heat that would require, and she decided she didn't want to know.

Finally, they reached a chamber. At first, it seemed fairly empty but for a flaming pit in the center. It was chilly in the room, and the fire seemed to give off no warmth. Beyond the pit, the floor seemed to be a tumble of large rocks.

The "rocks" moved, and a large, triangular head reared up, the red of the flames reflecting off the large, pointed teeth so that they appeared bloodstained. It stared down at them with a kind of contempt. A long tongue flicked out between the jaws.

So, you have come to steal my companion. Eleanor heard the words in her mind, but that voice she would have known anywhere. Doyle! She was not sure what it meant by *companion,* whether the Harp or herself, nor, indeed, if the words were directed at her or at Arthur. The pain in her temples was nearly unbearable. All she was certain of was that somehow the thing staring at her was Doyle. She pressed icy fingertips to her forehead to ease the pain.

She glanced at Arthur. "I want the Harp," he said.

You may want whatever you like, puny princeling, but you cannot have my companion.

The Harp materialized against the chest of the dragon, and Eleanor realized it looked very like the beast Doyle had become at Glastonbury, four legs and a pair of stubby arms. It clutched the instrument with a lover's embrace, scaly fingers stroking the strings. There was no sound at his touch.

"Your companion seems very silent," Arthur replied. "Perhaps she does not favor your caress."

The dragon looked down at the Harp, peered at the woman's head carved at the top of the upright. He clutched it closer, and Eleanor almost gasped, for the gesture seemed to press on her chest. She closed her eyes to get away from her fear that the big hand would snap the fragile thing into bits. Immediately, the pressure on her body vanished, along with the headache.

"Arthur, tell me what you see."

"What? I see a big winged worm, the color of sand, holding a golden woman in his claws. It has fangs, like an adder, and they drip venom."

"One or both of us sees an illusion, for the creature I see is a big, six-limbed dragon holding a Harp. Close your eyes."

"No! I know it is no trick. My eyes do not fool me. I have seen this worm before, in dreams."

This is a swell time to display Plantagenet pigheadedness, she thought. I have to open my eyes. I can't stand around like a lump. And besides, I know it's an illusion. So it won't bother me.

She opened her eyes and saw the Doyle-dragon and found it disturbed her a great deal. It crossed her mind that she might not be seeing any trick, but that Arthur might be the only one who was affected. The beast turned its gaze on her, and she was sure it was her Doyle, so certain that her heart pounded in her chest. It had to be! The goddess had not cheated her. All she had to do was touch him, and he would again be her dear husband.

Eleanor moved around the fire pit toward the beast, discarding her conviction that she was seeing an illusion in her desire to regain her lover. Arthur, on the other side, moved, too, removing the fire sword from its sheath. She stopped in mid-step. What was he doing with Doyle's sword? The blood pounded in her temples as she realized she had given it to him. Shame and guilt seized her. She closed her eyes again.

A smell filled her nose, a fetid, rotten odor, like an open cesspool. She turned her face toward it. It definitely came from the beast. Doyle never stank like that. She wavered again.

Sing for me.

The demand had a physical presence, all the songs she had never sung for Doyle, would never sing for him. Music to soothe the savage beast, clutching a silent harp. Eleanor opened her eyes and saw Arthur, sword upswung, halted in mid-motion, frozen in time. Her throat was parched, and her mind filled with scraps of tunes, including one about a magic dragon named Puff.

"Why should I?"

Perhaps I will trade you my companion for yourself, if you sing well enough.

Eleanor tried to find sufficient self-sacrifice in her to make such a bargain, but the idea of spending the rest of her life in this dank, chill cavern singing to a beast who probably had a tin ear was remarkably unappealing. She felt a laugh begin to bubble up in her belly, a trickle of humor that seemed to turn into a stream and then a torrent as it rose to her throat. It burst past her lips, a hideous, hysterical sound with no pleasure in it.

Arthur started at the noise, moving once again, lowering the sword and peering at her. "Eleanor? Is that you?"

"Why?"

"Because you look like a hag. Your hair is white, and your teeth are all rotten."

Eleanor held out one hand and found a wrinkled claw. The beast had cast some illusion on her, some shadow. It was, she realized, her own weakness and doubt that permitted it to happen. Without Doyle, she in truth felt like a tired old beldam, going through the motions of her quest without any real feeling. It was her duty to finish what she had begun, but she did not really care. Perhaps it would be simpler to trade herself for the Harp and let Arthur finish the job without her. The child stirred.

Anger fountained up within her, red fury. It burned with many colors. There was the rosy glow of her rage at Bridget, the ruddy tone of anger at herself for loving Doyle and yet being the cause of his death, the ember glow of her father's death and the betrayal that it yet seemed, and finally, the blue flame of her own despair and doubt. Her muscles twitched as if she were having a seizure, energy coursing through her body like a flash fire.

Eleanor felt something change within her, some burden burning away with her anger. She grasped the rowan staff tightly in one suddenly sweaty hand and extended the other toward the fire pit. The flames in the pit seemed to bend toward her palm like a hungry tongue, and she could feel the strange chill of its light. It touched her hand, and she was cold. The breath left her lungs, and the blood seemed to still in her veins. Only where her hand held the staff was there any sensation.

She struggled to draw that warmth into her, feeling her body grow colder each moment, her lungs screaming for air that no longer existed, her heart still. The moon-carved head of the staff seemed to glow with flames. They raced down the wood, up Eleanor's arm, across her chest and head, and down the outstretched arm to meet the cold fire of the pit. If she could have screamed she would have, for where hot and cold interfaced there was agony, each progress more painful than the last. Finally, a gout of fire gushed from her palm, reached the other flame, and there was an explosive thump. Sparks shot up into the air.

The flames in the fire pit flickered and bent. Eleanor screamed now, for the pain increased as she forced her fire onto the other, consuming it. There was a guttering sound, and the cold fire died. A moment later, a small blue flame twisted up, then burst into warm, merry orange.

Eleanor felt the pain subside until only her right palm burned where the fire had touched her. She shook all over and leaned against her staff for support. Then, against her will, she turned to look at the dragon again.

Doyle's dark face looked down at her. The dragon's head was gone, replaced by curling black hair and great beard. He smiled, and Eleanor's heart leapt in her chest. The blue eyes twinkled at her, and he reached a clawed hand out to her.

Arthur moved, bringing up the sword. With a great sweep of metal, he severed the head from the neck.

"No!" Eleanor screamed. "Doyle!"

The head arced through the darkness, and no blood

gushed from the neck. A slight trickle of some sluggish green stuff oozed out, and then the dragon seemed to disintegrate. First the scales turned to broken leaves, then the flesh curled away into smoke, and finally the bones became glass, shrinking smaller and smaller.

The Harp rested on the floor of the cave between two quartzy outcroppings. Eleanor peered into the darkness, looking for the head, and saw only a small ball of crystal. She bowed her head, relieved and grieved simultaneously. It had all been an illusion. She felt sick that she had hoped even for a moment that she could somehow get Doyle back.

Arthur bent over and picked up the Harp. His fingers touched the strings, and clear notes rang out. Then he stood up, took Eleanor by the waist, and led her up the tunnel into the golden light of early afternoon.

She walked a few steps from the edge of the hole, then sat down on the stony ground, unable to walk another step. Her right palm burned, and she looked at it curiously. The flesh was black, curled, and blistered, like a frostbitten orange. She felt sick, and she began to shake with chill, her teeth chattering.

Arthur wrapped his cloak around her, then held her against his chest, rocking her gently. He stroked her hair and murmured comforting things she barely heard. The cold burning in her hand seemed to fill the universe, and she wept until her mind darkened and she slipped into a black unconsciousness.

It was night when she opened her eyes again. The stars gleamed above her, and the darkness was full of the distant roar of the sea and a birdsong. The smell of the sea seemed close, near as her hand, which still throbbed.

Eleanor raised her hand and found it wound with wet kelp. She sat up and found herself looking into a small fire. Arthur sat beyond it, his back to her, staring at the star-pocked sky, and Sable crouched like a sphinx between them. They were still in the broken confines of the monastery.

"Arthur."

He turned and hurried to her. "How be thee?"

"Ghastly, if you must know the truth. And hungry."

"You have been three days asleep, if sleep you can

call what you have done, for it was full of screams. How is your hand?"

"Bearable. Where did the seaweed come from?"

"Sable dragged it here, hissing and saying, I believe, very vulgar things in his own tongue. He has no greater affection for water than most of his kind. I found a sack of grain, barley, I think, in the storeroom, and boiled it into gruel. It has no taste at all, except I burnt it a little, but it will nourish you." He filled a wooden bowl and handed it to her with a carved spoon. She looked at the handle, worked into a simple interlace, then fell to. He was correct in saying the gruel was flavorless, but it was hot and made her stomach stop complaining.

Somewhat sated, she held the spoon up. "I guess you have been exploring the ruins."

"Yes, a little. I found some old robes to make a bed for you, though your covering is as fine a vestment as I have ever seen. Fit for a bishop, at least. It is very strange, for some rooms are hacked to pieces while the next is untouched."

Eleanor fingered the heavy silk across her lap. "What . . . happened?"

"You mean, when you got your hand hurt?" She nodded. "It is hard to say. One moment you were an old crone, the next a pillar of fire. Your hair turned red, and there was a flame where your dear face used to be. It was so bright a light, my eyes were dazzled. Then you turned to face the worm and were old again. You screamed at me not to slay it and cried your husband's name. Then there was nothing but the fire glowing in the pit and the Harp lying on the floor of the cave. The worm vanished."

"I thought it was Doyle."

"And I thought it was my dragon-self. In that moment before I cut off its head, it bore my own face."

"You were very brave, then."

"Brave!" he snorted. "I nearly wet my tunic. But you had warned me it was illusion. And yet I am not certain. In that instant, I felt I slew my monster-self."

She leaned back onto the pallet of old robes. They had a faint scent of old sweat and incense clinging to their folds, good, real smells that comforted her. "Is the Harp safe?"

"Yes. I even found an old leather case to cover it. A poor thing for such a splendid instrument. It makes such songs as I have never heard at the slightest touch. They are... like sunlight in summer fields."

Her hand throbbed slightly, and her eyelids drooped. "I must sleep again."

"Yes. And pray, do not beg me to cut off your hand again."

"Did I?"

"Yes, many times."

"Poor Arthur. Arthur Pendragon, brave dragon slayer." Then she was asleep.

XXVIII

They returned to the Scottish mainland as they had come, two days later. The burn on Eleanor's hand had finally ceased to trouble her. The skin had sloughed away, and all that remained was a strange, black, flame-shaped scar running from wrist to the base of the middle finger. Where the creases of her skin crossed it, they seemed to be made of silver—head-, heart-, and life-lines touched by moonlight.

But she was tired, weary with a kind of bone-wracked grief that made her dark in sunlight. She made an effort to shake away the clouds of despair that threatened her, but to little avail. Eleanor wished no better fate than to lie down by the side of the trail and sleep forever. Even the child within her barely stirred her from her lethargy.

Arthur made camp, twisting pine boughs off to make a sweet bed for her, then left her to hunt for food. Sable curled at her feet, and she felt the life in him. It coiled up her body like some serpent, but it did not reach her heart. She dozed lightly in the sunlight, dreaming vague visions of Doyle.

When she awoke, Arthur was fixing dinner, humming to himself. Eleanor sat up, stretched, and gave him a wan smile. They ate in silence. Then he set himself across from her with a very serious face. She cared too much for him to laugh at his solemnity, but it was an effort.

"I have filled the pot with water. Can you conjure us some wine?"

"Yes, but why?"

"Because I think you will need some, and because it is the proper quaff for poets."

"All right." She did what he asked, creating a flinty

white wine with very little nose about it. It was so dry on the palate, the mouth nearly puckered. He tasted it, made a face, then grinned.

"That is a good wine for my song, I think."

"Your song?"

"While you slept, it came to me, back on Iona. I am not any great poet—at least, I have not been before. And perhaps I have just been ensorceled by this precious harp. But it is like a great...river, pressing against some dam in me, this song. It is not unlike to those lays you told me of—I hope."

"Which do you mean?"

"Of Beren One-Hand and Luthien."

Eleanor realized with a somewhat guilty start that she had often whiled away their journey with the tales of Middle Earth, judging them more suited to Arthur's world than the bomb dropping on Hiroshima. But she knew she had done it as well for the similarity between the Shadow over Albion and the terror of Sauron. She had used her own modest store of music, fitting words to familiar tunes as was her wont. Some were folk music, a few classical, for her mother had a great fondness for those. So she had fitted "Galadriel's Lament" to a piece by Fauré, and "Tom Bombadil" to an Irish folk song. Now she could not recall if she had made it clear that these were fiction, not history, and she did not know if it mattered.

Arthur removed the case from the Harp. The long twilight of northern summer was around them, but the instrument gleamed in its own light, as if it had an aura like a living thing. The firelight reflected off the bare breasts of the female figure on the upright, and they seemed to be flesh. He ran long fingers across the strings, and the notes seemed to spring into the air.

He fumbled for the melody a moment, then found it loud and clear. It was a tune she knew but so slightly altered as to seem new, and he played it through in a kind of overture. Then he started to sing.

Eleanor listened in amazement to the first verse, then dipped her cup into the wine pot. Arthur had been correct. It was not to be heard with complete sobriety, for he sang of Doyle the Dark and Eleanor Bright Hope, detailing their adventures as if he had been present, and her love as if he had partaken of it. Tears dripped into the wine at the lonely refrain of her unspoken longing for her beloved, and she was three bowls to the bad before he was done.

The music stilled, and there was a long silence, broken only by Arthur attempting to slake a dry throat with drier wine. Eleanor waited for the slight easing in her chest to pass, but it did not, and she found no words of her own to reply.

Finally she said, "I see it is true that the hands of a king are the hands of the healer. Thank you, Arthur. You have given me a gift more dear than the wealth of the world. I would shower you with all the diamonds of South Africa and still feel in debt."

He blushed and grinned. "Yes, but was it good?"

She laughed until tears streamed again, in that dreadful place between joy and sorrow where she could not say what brought the crying. "I don't know," she said. "I can't even tell you if it is 'art.' I found it wonderful—and terrible—as if you have looked inside me. It comforted me in a way I cannot say. For a moment Doyle was here, present, now—as if he had not died. Ah, Arthur, words are such feeble crafts to bear the weight of feelings. Your Uncle Richard should be green with envy, for he never made a song so splendid."

"I have eased your pain, I am content."

"Nonsense. That kind of mealymouthed garbage may have pleased your confessor, but it does nothing at all for me. Come on, tell the truth. You are pleased as punch, aren't you?"

"I am. I have tried not to be, for it seemed unworthy of me—I mean, I am not as great as the song I created, somehow. Do you think Lennon feels that way when he makes a song?" Arthur had a particular fascination with that music.

"I don't know. But I remember a writer who stayed with us once, a distant cousin of my mother's, and I asked her what it felt like to write a story. And she said that sometimes it was torture—when the words would not come—and sometimes it was ecstasy and always, afterward, she was amazed that she had done it. I was eleven, I think, and very curious, so I sort of spied on her, to see if she was different when she wrote.

And one day I peeked in her room, and she was leaning her head on one hand and writing as fast as her hand could go. She'd stop, cross out, swear, light a cigarette, pace back and forth. Her hair stood out around her face, because she kept running her fingers through it, and her hands were stained with ink and there were smears of ash on her forehead. She looked like a lunatic. Then she put the pen down, stared at the paper a long time, and she sort of sagged, like all her strength was gone. It was as if some fire I could not see had faded and died. She went away soon after that and did not come back, for the book she had written made my parents very angry. I found it in the library and looked at it, but it made little sense to me at the time." Eleanor drew herself out of this reverie with a shake.

"Yes, it was like that," Arthur answered. "I was almost afraid to sing it for you, but I had to."

"I am most glad you did." She rose and circled the fire and slipped into his lap. Nestling her head against his shoulder, she felt herself relax against his warmth. "I think I am very fortunate."

They had followed Sable eastward for three days when they topped a small rise and found a small circle of carts surrounding a camp. They had seen so few people that it seemed a town had sprung up out of nowhere. They crouched down quickly and peered somewhat anxiously at the camp, but it seemed quite ordinary. A fire blazed under a large cauldron; children frolicked in the skirts of women; men carried buckets of water to several shaggy ponies picketed to one side.

Something about it disturbed Eleanor, and for several moments, she could not say what. "Why don't they have any dogs?"

Arthur considered this question thoughtfully. "Perhaps one of the men has taken them off to hunt? But I agree it is a little odd. There are always dogs to give tongue if some stranger approaches in the night."

"I do wish Sable could speak, because I'm not sure whether to avoid them or walk down and say 'Howdy.' The men are not armed, which is also unusual, isn't it? A band of Reavers would make quick work of them, and even those savages we encountered would give them a fight."

"Perhaps they do not foresee any danger."

"Why have they stopped? It is just past midday."

"I think . . . they are waiting for someone who arrives even now."

A second caravan of wains inched into view across the valley. There were waves and shouts, gestures of greeting, and it was clear they were expected. Eleanor and Arthur crouched on the little rise for over an hour, watching more and more wagons arrive, until there were perhaps fifty scattered across the landscape. The major activity seemed to be gathering firewood, which puzzled her until she noticed that most of it was being piled in one place, a sort of bare circle off to one side.

Eleanor studied the circle, which was partially obscured by trees, as best she could and saw several stones around it. "I think they have come here to celebrate the Old Religion, Arthur. Let me see—it must be almost August—or did I lose track of the time when I was sick? Lammas, that's what it is."

"Yes, but do we go down and creep away? The local peasantry back in Brittany had not much care for intruders during their celebrations. In truth, they had a tendency to kill them on the sopt."

"The British are more phlegmatic than that. They give you a cup of tea first." Sable turned his golden gaze on Eleanor, rose, and pointed at the gathering below. "I think he means we go down there, Arthur."

"Yes. And I think it would be good if you put on that gown the Lady Bera gave you and see if we can get some snarls out of your hair."

"Do I look awful?"

"A bit travel-worn." Arthur took out the comb he had carved while she slept in Iona and, after a good deal of tugging, managed to tidy her black hair into a semblance of order. Eleanor pulled off her tired old tunic and took out the gift of the Hag. It fell gracefully to her knees, the soft violet linen falling in perfect gothic folds. She tied her cincture into place and was about ready to close up her pack when some inner voice told her to wear the starry cape as well. So she put it on and wondered why he looked at her sharply.

The panther guided them down into the vale, and they walked toward the encampment. The people turned and gazed at them sullenly until one man came forward. He was perhaps forty, pleasant-looking, and very cheerful. He smiled and smiled, and Eleanor felt a faint mistrust.

"Greetings, strangers. I'll bet you heard there was a fair, and you came to find a bargain or two. We have broideries from the Levant and fine steel blades; spices and silks from the East; Lombardy rice, said to be the best in the world, and wine from Provence." As he babbled, Eleanor decided he was the medieval equivalent of a used-car dealer, and she half expected him to step to one of the carts and say, "Here's a little beauty; formerly belonged to a widow from York who only used it to go to Mass on Sunday." She also realized she had not seen a piece of money since she had arrived in Albion and had not even missed it.

When he paused for breath, she put in, "No, we were not coming to see the fair." No one in their right mind would expect to find any business out in the middle of nowhere, unless there was a decent-sized town hiding in the hills somewhere.

"Where are ye goin', then?"

She suppressed an urge to be rude and tell him it was none of his business, or worse, to claim to be on a walking tour from Oxford, but she resisted. "We have matters to take care of in Lothian."

"Lothian? An ill-omened place. They say the wind howls out on the plain like a dyin' man. Others say it is the devil tryin' to break outta Hell. You don't want to go there."

The man was almost shouting, and she noticed that several women were staring at Arthur and whispering to each other. They looked quite delighted, and one came forward and plucked boldly at his sleeve. Eleanor caught a murmur, garbled words she finally understood as *le roi d'été,* though it was said with a dreadful accent. The Summer King. She did not bother to explain that the real summer king was a golden man, not a redhead, with one missing eye. Instead, she pondered the possibilities—one of which was the murder of the king of summer. A gaggle of women surrounded Arthur and sort of eased him into the enclosure.

Eleanor found the situation unwieldy after so many months of near solitude. There were too many people, many of them children, and she could not guess what the people would do. They seemed to ignore her and concentrate on Arthur, and that gave her the chills. She moved slowly between the carts, listening and watching. There was nothing specific to be afraid of, and she was left with nebulous fears. The people around her seemed to be in constant motion, after the used-cart salesman had left them, and she found herself becoming dazzled by the sun. She wanted to crawl under a cart and take a nice nap.

Closing her eyes, Eleanor thought of the clear waters of Sal's pool and the smell of willow. It clarified her thoughts and woke her up, but the next thing she knew, someone had popped a rather dusty hempen bag over her head, and she jerked aside just quickly enough to deflect a blow from her skull to her right shoulder. The pain ran down her arm to her hand, which held the staff, and she wished to loosen her grasp. She did not, however.

The anger that flowed into her a second later surprised her a little, for it was a hot rage. Unlike the attacks of the little savages, during which she had felt vaguely sorry to have to kill or injure anyone, she wanted to hurt these people. She took a deep breath to try to dampen that feeling.

Eleanor released a gout of flame from her mouth, which turned the bag over her head into ash without any intermediary combustion, though her brows were slightly singed. Then she turned on her somewhat dumbfounded attackers with the fire still flowing from her mouth. They fell back, two nervous-looking men with cudgels, and her breath touched the fabric cover of the wain behind them. As she saw it burst into fire, she wondered what she was doing to her lungs. As they scurried away, she turned to look at the rest of the camp and saw that they were barely aware that anything was amiss. Arthur was nowhere to be seen.

A scream from a woman nearby drew attention to the burning cart and Eleanor's conscious and unfettered state. After a hurried gabble, several men started to rush her, and her rage, starting to cool, flared up again. Bridget's fire leapt from her hands and spumed from her mouth in a way any dragon would have been proud of. The head of the rowan staff was a ball of golden flames. In seconds, there was screaming chaos as women snatched up babies and men ran pell-mell.

Eleanor fought to control herself and her magic, because she knew she could easily, between the dry grass and the fire, cremate Arthur in some wagon without even knowing it. The flames on her arms died slowly, and it cost her some effort.

Someone in the small mob had kept his head, for the panic subsided. Eleanor collected her thoughts, feeling utterly spent, as her friendly used-wagon dealer stepped forward. Now he looked less genial, however, with a smear of ash on his face and a singed tunic hem.

"You leave now, witch. We got the king and we will keep him until it is time." He sounded less certain than his words.

The fragile controls snapped like a stick. Eleanor saw the dark fear lurking in her mind that Arthur would perish as Doyle had, and it kindled her rage again. She struggled feebly inside herself, trying to suppress this convenient opportunity for relieving a host of pent-up demons in favor of rational, civilized behavior. It hardly mattered that her adversaries were neither. But she was too tired and too frustrated to manage the task of reasonability. Or too Irish, she told herself.

Still, it would not hurt to try for a little sweet reason. "The king is not for the likes of you. He has a greater destiny. Return him now, and I will stay my just anger at your miserable presumption." *I sound just like Mother,* she thought. It heartened her that she could take on any aspect of the formidable female, even if it was only to be quelling.

The man shifted uneasily, casting a glance over his own shoulder at the nervous people, then over hers, telling her that someone was sneaking up on her back. She gave a scant thought to Sable, who had faded out of sight as they approached the encampment, and was rewarded by the sound of the panther's cough. It was a noise to make any Kenyan shake, but the would-be

assassin did not know his peril. Aware that her back
was as protected as it could be, she returned her entire
attention to the fellow before her.

"A greater destiny? Fine words, but there 'tisn't any
better end than the one we are going to give that young
man."

It was a philosophical argument she had no energy
for. A movement beyond the milling crowd, toward the
pyre in the stone circle, told her where Arthur was.
"Give him back to me, or you will never light another
fire for the rest of eternity."

"Wha—"

"I serve Bridget, and what she provides she may also
withhold." Eleanor had not the faintest idea if that was
true, but it sounded good.

"You? Hah! She would never pick such a scrawny,
dark handmaiden—and maiden you are not." He pointed
to Eleanor's belly, which while not large yet, was obviously *enceinte* under the close lines of her clothing.

"Return him to me or you are dog meat, old man."

But he was no longer paying attention to her. He
stared past her shoulder, first with an expression of
anticipatory glee, followed by one of horror. The scream
of the man and the scream of the panther mingled in
the sultry air, but she did not turn.

Eleanor saw a sudden flare of fire in the circle, and
she bent her energy to snuffing it out. This was more
difficult, she discovered, than making it. The lifted brand
guttered and smoked, and she began to move toward
it. There were perhaps a hundred yards between her
and the edge of the stone circle, and that seemed about
ninety too many for her magic to be effective. She was
hardly aware that the man attempted to block her way.
She just shoved a flaming hand into his chest and left
him alight, a human torch.

The crowd parted before her, scrambling over one
another in their haste to avoid the figure of living fire
that charged at them. She reached the pyre and halted.

Arthur was trussed up like a fowl and lay faceup on
the stack of wood. He appeared to be asleep, though
whether he was drugged, hit, or already dead, she could
not tell. She paused, letting the Bridget fire die along
her body. Flickers of flame around the circle informed

her that they had only in part succeeded, though it was a sickly fire, anemic somehow, which she knew was almost certainly due to her own efforts. The air seemed terribly poor, and she gasped, feeling dizzy. The fire guttered and smoked, and Eleanor realized in a dazed fashion that she had somehow displaced a portion of the local oxygen supply. It was effective, but it was also awkward, for she could hardly breathe.

I despise stopgap magic, she thought as she released the subtle spell she had cast on the circle and felt sweet air flow into her laboring lungs. The fire, of course, flared into new life, and she heard a weak chant from some onlooker. She leaned upon her staff, defeated.

Eleanor shook herself all over, grasped her staff tightly, and shifted her weight from foot to foot, seeking a solution. She could almost certainly climb the pyre with impunity, but she doubted she could lift Arthur's weight. Some shape-change could enable her to have the needed strength, but it had to be something impervious to fire, and she was too tired to construct something. Without Doyle's assuring presence, she felt doubtful of that particular capacity.

The mob, seeing her hesitate, surged into the circle, and Eleanor went down in a sea of fists and kicks. She coiled fetally to protect the baby and felt tears sliding down her face into the dry dirt under one cheek. A booted foot thudded into the small of her back, and she knew that Death was there, waiting for her. It was so tempting, except that there was no surety that Doyle was on the other side, waiting for her. Or even that there was another side.

Eleanor felt a spatter of spit hit one hand, and with Celtic perversity, she was suddenly damned if she was going to roll over and die for a bunch of half-baked, degenerate pagans. She bunched her body smaller, pulling the starry cloak around her, ignoring the continued blows. Instead, she pressed an ear against the ground, listening for the voice of water. She touched her fingertips to her tears, drew her anger out, and called the storm.

The sonic clap of thunder rumbled over the low hills, and the wind rose from gust to gale in moments, sending sparks flying into the clothing of the mob. They paused in their efforts to kick her to death to slap out flames, and sheet lightning brightened the suddenly darkening day with an actinic glare that penetrated past her sheltering hands and into her closed eyes. A hiss like a nest of serpents whispered through the air, a rush of rain through the low trees and into the circle where it poured down with deluvian energy.

Eleanor crawled to her knees, then used her staff to stand up. The ground turned to mud beneath her boots as the mob milled in confusion. The wind rolled wagons off their wheels as the rain soaked everything. The pyre was a drenched pile of wood with a still-unconscious Arthur atop it. She drew a shaking breath and banished thoughts of pneumonia.

The sturdy ponies picketed throughout the enclosure decided that the lightning was too much for even their phlegmatic dispositions and began to rear and yank at their rope halters, whinnying eerily. One line pulled free, and there was a surge of still-connected horseflesh away from a burst of lightning through a group of people too dazed or too stupid to understand their peril. As they went down under sharp, shaggy hooves, Eleanor was filled with remorse. If only she could have just put out the fire.

The mob was now simply a collection of frightened individuals fleeing the little valley as quickly as possible. The storm rushed southward where it would dampen some farmer's summer crop, hopefully not fatally. Eleanor watched it move, an almost sentient presence, and wondered if it would drench London before it dissipated.

It hit her then that she had burned a man to death, caused a stampede fatal to who knew how many, and had let Sable tear up another man. It sickened her, for these were hardly howling savages. She watched the valley empty as every man fended for himself and felt her body rebel both at her own acts and the beating she had taken. She emptied her stomach onto the sodden ground, then leaned against the staff while dry heaves racked her chest. A feeble, shaking hand tried to soothe the pain in her kidneys where a kick had landed, but the throbbing continued.

Arthur moaned softly. Eleanor steadied herself,

clambered up the dripping wood of the pyre, and cut his bonds. He had a lump on his left temple, and when he opened his blue eyes, the left one was bigger in the pupil than the other. Quelling visions of curing a subdural hematoma by laying on of the hands and her taste for medical dramas, which had educated her into such fears, she helped him down off the wood.

Sable padded up to the circle, lifting each paw disdainfully out of the mire everywhere. "A fine guide you are, sending us into this den of yahoos," she told the panther angrily. Half-conscious, Arthur leaned against her, and he groaned, so she cut short her recrimination, which was as unsatisfactory as most exchanges with felines are, and half-dragged him to the closest deserted wagon.

The previous inhabitants seemed to have made no special fetish of cleanliness, for it smelled of sweat and unwashed blankets, but Eleanor could see no blatant filth, so she settled Arthur down. He closed his eyes almost instantly and was so still she could not tell if it was sleep or coma. Exhausted, she sank down beside him, kneeling on the floor and clutching his hand, until the chill of her garments forced her to move.

Eleanor struggled up and pulled off the violet tunic and the shabby shift under it. As usual, Bridget's cloak was not really wet, and she pulled it about her. Next she rummaged through the contents of a trunk at the foot of the bed, finding little in it but a shift that was dry but no more. Then she forced Arthur to sit up, pulled off his tunic, then removed his boots and hose. She tucked a rough blanket around his naked form and prayed his youth and generally robust constitution would keep him from any permanent harm. The bump on his head worried her.

Food seemed to be the next requirement, and she climbed out of the wagon to see how much damage stampeding horses and frightened people had done. Several wagons were overturned or their coverings ripped away by the wind and their contents tossed everywhere. It appeared quite random, for some were standing between two that were tumbled. One line of ponies was gone, but the other two remained, crunching wet grass with big white teeth. There were several abandoned cooking fires, and a large metal pot hung over one. It seemed to have a stew in it that was not too full of leaves or dust. She skimmed off the top layer, coaxed the fire to life by letting Bridget's fire leap from her hands for several minutes and tried not to remember that that same gesture had incinerated a man only hours before. When it was blazing cheerfully, she left it to find out what had happened to the Harp and the fire sword, as well as the rest of their gear. She thought she had dropped her pack on the ground, but she could not clearly remember where.

Sable moved shadowlike beside her, pausing to sniff at a bundle here and there, until Eleanor found her things shoved under a wagon bed. She bent forward slowly, groaned a little at the pain, and took it up, pressing the damp cloak everything was tied in against her chest. It was comfortingly familiar. When she turned, the blackened skeleton of a man lay on the ground, and she edged away from it.

She returned the pack to the wagon where Arthur lay, and held his pulse a long time. Then she took her willow cup, filled it with water, and pressed it to his lips. She dampened a strip of cloth and pressed it gently against the lump on his forehead, silently cursing her lack of medical knowledge. He seemed to slip into a more natural sleep, and she left him to continue her search.

"Why did you bring us here, Sable?"

The panther regarded her calmly as she paused by the stew pot to give it a stir and a taste. It was a bit greasy but not unpleasant, and she found a bowl and spoon and ate eagerly. Two bowls did a great deal to restore her composure, and she began an orderly examination of the remaining wagons. In the fifth, she found the Harp and sword, plus an embroidered tunic just about the right size for Arthur. It was very fancy, the wrists, hem, and throat exquisitely worked, the white wool as soft as a baby's breath. She tucked this obvious festal garment over one arm and carried the Harp and blade back to their wagon.

Arthur seemed restless, so Eleanor gave him more willow water. Then her tiredness and the food overtook her, and she spread out atop his blanket, pillowed her head on his shoulder, and slipped almost instantly into sleep.

It was dark when she woke up and pulled herself out of the wagon. Eleanor sniffed the air and listened. A cough that was very human sounded somewhere in the darkness. She stood very still and "sensed" around her, until she knew that several men crouched to one side of the stone circle.

Eleanor could hardly blame them for trying to recover their lost chattels, but she doubted somehow that this was their only intent. Again she wondered why the cat had led them here, and something answered, *To celebrate Lammas correctly*. What did *that* mean? That the wagon people were doing it wrong. How? Then she remembered Avebury.

With a swirl of hem and starry cloak, Eleanor grasped her staff and walked purposefully toward the circle. This proved difficult, because her sleep had allowed several muscles to stiffen, and there was debris in the darkness. Only the glow of her aura casting shadows before her kept her from disaster.

She shed the shift, shivering slightly, and stepped inside the circle as the moon edged its white face above the low hills. Walking widdershins inside the stones, she circled three times, listening for their voices. They were fainter than those at Avebury, but she finally paused before a rough-hewn slab almost twice her height. Then she drew several deep breaths, aware that a dozen yards away, an unnumbered group of very frightened, superstitious, and potentially murderous men crouched in indecision. She was pretty certain that the consensus among them was that they should have killed her and that they were puzzled at their failure. She could have slain them where they hid, but she remembered the charred skeleton and could not. The way she chose was not as easy, but it was, she believed, better.

Turning to the pyre, she sent a bolt of Bridget's fire racing along the staff. The wood gave a *whump* and ignited, sending a flame a good ten feet up. A half-dozen terrified faces reflected in the ruddy light. She turned back to the closest stone, hearing its song rise with the fire. It strained upward, as if its rocky spirit yearned for the distant stars. It was a poignant and unbearably lonely song.

She stood as still as the stars themselves, the rising moon silvering the unruly tangle of her dark hair and the fire staining her skin a sort of gold. Eleanor, listening intently, did not notice when the fire began to appear along her limbs, did not realize her face seemed a clear, gold flame. To the anxious onlookers, she was a figure of fire as tall as the stone beside her.

Eleanor lifted a voice rough with unshed tears to answer the chant. At the first phrase, the stone moved. Unlike the Avebury stones, it was not going to be content with being capered around. The grayish rock lumbered forward, and Eleanor heard very faintly the sound of at least one man bolting away in the darkness. She barely cared, swept away in the strange pleasure of the circle's song. It was a dance as old as time, a song much older, and the other stones began to move, too.

The pyre became a pillar of fire, blazing up where no wood remained as the moon sent her benign rays upon them. Eleanor knew nothing, remembered nothing, felt nothing but stone, until many hours later, as the sky lightened, they ceased their dance and the song faded. Dazed and exhausted, she stared around. Yes, the circle was definitely different. Reconfigured.

She stumbled back toward the wagon, knees trembling. Sable sprang down from the back, and she gave the panther a pat on the head. "I guess she can't resist having me tinker with any leaking faucets in the neighborhood, huh?" His rough tongue brushed her hand in answer.

Eleanor climbed into the wagon. Arthur opened his eyes. "Where were you?"

"Out dancing," she replied, and fell asleep.

XXIX

Six days later, they were still in the little valley, for Arthur had a truly magnificent concussion, and Eleanor found herself quite worn out. She had released the shaggy ponies and done a little more scavenging among the wagons, finding decent clothing for both of them, but for the most part she had done little but eat, sleep, and cook. The reason magic had never really caught on, she decided, was it took too much out of you. Merlin probably allowed himself to get trapped by Nimue because he wanted a rest.

She was returning to the camp with a plump grouse, her mind pleasantly filled with nothing but sunlight and a sense of well-being. For the moment, she felt no urgency. Her body was bruised from the beating she had taken, but it was healing, as her spirit was healing from Doyle's death. She still experienced moments of black despair and terrible guilt for simply being alive, but these were rarer, and she felt she might almost dare to be happy. So she hummed and gathered the dew from the grass on her gown's hem.

Eleanor barely felt the garrote before she was choked into unconsciousness. Her only instinct was not to struggle, since a broken neck seemed the only outcome of that. So she went slack and did not feel the leather thongs being tied around wrist and ankle, and was spared the ignominy of knowing she was slung like a bag of grain over a broad shoulder.

Eleanor opened her eyes and looked into Baird's ruined face. A scar bisected it from one brow-tip across the nose to the other cheek. The missing eye socket was a crusted wound. She wanted to look away, but she refused to. It was partially her fault he was in this pitiable condition, since she had not had the mercy to kill him after the rape.

She started to speak and found her mouth gagged. Eleanor tested the restraints on her wrists and ankles and found them very tight. Her sympathy for her brother-in-law faded in a burst of anger. She flexed her fingers and called for fire. None came.

"Surprised?" he asked. She gave a little nod, though she would have preferred to deny him the satisfaction. "Good." Baird reached out a hand and caressed her jaw roughly, running thumb and forefinger down to press against the arteries on either side of the throat. Darkness swirled in her mind until he released his grip. "I have several other surprises for you, dear sister."

Eleanor found she cared not at all for the tone of his voice. The fear crept in, coiling itself around her soul as she realized how helpless she was. Her staff was back in the camp with Arthur, assuming that he was not dead already. She forced a breath into a tense chest and looked around.

They were in a small glade. A large horse was tethered nearby, but there was no evidence of the Fire Sword. If he had killed Arthur, he would have found some way to obtain the weapon, even if he could not wield it. Baird was insane, but he was not stupid. The whole family was a little loony, she decided, and that made her smile under the gag, so the cloth cut into the corners of her mouth.

Baird saw her expression, and he looked a trifle uneasy. He relieved his frustration by dragging her head up and slapping her face several times. Tears started in her eyes, and she felt the soft brush of his lips and beard upon a stinging cheek. The quick contrast in his behavior almost undid her fragile control, and for a second she would have done anything to prevent him hurting her again. That passed, and she forced the tension out of her body.

"If you are wondering why you cannot resist me, why your fire is dead, it is this." His thick finger rubbed on a band around her throat. She had not felt it before, for it was not snug. It was, in fact, almost not there, except it was. "It took me some time to find it, but it makes you mine. And mine you will remain." He brushed her brow gently. "I shall take great pleasure in slitting the throat of that child within you with the very sword I shall get from you. Now, where is it?"

Eleanor sighed. The sword, always the sword. She damned the smith who forged it, the metal it was made of, and Orphiana, for being so arrogant that her lovers must make such things, so careless they were lost, and such a neglectful parent that her sons were single-minded boors at times, all with equal fervor. Though Doyle had, she thought, come to love her in the end, he never would have noticed her existence unless she had the sword. And Baird might lust for her body, though at five months' pregnant, she doubted it, but he lusted for the sword more. Although it put Arthur in peril, she was glad it was no longer hers to bestow. And Arthur, bless him, had not wished to possess the cursed thing at all.

Baird apparently found having a one-sided conversation unsatisfactory, for he loosened the gag. "No biting now."

Eleanor swallowed several times, for her mouth was very dry. Then she flexed her jaw and shoulders to ease her tension. "You really should not gloat, Baird. Your eyes get piggy." A slap stopped any further comments. She tasted blood from a cut lip and decided she was in no position to be sarcastic. She pressed her tongue against the wound and waited.

Baird reached for her face, and she flinched before she realized he only wished to stroke her cheek. He looked puzzled, as if his hand felt nothing. He cupped both breasts in his hands and looked even more confused. Eleanor shared his confusion, until she recalled the sprig of white heather that rested in her belt pouch. It was a charm against unwanted acts of passion, and it seemed to be working like one. Now, if he would just refrain from stripping her, she could at least avoid being raped again.

"I cannot remember why I wanted you so much," he said. Baird picked her up in his arms and set her in his lap, resting her face upon his shoulder so she could only see the unmarred side of his profile. She considered the blood pumping through his jugular and decided she was

not good vampire material. Instead, she rested against
him as if she were friend, not prisoner.

"Perhaps the collar hides my charms," she said slowly.

His hand caressed her throat, the metal across her
skin.

"How does it feel to be powerless?"

Eleanor considered the question seriously. "Okay, I
suppose. Don't forget, I've spent the greater part of my
life that way. Will you tell me about it?"

"What? The collar? Do you think that if you learn
its secret, you can overcome it? Banish the hope. The
goddess has no power over starstones. And Bridget would
not help you in any case. She is too flighty. And careless."

Eleanor did not inform him of her somewhat divided
loyalties as far as deities went. In her own mind, she
did Bridget's bidding, but she served Sal. It was a niggling distinction redolent of theological hairsplitting
and meaningful only to her own interior sense. Dis-
missing this, she concentrated on the term starstone,
assuming he meant it was made of meteoric material.
Why should nonterrestrial iron interfere with magic?
Or was it some other metal? She wished she had paid
better attention in her science classes. She solved the
riddle to her own satisfaction by realizing that in the
end, all goddesses were essentially of the earth, that
their power was connected to the planet itself.

She relaxed against him, wiggling her fingers and
toes and feeling needles. "What's this? Think you can
seduce me?"

"No," she replied. "You are just a more comfortable
resting place than the ground. And I wish we could
have been other than adversaries. I would like to have
liked you, Baird, truly."

He caught her hair and dragged her head back until
the collar pressed her larynx and she could see the ruin
of his beauty. "You didn't try very hard, did you?"

Eleanor gasped in pain and did not answer. Something of her mother's stern pride kept her from plead-
ing. She endured the agony as long as she could, then
whimpered a little. He loosened his grip and pushed
her head back against his shoulder with a kind of rough
tenderness.

She was silent, smelling his body scents awhile, until she said quietly, "It must be terrible to want to beat me and want to love me."

"Terrible? It is nothing to how you will be when I am done with you. I shall use you until you break and come to me like a pig to the trough. Now, where is the sword?"

"I don't know." That was true enough, since she did not know where Arthur was, or where she was if it came to that.

"I think I can improve your memory." Baird untied her feet and hauled her onto them. Then he led her over to the horse, mounted, and took up a length of stout rope. He brought it down against her shoulder and commanded, "Now run!"

Eleanor needed no urging to try to avoid the rope, and she stumbled away. The glade gave way to a rough heath, and as the blood returned to her legs, she ran. The horse was always behind her, the rope striking her back. Sweat stung her eyes, and she fell forward, rolling slightly to the side to protect her child. Having her hands bound behind her did not help her balance on the uneven terrain, and he pulled her up by the hair each time she fell. She lost count of her tumbles, lost any sense of anything but the need to keep moving.

Finally, her legs refused to move under her, and when he released her hair, she sank down on the hummocky ground again. Baird dismounted the horse, and she could feel him standing above her. Eleanor bowed her shoulders and waited for the rope to fall. She drew air into her lungs and felt her muscles tremble with exhaustion. After several minutes, he had not moved, and she risked a quick glance up.

Baird might have been carved from stone, so still was he. The one good eye stared at her emptily, and Eleanor felt a rush of pity. She knew instinctively he would hate that if he knew, and she suppressed it. Besides, it was not her fault he wanted what was not his to have. And she wondered if she had given the fire sword to Arthur just to spite Baird's ambition. Did she hate him that much? With a pang, Eleanor realized she had never even noticed Baird enough to care sufficiently to hate him. One look at Doyle's gloomy features and Baird had simply ceased to exist. And that was just not fair.

With a grunt, he bent forward and picked her up in his arms. "You are stronger than I thought."

She gave a shaky laugh, one a breath from tears. "I am stronger than I thought, too."

Baird kissed her, gently at first, then more deeply. She tasted his sweetness and wished the cosmos more fair. But there was only room inside her to love Doyle, with table scraps for Arthur, and nothing at all for this ruined, golden demigod. She shuddered, suddenly hating herself.

He took her shaking as revulsion. "Does my touch sicken you?"

"No!"

"I will choke the truth from you if I must."

"Baird, I am sick of myself." The hand closing around her throat stopped. He considered deeply, and she saw his good eye twitch suddenly.

"You gave the sword to that sniveling cockerel! You whore!" He flung Eleanor facedown on the turf. "Why?"

"Because he did not want it. He wanted me—just me! Because I was lonely, but mostly because he didn't see me as a way to that damn sword!"

Baird roared his rage, "I will kill him! I shall flay the skin off his bones! The sword is mine; you are mine!" For a moment, she was afraid he would turn into a beast shape and tear her limb from limb. The rope fell across her back several times, then stopped. He rolled her onto her back and crouched over her. "You never gave me a chance."

Eleanor felt the bitterness in his voice and found an echo within herself. *There are no chances; just moments in between disasters. I don't have any moments in me for him. Goddess, why is compassion such an empty feeling?* Tears filled her eyes. "I have no song to give you."

For a second, they shared the empty space that yawned between them. Then there was a great rush of wings, and Baird was lost in a flurry of golden griffin feathers. He fell backward in surprise, hit his head, and stayed down. The horse reared in fright, and the griffin sank long talons and claws into the proud throat. The horse screamed as blood fountained up. It sagged to its knees as the beast turned to Eleanor. With a brazen squawk, it grasped her shoulders in its eagle claws and leapt into the air. She gasped in pain, but he bore her higher and higher, so she held herself very still. As they flew away, she looked down at the dying horse and the still figure of the man. She saw his arm move and felt the relief of knowing he was not dead. Then she let herself go into the care of whatever the fates had prepared for her.

Eleanor lay in the wagon, Sable back in panther form, stretched across the bed at her feet. Arthur whistled shrilly as he brought water or gathered firewood, a cheerful sound that contrasted irritatingly with her black mood. Outside the wagon she could see the heartless sunshine, and it annoyed her. It ought to be raining, at least, to match her mood.

Eleanor turned her head away from the offending sunlight and winced. Where the eagle claws of the griffin had gripped her through her clothing, she had two painful wounds, small but very real. Her back was bruised badly from Baird's rope, though the skin was not broken. Her legs were cut from numerous falls, and she was one large ache all over.

For three days she had lain in the wagon, barely responding to Arthur's questions from her bruised lips, and sunk in gloom. She had a kind of cold rage churning within her, most of it directed at herself with a goodly portion left over for Bridget. She knew it was irrational, for had she had the foresight to know that the moment she grasped the sword in the priory she would set in motion a series of events with terrible consequences, she would still have taken the sword. The Fates had a nasty sense of humor.

Eleanor forced herself up on one elbow, leaned over the edge of the narrow bed, and picked up the strange collar that Baird had used to neutralize her. It was heavy, dense metal, a shiny silver color, incised with some reptilian creature, neither serpent nor dragon. She rubbed a finger over the design, and it was warm, though the metal of the collar itself was cool. Something in her wished to put it on again, so she could do no more harm.

She dropped it with a thunk, glanced at the golden-eyed cat at her feet, and lay back down again. It was too late to stop. Doyle was dead, Baird was crippled, and there was still a Shadow over Albion. She patted her growing belly and tried to be optimistic. Perhaps all the tragedies were behind her. She wasn't quite sanguine in that hope, and hope, she remembered, can break the heart. She made a wry face at this unintentional pun on her last name, wriggled sore toes against the panther's sleek belly, and snuggled back down. Things were bound to look better in the morning.

XXX

Eleanor always remembered the next few weeks as nearly idyllic. They had taken the sturdiest wagon of those undamaged by the storm, caught four of the ponies still wandering in the valley, loaded up anything that seemed useful, and set off to the east. It was more comfortable than walking, though they rarely managed more than ten miles in a day, and they often went on long detours to find fording places across Scotland's numerous rivers. She found her spirits restored as her body healed and regaled her companion with occasional tales of pioneers crossing the Great American Desert in similar conveyances.

August passed into late September, the days growing shorter and the temperature getting brisker. Only the insistent presence of the panther reminded her they were not on a prolonged camping trip. Sometimes at night she toyed with the collar, remembering her powerlessness, and wondered what had become of Baird. That was not over.

One day in late September, the terrain changed subtly. The heather grew in twisted shapes and was a sickly gray. The birdsong that had accompanied them across the land faded into eerie silence. It was a perfect setting for the opening of *Macbeth*, a notion Eleanor did not find particularly delightful.

They crawled across the uneasy landscape for three days, both of them edgy in the oppressive silence. Eleanor tried singing but found her choices running to the gloomier and more tragic pieces in her repertoire, so she stopped. Arthur was very quiet, his eyes constantly scanning the horizon for some invisible threat.

The fourth afternoon, Eleanor heard a sound that chilled her blood. It was a brazen horn, distant but not distant enough. There were Reavers somewhere on the plain. And there was a second noise, a kind of shrill whistle that frayed the nerves. It grew louder, a constant whining shriek, as if the wind had found a voice.

A modest tor shoved its shoulders out of the heath. The dissonant piping swirled out from it, accompanied by a biting wind that seemed to come from all directions. They drew the wagon to a halt, since the ground sloped upward rather steeply.

"Let's camp here," Eleanor suggested.

Sable growled.

"I do not think camping is what he has in mind," Arthur answered.

She regarded the panther unfavorably. "Pushy beast. We'd better go on foot. That noise is going to give me a headache. I never thought I'd hear anything that sounded like a bagpipe being tortured by the Inquisition. It is worse than my cousin Colin, who used to get drunk and play his bagpipes on the roof. He swore it kept the banshees away." Then she wished she had not mentioned banshees, for they wailed to announce the death of royalty. Eleanor decided, not for the first time, that there was such a thing as being too Irish.

They climbed out of the wagon, Eleanor taking her staff. Arthur put on the sword, his face grim. "Eleanor, I do not like this."

"What troubles you?"

"My dragon...is very restless here."

She wanted to chide him for being afraid of himself, but since she shared that fear, she did not. "I am sure it has reason. Those pipes would disturb a saint."

"No. It is more than that. I am going to do something terrible."

Eleanor studied him in the fading light and found him subtly altered. His aura seemed charged with a new energy, and his eyes gleamed with a light she had seen in Doyle's before Glastonbury. She could not decide if he was fey or berserk, or if there was much to choose between them. Nor could she find any way to reassure him, for she remembered now her fleeting vision of

Arthur in battle with some unseen adversary and the unharmonious scream of the pipes behind him.

"Terrible?" She gave a laugh that had no merriment. "Shall we abandon the quest, then? I will not force you to continue. This is your choice. I am living with the consequences of mine."

He paused, then rested his hand on the hilt of the sword. "It speaks to me, you know. It whispers of bright blood and a brighter destiny. Did it ever speak to you?"

"No." She did not say that this revelation was both disturbing and unsurprising. "Do you believe what it says?"

"I want to." He drew a deep breath. "Let us go."

They moved behind the panther, through the unhealthy vegetation, the twisted branches snatching at ankles and hems. The twilight faded slowly as they climbed toward the screaming pipes, the wind spitting particles of dust into eyes and skin. Both of them moved stealthily, peering at shadows with tearing eyes, so it was a march of furtive movements and abrupt halts.

A hunting horn clamored across the howl of wind and pipes, and a pack of Reavers seemed to leap out of the ground on all sides of them. A boar-man snorted and charged the woman, and Eleanor sent a fireball into its slavering maw. The flame flared along the tongue, and a second later, the skull exploded in a mass of sparks and flesh. The falling fire touched a bear-creature and started the dry heather burning. The wind fanned the flames as Arthur beheaded another bear.

Some of the Reavers hesitated, for the fire leapt into their fur with the aid of the wind. A pair of boars, braver or stupider than the rest, charged Arthur while a bear lumbered toward Eleanor, curved claws slicing the air. She did not dare use her power to cast more fire, for fear the wind would bring it back into her face, so she shoved her staff into the oncoming form. A huge paw pushed at the staff. Then the beast shuddered, stiffened, and fell backward. The rest of the pack seemed to lose their enthusiasm and began to depart as best they could through the spreading fire.

Eleanor caught her breath against the buffeting wind and saw Baird striding toward her across the flames. He seemed enormous, the fire reflecting in his golden hair and beard. Then she saw the ugly scars below his missing eye where the griffin's eagle claws had raked the flesh, and she wondered for a moment how much more she would mar him before the end.

Arthur turned and saw him, and the light in his eyes darkened. Baird smiled, twisting the scarred portion of his face into a hideous mass, and drew something from a shabby sheath at his side. It was a sword, the blade as black as pitch. It did not reflect at all in the firelight. Baird's sword was shorter by several inches than Arthur's, but his greater height and arm length evened out the disadvantage.

"I have come for what is mine, cur. The woman and the sword."

"Eleanor belongs to herself," Arthur replied, eyeing his adversary, a man he had not killed in a stream months before, now returned larger and somehow monstrous.

She considered this liberated and unloverlike statement with half her mind as she tried to decide how to put out the fire with the balance. The idea of being cooked alive was not appealing, and she regretted that her immediate response to danger was to incinerate everything in sight. What would Doyle have expected her to do? As she thought this, the low-comedy aspect of the two males squaring off before her struck her. They were, in one sense, fighting over her, and she was not only not complimented, she was also annoyed. Neither of them was the man she wanted, and she did not deceive herself that their motives were either honorable or noble. An excess of male hormones seemed a stupid reason to kill a man.

Then the very real seriousness of the situation struck her. Short of teleporting one of them to the dark side of the moon, there was no way to stop the confrontation. One of them would die. And it would be her fault, just like Doyle's death. She forced her attention back to the fire, for it presented a greater danger at the moment than two men shouting insults at each other. In that instant, she "saw" Arthur again, outlined only by his aura against the darkness, swinging the bright sword under the black sky while the pipes screamed. There was no fire in her vision.

Eleanor was torn with indecision. Put the fire out? Let it burn? As the two men circled each other warily, she decided that the fire had to go. With a clumsy gesture of her staff, she pointed at the slope of the tor, and a few cubic feet of earth tumbled outward. It was an unwieldy mass to manage in the ripping winds, but she got it to crash down on a patch of heather burning nearby. Twice more she tore out parts of the ancient hill, until she had a modest firebreak.

Perhaps a minute had passed and Eleanor stopped, for she lacked the strength to continue flinging dirt around indefinitely, and she looked at Baird and Arthur. The exchange of insults was over, and the ritual sizing-up about finished. Baird had the disadvantage of only one eye, and Arthur of being the smaller, but they were probably well matched in skill and stupidity. All she knew was she wanted it to stop.

The heroines of romantic novels, she knew, would have thrust themselves in between the combatants and almost certainly gotten unkind cuts from both sides. So she screamed at them instead. "Will you two stop being a couple of pricks!" She was surprised at her own vulgarity, but the wind tore the words away, and neither of them acknowledged her existence.

Frantic now, Eleanor tried to think of something useful to do, but there was nothing. The swords came up and crashed together, though there was no sound. The wind shifted suddenly, sending dirt and ash into Arthur's eyes and fanning the fire behind him. Baird gave a great shout, leapt forward, and found his dark blade slicing empty air. Arthur had sprung sideways, toward Baird's blind side, and he wiped his own eyes and kept moving.

Baird swung around with his blade raised again, and Arthur sent the edge of his sword deep into the muscles under the right arm. Then he leapt aside again as Baird brought his sword down where Arthur had been a moment before. Arthur struck at the exposed thigh, and blood spurted into the wind as he pulled away. Baird bellowed above the gale and charged again. The wounded leg gave way and he stumbled. The fire sword came down on his right forearm, severing the hand away completely.

The pipes on the tor gave a mind-searing wail as the golden man fell to earth. Arthur lifted the sword as if he would behead his foe. Then the energy seemed to leave him, and he let the sword hang from limp hands.

Eleanor was frozen for a second. Then she knelt beside Baird and took his head into her lap, smoothing dirt and smuts off the scarred skin and out of the sun-colored hair. Hot tears welled from her eyes and fell onto his face. "Baird, I did not wish you dead."

"Mother told me not to come. I did not listen. Tears for me? She'll give me no peace. She never does. Why couldn't you have loved me?"

"I don't know, Baird, I don't know."

He caught her hand in his remaining one. "How will you remember me?"

"Golden and whole and...laughing."

"Then kiss me once before my mother takes me home."

Eleanor bent forward and kissed his mouth, feeling the soft, golden beard under her lips. She felt the shudder as the life passed from his body and caught the trembling of the earth under her knees as the earth serpent came to claim her child. Putting his head gently off her lap, she crab-walked away slightly as the ground began to open. Baird slid away, and then there was nothing but the wind, the fire, and the maddening scream of the pipes on the tor.

Eleanor and Arthur struggled up the tor, slammed by fiercer winds with each step. They could not speak, and it often felt as if they took two steps back for every one forward, so that they were both gasping and exhausted when they achieved the summit. The near-dark moon cast slivers of silver onto the rocky earth.

A frame of wood stood on the top and, hanging from it, an object no bigger than two hand-widths held up with leather thongs. It looked like a miniature raft, and Eleanor was astounded at how much noise it made. It took her a moment to realize it was a pan pipe, or syrinx, not the bagpipe she had expected.

The sounds it made made bones ache, the skin crawl, and the eyes tear. She wanted to run away down the tor and into the steady beat of the flames. Arthur, beside her, was shaking, and his brow gleamed with sweat. He forced a hand up and reached forward. The wind shrieked; and the pipes wailed more loudly, though Eleanor would have thought that impossible. He snatched his hand back as if burned, and screamed.

Eleanor probed with her staff and found a sort of force field. It sparked where she touched it. She moved the staff around, seeking the perimeters. Arthur stopped screaming and looked at his hand in the faint moonlight. It was black as ash. He flexed his fingers cautiously.

Eleanor had discovered that the resistance to her probing did not extend beyond the middle of the leather thongs holding the pipes aloft. She started to move toward the nearer one and discovered her legs were frozen in place. That was too much. She panicked, clawing at herself and whimpering.

Arthur lunged at her, grabbed her shoulders, shook her, and finally struck her. In the pale light, he seemed to be Baird, reborn somehow, and she fought him. He seemed then to be a skeleton, a bunch of burned bones, and she struggled to get away from his touch. A clenched fist moved toward her face in slow motion, and she felt its impact on her jaw. Everything went a murky gray before her eyes.

When her vision had cleared, she found herself looking up from the hard ground. Arthur stood above her with the sword over his head, straining every muscle so the cords stood out in his neck. He was on the balls of his feet, and she flung an arm across her face to resist the blow she was sure would come. The wind snatched the cry away from dry lips.

Inch by inch, he lifted the sword. He leaned his torso forward slightly from the hips and stretched so the muscles knotted along his bare forearms. The tip of the sword wavered as he grunted and strained. Finally, it rested on one leather thong. He gave another grunt and forced his weight downward. The thong snapped, and the sword, so slow before, crashed to earth a few inches from her head.

The pipes and the wind redoubled their fury, so that Eleanor could do nothing but cover her ears and cower. Then one of the wooden uprights of the frame snapped like a matchstick, pulling the thong on it apart, and the pipe arced on the remaining tie, swinging down with a dying squawk, like the dissonant moan of drones when putting a bagpipe down. The wind faded, and Arthur tumbled onto his backside.

He sat there, his legs splayed out like a child's, the fire sword on the ground between them. He forced himself onto his knees and crawled over to where the pipe hung murmuring to itself in odd harmonies that made the skin shiver. Arthur yanked it free with a vicious gesture, then wrapped it in his tunic.

The silence was incredible. Both of them sat breathless, appreciating the absence of sound as the desert dweller looks at the oasis. After a time, they both rose and started down the slope, still wordless. The fire was burning itself out as they picked their way out onto the heath.

The wagon stood where they had left it, the placid ponies either too stupid or too phlegmatic to dash away from the excitement. But the fire had burned in a different direction. They tumbled onto the back of it.

Eleanor rubbed her jaw tenderly. "You have a mean right cross, Arthur."

He extended his arms. "And you have sharp nails."

She looked down at his hand, still black, and touched the skin tentatively. It felt fine, warm and pliant. "Does it hurt?"

"No. It is sort of cold, but nothing more than that. I wonder what happened to Sable? I saw him in griffin-shape when those beasts attacked, but he seemed to vanish...along with Baird."

Eleanor flogged her weary brain into motion. "You said you had a premonition you would do something terrible, and I think you did. You killed summer, Arthur—sort of. But if that is true, then Sable stopped, too, because he was part of that time. I am too tired to try to explain it tonight. But I think we let the...cat out of the bag." She gave a half-chuckle, snuggled down in her filthy, torn clothing, and was asleep almost immediately.

Arthur sighed, pulled off her boots, and drew the covers up around her. He stepped down out of the wagon, picketed the horses, watering them and feeding them a handful of grain. Then he washed the sweat off his face and upper body, turning the dark hand back and forth in the light of the sickly moon. The air still smelled of the fire, but it carried a damp chill on it, too, which made him rub himself dry quickly and pull on his other tunic.

He got back into the cramped confines of the wagon and looked down at the sleeping woman. Her spirit's light shone in the darkness, so he could trace the tracks of tears across the dirty face, the tiny upright lines between her eyebrows and the slight creases at the ends of her mouth. She showed the strain of the quest only in these small ways, but Arthur realized as he gazed at her tenderly that she was doing it all with no thought of reward. She just went on. No wonder she shone brighter than anyone he had ever seen. No wonder she nearly blinded the eye.

Arthur tugged off his boots, lowered himself carefully onto the narrow bed, and slid under the covers. Eleanor murmured in her sleep, stroked his cheek with her hand, then turned on her side with her back against his chest. He held her, his hand resting on the curving belly, feeling the fishy movements of the unborn child, and wished that he could say to her the words that filled his heart. But he would not. He had but the briefest memory of the great, dark man who had died releasing him, but it was enough to know that no living person could compete with her reminiscence. But he was determined that if he survived to claim his throne, she would never again suffer more discomfort than having to decide whether she wanted to wear a green gown or a blue one. With that pleasant thought, he drifted into sleep.

XXXI

It was perceptibly colder the next morning, as if the autumn had vanished in the night. They woke stiff and chilled, except where their bodies pressed together, and went about their morning tasks briskly. Eleanor got a voluminous gown out of the chest scavenged from the encampment and belted it around her. It was as drab as the day, its original color faded to a grayish brown, but it was wool, and that was all she cared about.

There was no sign of the panther. She mulled that over as she bent her hands over their small campfire. She wondered if Wrolf would return to her, for winter was his time, but she was not sure he could. She worried, too, over the consequences of killing Baird out of season, but it was too late to do anything about it. They smothered the fire, hitched up the ponies, and turned their faces southward.

It seemed to Eleanor that the following weeks were an endless repetition of the same day over and over again. The wind blew from their backs, icy and knifing through cloaks and tunics, and the rain fell with dreary consistency. Their boots were permanently damp and caked with mud. They passed Hadrian's Wall where she had slumbered a week, exploring the infinite in a chilly mist, and continued onward.

The mild barrier of the Cheviot Hills was broached, and they were in Albion, though it was not too different from the land they had just left. There were more people, a few hamlets, and then the somber bulk of Norman keeps on rises of land. Flocks of sheep dotted hillsides, and a few fields lay fallow but clearly bearing the mark of human hands by the hedgerows that delineated them.

Passing through the small villages was nerve-racking to Eleanor, for she had grown unaccustomed to the yap of dogs, the lisping accents of toddlers, and the harsh voices of adults. Their thick dialect was almost unintelligible, and they were a dour, suspicious kind of folk, eyeing the worn wagon and the shaggy ponies cautiously. But they did not seem hostile, just wary, and she saw few who were touched by the Shadow, as if the mixture of native and Viking blood was more resistant to the pestilence than their southern relatives. Still, she preferred to keep to the inside of the wagon when they passed a town.

They entered the North Riding of Yorkshire in a fog of wet snow, and she knew it though no signpost marked the arbitrary line between it and Durham. But a sense of uneasiness she carried in the weeks since the Tor faded suddenly, as if she sensed the presence of her mother's people, her own tribe. On their northern journey, she and Doyle had passed around the county, traveling, by her guess, through Lancashire and Cambria.

The town of Richmond seemed like a metropolis after months in the wild, though it was little more than a small keep and perhaps a hundred dwellings nestled on a hill. A tall, fair man studied Arthur for a long minute, then turned and strode briskly away toward the castle.

A few minutes later he returned with several leather-armored men-at-arms who broke into two ranks flanking the wagon. The fair man caught the ponies' harness, and Arthur clucked the steeds to a halt. The man smiled and nodded. The wind gusted and sent a swirl of mushy snowflakes into the grinning face. He just laughed and swiped at the moisture.

"My lord, my mother would be most pleased if you would pass the night with us." He waved a slender hand toward the castle.

Arthur was unsure how to treat this friendly reception. "Milady," he hissed.

Eleanor had been resting in the back, for she found herself tired a great deal now. She sat up and came to the front of the wagon, took in the smiling man and the armed escort in a quiet glance, and nodded graciously. "If I did not know better, I would say we were expected," she said quietly.

The fair man apparently possessed very acute hearing. "You are, my lady, you are."

Since he seemed disinclined to offer further explanation, they did not ask for any but followed him up the rather windy street to the thick walls of the keep and through them. Arthur pulled the wagon to a halt inside the courtyard, leapt down, and turned to assist Eleanor. She felt awkward under the weight of the child, shabby, worn, and terribly tired. Her right hand on the shaft of her staff trembled a little. Arthur supported her against his chest for a moment while the fair man watched curiously.

Eleanor realized no names had been exchanged, and she wondered why. Then a groom appeared to draw the wagon off to the stables, and she had a mild panic for its contents. Arthur smiled, patted her arm, and said, "Do not worry, milady, I will see your good gown gets to you. Now, go inside out of the cold." With those words, he turned to follow the wagon, and she gave a silent thank-you to the kindly deities who had endowed him with a quick mind as well as a strong body.

The fair man offered his arm, so Eleanor took it, the cobblestones being somewhat treacherous under her worn boots. She felt the strong muscles under her fingertips and wondered what the devil was going on. Who was he, and why were they expected? Then, more important, could she get a hot bath? She chuckled to herself at the odd order of her priorities and felt almost lighthearted for the first time in weeks. Or was it months?

The hall was long and dark-beamed with two huge fires roaring on each sidewall. It smelled of straw and cooked meat and babies and dogs, a combination she would have found distasteful a year earlier but which simply had a homey feel to it now. Several toddlers were rolling a ball back and forth between their fat, outstretched legs, supervised by a plump servant holding a sleeping infant. A puppy of the mongrel kind kept darting into the circle to grab the ball, sending the children into giggles.

A tall, grave-looking woman rose from a high-backed chair and moved toward Eleanor. The sweep of her high brow beneath still-golden hair and the long, narrow

nose marked her as the mother of Eleanor's escort, so
she bobbled as much curtsy as tired limbs and a large
belly would permit. A slight smile touched the rather
stern mouth.

"Come sit by the fire, child. You look half-frozen."
She had a low voice, almost a tenor. "Winter has come
early and fierce as a wolf this year."

Wolf winter, Eleanor thought, and without a master,
then shook her head to clear away the cobwebs of uneasiness that brought. Wrolf and the Fenris wolf and Rag-
narok all danced in her mind. "Thank you, milady. I
think I have forgotten what it feels like to be warm."

"You will sit for a while, and then you shall have a
hot bath. My servants are warming the bathing chamber."

"I cannot think of anything I would enjoy more,"
Eleanor replied sincerely. How long had it been? She
thought of Sal's well and felt the presence of the Lady
of Willows within her, as reassuring as a mother's hand
soothing her brow. In that instant, she also knew her
hostess's name, and that of the handsome son. Sal's
whisper withdrew, and she sat down, wondering what
to do with the information. A name had a curious power
of its own, and she was reluctant to abuse it.

A toddler, bolder and more curious than the rest, got
up from the circle and staggered over to her, still being
in that stage where walking is a matter of falling forward. He regarded her with wide blue eyes, and im-
pulsively Eleanor scooped him up and balanced him on
one knee. He patted her belly with a chubby hand, and
the baby moved under his touch, so he crowed with
delight. "Fish," he lisped, patting again. She considered
her unborn child's aquatic adventures, almost from the
moment of his conception back in Ireland, and found
no argument with the youngster's opinion.

Arthur, accompanied by two manservants bearing
the wagon's worn chest between them, entered the hall,
snowflakes melting in his russet hair and beard. The
wind was rising outside the thick walls of the keep, and
she was glad to be out of the weather. He bowed to the
lady, the length of the fire sword banging his leg and
the firelight playing on the jeweled hilt. Then he un-
clasped his tatty cloak and swept it off as if it were the

finest silk, looking every inch a kingly man. He strode over to Eleanor, eyes watchful, and stretched his hands to the fire.

Eleanor realized that the lady and her son were staring at the oddly blackened flesh of Arthur's left hand, and stirred nervously. It was like the dark flame on her right palm, a token of an experience that would not be denied, but she wished his was less visible. The son took a deep breath and seemed to relax, which she found strange. Arthur was oblivious to their interest.

"Some wine for our guests," the lady ordered a servant, and a moment later they were served a warm, mulled drink, redolent of spices and burned sugar. Eleanor sipped hers and found it tastier than her own attempt, months before.

But the silence of the adults was maddening over the cheerful babble of the children. The one on Eleanor's knee demanded a sip, which she gave him. He then snuggled into the curve of her arm, around her stomach, and closed his eyes. "This is delicious...Lady Elfrida."

The woman started, then broke into a broad smile that made her face look very young. "You are she." There was great relief in her cryptic reply.

"I told you it had to be them, Mother. How many ...black-handed men do you think there are?"

"Is that what you were looking for, Leofric?" Eleanor asked.

He gave her a wide grin, very like his mother's, and nodded. "A messenger came to Richmond from the Marshal, oh, five weeks ago. He said we should be on the lookout for a red-haired man with one black hand and a woman with hair like night. They would, he said, know us without introduction. Two days ago, a rider came from Darlington saying such a pair had been seen, but my mother was not convinced. She rarely is."

Eleanor remembered her conversation with Brother Ambrosius at the priory and his mention of Guillaume the Strong, defender of the realm, and wondered how the Marshall had known of their coming. "I see. Did he say how he knew?"

"The Virgin came to him in a dream."

Eleanor sipped her wine and speculated on whether it was fair Bridget or dark Sal who had disturbed the

Marshall's rest. The child rested heavily against her
body and snored lightly. "I am glad he ensured our
welcome."

"He travels north to meet you," Leofric added. "So
you will rest here until he arrives." It was not a request.

Eleanor turned to Arthur, who was masking his confusion with wine and silence. "You will be glad to see
your childhood friend, the son of your master, will you
not?"

Arthur considered this tidbit of information. "I will,
indeed. And I hope he does not hurry too much, for I
am glad to be warm and dry again."

They finished their wine, and Lady Elfrida bustled
them off, Eleanor to the bath chamber under the care
of a sour-faced servant who obviously viewed the steaming vat of water with suspicion. Eleanor soaked the ache
out of her bones, dried herself on a rough towel, and
put on the cleanest shift she had, plus the violet gown
that had been the gift of Bera the Hag, belting it above
the swell of her belly. The servant sniffed at her, then
grudgingly produced warm hose and a pair of leather
shoes, a little large in the toe, which Eleanor donned
with pleasure. Then she suffered the woman to yank
the snarls out of her hair, braid it, and coil it on the
back of her head.

A trestle table had been erected in the great hall,
draped with a linen tablecloth and set with metal
trenchers and real glass goblets. Eleanor knew this was
meant as a great honor and wondered only if it was
meant for her or Arthur. Leofric took the head of the
board with his mother to the left, and Arthur and
Eleanor to the right, while an assortment of family and
chivalry, men-at-arms and wives, filled out the rest. A
merry, red-cheeked girl of twelve turned out to be Leofric's sister Hilde, while a wizened beldam who gummed
her well-hung mutton with the concentration of one
who values life's flavors because there were few left,
was his father's mother.

Sharing a plate with Arthur, Eleanor worked her
way through a hearty array of meat, fowl, and fish
dishes, all a little sweet and spicier than she liked,
while a sort of desultory conversation whirled about
her. There was the ever popular topic, the weather,

which branched out into whether the roof on the Three
Acre Barn needed repair, was there enough fodder,
would wolves come down from the hills, and other matters of intense interest to the agriculturist. Neither of
them were addressed directly except to ask if they
wanted more food. It was a feast of welcome but a tentative welcome, and Eleanor noticed more than one curious look at Arthur's hand. Obviously, the Marshall's
message had been somewhat ambiguous.

Replete with more food than she had consumed in
weeks, Eleanor enjoyed the warmth and the commonplace chatter of the people around her. They were a
healthy, hearty lot; good, stout Yorkshiremen to whom
the Shadow was a distant rumor. Leofric looked as if
he would like to ask some questions, but Lady Elfrida's
rather stern countenance prevented that. She sipped
hard cider and listened.

Finally, Leofric pushed his tall chair back from the
table a little and stretched out his lanky frame. "My
lord," he addressed Arthur, "my servant tells me you
have a harp. Could you be persuaded to play us some
music? Our harper died last winter, and we have missed
him."

Before Arthur could reply, a groom appeared with
the shabby, leather-covered instrument. He exchanged
a quick glance with her, and Eleanor shrugged slightly.
"I think we have to play it by ear," she murmured, and
he gave her a broad grin, then began to unlace the
bindings. A rush of servants cleared the board in record
time, then hauled the table off its supports, leaving the
diners holding goblets, mostly wooden or metal, for the
fragile glass ones were only for the lord and his guests.
The old grandmother complained at this for a moment,
then went silent as Arthur removed the Harp. A slight,
rustling sigh went around the hall, and the fireplaces
seemed to burn more brightly.

Arthur seemed a little unnerved by the intent regard
of his audience, but he was too much a Plantagenet to
let it show for more than a second. He touched the
strings lightly, twisted a peg here and there, though
Eleanor could detect no need for tuning, then ran his
fingers up the scale.

An uneasy melody hummed on the strings, and

Eleanor sipped from her cup to cover her confusion. It was very like the music he had written about Doyle but subtly altered, so that the nerves were jangled. Then it changed again, going from the minor to the major key, speaking of sunlight and summer. Arthur's voice rose, and Baird was present, two-eyed and golden, though Arthur had never seen him like that. The words floated out onto a bittersweet lay of rivalry and defeat. As she listened, Eleanor felt a pain she had been unaware of ease and reflected that Arthur could have chosen no more perfect entertainment for these descendants of the fierce Norsemen. Doyle and his brother were the stuff of scaldic song, and any other form was too fragile to support the weight of their lives. He must have made the verses as he sat on the wagon's hard seat, and she wondered what kind of ruler he would make who could command such music.

A brittle silence greeted Baird's passing, and Eleanor looked around to see several sleeves being used for hankies. Leofric grunted, cleared his throat, and sipped some wine with a hand that shivered slightly, so droplets of wine dripped on his tunic. "That will teach me to be careful what I ask for. Strange. The man you sang of passed through here, I believe, just before midsummer. Some said he was Thor, though all know the old gods died with the birth of the Savior." His voice carried little conviction on this theological matter. And the expressions on the faces of some of the men-at-arms showed they had not forgotten their berserker patron.

"It was not my choice, precisely, Lord Leofric. The Harp...has a mind of its own." And with that, he struck up a brawl-gaye which had a circle of dancers out on the floor in a flash of skirts and booted feet. This was more to their liking than sagas, however heroic. Eleanor relaxed a little and hoped the Harp wouldn't veer off into "Eleanor Rigby," which would bemuse this audience beyond endurance. Beyond the thick walls, she could faintly hear the wail of the wind, and she was simply grateful to be warm, clean, dry, and, for the moment, safe.

The second morning at Richmond brought a frost that turned the earth to iron. The wind rose, and before nightfall, there was a real snowfall of a few inches. Lady

Elfrida looked anxious, as if anticipating that she might have to house her guests over a snowbound winter, for by mutual consent, Eleanor and Arthur had remained anonymous. She helped with a case of chilblain, fondled children, and oversaw the making of a new outfit, for Lady Elfrida had declared everything in her wardrobe useless but Bera's tunic. She gained an enormous respect for the occupation of medieval homemaker and was a little ashamed at her lack of domestic skills. What passed for scissors was an awkward U-shaped spring with two small blades at the ends, quite useless for cutting anything more than threads, and she watched a little awed as twelve-year-old Hilde cut a tunic from thick woad-dyed wool with the edge of a knife. No measuring tape, either. The girl used her hands and arms to gauge Eleanor's form.

Just before nightfall their fourth day at Richmond, there was a muffled clamor on the cobblestones in the courtyard. A hubbub of voices rose and fell, and a few minutes later the doors of the hall opened to admit a dozen brown-caped men stamping snow off their boots and dragging damp leather gauntlets off cold-reddened hands. They scattered to the fireplaces, revealing Leofric and another man still poised under the lintel.

Eleanor studied the man and wondered how even a war-horse could bear him, for he was a giant, larger even than Doyle or Baird. He swept off his cloak as Leofric shut the doors, and she saw his hair was brown and curly, touched with gray, with a shiny scar on the brow running into the hairline. She guessed his height at six feet eight and his weight at two-fifty plus, though all of it was hard, fighting muscle. His eyes searched the dimness of the hall and paused on her for a second.

Then they swept past to Arthur, who was just entering. As restless as herself at enforced inactivity, he had spent the day cutting wood with several other men. He was licking a blister on one palm, and his hair was darkened with moisture. Dressed in a leather tunic and cross-gartered leggings, he might have been anyone.

The big man gave a bellow of greeting and loped across the hall in a few strides. "My lord. My king. You are returned!" With these words, he knelt on one knee and kissed Arthur's somewhat grimy hand.

Arthur urged him up, ignoring the startled reactions of the men-at-arms, and embraced him, becoming almost invisible in the larger man's bearlike hug. Eleanor let out a great sigh at the obviously joyous reunion and watched her companion emerge from the hug with his eyes bright with tears. "William! For a moment, I thought you were a ghost, so like your father are you." He patted a great shoulder as if to reassure himself that it was flesh and bone.

Then he drew William toward Eleanor, brushing aside a tear and leaving a smear of dirt on his cheekbone. "My lady, this is William, Marshall of Albion and Earl of Pembroke."

"Nay, sire. They call me Lord of Striguil but earl no more. King John has removed that honor, as he would have taken the marshall's, could he have found anyone to put in my place." He made a wry face and spat on the floor. Then he bowed over Eleanor's hand and rose with a wide grin. "So, you are the little lady who has been walking in my sleep."

Amused by his bluntness, she replied, "Have I? I hope I did not disturb your virtuous rest."

He laughed, a gusty rumble. "Nothing disturbs my rest, virtuous or nay, and some might argue that I have none, though I am as God-fearing as the next, as long as the next is not a bishop." The thought of bishops seemed to tickle some fancy, for he chuckled again. Then he sobered slightly, though his gray eyes remained alight with merriment, and Eleanor thought she had never met anyone who crackled with quite such energy. "'Twas the feast of St. Bridget when first I dreamt you, and but for your dark hair, I would have thought it was the saint herself. Then again on May Eve, all bright with moonlight, and finally on the Feast of the Ascension. My good wife was not pleased, for she does not approve of my dreaming of pretty women, even on saints' days. But she has ceased to be vexed by my visions, having become accustomed after many years, for she knows they are a favor of our Blessed Virgin."

Eleanor warmed to the large man, blessed of the goddess by whatever name he called her. "I am glad you came and that you have faith in your dreams." She did not add that she was relieved that someone who knew Arthur had appeared, for she had begun to fear it was another untidy loose end that Bridget had over-looked. She had a foolish nightmare of knocking on the walls of London, saying, "I've brought King Arthur," and being laughed at.

"A man who does not have faith in the Blessed Lady is hardly fit to be called a man. Now, my lord, we must go to York."

XXXII

Eleanor had heard the Marshall's words with a sense
of release, that her part in the adventure was safely
past and she could settle down to the real job of com-
pleting her pregnancy. William was clearly better
equipped to stage-manage the young king's return, and
except for the small matter of the fire sword, an object
that she considered a very two-edged weapon indeed,
there seemed to be no reason for her to go any farther
on what promised to be an arduous journey.

She said as much to Arthur that night. The vehe-
mence with which he disagreed surprised her. "Oh, no,
you don't. I will not go a step without you, and that is
final."

"But Arthur," she answered reasonably, "your duty
is to Albion and mine—"

"Albion be hanged. I have spent less than a year of
my life in this land, and I have less feeling for it than
I do for a good horse. I will do my duty but not without
you. You, I trust. I need your sharp eyes and quick wits
with me as much as I need William's hefty arm. The
matter is settled. We leave in the morning."

"Now just a minute, you arrogant—"

"Shh." He put his black hand over her mouth lightly.
"You are dear to me, and I will not lose you, nor leave
you among strangers, however kindly disposed." He
stroked the dark hair with his other hand. "I can fulfill
my destiny with one blighted hand, but without you I
would be missing an arm."

Eleanor leaned her head against his shoulder, considering this declaration if not of love, then of something as worthy. It was true he trusted her, and she
him, and that they worked well together. A look between them spoke volumes. Still, she recalled her flight

of visions, the moment Arthur faced Baird, which had already passed, and the moment she had foreseen when she might wed him. Then she drew a deep breath and surrendered. She played with his red beard and said, "Well, if you insist...and I won't be in the way."

"A man could not ask for fairer *impedimenta*."

The wagon she rode in to York was sturdier and warmer than the earlier one, but as Eleanor huddled inside it while a man-at-arms drove, she regretted the comforts of Richmond Keep. The wind roared down from the north, cutting past cloaks and tunics with icy knives. It rained, snowed, sleeted, and hailed. The road was alternately a mire and a frozen slide. The only respite was that there was a keep or castle or farmstead to stay in most nights.

It amazed her how cheerful the followers of the Marshall remained. More swelled the ranks daily, for William had sent several of his knights off to gather forces. Her driver changed daily, and to ward off boredom, she often sat on the seat and tried to engage them in conversation. A few were loquacious and regaled her with their master's exploits against the Darkness. Each night she searched the faces of the newcomers for those who might be Shadow-touched, for she feared some treachery, and if she singled out a man to Arthur, he was gone in the morning, usually upon some spurious errand. Eleanor felt she could do no less than surround the young king with men whose light was clear and untainted, even if it cost her some suspicious looks.

Her position was anomalous in any case, for she had Arthur's confidence, but she was not part of the recognized hierarchy, and pregnant in the bargain. There were some knowing smirks when it was explained that her husband was dead, and she learned to live with the fact that a man may be good and true and still be a jackass. She enjoyed brief fantasies of endowing the smirkers with braying heads, like Bottom, and was ashamed of herself for contemplating such a misuse of her powers. And Arthur met demands for further elucidation about her with curt arrogance.

A week beyond Richmond, they came to the walled city of York, two hundred strong, forty knights and the rest sergeants and bowmen. The squat motte the Conqueror had constructed to aid in quelling the rebellious north made a dark obtrusion against the leaden sky. The city itself was swathed in smutty smoke, and the half-frozen Swale was choked with refuse.

Eleanor studied the walls, trying to see if she could distinguish the Roman from the Norman parts, and wondered just what the Marshall had in mind. It seemed unlikely that two hundred men, however valorous, could take this fortress town. She remembered that the Roundheads under Cromwell had breached the wall with cannon, but it would take siege weapons at least. She might, she realized, be able to magic the stones out of the wall, but the moon and sun were hidden behind the wind-driven clouds, and she needed the lunar orb. Besides, she was fairly certain the walls contained the kind of living dead she had seen at Glastonbury, and she had no desire to give them an exit other than the gates. Eleanor cursed herself for a managing female and reminded herself that her job was to advise Arthur, not to do it for him. She made a wry face, remembering how Doyle had had to force her into independence and thought she had learned his lessons too well.

There were half a dozen wagons in the train now, full of corn for the horses, linen for bandages, blankets for sleeping, and kegs of ale for drinking, as well as mutton and venison in no danger of spoiling quickly in the frigid temperatures. They had also acquired a handful of camp followers, hard-faced women who cooked and swore with astonishing fluency.

Eleanor was watching the camp sort itself out from the wagon seat when she saw the gates of the city swing partly open. A handful of riders trotted out and came purposefully toward the encampment. The wind had died to a breeze that barely stirred the bannerets, though it felt as if it might burst out again at any moment. The air was almost tense, and she found herself listening for a boom of thunder.

Arthur appeared beside the wagon, his chain mail jingling a little over his leather jerkin. He put his dark hand over hers. "We are about to have company, milady."

"They don't look like they are coming to sue for peace, but there's too few to fight. I wonder what—"

"Bring your staff and come meet them with me and the Marshall."

"Yes, my lord," she said with a quick grin to take the sting out of the words. Arthur had become a bit abrupt and autocratic over the past week, but she knew it could hardly be otherwise. His Plantagenet nature had combined with the demands of a tenuous position—for the men were loyal to the Marshall and not without reservations about the young king—to bring out both the best and worst in his character. The rest of the time he commanded, which was the best way to gain the respect of the doubtful and indecisive.

He grinned back and waited to help her down from the wagon, a task that grew more awkward with each passing day. Eleanor shivered a little outside the wagon and hugged around her the heavy brown cloak Lady Elfrida had given her, though her hand on the staff left a vent through which the breeze entered. Arthur put a sheltering arm around her and led her toward the magnificent bulk of the Marshall silhouetted against the sky.

The delegation from York was six men-at-arms and a seventh in the garb of a priest. The priest slid off his horse with ill grace, landed his foot in a half-frozen puddle, and promptly fell on his butt. The dozen or so knights who had gathered behind William forced back smiles, but no one made any move to assist the fallen man to his feet, and the six mounted men sat as still as statues. Their hands rested slackly on the reins of their horses, and their eyes stared at nothing.

The priest rose with what dignity he could muster, his garments wet with mud. He shook out the skirts of his robe with a dirty hand, straightened his shoulders, and drew himself up to his full five-foot-nothing, arranging his face in a caricature of a smile. His eyes were like dabs of blackberry jam in his wizened face. "I have come to accept your surrender," he began without preamble.

William's laughter rumbled like distant thunder. "Now, Père Gerard, why should anyone surrender to a little raisin of a man like you?" he bellowed.

The priest jumped, and a look of confusion crossed his face. Eleanor almost felt sorry for him, for it was obvious that whatever power had sent him out had not prepared him for anything but capitulation. "I speak for the Mouth of York, and I will accept your swords as—"

"The rector of York speaks for the rectum," a knight behind William interrupted crudely. He got a quelling look from the Marshall, though his fellows grinned among themselves.

"...As a token of your surrender to the lawful authority of my master," the priest continued as if he had not heard. "I will take that man and the woman as hostages and—"

"You will take nothing but a swift boot on your shrunken backside," the Marshall interrupted. "You were a poor excuse for a priest thirty years ago, but you are an even worse one for a servant of the Shadow."

"I serve the Power, the Great Power of the Almighty." The words were spoken tonelessly, by rote.

"Do you remember me?" Arthur asked, peering at the face of the priest.

"Certainly. You are dead." He smiled. "I helped kill you, so I am quite sure. Good John is a true servant of the Great Power, and we could not let a wicked..." He faded off, confused by Arthur's presence. "Evil! Abomination! The Lion's whelps are all dead, dead, de—" Spittle drooled out of the nearly toothless mouth, and he ground to a halt like a windup toy running out of turns.

"Go back to your master and tell him we do not surrender but await his personal presence on the battlefield tomorrow." Arthur's voice was kind but firm.

Gerard blinked. "You mean you will not give me your swords?"

"Only between your ears, old man," William snarled.

"But you must. I have my orders. Collect the swords and bring the woman and the dead man. It is so simple, you see." With surprising quickness, he made a dart toward Eleanor.

Eleanor had no more devout wish than to avoid any contact with the Shadow at all costs, so she grasped her staff in both hands and extended it toward his bony hands. He curled his fingers around it, as if to pull it from her, and then screamed when lines of blue fire began to crawl up his forearms. He snatched his hands back and did a hoppity-dance, flailing his scrawny arms like a drab scarecrow. The knights behind William laughed at his antics, although it had an uneasy edge to it.

The fire faded, and Gerard stood quivering with indignation, his cheeks puffed out into sallow balloons. "Witch! Kill her!" The still-mounted men stirred in their stupor, and she heartily wished she had stayed in the wagon, for while Arthur would defend her, she was not sure anyone else would.

The mounted men were terribly slow in their movements, like sleepers barely aroused, and Eleanor found she was angry. Her feet were cold, her back hurt, and she could hear real thunder rumbling in the distance. She wanted to be warm and out of the weather, and she was totally uninterested in the nicer points of chivalry. Her resolution to keep a low profile and not be a managing female vanished in a surge of adrenaline.

With a sweeping gesture, she thrust her cloak back, lifted her arms, and let the divine fire of the goddess course through her veins. Her body was a vessel of anger, righteous anger, her face a flame. She flew at the mounted men like an outraged phoenix.

The horses were more alert than their riders, and they found this apparition not at all to their liking. Two reared, and one turned tail and galloped toward the chilly waters of the Swale, screaming with equine hysteria. Gerard's horse bolted in the other direction.

One rider of greater purpose than his fellows got his sword out, mastered his capering steed, and rushed at her. Eleanor brought the staff across his helm with a bright flare of light. The horse took matters to himself, dumped the rider, and sped away toward the city. A sword cut through the air beside her, and the fallen man was half-beheaded.

Eleanor glanced up, expecting to see Arthur or the Marshall, but it was a grim-faced knight, helmless and unshielded. The two remaining riders were dragged off their white-eyed mounts and slain in the next instant, and she was surrounded by four of William's men.

Her fire faded, and she saw the priest had tripped and fallen into the mud. A knight hauled him upright and dripping by the cowl of his cloak, so Gerard made gabbling noises, and shook him like a pompon. Then he released the priest and wiped his hand distastefully on his leg.

Gerard staggered, coughing and sputtering, as Eleanor turned to find the Marshall firmly holding Arthur from the brief affray. She grinned and drew her cloak back around her as a flash of lightning made the falling dusk bright. Thunder boomed, and a throaty gust of wind swirled cloaks like dervishes. The heavens opened up with enthusiasm.

"Go back and tell your master we will see him in hell," a knight bellowed at Gerard, the storm almost drowning his words. The priest scurried off toward the city.

Arthur came to her, smiling slightly as rain drenched his ruddy hair. "You are too quick, my lady."

"I haven't been getting enough exercise," she screamed back at him. And Doyle taught me to take care of myself, she added silently. As Arthur drew her back toward the wagons, Eleanor realized that it was impossible for her to maintain a passive posture, that she had changed so much that neither pregnancy nor the lack of the fire sword could prevent her from combat.

That was wrong. She was a woman; women made life, not took it. She laughed a little hysterically at this sexist notion. Why should men do all the dirty work, just because they were bigger and stronger? If there must be wars, then every able-bodied person should fight. And having solved this philosophical point to her own satisfaction, she climbed into the wagon and removed her soaking clothes and dried herself before putting on dry ones. She patted her belly and promised the unborn child—a son, she was sure—that she would always fight beside him.

The rain drummed on the wooden roof of the wain, almost drowning out the thunder, but the lightning flashed. She stretched out on the bed and wondered if

Arthur felt unmanned by her precipitous actions. It had been so much simpler when she'd been just her father's little girl.

Morning brought warm, wet snow that melted almost as soon as it hit the ground. It also brought Arthur and William into the wagon for a war council, so the cramped space was filled with the dank smell of wet leather and mutton-greased mail. The Marshall sat on the wagon seat, his huge legs inside and his torso and head filling the opening. Eleanor and Arthur sat together on the bed.

"How great a force do you think is in York?" she asked, for she had not been privy to that information.

"Two thousand or a few more," William replied.

"And we are two hundred. Why don't we just go on, then?"

"Because I do not want a force that big at my back." He studied her with intent gray eyes. "Tell me, milady, what are you?"

Eleanor considered the question carefully. She discarded several easy, flip answers, trying to find a bridge between her service to the goddess and his reverence of the Virgin that would not seem heretical. Arthur's discretion had been admirable, but it gave her no clue how to proceed. Despite the liberal proclamation of the multiverse by the pope, she was fairly certain that magic was still frowned upon in polite circles, and Gerard's naming her "witch" was now known to all in the camp. And, remembering what had happened to Jeanne d'Arc—or would happen, she reminded herself—she was not going to claim divine guidance. The French heroine had always struck her as well intentioned but incredibly naive.

"I am Arthur's friend."

The hamlike hands of the Marshall slapped onto his thighs. "That is all very well, but it does not explain how you turned to fire before my eyes."

Eleanor felt herself stiffen. "I am working toward the same end you are."

"Aye, but for whom? People do not burn but demons do."

"Of all the stupid . . . you don't have enough problems with a city full of those gibbering apes of Darkness, but you must suspect me of being in league with the Devil. You certainly will be doing his work if you get rid of me. Or if you try to. I am not sure you can. I might have to kill you, which would grieve me, sorrow Arthur, and be fatal to our cause."

"Kill me?" He seemed amused.

Arthur looked at him. "Do not doubt it. I have seen her burn a man to death without touching him. And do not threaten her. I have told you of my thoughts in these matters, and I will not be gainsayed."

"We want no Melusines in Albion."

"I am not in the habit of turning into a dragon on Saturday, or any other time, Marshall. In any case, the matter will not arise, for I have no intention of marrying Arthur or anyone else. No, my lord, I will not be queen, nor have the child within me superseded by his brothers or sisters. So, if that is all that troubles you, Lord William, you may set your mind at rest. Arthur must marry a lady of noble birth. It is only right. And he won't marry anyone if we cannot stop squabbling and find a way to take York."

Arthur was glaring at her, so she raised a hand to his cheek. "It is not that I do not care for you, my lord, but that I would find being queen a dead bore." She did not say that Bridget might haul her back to a world she had almost forgotten on a whim, baby and all. *That* would be quite a shock to her mother. "You really must not get into the habit of announcing your intentions before you have inquired whether they will be met with approval." She turned a bland face to William's frown.

"There was never any question that such a thing would happen," he rumbled. "Kings may not marry as they please. But you have not answered my question. What are you?"

"Right now I am a very cold, tired, pregnant woman who wants nothing more than a warm, soft bed in a room with no drafts."

"How did you make the fire appear in your face?"

"Did I? I could not see it." That was true enough. "I pray . . . to Saint Bridget, and she strengthens me." That was true, too, as far as it went. It was also a simple answer with no visions or voices.

The Marshall was not completely convinced, but her

reply assured him slightly. "Tell me, can you make a fire onto the city of York?"

"Are all who dwell in York in Shadow?"

"No, no. Many there are who live under the Shadow but are not of it. This is true all across the land."

"Then, no, I cannot do anything. I will not use my gifts in any way that might hurt innocent people."

William nodded. "'Tis true. Yesterday you but defended yourself—and right well, I might add, though your quarter-stave work would not aid you against aught but a priest."

"Then, after I have the baby, you must show me how to do it right."

He looked shocked and pleased. "My lady!"

"Why not, William? You were wont to spar with my sister years ago."

"True, but she was yet a child, not a woman."

"How is she?"

"I cannot say, for no man can say where she dwells, or if she is still alive. She vanished from her bed nineteen years ago."

"My uncle John's hand again?"

William looked thoughtful. "No, I do not think this can be laid at his door, though many, including your mother, have. But that is something to ponder another time. I am satisfied, for now, that your intentions are pure, milady. For if you were in league with the Devil, you would not hesitate to kill the innocent. Now, let us see if we can find some other way to bring York to its knees."

Eleanor wriggled her toes in her slightly damp hose and did not disabuse him of his simplistic attitude toward Satan. Her own opinion was that the Prince of Darkness was a lot sneakier and more subtle than most people gave him credit for. Instead, she was content to have eased his mind as to her own motivations, though she had several doubts and sincerely wished she knew herself a little better.

Three nasty days passed, and the gates of York remained closed. Whatever intelligence guided the master Gerard served seemed to have been stymied by their refusal to capitulate. Either that or it had decided to let the cruel weather do his work for him. Chilblain, frostbite, and pneumonia made their presence felt in the camp, and Eleanor spent some time ministering willow tea and comfort to the sufferers.

The fourth morning dawned dark and cold, and there seemed to be a black cloud rising from the city and stretching out to the horizon. Eleanor studied it and noted that the driving wind did not stir its edges. She pointed out the phenomenon to Arthur, and he agreed it probably meant that something was about to occur.

"By the way, milord, I have lost all track of time. Do you have any idea what the date is?"

"All Hallow's Eve, my lady."

She made a face. "That figures, I suppose."

"Why?"

"I don't know—except from Glastonbury on May Eve to here on Halloween makes . . . good poetic sense. What is that?"

There was a disturbance on one side of the camp, a guard shouting and someone bellowing back. Moments later, a cluster of mounted men came into view, followed by a number on foot. At their head was a slender man who swept his helm off as he dismounted, revealing black hair and a crooked nose. His eyes were dark, and he moved like a cat. He moved toward Arthur purposefully and bent an elegant knee into the snow.

"My lord king," he began in a light tenor voice, "I have come to offer my sword."

Arthur stared at him blankly for a second. "Giles de Repton! I see you have not grown much since last we met. Get up, man." He clapped the short fellow heartily as Eleanor studied him. From their chatter, she gathered that Giles had been an esquire at the birthday banquet where Arthur had drunk a glass of wine that gave him a twenty-year nap. There was some raillery about a sister, now married and fat according to Giles.

A shout from the pickets ended the reunion. It was followed by the hollow moan of a war horn. The gates of the city began to open, and men scurried to arm themselves and saddle their mounts.

A figure in golden armor rode out of the gates, followed by a dark tide of infantry with only a few mounted men among them. The man in gold had his helm under one arm, and his blond hair seemed to glitter faintly in the somber overcast. Even at this distance, Eleanor thought she had never seen a man so fair, for he laughed as he rode. He seemed more an elfin prince than a creature of Shadow, and she was not surprised that Gerard followed him. But the horse beneath him was skittish, as if the burden he bore was unwanted, and she could see it was dark with sweat despite the chill of the day.

The foot soldiers flowed out in two arcs to surround the camp, and Eleanor watched as the Marshall arranged his men to confront this attack. It seemed to her that there was chaos all around her, and for a second she was undecided as to what her part, if any, should be. Then she returned to the wagon, got her staff, and started looking for Arthur, who had vanished in a flurry of orders a few minutes before.

She found him waiting impatiently while an equerry saddled his horse, drumming on his helm with his black hand. She caught the free hand in her own, searched his face, and found him bright-eyed with battle fever. Eleanor touched his face with her fingertips. "I think you may safely let your dragon out for the occasion, my lord."

He went as still as a statue at her words. "I should be afraid, but I am not. 'Tis foolish to not fear death, but I do not. And the beast seems less terrible, somehow."

Eleanor remembered that Bera's boon to Arthur had been that he would not be afraid of his mortality and found it a very chancy gift. "There is nothing to fear," she replied, knowing that what she said was both truth and lie.

Then he mounted, and a dozen men fell in behind him on their horses, including the newly arrived Giles de Repton. She gave the dark man a hard look, wondered if more was crooked about him than his nose, and decided he might bear watching. He might not be Shadow-struck, but that did not eliminate the possibility that his motives were less than pure. She trudged through the snow in the wake of the horses as minor battle was engaged on the right flank.

William had deployed bowmen on that portion of the camp, and they released a flight of arrows against the tide of Shadow folk. They struck but did not halt the onslaught. The wind was picking up a little, sending the arrows farther on their course.

"Okay, Bridget. It is now time to do your stuff." She felt a slight glow inside her, like a swallow of brandy, which she took for assent. Eleanor closed her eyes a second, visualized the essence of fire, then sent it flying from herself. It caught a shower of arrows as they arched from the yew bows, and they sparkled against the grim sky. For a moment, she was afraid she would incinerate them in midair, but they continued burning as they fell to earth. Where they found fleshy target, they exploded into flame, and the wave of Shadow folk became a death dance. They screamed and leapt and beat at their bodies while those untouched turned to retreat and found their way blocked by those behind.

There was some confusion in the bowmen's ranks as well, though several shouts of glee indicated that the sturdy yeomen were not about to look a gift horse in the mouth. A troop of sergeants trotted forward into the melee to hack off heads and arms, which dissuaded her from sending up any more fire immediately.

She hurried after Arthur, regretting her lack of a horse but aware that she would be a clumsy rider in her current state. Besides, they were not racing forward, for the ground was irregular beneath the snow, and the horses were in danger of broken legs at any greater pace. Eleanor contrasted the reality with her impression of medieval warfare gathered from movies and found it a drab picture. Brown cloaks, gray sky, white snow, and the skeletal silhouettes of a few trees, with a dab of blue here and green there. Blood, she knew, would soon brighten the snow, but she found that no enhancement.

The wind was getting stronger, pressing her cloak against her shoulders, and it had a bite to it. Eleanor suspected they would have an ice storm before too long. Fire and ice, she thought with a glance at the growing confusion on the right flank. I gave them an advantage, and they are making good use of it, but it is still murder.

Eleanor came to a small rise, which gave her a slight vantage point. Arthur and the knights around him were perhaps two football fields ahead of her. The golden man sat on his horse as far beyond, apparently unconcerned with anything. The fire was spreading in the Shadow ranks on the right, and those on the left seemed to be milling around in confusion.

She considered them, wondering if a fireball in their midst would be a good idea, when a shout and the crunch of hooved feet on snow caught her attention. The hefty bulk of the Marshall on his enormous horse appeared leading a bunch of knights, bearing down on the left. Eleanor turned away from that carnage, for the Shadow people seemed to have little power to flee. Battles, she thought, were not exciting. They were ugly and confusing. And the Shadow folk, while they had greater numbers, were very slow to respond.

Eleanor sensed something was missing; some element or component of a battle was not there. It came to her that it was a very quiet encounter, for the Shadow people made no cries, except those who were on fire, and William's men seemed to pursue their objective in a kind of grim silence. The snow muffled sounds as well, so she had the sense of watching a silent movie. She found that eerie and exhausting.

She hurried to catch up with Arthur and the men around him, following in the track left by the horses. When she was perhaps three hundred feet away, he reached the golden knight, and she could hear them shouting at one another. The golden man tossed his head back in laughter, looking splendid. He seemed every inch a prince, and Arthur a shabby peasant.

With a flash of gold, the man clapped his helm on, pulled his sword out, and urged his reluctant steed forward. Arthur, already helmed, drew out the fire sword. She felt it slide from the sheath like a man withdrawing, all passion spent, and knew that the sword was no longer in her charge, that it was Arthur's now, his Excalibur. She sensed Orphiana shudder slightly beneath her feet and knew she was correct. Doyle had died because of it; Baird had died wanting it. Now it was beyond her power forever, and she was relieved. She would untangle the mystery of what had happened some other time.

His blade flamed, and the dark, heavy clouds seemed to boil above him. The golden knight hesitated a second, then urged his horse forward. The men around Arthur turned to engage the dark riders of the gold man's entourage, all but Giles de Repton, who crowded close behind Arthur's mount. Eleanor found that odd, though she reminded herself she knew little of medieval warfare.

The two men circled each other, the horse's hooves making a dark mess of the snow. There was a jingle of mail and harness, equine snorts, and the wail of the wind but little else. Eleanor moved closer, aware that she was in some jeopardy from the mounted men around her, but determined to get as close as she safely could to the young king. There was a clang of metal meeting metal as various knights got down to serious combat, but she had eyes only for Arthur and Giles de Repton.

His maneuvers, she decided, were hampering Arthur's movements. She darted under the nose of a horse, felt a swish of metal behind her, and looked up to see a Shadow rider above her. Eleanor thrust her staff into the horse's sternum, then slammed it into the rider's arm as he came down with another blow. There was a wild scream, though from rider or steed she was not sure, since they were both engulfed in a burst of white light.

Without pausing to examine her handiwork further, she moved across the churned-up snow to grasp de Repton's bridle. He jerked at the reins, bringing the horse's head back, but Eleanor's weight was too great. She could feel him glaring at her. He leaned forward to pull her hand away.

"You are getting in Arthur's way."

"And you are in mine, bitch. Let go."

"I think not." She released her hold with a whisper of mind to the horse as his sword whistled down to cut off her hand. It met air as the horse started capering like a Lippazaner. Giles swore loudly and tried to get control, yanking at the reins until bright blood flecked the horse's mouth, and it screamed in protest.

Eleanor turned around to see that Arthur and his foe were finally coming to blows. The golden knight had a shield and a shorter sword than Arthur, and she admired his skill as he deflected the fire sword. It sheared off a chunk of the shield and lopped off one ear of the horse in the sweep. That steed decided it had had quite enough, reared, and dumped the unprepared knight into the mushy snow.

As the gold knight struggled to his feet, Arthur dismounted, slapped his horse on the rump, and sent it out of the way. The light of the fire sword glittered on the knight's armor and cast red reflections in the dirty snow.

A slight movement behind her made her spin around and trip back onto the snow. Giles de Repton's sword met nothing as it passed the place where she had been. Eleanor rolled out of the way of another blow, sat up, and swung her staff like a baseball bat as he raised his arms to strike again. The head caught him on the side of the chest with a loud crack. His face was hidden beneath the helm, but his body registered surprise. There was a popping noise, like a lightbulb burning out, and he sank back into the snow. Eleanor got to her feet and looked down at him. A slight mist rose and fell above his mouth, so she knew he was not dead. Hastily, she removed his sword and small belt knife and tossed them away.

"Perfectly shocking," she muttered as she got to her feet again and turned to observe the rest of the combat. "At least I had time not to kill the bastard." She gave her staff a kind of pat.

Arthur had hacked the other's shield into a jagged rondel of scorched metal, and as she watched, the gold knight cast it aside and crouched slightly. Arthur caught the golden helm a glancing blow that sheared one side away and singed the yellow hair beneath. The knight gave a bellow and charged madly forward, catching Arthur's forearm with the edge of his sword. Blood darkened the sleeve as Arthur rammed his shoulder into the knight's chest with a grunt. They both sprawled onto the snow for a second, the knight springing up a moment before the young king.

Arthur brought his sword up quickly enough to deflect a blow as Eleanor lifted her hands to bring a quick end to the combat. *No!* The whisper in her mind was like a blow. *He must fight his own battle now, child.* She lowered her arms, swallowed in a suddenly dry throat, and watched them stumble on the uneven footing. The gold man was very quick, and he danced around Arthur just out of sword's reach now, as if to tire his opponent.

The young king seemed to pause, as if drawing a deep breath. The gold man sprang forward, and the flaming sword parried as if it were guiding itself. Eleanor once again had the impression of time slowing, as she had in Arthur's fight with Baird, and she watched the fiery blade descend, slicing through flesh and bone. The gold man's shield arm parted from his body as the arc of Arthur's weapon continued into the mailed chest. Blood gouted onto the mushy snow as the knight crumbled onto one knee, then folded into a heap.

A wild sound rose above the whipping wind. Eleanor turned toward it and saw there were many small figures moving along the top of the city wall. They were cheering and casting bundles down from the wall. It took her a moment to realize that the objects were people. The good folk of York were doing some rough and ready housecleaning. She felt sick as she watched. Swallowing a bile-bitter mouthful, she turned back to bind up Arthur's arm.

The Shadow people seemed to have lost what little power they had with the death of the golden knight, and William's men moved among them like grim executioners. The Marshall himself rode up after a few minutes and swung off his horse.

"My lord. You are hurt."

"Not badly. My lady here can take care of it."

"Good." His keen gray eyes swept the field. "What?" He pointed a large finger at de Repton's unconscious form. "How did that little rat get in here?"

"He rode in just before the battle," Eleanor answered, "and we did not have time to tell you. Why?"

"He is King John's man."

York was a warren of crooked streets, and Eleanor found herself looking for the lovely gothic spires of the minster, so much a part of her memory of that ancient city. Where it should stand was the fire-blackened remnant of a Romanesque church. The narrow streets were full of half-starved people shouting, laughing and weep-

ing, waving and leaping about, rushing up to touch
Arthur's muddy boot or pat his horse. Eleanor, perched
awkwardly on the broad back of a destrier, watched
their pleasure with a jaundiced eye, trusting no one
after Repton's planned treachery. The stone walls echoed
with the cry of "The King has returned," and she wondered if they thought he was the legendary Arthur.
Then she reflected that if she had not known him and
had seen him with the fire sword aflame, as he must
have appeared to them from the walls of the city, she
would have thought him a hero out of legend.

The keep was filthy, but several purposeful burghurs
quickly organized a cleanup crew. They carried refuse
into the courtyard where a bonfire consumed the stuff.
By nightfall, the stone floors were washed clean of muck,
the fireplaces cleaned and burning brightly. The place
smelled of soap, damp stone, burning wood, and sweaty
people. Over that was the scent of cooking meat and
bitter ale. Eleanor ate and drank without tasting, at a
banquet that seemed to appear in the hall by magic.
She noticed that the Marshall seemed to hover near the
young king and knew he shared her fear of an assassin
in the merrymakers.

She was tired but wide-awake with a sense of some
task unfinished. *Come to me,* came a mental whisper.
Eleanor glanced around, then saw a small door on one
side of the hall. She got up and left the table and pushed
it open. A faint rotting smell met her nose as she peered
into the darkened chamber.

Her body's light pierced the gloom, and she could
just make out the shape of a long table at the far end.
Her foot slipped on something round and fat, a candle
hacked in half. The decaying carcasses of several rats
lay in a heap upon the chest of a body in the torn remnants of an alb, one hand still raised in benediction.
The glittering eyes of another rodent glared at her, then
it scurried away into the shadows.

An uneasy townsman came into the doorway, and
she jumped and gave a squeak when he cleared his
throat. "So, that is what happened to poor bishop Geoffrey. Still, I suppose it is best to die in a chapel, if yur
a priest. Those bastards! They pissed in here. You can
smell it. I wonder what happened to the statue of the

Virgin. 'Twas stone, so they could not burn it. Ach. This was a lovely place once." He spoke in the long, slow accents of the north, swaying slightly over his tankard.

"Go get me servants with buckets and brooms," she ordered.

"Now, milady—"

"This is a desecration of a holy place. I want it cleaned now!"

He sobered a little, considered the matter, and nodded. "Yur right. It should be clean for All Saints', though unless you have a priest in your train, there is none alive to bless the place, 'less you count that creature we found hiding in the linen press." He referred to Gerard, now languishing in a dungeon. Then he turned and walked off.

Eleanor picked her way carefully among the refuse, finding that the combined odors of old incense and urine grew stronger as she moved toward the altar. She wrinkled her nose and looked behind the long altar. The statue lay on its back, staring blankly at the ceiling, a sweet smile curving from a serene face. One graceful hand rested on the chest, the other uplifted, palm outward. There were a few chips out of the folds of the cloak painted blue and edged with gilt, but otherwise she was undamaged.

Knowing it was just a figure, Eleanor yet felt herself in the presence of the Lady. She took a deep breath and knelt down beside it. The calm face shifted, and Bridget looked up at her, bright-eyed and merry.

"You have done well, daughter."

"I tried." The words were bitter on her tongue, because Baird's death still troubled her mind, that and the terrible winter it had released. "Now what?"

"So hard-eyed and unforgiving. So cold and abrupt."

"Perhaps. I don't recall you being exactly loquacious back in February yourself. Go here, go there. Do this, do that. So I did, and Doyle is dead and Baird is dead and I'm a little—"

"I know. I even understand. But remember that it was their choice, particularly Baird's."

"If you hadn't given me that damn sword—"

"Ifs are for weaklings." The words were sharp. "Be quiet and listen. You will take the Heir to London."

"Yes."

"Now, when the time comes, remember this. The harp makes and the pipes unmake. I will keep my eye upon you, though you hardly need me, and I forgive your unwonted affection for my reclusive sister." The shining face turned back to dull stone.

"Damn you for an unrepentant, meddling, cryptic Irishwoman, Bridget of Hibernia." Eleanor thought she heard a faint chuckle among the stones, but a clatter of footfalls and buckets interrupted her.

"Milady?"

"I'm here." Eleanor stood up behind the altar and saw several kerchiefed women with brooms and mops and buckets of soapy water. "I found the statue."

"Good, good."

Two men carrying a stretcher came in and removed the corpse of the dead bishop while the servants began cleaning up the mess. Someone started a plain chant in a very broad Yorkshire accent, and Eleanor smiled as she recalled the snatches of bawdy song that had wafted through the hall earlier in the day. It gave a rhythm to the work and, tired as she was, Eleanor felt refreshed by the energy of the servants. They had cleaned the hall out of need; this task they undertook with a joy that spoke of their affection for the Virgin. They attacked the stones at the base of the altar with stiff brushes and enthusiasm, sending a rather dull-witted boy back to the kitchen for water again and again, until the chamber smelled of only soap and hard-working humans.

Eleanor did not depart until the altar was cleansed, a white linen cloth spread on it, and the statue set up on it by two sweating manservants. The women paused, leaning on their brooms and mops, rising from their scrubbing brushes with soaking knees, and a smile seemed to spread from face to face. A kind of sigh echoed. Lips moved in subvocalized prayer as the benevolent gaze of the statue seemed to fill the room.

Heal, always heal, my daughter. Eleanor could not mistake that voice. Content in Sal's affection, she went off to find her bed.

XXXIII

The journey toward London was a nightmare of blowing snow, driving rain, and an increasing, icy wind from the north. In spite of this, they pressed ahead, their ragged army growing daily as word went out that Arthur had returned. Many who joined them had been babes in arms when the Heir had vanished, and they seemed to be of the mind that he was that previous Arthur, come to rescue Albion in its hour of need. Eleanor found herself in the company of legend and wondered if there was more truth in their belief than she knew.

Despite her continued vigilance and that of the Marshall, there were two assassination attempts on the young king's life. After the second, the Marshall put a guard of handpicked men, whom he trusted utterly, around Arthur at all times and kept everyone else at a distance. This led to some grumbling, since the newcomers wanted to meet Arthur personally, to kneel before him and offer fealty. One could hardly insult a member of the chivalry by demanding he disarm before coming into the presence of the king. They worked out a compromise of sorts, so Arthur sat on the back of a wagon with two armed men at his sides each day when they halted, unless the weather was too awful, which it often was. Eleanor considered this a mercy, for the young man was fearless and a bit too cocky for her peace of mind. William just shook his head and said the whole family was either feckless or heedless, and there was naught to choose betwixt them.

Eleanor decided Arthur needed some sense shaken into him, and one evening she bearded the young lion in his den, going immediately on the offensive to be sure she had his attention. "I wish you had told me when you were dipped in the River Styx and made invincible, my lord."

The reference was lost on him, but he caught her meaning. "What do you mean?"

"I mean you are behaving like a fool, rushing to embrace every Tom, Dick, or Harry who calls you king. If someone shoves a knife in your heart, I won't be able to save you."

"No, I suppose not. If you could have healed such hurts, your dark Doyle would be living. Oh, forgive me." He hugged her shoulders. "That was cruel, but I feel as if you and William would tie me up in a sheep's fleece to save me from harm. I never knew him, yet he is my rival for your affection, and I think it makes me do stupid things. He was such a man as casts a great shadow. I have this hunk of metal by your grace and love, but I do not have you, and it is cold comfort. I know what demons drove golden Baird, for I feel their whips on me also."

Eleanor thought her heart would still in her chest, and she felt ashamed that she could not return his love. She knew she cared for him sincerely, but it was nothing like the emotions she still bore for her dead spouse. Doyle never had but one rival, and that was a goddess who wore the willows. The unfairness of it had the bittersweetness of mead on her tongue.

She rubbed her head against his shoulder, forced tears away, and made herself chuckle. "He was a close-mouthed, stubborn son of a snake. Don't let his shade touch you. I wish I could love you the way you want, but it might be fatal. I don't have a very good track record. Just be careful, please—for such love as I do bear you." They left it at this unsatisfactory point, and Eleanor found herself weeping later: for Doyle; for Arthur; for poor, bright Baird; and for her unruly heart. And afterward Arthur kept his guard up, and she was relieved.

They paused at various strongholds, some friendly, some filled with Shadow and needing a good cleaning. By the time they reached Oxford, their numbers were more than a thousand. The town welcomed them, and she was relieved to find it a bastion of light in the Darkness, uncorrupted by Shadow. They rested there

two days, and she stood on Folly Bridge and watched
the ice-floed river, glad that it had remained untouched.
Then she laughed at herself for foolish notions about
intellectual purity and went to warm her feet by a fire.

It was while she was half-sprawled in a high-backed
chair, toasting her toes and enjoying the feel of a seat
that neither bounced nor jiggled, that the Marshall found
her. Eleanor had requested—politely—that he speak
to her, but it had been several days, and he had not
come. She understood. The press of his duties was great,
for not all who joined Arthur's train did so out of love
or loyalty. That was a trait of minor landholders and
landless knights, afraid of the growing Shadow and
looking to the young king with hope. Wealthy barons
and earls wanted something more, and William had
taken on the task of promising them the moon while,
in fact, offering nothing.

He sank wearily into a chair beside her, looking older
than he had a few weeks earlier, and she felt guilty for
her comfort. "You wished to see me."

His abruptness stung, and she knew he was still
suspicious of her. Eleanor sighed. She pulled herself
more upright and gestured to the now nearly omnipres-
ent Yorick, who had started off as her driver and somehow became her personal majordomo on the long trip
toward London, to get the Marshall some refreshment.
Yorick was dour and silent, a North Riding man of
grunts and shrugs, but somehow he always made sure
her clothes were dried, her bed warm, and her person
respected. He reminded her of her Uncle Richard, her
mother's brother, lean of face and long of limb, and she
found in him a comforting if untalkative companion.

When the Marshall had a goblet of wine, she spoke.
"I wish to know what manner of man John is. Does he
serve the Shadow?"

"No. At least, his light still gleams, as those under
Darkness do not. A good question you ask me. I would
say he is subtle and cunning...and a witch, like yourself."

"That, at least, is plain speaking."

"I am a simple man, milady and—"

"Oh, stop! You are a brilliant strategist, as canny as

your father, and there is nothing simple about you. Spare me a humility that fits you like hosen on a cat."

He chuckled. "My good wife always gets sharp-set as she comes to her time. But its been ten years, and I had forgot. I've rarely been to Striguil enough to bed her for more get these past three years, and if she gives me a lusty son, I will know she played me false. Hosen on a cat. Very well spoke."

"I'm sorry. Yes, I am irritable. My baby kicks and squirms and I feel like...a wallowing ship. Before York, you said something that struck me. About being under Shadow but not in it. And would it reassure you at all if I made you free of my name?"

He leaned forward, piercing her with sharp gray eyes. "That has rankled, *milady,* more than I wish to admit. You have such power over Arthur that he lets you go nameless amongst us yet seeks your counsel. I have watched you. I have seen the fire in you. I have seen you give a man a quaff from your bowl, and lo, he is well and hale. He sings your praises, that fellow, and yet I smell sorcery about you and trust you not."

"Again, I am sorry. Of all the men in Albion, I should depend on you most, but the Shadow makes us both untrustful. And names have power in them. For instance, I do not know your wife's name, though you speak often of her. Your instinct is to protect her from me, as if I could reach out to the marshes of Wales and touch her. I cannot, I assure you, and I would not, if I could. But any words are empty, and promises get broken." She took as deep a breath as her advanced pregnancy permitted, and the baby flexed, pressing hands and feet to each side of her swollen abdomen. She put her hands on the child's, pushing inward to make it go to sleep. In that instant, she knew its name and nature, as if he had spoken to her, and she smiled. Whatever the moment of his conception, he was Dylan, a wave of the sea, a mighty fish, and she rejoiced in his essence, that he had of his father the water and of her the earth, joined in a harmonious person. He would have her song and Doyle's seriousness, and she would have cried but for her pleasure. *Sal, will you be godmother to my baby?* The thought rose unbidden in her mind. *Of course, be-*

loved, came the reply, a rustle of willows. But all she said was, "I am Eleanor."

"Is that your true name?"

He was, in some ways, as simple a man as he claimed, and he needed more assurances. She remembered another Eleanor, a dramatic figure who ripped her sleeve and promised to write a will on her arm in blood and wished she had the stomach for such hijinks. "I am Eleanor Darlington Hope, and my mother came from Yorkshire, my father from the land you call Hibernia, but not in this time or place. I am from another future, another world, and that you will have to take as a matter of faith."

"Hope. Then you are she whom I dreamt of, and not some evil phantasm as I have feared." He made a wry face. "I should trust more in the Lady, but it is hard."

Eleanor cast a quick glance at dour Yorick, standing within earshot, and he gave her his shrug, which said "I don't gossip," as plain as houses. She gave him a nod and a smile and hoped she would never be tempted to do *Hamlet* over his bleached bones. "So, John is a magician. Tell me more."

The Marshall gave a great, gusty sigh and rearranged his extended legs toward the crackling fire. "More? 'Tis difficult. He consorts with ghosts on the White Tower, some say. I have, myself, seen him walk those ramparts, speaking to air. He is tall and fair and well proportioned, a handsome man, but he has never taken a wife who lived more than a year, and he has had three. Several bastards claim him for parent, but who can say? I would say he serves neither the Light nor the Darkness but some other master. Mischief, perhaps."

"Does he possess some object—a ring or wand— which he is never without?"

"You mean, like your staff?"

"You don't miss much, do you?"

"No." It was a simple statement of fact with no arrogance in it. "Yes, he does. 'Tis an odd thing, but I have never seen him without it. It is a wide bracelet upon his right arm with a face of some rude beast repeated around it. Sort of lionlike but with the tongue lolled out. Ugly thing. I cannot swear it is what you seek, but I think it is. Now, tell me why you're curious about this."

"One should always know one's adversary."

"True."

"Also, I think you and Arthur have been thinking purely in military terms. All the hours I have spent in the wagon have given me a lot of time to think, and I realized that I did not know enough about John. William, I doubt he can be defeated by the sword."

He gave another gusty sigh, sipped his wine, and said, "I suspect you are right. Several have tried to murder him over the years and failed. He seems invulnerable to knife or poison. And you are right, too, that I think only of the sword, for I am a fighting man."

"I think enough people have died already. How great a force can John muster?"

"Five thousand, perhaps six."

"And we are a mere thousand."

"Yes. Though I am the better general than John, we do not have the advantage of numbers. I had hoped we would be greater, but this winter has ruined that."

"It wouldn't do any good if we were ten thousand, if we cannot topple John from his throne."

"I think I begin to be glad to have you for a friend, for I believe you would be a deadly foe, my lady. There is steel in your voice and in your eyes. Indeed, you put me in mind of good Queen Eleanor, who was a most redoubtable woman, even in the last years. Do you have some plan to defeat John?"

"Not yet."

Eleanor turned the matter over in her mind a great deal in the following week as they crawled to London. She thought of invisibility, then realized there was no way to make her body's light vanish. The very act of making the body disappear seemed to enhance the aura. She went over every lesson Doyle had taught her of magicks and found no answer.

After a particularly filthy day of driving through near blizzard conditions, they stopped. There was no keep or castle nearby, so they camped out as best they could, and Eleanor opened up her clothes chest to get another tunic, though she already wore so many she looked like a bear.

Something clunked as she pulled out the garment, hitting the wood with a thud. She felt down to see what it was and found it was the ugly collar Baird had used to neutralize her powers. Turning it over in her hands, she pursed her lips thoughtfully. I'll just nip into his bedroom and put it on his scrawny throat.

Eleanor chuckled at herself, but she puzzled over how the collar might be used to advantage. She thought of several daring but impractical plans, all of which she discarded with mild regret, and took to carrying the thing in her belt pouch. Something would occur to her, she was certain.

It had not by the time they made camp across the Thames from the walls of London. Eleanor stared at the frozen waters of the river and the snow-clad ramparts of the city and felt exhausted. The cold seemed to sap her strength.

William drew up his battle lines in the bleak wilderness of snow and waited. His face as he walked the pickets was grim, almost haggard, and Eleanor realized with growing horror that he was defeated before he even began. She could feel the despondency spread and knew that a subtle magic was at work.

"Yorick, help me down. I must find Arthur instantly."

"Naw. You sit. I seek." He clambered out, sank into snow to his kneecaps, and plowed away determinedly. About half an hour later, he returned with an anxious-looking Arthur and his grim attendants.

"What is it, milady?" He sounded annoyed.

"Come into the wagon."

He joined her with ill grace. "Can't you see I'm busy?"

"Yes, busy getting ready for your cousin to win."

"What?"

"Can't you feel that the heart is going out of the men? There will be desertions before morning if you don't act now."

"Would you suggest I tie them down?"

"Stop being a sarcastic ass. Honestly, Arthur, sometimes I could box your ears, just to get some blood into

that thick head of yours. Get off your Plantagenet high
horse and listen to me. Use the Harp."

"This is hardly the time for a musicale."

"Shut up!" She was weary beyond endurance, short-
tempered and at the edge of her control. Arthur saw
her face waver toward flame for a moment and drew
back.

"I am sorry, Eleanor. I feel surrounded by enemies,
silent, invisible enemies. I jump at shadows. A hare
running through the snow nearly panicked me."

"Yes, and the knights and men-at-arms feel that way
even more so, because they lack your strength."

"Or thickheadedness." He gave her a weak grin. "I
am afraid of...nothing."

"Yes, I know. I think your bastard cousin is putting
the whammy on us and—"

"Whammy?"

"A wicked spell. Remember how your harping healed
me of some of my grief for Doyle?"

"Yes."

"I want you to heal this fear, or there won't be any
fight tomorrow or any other day. Bridget told me the
Harp makes and the pipes unmake, which makes me
real glad, because I was starting to think she made us
get them out of sheer perversity."

"The pipes unmake. They would. All right, I'll do
what you say. I just wish I could make it be less cold."

"We can bear the cold a few more days. The fear we
cannot."

He was still doubtful. "I suppose it will not hurt."

"Believe me, it will work like magic." Then she started
to laugh, an ugly, hysterical laughter that frayed the
nerves. Her body trembled. Arthur shoved her rudely
onto her bed, heaped blankets over her, and tromped
off to his own wagon. Eleanor huddled, shivering under
the blankets, swearing under her breath that she was
going to freeze one side of John and boil the other in
oil. She fought the nibbling despair with all her strength.

It was gone as suddenly as it had come, dissipated.
Eleanor could not hear the Harp, but she knew it was
being played. She took a deep breath and discovered
she was not quite so cold. Yorick sat on the wagon seat,
and she could hear him sniffing loudly. "Roses, milady."

Eleanor realized he was right. She sat up and pushed the covers aside and felt almost dizzy from the heady scent of roses. She felt refreshed and energetic for the first time in days. Her mind cleared of a fog she had not even noticed, and she scrambled off the bed and up to the almost smiling Yorick. She had never seen him quite so cheerful-looking.

Eleanor knew Arthur couldn't play the Harp forever, so she set her mind to finding another solution to the problem. His wicked cousin could continue to send despair or any other mischief he could design at their camp, and Eleanor needed to find some way to prevent it. "A mirror!" she said so loudly that Yorick started in surprise. "Come on. We are going to walk the pickets."

"Snow's deep," he grunted.

"I don't care if it comes to my belly button, we are going."

"Reet. Ya sure gotta spiky temper for a Yorkshire woman."

Since this statement was perhaps the longest he had ever made to her, she gave him a quick smile. Then she got her staff, and he helped her down, glad she had someone around who neither argued nor smothered her with solicitation, as Arthur had developed a tendency to do when he thought of her at all. It was cold, though the wind had faded a little, and for once the snow had stopped.

They trudged around the perimeter, greeted by cheerful guards, seemingly unaware that an hour earlier they had been ready to jump at any sound. Yorick moved ahead of her, clearing a path with his legs, while Eleanor concentrated on making an utterly simple spell that did nothing but reflect. When they returned to their starting point, she paused to sense her handiwork and found it good. She turned toward the snow-cloaked walls of London and smiled. "I hope John chokes on his own filth." Then she leaned on her servant's arm wearily.

"Tha Marshall's reet. A bad foe." He patted her hand on his arm affectionately. "A good friend."

Eleanor slept a deep, exhausted slumber, full of strange dreams. It was a beautiful spring day, and the grass was dappled with golden daffodils and blue iris. She moved around the stones of Avebury, hearing their song mingling with a faint murmur of bees. A shout made her turn, and Doyle strode across the grass toward her. He smiled. On one wide shoulder he carried a girl child, squealing with delight and clapping plump hands. She reached for him, and her hands met the rough wooden wall of the wagon.

She pried her eyes open, still full of the warmth of the dream, and took a deep, shuddering breath. Knuckling her eyes, she sat up. "Talk about wish fulfillment," she muttered. "I even knew her name—Rowena."

The night was full of sound, the stamping of horses and the movement of men, along with a few dogs. The wind sighed, as if it had tired itself out in the past few weeks. Eleanor listened, then got up. Something was wrong. She pulled her cloak around her and crept to the front of the wagon, hoping not to disturb her faithful servant.

Yorick's lean shadow crossed the opening of the wagon. "What?"

"Don't you ever sleep? I don't know. Something's amiss. I had a dream and—"

"Laughed," he replied.

"Yes, I did, didn't I?" So powerful had the dream been, she still carried the sense of well-being it had given her. Eleanor could not decide if she thought it kind or cruel, to have visions of what could never be.

He extended a long hand to help her onto the wagon seat, then sat beside her in companionable silence. Eleanor enjoyed that, and the good man smells that enveloped him, work sweat and damp leather and cloth. His body light was clear, a diamond light around a jewel of a man.

She looked across the river toward the walls of London. They had camped at one end of the stone bridge, the span that would give rise many centuries in the future to a children's rhyme. Now it was brand, spanking new—barely passed its fifteenth year, the Marshall had informed her. Already there were wooden houses on each side of the wide roadway, though she had only caught a glimpse of them in the gray daylight. She checked her "mirror" above the camp, surprised at its existence and at her own capacity to weave such a thing. *You still do not know your own strength, daughter.*

Eleanor smiled at this whisper, feeling that special acerbic affection she associated with the Mistress of Willows. A good thing, too. I wouldn't want to get stuck-up.

Goose! Arrogance is not your vice, but humility.

Eleanor felt she had just been slapped a stinging blow on the face. Humility a vice? She frowned over it, until she remembered a certain Dr. Hoffman in the history department at her father's university, an absolutely brilliant scholar who deferred to everyone, even the school janitor, in a perfectly maddening way. She would let her colleagues attach themselves to her work like leeches in exchange for a footnote, until she became a kind of departmental workhorse, always publishing but never alone. I don't do that. But she knew how eager she had been to hand Arthur over to William and stop with the job half-done. Her pregnancy was just an excuse to get out of the responsibility of finishing the task.

Sighing, she thought, Why can't things be all clear and neat?

They never are, even for the gods, child.

A faint thud caught her attention, and she looked up toward it from the meditation on her wind-chapped hands. A tiny movement in the darkness of the city. Eleanor stood up awkwardly and tried to penetrate the gloom. Something darker than night seemed to creep along the base of the wall, a black serpent coiling around the city with sinuous stealth. She studied it, feeling her energy stopped as if by a barrier at the edges of this darkness.

For perhaps half an hour she stood and sensed the thing, until her spirit felt bruised from hammering at the darkness. Yorick's gnarled hand held her elbow, and she could feel his warmth and loyalty upholding her. For a moment, she wondered why he had attached himself to her. As if this distraction released her mind, she suddenly found an answer to the question of what was going on.

"Nevsky!"

"Milady?"

"John's going to send his men across the river in the

cover of darkness. Or that is his plan. We have a small surprise for him. Go wake Arthur, and tell him...to bring his pipes." A slight smile touched her face.

Yorick returned with the young king still rubbing sleep from his eyes, a cloth-wrapped bundle pressed against his chest. William lumbered out of the shadows, alert and sharp-eyed.

"Milady, this is the first good night's sleep I have enjoyed in a week," Arthur complained. The camp was astir now, though mutedly.

"Yes, my lord. Look to the river. What do you see?"

"Nothing. No, moving darkness. What is it?"

"Your cousin sends his troops, I believe."

"But what of their light? Does he command Shadow men now?"

Eleanor sat down with a thump. It suddenly came to her that these approaching troops were not lightless zombies but living men, ordinary men who followed John out of fealty or love or greed. "His magic cloaks their lights, I think."

William snorted, cleared his throat, and spat into the snow. "Yes, milady. He can make himself almost invisible, though I think it costs him dearly."

Eleanor nodded, for she had not solved that problem herself and knew it to be a difficult one. She realized that while John was a very bad man, he was also the only person alive who probably knew more of the uses of magic than she did now. In some other circumstance, she would have sat and learned from him. Now she would send several hundred or thousand men to a chilly death.

It was hard, the choice to use her power, Arthur's power, for there seemed no way to do so without killing. Those men creeping out onto the frozen river probably had wives and children, mothers and fathers who would mourn their passing.

Arthur shifted his hand, and an eerie moan slipped from under the cloth. He clapped a hand around it, and the sound died. "I do not like this accursed thing, milady."

"No. But with every harmony, there is an equal disharmony. There is God, and there is the Devil. There is the Harp, for healing, and the pipes, for illness. Such things keep the cosmos in balance."

William guffawed. "I did not know you were a philosopher."

"Me? No, I'm just a simple wench who—"

His laughter broke over her words. "I am repaid for my attempt to gammon you. Simple wench, indeed."

Arthur ignored this byplay, still turning the matter of harmony over in his mind. "If I play these in the camp, there will be madness."

"True, my lord, and I had not thought of that." She had but felt a need to protect his pride. "Let me think. We will go beyond the perimeter to use them. That should suffice." But she did not stir, aware of some detail overlooked. Then she moved back into the darkness of the wagon and drew the silky blue cloak of Bridget over her, took her staff, and dismounted.

They were two dozen as they stepped outside the confines of the camp. The air seemed heavier, as if charged with lightning, but it was not unbearable, just a bit stifling. The lingering smell of roses vanished, and there were the odors of cold, nervous men, the clean bite of snow, and a slight, burning, woody scent from the city.

The blackness spread out in a thick line across the river. It wound under the arches of the bridge like a swirl of velvet on the slightly shining ice. Several knights ranged themselves on either side of Arthur, and Eleanor stood behind him. "I would suggest you gentlemen stop up your ears."

Then they waited silently for a few minutes, the men stamping uneasily in the snow, watching the dark line move forward until it was in the middle of the frozen river. Eleanor used the time to wrestle with her conscience, trying to see if she had overlooked some less violent solution to the threat. But she knew that John could sit in London while they froze, harassing them and wearing them down, unless they forced him to do otherwise. She speculated why he had not chosen to do just that and decided that it was her own presence that unbalanced his calculations. He must have been startled, at the very least, by the sudden appearance of the mirror. Or perhaps he felt his power waning and moved to stop the process.

Guide me to do right, Lady. It was a heartfelt prayer offered to Bridget and Sal and the Virgin Mary and all the faces of woman. The answer was an uplift of pure joy, so her aura fountained up, casting shadows on the snow. She raised her hands together. "I think we need a little light on the subject," she said, and cast a fireball into the air above the river. It burst like an Independence Day display, and the figures of the men on the river were cast in gold for a second. They turned their eyes toward the sudden brightness, then away, dazzled.

"Now, Arthur!" She gasped the words, for she felt her heart struggle suddenly, as if squeezed by a dark hand. She snatched the blue cloak across her chest, and the pain passed as Arthur dropped the cloth and lifted the pipes to his mouth. At the first tone, half the knights clapped their hands to their heads and howled, and several others fell down senseless.

Eleanor set her feet apart, at shoulder width, drew a deep breath, and spread her arms, holding the cloak out around her like a field of stars, her aura flaming like a beacon. The strength of earth flowed into her feet, up her legs, and into her body as Arthur played six notes, over and over. She could see his shoulders tremble. William stood rocklike beside him, one hand over an ear, the other on the young king's shoulder.

There was a cracking sound, and the bridge trembled. Then the ice began to craze like a shattered mirror. Screaming panic hit the ranks of men on the ice, though whether it was from the pipes or the sudden unsteadiness of footing one could not tell. Eleanor felt the panic, too, but detachedly, as if it were someone else who was screaming from a raw throat.

The river under the ice churned, first sluggishly, then with greater turbulence, smashing blocks of ice and bodies of men into the arches of the bridge. It swallowed struggling, armored men, the black waters closing over their heads as they fled back toward the far bank. Others ran toward Arthur's camp, and a few made it, crawling out onto the icy shore, howling.

Eleanor's arms ached, and her hand around her staff was stiff. She felt a sudden warmth upon her back, and

two bony hands raised her elbows. Yorick's familiar
presence steadied and refreshed her, though her heart
was heavy.

The pipes made a particularly shrill cry, and the city
wall seemed to tremble. Then great blocks of stone leapt
into the air and fell back to earth with loud thuds, which
echoed even above the confusion on the river. A gap in
the wall widened.

"Arthur! Stop! You'll bring down the whole city!"

He stood limply with his back to her, the syrinx
hanging from his black left hand. It fell into the snow
with a few faint squeaks. Water crested up from under
the undamaged ice upriver, pushing the debris of dead
men and floes down to the cracked arches of the stone
bridge and beyond. Pale dawn grayed the east as they
came back to the silent present.

The Marshall cracked his jaw, as if his ears needed
popping, then bent down and wound the damp cloth
around the pan pipe. "I never knew it 'twas of any
use to be tone-deaf," he said, holding the bundle distastefully. "Give me a grand headache though. A fair
sickening way to fight."

Eleanor was too tired to argue the niceties of sword-
fighting over drowning. All she said was, "God willing,
we will never have to use that thing again." Then she
turned and let Yorick help her back to the wagon.

XXXIV

It was a bitter-flavored victory, and Eleanor found herself once again the object of curious and suspicious glances that slid away anxiously when she met them. A number of surreptitious signs of the cross touched brows and shoulders as she moved about the camp with dour Yorick constantly beside her. She could hardly blame them, but that did not lessen the pain it caused. She wanted to say, "I did what I had to," but the refuge of expediency was unpalatable. The men around her would have felt no sense of shame to have gone out on the ice and hacked their way through King John's men, but fireballs and pan pipes and cracking ice were somehow dishonorable.

She saw, too, that she could very rapidly become more a liability to Arthur than an asset, if his followers thought him too subject to her influence. A baron who almost sweated avarice approached her with oily enthusiasm, hinting that she was in danger and that he would give his offices to protect her for a consideration.

Eleanor, tired beyond endurance, short on sleep and chilled, just leaned into his ear. "Would you like to be minus your left testicle or your right?" He scurried away, and she found the ever-present Yorick grinning.

"That will learn him to suck up to his betters," he said slowly.

"My dear friend, you are a snob." His blank expression told her he did not know what she meant. "Never mind." She cast a glance at the ruined wall of the city. "I would give a lot to sleep in a real bed tonight. I wonder what John will do now?"

"Parley."

"You are probably right. I don't think he expected to be stalemated this way. Oh, by the way, the ... music didn't seem to affect you. Why? Are you tone-deaf like the Marshall?"

"Naw. No sound behin' thee. All caught on thy star cloak."

"Really. How interesting. Thank you for holding me up. I was ready to drop. I still am, except that at any moment, something is going to happen."

Yorick nodded. He held a hand up. "Storm." A snowflake clung to his knuckle.

Eleanor looked toward the west, where storms came onto Albion from the Atlantic, then north. The sky was its usual leaden gray, the pale winter sun hardly even a blur overhead, but there was no massing of clouds to signal any disturbance. The wolf winter, indeed, seemed to have exhausted itself for the moment, which she was grateful for.

As she had several times before, she wondered what had prompted this silent man to attach himself to her. Eleanor knew only that he was widowed by the Shadow and that his two sons were grown, that he could turn his hand to any task from driving a team to mending a broken wheel, and that his loyalty was as steadfast as anyone could wish for. She almost asked him, but a "halloo!" broke the relative quiet of the camp.

There was movement on the stone bridge, and a single file of riders picked their way across. The pipes had split the stone span along its center from shore to shore, so it was passable if one took care. A red banner with two crouched lions fluttered in the slight breeze. The horses reached the end of the bridge, and she could see perhaps a dozen riders in the slight drift of wet snowflakes cascading down.

They drew up before the guards at the perimeter, and one leaned forward and spoke. Their cloaks were blue, a wonderful splash of color against the dismal gray of the day, and the metal of their chain mail gleamed. Eleanor thought they looked like an illumination, and she realized that this was the first time she had actually seen anyone who resembled her mental impression of the Middle Ages. She glanced around at the muted browns and soft greens of her companion's clothing, the iron mail showing rust where it had been inadequately greased, at boots rimed with mud and old, dried blood, and knew that her picture book idea was a thing of cities and peace. The real Middle Ages was muted in its colors and violent in its life.

A man-at-arms loped across the camp, sending up spurts of mushy snow, hurrying to Arthur's wagon. The Marshall met him, and she watched their heads come together, conferring. Arthur, a little white-faced and fey from his piping, leaned out. He climbed out, twitching his drab cloak around him, saw her watching him, and gestured at her. He looked wan, and she understood that she was not the only one who found the experience changing them. He could destroy a city full of people by putting a pipe to his lips, and if she had not spoken, he might have. It was almost too much power to entrust to one headstrong young man, and she was sure he knew it.

They arrived at the point where the messengers waited on the horses, Arthur with his bodyguard and William, Eleanor, and Yorick. A number of the knights and barons in Arthur's train assembled behind them. For a long moment, there was no sound but horse snorts, hoof falls, the rattling cough of someone with a cold or incipient pneumonia, and the metallic chink of arms.

Then a man swung off his horse, swept back one side of his cloak, and revealed an embroidered tabard with two gold lions crouching on a red field. He wore a small knife in his belt but no sword and no mail, and he swept a casual glance across Arthur, the Marshall, and Eleanor. His eyes seemed to linger on her a moment, but she could not be sure. He must, by his lack of weapons, be a herald.

"Greetings, William of Striguil."

"Well, if it isn't Henry de Camber. When did you put on the pursuivant's tabard?" The Marshall ignored the absence of any title and returned the mild insult.

A quick movement, a hand reaching for a hilt that was not there, displayed Henry as a hasty man unused to his current office. The mounted men behind him shifted uneasily in their saddles, though their faces were hidden under their helms. One horse shook its head suddenly and blew its full lips, and Eleanor could hear sniggers in the barons behind her.

Henry flushed an ugly red. "I come with a message from King John."

"Then speak it. We are all ears and cold feet." William spoke lightly. Eleanor glanced over her shoulder and saw a number of wide grins.

"The King, in his mercy, forgives your treachery, William, knowing you were ensorceled by this pretender. Therefore, he bids you kill the woman. Burn her. As for the man who calls himself Arthur, you will surrender him to King John forthwith."

Arthur started laughing. It was a rude, raucous, unexpected sound. "That's my cousin John, commanding the moon and expecting it to shine on him. I think I remember you, Camber. About twenty years ago, you were a page who was forever breaking crockery. My cousin must be in dire need to use such a clumsy tool. Still got that big birthmark on the back of your neck? It used to fascinate me when you served at table. Took away my appetite, really."

Henry de Camber turned an unpleasing red, and Eleanor could tell by the shaking of their shoulders that a number of his escort thought this was a good joke. Knightly guffaws churned the air behind her.

"Where is the real herald, Geoffrey of Brideswell?" William asked.

Henry mastered his rage and gave a shrug. "In the Tower for his treachery. As you will be soon."

"And you were the only one willing to do the King's dirty work? Arthur is right. He must be in trouble."

"Will you accept the terms?"

"No." Arthur was serious again. "We will meet John here at midday. Tell him."

Henry went very white. "The King never leaves the city," he said hoarsely. He shifted from foot to foot. He obviously did not like the message he was to carry. John must be a difficult master to serve.

Arthur considered this. "In the middle of the bridge, then. Tell him if he is not there, I will not stop until every stone in London is broken." His face was calm and serious, and there was a light in his eyes that left no doubt of his intent. Despite his worn clothing, he looked like a man of purpose, a hero, in fact, and every inch the king he claimed to be.

Henry seemed to shiver all over. "I beg you to re-consider." All the arrogance had leaked out of him, leaving a very frightened, very human man behind.

Arthur did not answer but turned his back and began to speak to William. Camber hesitated a second, then whipped out his knife and hurled it at the young king. It hit and bounced harmlessly against the mail under-neath, leaving a jagged tear in the cloak. One of Ar-thur's bodyguards brought a clenched, mailed fist down on the hapless herald's skull, and the man fell to his knees, dazed.

The young king turned and looked at him. "Coward. I should make you crawl back to John on your hands and knees, but I shall be merciful. Get him on his horse and away." He raked the helms of the mounted men who had made no move to aid the fallen herald. "I see John commands great loyalty and devotion in his fol-lowers. What is it they say? Like master, like servant?"

A man-at-arms hauled Henry up, slung him across the saddle like a sack of meal, and slapped the horse smartly on the rump. One of the mounted men grabbed the reins and led the pack away. Eleanor watched them go and saw more than one turn and look back. She felt a little sorry for them, caught between John and Ar-thur. Men who changed masters with the wind were never trusted.

Then she caught Arthur's words. "I want all the buildings on the bridge burned or otherwise destroyed. My cousin is overfound of ambush, and I wish to give him no opportunities."

The smoke was still rising from the ruins of several buildings as they approached the center of London Bridge. Eleanor had given much thought to the coming confrontation, aware that Arthur and William were still apt to think in simple terms of winning and losing. Neither was subtle, and their cunning was that of the hunter, not the statesman. John, whoever or whatever he was, was more like herself, seeing devious paths on every side of the highway. She had not forgotten the way her heart nearly stopped the night before, and she judged him to be an experienced and deadly opponent.

Under the pretext of smoothing his tunic, she had bound Arthur in a small mirror spell, for now that she

had devised the trick, she knew how to use it on any-
body, large or little. She did not tell him what she did,
knowing he would feel it unmanly. Nor did she tell
William when she did the same to him. She managed,
with some difficulty, to brush against or touch everyone
in the immediate party. Yorick gave her a grave nod
of approval, and she was fairly certain he knew what
she was up to.

They waited in the middle of the bridge, on the north
side, so the cracked and broken center was on their left.
It gaped from six inches to a foot, and the swirling gray
waters churned under them. They were twenty in number, barons, knights, Arthur's bodyguards, William,
Yorick, and herself. Farther down the span, both sides
of the bridge were crowded with about a hundred carefully chosen fighters. The Marshall was not taking any
chances.

Eleanor had also made some subtle changes in her
appearance, because she did not want to draw attention
to herself. Arthur commented that she looked tired but
in a voice that seemed almost surprised at her presence.
She thought of it as looking nondescript, herself, and
was moderately pleased with her first attempt at social
invisibility. It was not very different, she decided, from
being her father's daughter. She was glad for the pale
daylight, which masked her aura. She patted the pouch
on her belt, assuring herself that the collar was within.
She also felt along her right sleeve where, in the confines of the tight underrobe, her staff had been transformed into a wand and hidden. It was a bit awkward,
but she felt it a good trade. Bridget's starry cloak hung
under her wool cloak.

She found as she stood waiting that she was not
terribly happy or impressed with her little devices.
Eleanor kept thinking of the times with Doyle and with
Arthur before William came to him, when her actions
did not have political implications and when she had
not felt driven to various shifts to salvage anyone's
pride or dignity. She resolved that at the first opportunity she would remove herself from Arthur and the
court. She would go back to St. Bridget's Priory, or
better still, to Avebury where she could be near to Sal.
Then Arthur could settle down to being king without

the embarrassment of her presence, marry whatever noblewoman seemed a good alliance, and get on with his interrupted life.

The smoke curled down the river to the sea as two fairly nervous-looking pages walked up the bridge from the London side. They were ten or eleven, one fair, one darker, and they stood with their shoulders close together, clutching the poles of the banners with tense hands. Two older boys, sixteen or so, followed them. Men-at-arms filed up to flank the pages and squires, so they stood four abreast. A chair litter came into view, borne by four yeomen sweating in spite of the chill.

The wind plucked at the embroidered coverings of the conveyance. A body of knights followed it, some, Eleanor suspected, the same that had accompanied Henry de Camber, notable by his absence, earlier in the day, though with the anonymity of their helms, she could not be certain. The yeomen set their burden down, and one of the supporting poles snapped with a loud crack. The man stared at the length of wood in his hands, then cast it to the flagstones with a noisy clatter.

One of the young squires nipped back and held the curtains aside. A long, lean leg came out, then another, and finally the king unfolded himself and stood up. He was tall, very well formed, and dressed in a fur-lined cloak of bright blue brocaded with golden flowers. Under it he wore a full-cut, flowing robe that fell almost to the pavement, scarlet and worked with lion heads, held around his small waist by a metal belt with another lion snarling from the center. He wore no crown, but a slender circlet rested on the high brow.

Eleanor studied him carefully, noting the wide-set blue eyes and the sweep of a long nose above the mouth of a sensualist. She also noticed that there were stains at the hem of his robe and that the fur lining of his cloak was a bit motheaten. Still, he was impressive and no doubt formidable.

John curved his soft mouth into a smile, displaying large, yellow teeth. He twitched at his wide sleeves with long fingers, and she caught a glimpse of metal on his right wrist. The hands were not completely steady, and she suspected he was tired. There were slight circles under his eyes, as if he had not slept in some time.

John searched the faces of Arthur's party, looking for something and frowning slightly. Eleanor found that she had been holding her breath, and she released it. He knew she was there, but he couldn't quite focus on her. He took two paces forward, so he was in arm's reach of Arthur's guard.

"I am glad, Marshall, that you have realized your folly and brought this troublemaker to me." He turned slightly and motioned to his men. "You may take him to the Tower now."

For a moment, it all seemed perfectly normal. Arthur was William's prisoner, about to be delivered into the rightful king's hands, a subtle illusion made of arrogance and persuasion. Two of John's knights started to move, but the men in front of the young king slapped their long halberds together in an *X* and shifted their hips to bring their sword hilts more forward. They were perfectly coordinated in their movements, and the illusion vanished in their motion. Eleanor whispered a tiny "thank the goddess" under her breath.

Arthur shook his head. "No, cousin. I have come to claim what is mine. Your reign is over."

John seemed to consider the possibility. *"You,* on Albion's throne. A sniveling, weak-minded coward who shelters in a woman's skirts. A jest, surely." He seemed to be taller, handsomer, and wiser, the most gracious of men. "Tell me, how did you escape the prison I made you?" Eleanor watched his eyes and knew he was baffled and anxious.

"That is too long a story for a windy bridge. I am released, and I will take what you have stolen from me."

"You will not take anything, you misbegotten whelp. I am king, and I will be, forever. I am that promised once and future ruler."

"Who cannot leave the confines of London," Arthur replied. "Who permits the Shadow to troop across the land, laying waste the fields and fouling the rivers. What bargain did your mother make with the devil she slept with, I wonder."

"It is not true. I am the rightful king and—"

"You are a bag of pus, whore-son."

Eleanor suppressed a grin. Arthur was coming on

with a vengeance, and she was pleased. True, it was only words, but John had a forceful personality that might have cowed another. And the words were having an effect on John's entourage, for they shifted restlessly in their places.

"No. You are in my power. You have walked into my trap, for I cannot be defeated in this place."

John lifted his right hand, and the sleeve slid back, revealing the bracelet. The halberds in front of him cracked and splintered onto the stones, and the two guards clutched their chests. He caught Arthur's throat in his long hands and began choking.

Eleanor felt like she was swimming in glue as she forced herself to move toward John, yanking the collar from her pouch. She was barely aware that no one else could move at all as she reached him. She stepped behind the king, put the collar around his neck, and tried to close the clasp.

John struggled as Arthur pulled himself away gasping. He coughed and drew ragged breaths as John clawed at his throat while Eleanor hung on. He was strong, and she felt as if she were wrestling an octopus. He humped his shoulders and lifted her feet off the bridge, and she almost lost her grasp. The collar was slippery under her fingers.

Suddenly, he fell backward, pinning her beneath his weight. Eleanor had the breath knocked out of her, but she forced her fingers to hang on. John jerked his torso up, so all his weight rested on one of her legs, and she screamed.

Arthur yanked the sword out of its bright scabbard and brought its flaring blade down on John's left arm and chest. It shivered and bounced.

"The bracelet, my lord! Cut off his wrist!" The Marshall's shout rang out as Eleanor snapped the clasp shut.

John made a high-pitched keening noise and flailed, catching her breast with a sharp elbow as he clawed at his bond. She shoved at his shoulder blades. The fire sword descended, severing John's hand from his wrist. Blood spurted into his face and spattered onto Eleanor. His right arm drooped, and the bracelet slid off the amputated limb into a widening red pool.

Yorick's strong hands gripped her under the arms, and Eleanor found herself hauled upright from under the body of the dying man. John's handsome face faded. The skin cracked and wrinkled, and the brown hair turned gray. With something of a shock, she realized he was several years past forty in real time, though he had not looked much beyond his mid-twenties. She turned her blood-smeared face into the rough cloth of her servant's cloak and cried like a child.

XXXV

"No, Arthur, I will not marry you, and that is final. I don't want to talk about it anymore. Please, Countess Constance, can't you talk some sense into him?"

The raddled face of Arthur's mother regarded Eleanor with the benevolence of a hungry spider. The Countess of Brittany had arrived a week before, descending on London like a plucked crow, and Eleanor had taken the woman's measure in an hour. She was ambitious, domineering, and rapacious, and Eleanor had spent many trying hours avoiding answering her questions while deferring politely to her monumental ego. It had been effective in as far as she no longer regarded Eleanor as a threat to her plans to be the actual power in Albion, but neither Constance's council nor Eleanor's insistence had dissuaded Arthur from his absolute determination to make her his wife.

"He is his father all over again," the countess grunted. She had crossed the Channel from Brittany in a winter storm and still looked a little seasick, but she carried her sixty-five years with dignity, and Eleanor could see glimpses of a former beauty that must have been wondrous. Her periwinkle blue eyes were almost violet, and they were very sharp.

Eleanor, remembering her vision months before of this woman handing her a fatal goblet, ate no food Yorick did not prepare and took no drink from the countess's hand.

London was abustle with restoration and preparations for Arthur's coronation, planned for Christmas Day. It was the twenty-first, and it had been three weeks since John had died on the broken bridge. The terrible winter, after a short pause, had come back with renewed vigor, but the happy inhabitants of the city were not about to let a few feet of snow dampen their enthusiasm.

As much as possible, Eleanor stayed in the chambers assigned to her in Westminster Palace. Reluctantly, she had accepted the services of a tiring-woman, Berthe, a plump, cheerful dame in her forties who flirted mercilessly with the imperturbable Yorick, and a page in the person of one of the Marshall's nephews. She had folded away into a trunk the starry cloak and the now worn gown Bera had given her, leaned her staff into a corner, and waited for the birth of her child.

Arthur had thrown himself into the ordering of his kingdom with energy and the kind of intelligence his grandfather, Henry II, was remembered for. He listened thoughtfully to the Marshall, the frail and saintly Thomas of Salisbury, Archbishop of Canterbury, released from a long imprisonment in the Tower, and other advisers on matters of state, restoring domains seized by John's men, and generally behaving with wisdom. Eleanor refused to even discuss these matters with him, insisting she didn't know the first thing about kingship, and besides, she had a backache, until he finally let her be. Except in the matter of marriage.

"Isn't my kingdom good enough for you? Come spring, I'll cross the Channel and conquer France."

"How can I get it through your thick skull that I don't want to be queen of anything?" A sudden pain shivered her limbs and abdomen. Eleanor blinked, outraged. Nothing could hurt that much. It passed, and she breathed again.

Arthur sulked. "Stop treating me like a spoilt child."

"Stop behaving like one."

"Why don't you love me, Eleanor?"

It was an echo of Baird, and it hurt. He knew it, too, and Eleanor realized she had to end this argument before it got any worse. "I do. But I still won't marry you." She felt another pain. "And I think my labor is beginning. Yorick, help me to my room. If you will excuse me, Countess."

Constance nodded grandly, and Arthur was instantly contrite, fussing over her until Eleanor could have screamed, except it took every effort just to walk.

Settled into her bed, Eleanor sought to ease the now

more frequent pains. Berthe clucked around the huge bed, a remnant of one of John's mistresses, as were the gaudy tapestries that adorned the walls. She had come to a sorry end, Berthe had informed her, as had all of John's companions, wasting away. That and the fact that there wasn't a mirror to be found anywhere in the palace made her wonder if he had not been some sort of vampire, a speculation she kept to herself.

Hours passed, and her shift was damp with sweat. Berthe brought a toothless beldam to be midwife, and Eleanor shrank from the wizened visage. Then she saw that the wrinkled old hands were pink with scrubbing, their touch gentle, and she was reassured. She groaned and grunted, shifting her hips to find a comfortable position, dozing fitfully.

She heard the cathedral bells toll the midnight hour and found herself wide-awake. The room was dark but for the cheery light of the fire and a few tapers. Berthe and the midwife were gossiping before the flames, and Yorick stood benevolently at the foot of the bed.

A pain sharper that before made her cry out and bite her lip. She felt a cool hand on her brow and another on her clenched fist. The Lady of the Willows shimmered before her eyes, dark hair framing the white face. A smile graced the berry red lips. "Sal," she whispered.

I am here, daughter.

Eleanor could smell the damp, clean scent of willow in the air, over her sweat and the ever-present wood smoke. A pain rippled through her, and she screamed, bringing Berthe and the midwife scurrying. She pushed her knees up and tried to force the pain away. Vaguely, she heard voices commanding her to do something, but all she did was scream and press. Then she felt a single, tearing agony that seemed to last forever.

It stopped, finally, and the room was silent except for the murmurs of the two women bent over her knees. Then there was a coughing sound, and a healthy yell broke the quiet. A damp, dark-headed bundle was thrust into the crook of her aching arm. It bellowed in outrage.

"I never saw such an easy birthing," the midwife told her.

Eleanor looked at the wrinkled face in wonder. If that was easy, she never wanted to find out what hard was. Then she looked down at the red-faced infant making his presence known in the cosmos and said, "Hello, Dylan. Welcome to the outside world, my little fish."

The cries stopped. Blue eyes regarded her intently. Eleanor kissed the brow and felt a surge of joy. Dylan closed his bright eyes and slept in an instant. She patted the little form as Berthe tucked the blankets around them, and Yorick grinned until his face nearly split.

There was a rumble, and the room shook. Berthe and the midwife clutched each other, shrieking shrilly as a large stone popped out of its place in the floor. Eleanor sat up as a mound of dirt fountained into the room, clods pelting down on the bed. A dark head came out of the hole, then broad shoulders and a huge chest.

Doyle climbed out of the soil, mother-naked and grimed with dirt. He brushed his beard clean, grinning, and Berthe and the midwife fled, yowling. Yorick clutched a bedpost, unable to decide if running or defending his mistress was the better course.

Eleanor blinked twice, then reached out a hand. She found Doyle's strong fingers closing around her wrist. "I told Arthur I could not marry him," she said stupidly. "Oh, Doyle, is it really you? Or am I having a very dirty dream?"

He kissed her, and she could taste his sweetness mingled with bits of grit. She felt his hands in her sweat-rimed hair, and the baby in her arm suddenly wriggled and protested this intrusion. Doyle rolled an eye to look down at the squalling infant, released her mouth, and touched a rosy cheek with one large finger. "Ugly, isn't he?"

"No, he isn't. And what the hell are you doing here? You were dead! I've spent six months grieving for you, dammit!"

"Such sweet words from my gentle wife, the light of my life."

Her lips quivered in a smile in spite of herself. "There is nothing more maddening than an Irishman being coy. Now, tell me what's going on or I'll box your ears."

"As I sat there in my mother's bowels, I have tried to decide if I missed more your tart tongue or your lusty limbs. Now, now"—he laid a finger on her lips—"patience. I had to die, Eleanor. It was my time. That part of me which was the season had to pass. But, because of this strange little creature screaming at me—will you please put him to breast and quiet him—I must also return and live out the span of a mortal man. So, here I am—unless you have a yen to wear a crown."

Eleanor fumbled the child onto a sore breast, then turned sparkling, tear-bright eyes to the man. "Monster. I would rather live in a hut in the woods with you than a palace any day. I still don't understand."

"Winter has a new king."

She felt fear clutch her heart, recalling that it was the solstice. "Not Dylan!" She squeezed the infant against her.

"No, not our little fish. And by the way, I'd as lief you hadn't killed Baird. He made a poor companion, moaning and moping around."

"I didn't want to!"

"I know, love. Sleep now. We have a lifetime to talk." He pressed her back into the pillows.

She looked at him and held his hand. "If you die one second before me, I swear I'll hunt you through eternity until the stars gutter in their orbits, and the void vanishes."

He bowed his huge head, and she felt a hot tear fall on her hand. "I know. I do not know if I deserve such fierce love, my love, but I accept it—with as much grace as I am able."

"Flimflam," she murmured wearily. As she slipped into sleep, she heard the watery laughter of the Lady of the Willows. *I told you dark men were the best, daughter*. Then she knew nothing put peace.

Eleanor and Doyle stood in the chilly and drafty confines of the cathedral and watched the nobles and landed gentry flow in, a brightly feathered flock of birds. She shifted the baby a little, took a quick sidelong glance at her husband, and smiled a little. *And I thought things would stop being exciting after I had the baby!*

The past three days flitted through her mind in a montage of moments. Arthur's stunned expression when he saw Doyle. An unseemly haste to withdraw his marriage offer, which had led her to believe he had made it as much from obligation as from affection. Then there had been that moment when he grudgingly began to give her back the fire sword, when Arthur showed himself to be as venial as any man, though more gracious than most.

"I suppose you want this back." He touched the hilt uneasily. She looked at the sword and remembered all the events it had played a part in and found she had no affection for it. The weight of Baird dying in her arms still lingered. It had caused her too much trouble, and she didn't want it.

"No. I don't think it has anything to do with me anymore. You keep it, Arthur. If Bridget wants it back, she can come get it herself. I don't have the energy to be her errand girl anymore. Let it be an heirloom of the men of your house. Women don't enjoy killing enough to need swords, you know."

Arthur caught the bitterness in her words and understood. "I owe you so much," he began haltingly.

"Then give me Avebury, to make a home for me and Doyle and the baby. Really, Arthur, my tastes are very simple, and I don't want more. But, perhaps you ought to let me take that collar and John's bracelet away. I find I don't approve of objects of power lying about in royal treasuries where they can tempt people." She almost regretted her words the next instant but decided it was probably the right thing to do.

He looked relieved, as if the things had preyed on his mind. "That's a good idea. Thank you, dear Eleanor. Will you still be my friend?"

"Oh, Arthur, of course I will. And don't be sad that I want to bury myself in the wilds of Wiltshire. Doyle and I will come to visit. I just think it will be a lot better for everyone if I go away, until people forget about my part in your story. You get enough odd looks with your black hand without having a witch at court as well."

He sighed. "Practical to the last. Women!"

Eleanor could not tell if that last comment was directed at her, at his mother, or at the female sex in general. She simply marveled at the complex intelligence that could have conceived the two sexes and given them such wondrous strengths and weaknesses, so much good and such great evil.

The crowd around her stirred and rustled in the great

chamber. It smelled of burning tapers and musty finery, for the people of London had had few festive occasions during John's reign, and the nobles not many more. Eleanor took a child's delight in the bright colors.

The brazen blare of trumpets turned all heads toward the rear doors. Pages first, small, proud boys, solemn or grinning as their natures led them, then squires, knights, barons, and earls. Finally Arthur appeared in a blue silk robe, a scarlet cloak billowing behind him, held by four knights. William the Strong, Marshall of Albion, strode behind him. A great cheer made the candlelight waver from the turbulence. The procession wound through the crowd, bringing Arthur to the foot of the altar where Thomas, the archbishop, stood garbed in a white chasuble.

The old man's voice was too frail for the cathedral, so it took on the aspect of a pantomime. He blessed the king, then the congregation. Two honored nobles— Eleanor had quite given up trying to remember all the names—bore the Harp and the pan pipes, now sewn into a sack, and these were blessed and carried up to the altar while Arthur knelt patiently. The mass stretched on and on with plain song echoing sweetly against the stones. People coughed and shifted respectfully.

After what seemed an eternity, Thomas of Salisbury lifted a crown up in his frail hands. His lips moved in benediction, and he lowered the golden circle onto the young king's brow. Arthur kissed an aged hand, then stood and turned to face his people. A great shout of *"Vivat Rex!"* leapt from the mouths of the congregation.

Eleanor looked at the great iron candelabrum that stood behind the altar and saw a figure, a grave, fair-haired woman in a very familiar blue cloak. The cheering died around her, so she knew the apparition was not solely her own. People went to their knees with whispers of "Ave Maria" on their lips. Doyle helped her kneel, for the sleeping Dylan made an awkward burden, as Eleanor thought a bit cynically that Bridget was up to her usual tricks. Arthur seemed a little puzzled by this sudden homage, but he could not see what was happening behind him. The archbishop turned, stared for a second, then slipped onto his knees as if he had been struck.

The vision smiled, and every heart was lifted. She raised her right hand in blessing. Arthur finally craned his neck around to see what was drawing everyone's attention, gave a sharp glance in Eleanor's general direction, then knelt again. She shimmered in the candles for perhaps a minute more, absorbing the awed admiration of the onlookers.

Eleanor felt the now familiar brush of the goddess in her mind. *Well done, daughter. Come to me on my day.* Then she was gone, leaving Arthur with a legacy of divine approval, which would tint his reign a golden hue.

XXXVI

St. Bridget's Priory looked very much as it had a year before, a little more weatherworn but nothing more. Eleanor got out of the wagon and reflected on the contrast between the two occasions, for there were a dozen wagons in her train instead of one large wolf, a greedy baby at her breast, and a husband who was gay and morose by turns. She would have gladly traded her rather hefty entourage for Wrolf in a minute, for she found that being Eleanor d'Avebury was a bit trying but not for the child or the man.

As they had traveled, it had occurred to her that this audience might be disastrous. Bridget might just ship her back to her own time and place, and while she tried to believe that the goddess would not be so cruel, she still fretted over it. So she clung to Doyle in the nights and to the baby in the day and was sharp-tongued and short-tempered.

On the journey, they had seen remnants of the Shadow, for it had not departed Albion entirely with John's death. They met two ragged bands of listless folk, starved-looking and sad. Doyle and the dozen men-at-arms who served her gave them the mercy of death, and Eleanor was left depressed.

So she was sober and somewhat careworn when she greeted Brother Ambrosius, glad that he still trod the earth, but apprehensive. "I'm back, like a bad penny."

"I see that, but I knew already. We heard that John was dead and Arthur returned, and I knew you had accomplished what tasks our gracious lady had set you. But come in from the cold. You seem weary."

"A little. I lost the book you gave me, and I'm sorry. Stop wriggling, Dylan. I'll change you in a minute. Babies are a lot of bother," she added fondly.

Ambrosius chuckled and led her inside. "You still say unexpected things, I see."

"Do I? I want you to baptize my son, Brother Ambrosius." It was the ostensible reason for their halt, though Eleanor had some doubts that a child with a snake for a grandmother was subject to the rituals of the church. And gracious was not an epithet she was willing to apply to Bridget. High-handed was closer to the mark.

"Me? I am honored, milady. You could have had one of those London priests do it." His voice carried his low and uncharitable opinion of London's clergy, for which he would undoubtedly do penance later.

"No. You were my first friend."

They sat and talked while Yorick oversaw the unloading of barrels of salted fish, bags of corn, bolts of cloth, jugs of wine, honey and perry, and much else, for Eleanor had not forgotten her first meal nor the bare state of the priory's larder. It was the first time she had retold her entire adventure in one sitting, and she drew it out to avoid the inevitable. Also, she had promised to tell him the story a year before, and she felt she might have no other opportunity.

But finally, her household was settled in, filling the priory's modest facilities to the bursting point, and she knew it was time. She followed Ambrosius to the chapel, the starry cloak over one arm, the baby in the other, with Doyle close behind. It was dim and cool and just as she remembered it, the large figure of Saint Bridget dominating the whole.

Eleanor stared up at it and shivered. Doyle touched her shoulder with a gentle hand, for though she had not spoken her fears, he knew them. The statue shimmered, and the face became animated.

"Welcome, daughter."

"Greetings, Bright Bridget. I bring you back your cloak. The sword I have no more."

"Yes. It passed beyond you when you bestowed it on a man of woman born. 'Twas well done, that giving."

Recalling her own confused reasons for giving Arthur the sword, Eleanor was not sure she agreed, but she wasn't going to argue. "I am glad you are pleased."

"You have done well, more even than I dared hope.

Give to me those objects, the wristpiece and the collar, which you so wisely bore away from Arthur."

"Happily." They were in the belt pouch, a dark, heavy burden. "Now what?" she asked as she put the cloak and the other things at the foot of the statue.

"Now you live your life."

Eleanor stood up and looked directly into the glorious face. "Here? With my husband and my baby?" She felt a pang of guilt. "What about my mother?"

"Yes, here. How will Rowena and Beatrice and little Eleanor be born else? As for the other, it was all a dream. You were never really there, child. You will go to my solemn sister and sing her songs, bringing the healing of the Willow into the world and bearing your children, so they can finish what you began."

"What?" She knew she wasn't going to get any explanation of how she had "dreamed" her first two decades, for Bridget reveled in obscurity, but Eleanor was determined to get some further elucidation of that final cryptic statement.

"There are other swords to be brought from the realms of the gods into the world of heroes, and the Shadow still darkens many places. But that is not your task." The goddess gave a kind of sigh. "I would that you had loved me more, but you are the Light which breaks the Darkness, and always will you seek to bring laughter to those who are merry with difficulty. That is your special gift. It is a great power, Eleanor, greater than you know. You have served me well, if not always with respect, and I now release you. I thank you for your boundless joy, for the living person you are." Bridget faded, and the chapel was still.

Eleanor turned into Doyle's arms, burying her face against his chest while she felt tears flow. "Why can't I just love everyone?" she whispered.

He stroked her hair. "Because even the gods cannot command the heart, my dear, foolish Eleanor."

FANTASY AND ILLUSION

A READER'S GUIDE TO FANTASY   80333-X/$2.95
Baird Searles, Beth Meacham and Michael Franklin
A comprehensive source of writers and works—from the magical
to mystical to supernatural—for every lover of fantasy, with full
listings of authors, titles, series, categories and award-winners,
plus a fascinating overview of fantasy's past, present and future.

THE FANTASTIC IMAGINATION:
An Anthology of High Fantasy   32326-5/$2.25
Edited by Robert H. Boyer & Kenneth J. Zahorski
THE FANTASTIC IMAGINATION II   41533-X/$2.50
From another world beyond our own where epic quests and ritual evil
challenge the gods and seduce the spirit...where witchwomen and
unicorns, sorcerers and swordsmen vaunt and court and do battle...
come these brilliant collections of the best in fantasy literature,
chosen from the most popular works of the past 150 years.

THE PRISONER OF BLACKWOOD CASTLE   88005-9/$2.50
Ron Goulart
When an American millionaire is mysteriously kidnapped, ace detec-
tive Harry Challenge is called on to rescue him...but finds himself up
against a team of deadly robots and a mad doctor, amidst swords and
sorcery, werewolves and automatons.

QUARRELLING, THEY MET THE DRAGON 89201-4/$2.95
Sharon Baker
A compelling fantasy novel of mystery, passion, and horror on a distant
planet where a slave's quest for freedom takes him on an unforgettable
adventure into the realm of the Off-Worlders...and to a destiny
stranger than dreams.

THE FIRE SWORD   88718-X/$3.75
Adrienne Martine-Barnes
An epic fantasy novel of pageantry and ritual, of a beautiful young
woman transported into the mysterious world of 13th century England,
and of her mission to reinstate the King of Light to the throne using
the magical powers of faith, courage and love.

AVON Paperbacks